THE LIGHTBODY BEQUEST

*Book Two in The Lightbody
Mystery series.*

Carolyn Ruffles

for Liz
Enjoy!
Carolyn Ruffles

Carolyn Ruffles

First Printing: July 2024
Publisher: Carolyn Ruffles

ISBN:978-1-9163913-7-6

https://carolynrufflesauthor.com.

Cover designed by Rob Ruffles.

For Harry, Max & Georgia.

AUTHOR'S NOTE

This is a work of fiction. All the characters in *The Lightbody Bequest* are creations from my imagination and bear no resemblance to anyone, living or dead.

Martha's story is mostly set in the 1640s against the backdrop of the English Civil War. Historical details mentioned in the book are based upon research, but I confess to reinstating the Duke and Duchess of Suffolk. Historically, there has been no Duke of Suffolk since 1554 when Henry Grey was executed by Mary I after his participation in Wyatt's rebellion so these titles did not exist during Martha's lifetime.

Real places in Suffolk and Norfolk are an integral backdrop to the narrative but I have added imaginary locations of my own, such as Little Horseshoes, Tocklewood, Bathersford and Wickthorpe itself. The legend of the Wickthorpe Witch is entirely fictional. Readers from Suffolk may spot similarities between Wickthorpe and the beautiful village of Woolpit – my childhood home. Woolpit was originally intended as the location for *The Lightbody Mystery* series but I soon realised I was taking far too many liberties, both historical and geographical, for that to be credible. Therefore, although I could not resist keeping some of Woolpit's features, the village name was changed to Wickthorpe. Indeed, Woolpit has its own fascinating legend, *The Green Children of Woolpit,* which is well worth researching.

PROLOGUE

It had taken hours, sifting through boxes, but she had found it. *The book. About Martha Lightbody.* Her fingers stroked the worn, green leather. Only recently had she recalled the book's existence and her late father's words:

'The witch was real. The curse is real. The book is the proof.'

As a child, she had not been interested. With the scorn of youth, she had dismissed her father's obsession with the Wickthorpe curse. Her preoccupation had been with the present and the future, not the past and some old legend. Life had been exciting, full of promise, and she had scoffed at her father's warnings. She knew better, or so she thought. How naïve she had been! How was she supposed to know of the disappointments awaiting her, and the bitter taste of disillusion?

Now, with the weight of old age and harsh experience hanging like a noose around her neck, she knew her father had been right. Her family was cursed. The danger was real. There was no escape from the past ... unless the answer lay in the book.

Her father had been a hoarder. He would never have thrown such a treasured possession away. It was too important. She ordered the boxes of his things to be brought down from the loft, where they had lain untouched for many years. Impatiently, she sifted through them, one by one. It had taken a long time, but at last she held the book in her misshapen hands. It would provide the proof she needed. And those heedless sceptics in the village would realise she had been right all along.

Gnarled fingers turned the front cover. The spine was damaged and some of the yellowed pages were loose inside. She hoped the book was intact. Just a few, crucial pages missing could ruin everything.

She picked up her reading glasses and began ...

The Life & Times of Martha Lightbody

Written in 1845 by John Littlebody

Foreword

Herein follows the life and times of Martha Lightbody, a woman whom history has vilified as a witch and a harbinger of evil. It is my strongly-held desire to rectify the many wrongs done to her and to present her to the world as the God-fearing, Christian woman she was. The world deserves to know the truth of the men culpable of her wicked persecution and history should pass judgement on their vile actions.

What a load of rubbish! With a grunt of annoyance, she thrust the book aside. Clearly, it was written by a fool who believed in the witch's innocence. Huffing to herself, she picked it up once more. She would have to read it, despite the false voice of its narrator. At least it was short. Her father's voice sounded once more in her head, almost as if he were right there alongside her. *'The witch was real. The curse is real. The book is the proof.'*

With a sigh, she turned to the rest of the foreword ...

My writings are taken with the utmost attention to accuracy from letters passed down within the family and a diary kept by Martha herself. That diary has since been lost but her great granddaughter, Elizabeth Croft, most diligently recorded information in a series of letters to her own granddaughters, as repeated to her by her grandfather, Josiah Lightbody, Martha's son. Many of these fascinating epistles remain and have, after more than a century, fallen into my unworthy hands. It is a true account, to the best of my knowledge, but the lapsing of time may have produced some minor inaccuracies and, for that,

I beg you, my dear Reader, to forgive me. The heart and soul of the story I swear on my life to be truthful.

Martha's tale will now commence in the hope that the telling of it will restore her good name and reputation.

The old woman closed the book with an ironic chuckle. *Good name and reputation.* Little chance of that! Not if she had anything to do with it. She had *very* different intentions for the information she would discover. Soon, the Wickthorpe Witch would receive her just desserts, once and for all.

CHAPTER 1

August

Wickthorpe, an historic village nestling in West Suffolk between the towns of Bury St Edmunds and Stowmarket, had become notorious. The death of a young girl, followed by the attempted drowning of successful businesswoman, Deborah Ryecroft, had made the headlines on national news. Anyone interested in such matters now knew of the Wickthorpe curse and its supposed history. Debates as to the validity of such a curse had even aired on national radio stations.

Throughout August, reporters swarmed the streets, speaking to inhabitants keen to give their opinions. As President and Founder of the Wickthorpe History Society, Honoraria Simpson-Fairchild was much in demand. For almost a week, her plump face and carefully-coiffed, red curls appeared on television screens across the nation, as she expounded further upon the legend of Wickthorpe's curse.

'In 1645, a young woman called Martha Lightbody was accused of witchcraft. She was subjected to a trial by drowning which meant she was tied to a chair and thrown into Dark Water Lake. If she drowned, she would be declared innocent – not much of a consolation!' She chuckled at the camera. 'If she floated, she was a witch and would be sent for trial at Bury St Edmunds, where she would be convicted and hung. Before Martha was thrown into the lake, legend has it that she cursed the whole village and its descendants. She was never seen again. The chair surfaced, but empty, and of Martha there was no sign. Most believed she must have escaped and swum to freedom. Some thought she may have drowned, although her body was never found. It is said that Martha's husband and young child left Wickthorpe shortly afterwards and no one knew what became of them. For a while, villagers worried about the curse but, as weeks passed, their fear eased … until the following year when a woman was found drowned in the same lake. The dead woman's husband was one of the ringleaders of Martha's initial arrest. The whole village believed the curse was responsible. And so the legend was born, passing down through subsequent centuries. Renowned historians, such as Dorothy Fairbanks, suspect the legend of the curse may have been fuelled by foul play. For example, any villager wanting rid of someone, for whatever reason, could drown their victim and dump the body in the lake. There would then be the inevitable claims that the fault lay with the curse and the perpetrator of the crime would thereby be absolved of culpability. It is certainly true that Wickthorpe has recorded a much higher number of deaths by drowning than other, similar villages.' Honoraria favoured the camera with an eloquent shrug. 'As years passed, so the legend grew. Villagers came to believe the witch continued the curse by inhabiting the bodies of other women and that was what led to the accusations against Deborah Ryecroft. In 1988, a sixteen-year-old girl, Ayesha Khan, drowned in Dark Water Lake. Deborah was deemed by some to be responsible, although she was never charged. Shortly after that, Deborah left the village, but returned at the beginning of this year. Some villagers persist in the belief that Deborah is the Wickthorpe Witch. As you know, the Hampton-Browns tried to drown her for that very reason and are currently detained, accused of attempted murder.'

'What do you think?' asked the reporter.

Honoraria's scarlet lips curved as she prepared to give her well-rehearsed response. 'I am a historian. As such, I consider all the facts in my possession and form conclusions based solely upon them. As I said, Wickthorpe has recorded a higher incidence of unexplained deaths, especially by drowning, than other villages, and this *could* be attributed to the curse.'

'You believe Deborah Ryecroft is a witch?' the reporter jumped in, gleeful at the prospect of a real scoop.

'I did *not* say that.' Honoraria shook her head, her tone patronising. 'I said it *could* be, but there are countless other, more likely explanations. I concur with Dorothy Fairbanks. At a very well-attended History Society meeting a few months back, she mooted that curses have been employed by people as a means of controlling others to achieve a specific end. Martha Lightbody's curse was aimed at the men persecuting her. Understandable, really. In her situation, tied to a chair and about to be thrown into a lake, I would be tempted to do the same! The fact that the curse has been believed, even through the centuries, means it has worked. People continue to fear it. My view is that the power of a curse lies in the belief of the person or people cursed. Without the belief, the curse loses its threat. People are very superstitious in this village and the curse gives them a reason for the recent tragedies. It has been a truly terrible time for many. The Hampton-Browns, for example, believed the curse was responsible for the tragic death of their son in a car accident near Dark Water Lake in 1988. That was probably ...'

'But do *you* believe in it?' the reporter interrupted again, wearying of Honoraria's long-winded diatribe, and hearing a voice in his earpiece, instructing him to wrap things up.

'To answer your question,' Honoraria composed her features into an expression of learned sincerity, 'no, I don't. I'm a historian and ...'

'I'm afraid that's all we have time for.' The camera shot swivelled to capture the face of the reporter as he signed off.

'Well!' Enid Green spluttered into her teacup as the news moved on to a piece about a llama in Lincolnshire. 'Trust that woman to talk a lot of nonsense! They should have asked me what I thought. I would soon have put them right.'

'I'm sure you would, Mother,' her long-suffering daughter, Ava, responded, rising from the sitting-room sofa. 'Would you like another cup of tea?'

'Fancy saying the curse was rubbish! She just says what she thinks people want her to say, that one! When she was talking to Valerie and me in the Post Office, a few months back, her tune was very different. I intend to give her a piece of my mind when I next see her.'

'I'm sure you will.' Ava sighed and left her mother muttering at the television screen. Privately, she thought Honoraria had done a good job. Hopefully her interview would help take the heat off Deborah Ryecroft, who was still recovering from her awful ordeal.

CHAPTER 2

Three months later.

Grey November mist hung a murky veil over Wickthorpe. Three months on, the village had got over its flurry of fame, and life for the majority of its residents had returned to its normal routine.

Deborah Ryecroft had recovered from her physical injuries and returned to work. She continued to receive counselling, hoping to diminish the nightmares which still haunted her after her ordeal, but she did not think she would ever forget the horror of being bound to a chair and thrown into Dark Water Lake. The love and support of Tom Oldridge had helped but her mental scars remained.

One recurring image was that of a dark-haired woman in a long, flowing nightdress, who silently urged her to fight as she struggled in those black depths. This woman held out a hand, guiding her to rescue. Much as she tried to dismiss the memory as a figment of her imagination, it would not go away. The face haunted both her sleep and her waking moments. Her counsellor, an empathetic woman named Helen, with whom Deborah soon felt at ease, had explained it all for her. She was superimposing her knowledge of Martha Lightbody onto her own experience. When she suffered a terrible, near-drowning incident, she had inevitably thought of Martha Lightbody, and her mind had constructed an image of her. Deborah had always believed that Martha survived her trial by drowning in 1645. Therefore, it was only natural her subconscious should summon her in her own efforts to escape. This all sounded very plausible. She could almost believe it. But there were so many tiny, realistic details in her dreams, and she still wondered …

'Knock, knock.' Emma Oldridge, Tom's daughter, poked her head around the door, interrupting her thoughts.

Deborah smiled. 'Good timing. I was just about to have a coffee. Do you fancy one?'

'Great, thanks. I haven't seen you for a bit so I thought I'd pop round to see how you were doing.' Emma slid comfortably onto a bar stool, surveying Deborah with shrewd, green eyes. 'You look well.'

'I feel well.' Deborah set two mugs on the kitchen island and settled opposite Emma. 'How about you? I understand things have quietened down on the farm, now the autumn drilling is finished.'

'Yes, thank goodness.' Emma worked for the family farm alongside her dad. She shook her thick mane of auburn hair. 'It's been a tricky autumn, but we're all done for now. Actually, that's what I wanted to discuss with you …'

'Are you intending to make a start on my paintings?' Deborah asked. 'I'm so sick of looking at these bare walls.' Emma liked to paint in her spare time. Deborah had seen some of her work, hung in the Oldridge farmhouse, and fallen in love with it. She had asked Emma to create some pieces for her.

'I am. But also, I could do with a break. Get away from here for a bit.'

Deborah nodded. 'Good idea.'

'And I was going to ask Rick to come with me. What do you think? I wondered if a change of scene might help him to think of me in a romantic way.' Emma gave a self-deprecating laugh. 'I know … I'm getting desperate. We get on so well and I had hoped, when he moved in, things might develop. But they haven't. I'm beginning to wonder if they ever will.'

Emma had loved Rick Billington, a local vet, since she had first laid eyes on him, five years earlier. They had formed a strong friendship and when Freya, Rick's sister, had drowned in Dark Water Lake earlier that year, Rick had moved into the Oldridge farmhouse. This gave him some respite from his grieving parents, who ran the village pub, *The Lamb Inn.* It also provided Emma with some company, after her father had moved in with Deborah.

'All things are worth a try,' Deborah gave her an encouraging nod, 'and I'd say you could both use a holiday, after everything that's happened. Ask him and see what he says.'

Emma grinned. 'That's what I thought. I'll ask him tonight.' She finished her coffee and jumped up to put her mug in the dishwasher. 'I will have to wait for him to be able to get time off work though.'

'Great! That will give you a chance to get painting!'

'I will. I have some ideas. Anyway, thanks for the coffee. I'm off to check on holiday destinations.'

Deborah responded to Emma's cheery wave with a smile but her heart ached for the girl who had become so important to her. Privately, she despaired of Rick Billington – a lovely lad but he couldn't see what was under his nose. And she hadn't had the heart to tell Emma that Rick's ex-girlfriend, Amelie Charles, was back in the village, staying with her parents. Hopefully, she would be gone again before Rick knew about it.

A muffled thump from her front door heralded the arrival of the post and she set down her mug to retrieve it, surprised to see an A4 padded bag amongst the usual assortment of bills and junk mail. Intrigued, she picked it up and turned it over. There was a solicitor's stamp on the envelope. *Something to do with Mother's will? No, not the right solicitors ...*

Suddenly, she knew who had sent it – the solicitors acting for Mabel Littlebody's estate. Mabel had lived in the bungalow opposite and had been a salvation for Deborah during her unhappy childhood. When Deborah returned to Wickthorpe, she had visited the old lady several times before Mabel had died peacefully in her sleep. In a letter left to her by her mother, Hannah, Deborah had made many important discoveries, including the fact that she and Mabel were distantly related. She was also told that Mabel possessed a book, written in the nineteenth century, about Martha Lightbody, the original Wickthorpe Witch. Deborah had contacted the solicitors and promised a generous finder's fee should they succeed in locating the book so she could offer to buy it. They had written back and promised to check with the house clearance company responsible for emptying Mabel's bungalow. They would do all they could, they said, and named their prices, one for doing the work and another should they achieve success. Deborah had agreed but had not held out much hope. However, the appearance of the package caused a surge of excitement. *Had they found it?*

Tingling with anticipation, she carried the bag through to the kitchen and cut the top open with a pair of scissors. Inside was a further package – book-shaped, encased in brown paper and bubble wrap – and a white envelope with her name on the front. Difficult not to get too excited. She could be holding Martha's story in her hands right now! Turning to the envelope, she found it contained a single sheet of paper with the letter heading Grantley Jolson Solicitors, and a brief paragraph of text:

Dear Ms Ryecroft,

We have great pleasure in enclosing the copy of The Life & Times of Martha Lightbody as you requested. You may be interested to know we located a sheet of paper within the book, presumably written by Miss Littlebody, bequeathing the book to you. We have included this also.

Please let us know if we may be of any further assistance.

Yours sincerely,

Humphrey Jolson.

Heart thumping, she turned to the package. They *had* found it. Against all the odds, the book had found its way to her hands. She could almost believe in fate when such things happened. It was meant to be. Almost reverently, she snipped at the tape holding the parcel together and unwrapped it, layer by layer, until she was left with the book itself. Tucked inside, its crumpled edge protruding from the pages, was a single sheaf of paper containing two lines of spidery, blue ink:

To be passed on to dear Deborah Ryecroft.
With my love.

With a lump in her throat, Deborah turned her attention to the book. It was small and slim, bound in battered, green leather with the title engraved on the spine in scratched, gold lettering. *The Life & Times of Martha Lightbody.* With careful fingers, she stroked the cover. The book was almost two hundred years old. Very fragile. It was a miracle it had survived. She turned it over to inspect the back. Just the green cover, marked with stains and splodges. Worn, loved, read many times over those two centuries.

And now she could read it too.

The Life & Times of Martha Lightbody
Chapter 1

Martha Lightbody was a kind, homely woman, born Martha Sturry in 1622 to parents, Solomon and Mary. She was one of seven children and lived in the town of Kings Lynn where her father was a wool merchant. In 1643, she married John Lightbody, the younger son of a farmer, and they moved to the village of Grimston. In July, 1644, their first child, Josiah, was born but, shortly afterwards, the family were forced to flee when accusations of witchcraft were falsely levelled against Martha. The family travelled through Norfolk and into Suffolk where they sojourned briefly in Framlingham. They hoped to settle there until they heard tales of an elderly vicar, imprisoned in Framlingham castle, accused of sending imps to sink a ship at Harwich. It seemed impossible that a vicar should be so accused but the persecution of innocents in East Anglia in the name of witchcraft was rife. This tyranny was led by the son of a Puritan vicar, Matthew Hopkins, a self-titled Witchfinder-General, a man who had bestowed upon himself an authority which none thought to question. Upon this horrifying discovery, John and Martha decided to tarry there no longer and journeyed on, finally settling in the village of Wickthorpe.

Deborah sped through the early pages, and discovered that John secured employment with a farmer, Jed Finch, enabling the family to live in a small cottage on Finch's land. She wondered why Martha had been accused of witchcraft in Grimston, but soon learnt that the young woman was skilled in the use of herbs for treating the sick, and it was such knowledge that provoked suspicion. Once settled in Wickthorpe, Martha was understandably cautious in revealing her abilities to others, but she felt obliged to help a young woman she had befriended, Prudence Harkness, when Prudence was in danger of losing her unborn child. After that, it seemed, word of Deborah's skill spread through the village, and she was called upon increasingly frequently to help those in need.

Deborah felt the first glimmerings of concern. She could already see the direction the book was headed. One paragraph, in particular, caused her heart to beat faster:

On one occasion, when Martha and Prudence were on their way back to their respective cottages, they encountered the man who was to become Martha's nemesis, namely Roger Holley. On that occasion, he was polite enough, bid the women a good afternoon and questioned Martha as to the nature of her settlement in Wickthorpe. She found him pleasant enough on the surface but there was a certain arrogance about his manner. He was certainly a fine-looking man, a few years older than her, tall and golden-haired. But the way in which his blue eyes sought hers made Martha uncomfortable. Even upon that first meeting, there was something about him she did not trust.

Deborah shivered. The description of Roger Holley called to mind her own first encounter with Dr Seb Holley. *Tall, golden-haired, blue eyes.* They even shared the same surname! How strange, too, that Martha's reaction to Roger, mirrored her own feelings about Seb. She shook her head. Pure coincidence, nothing more. Martha's story took place centuries before, and Deborah's sole connection to it was villagers' superstitious belief that she was a reincarnation of the Wickthorpe Witch.

However, as she read on, reaching the conclusion of the first chapter, that initial knot of anxiety tightened in her chest.

News of Martha's talents and knowledge became widespread and she received several such requests for her help, much to her dismay. It was on one of such missions that she had the misfortune to encounter Roger Holley once again, and this time she was alone.

Dismayed at her own visceral reaction to the final sentence, Deborah cast the book aside.

14

CHAPTER 3

Honoraria Simpson-Fairchild had been busy. First, there had been the clamour for interviews in the summer. She had become considered *the* expert on all matters concerning Martha Lightbody, the Wickthorpe Witch. Quite right too. She really was the *only* person eligible to discuss such a sensitive subject in a knowledgeable and objective way. And she had been more than happy to do so. It had been incredibly exhilarating. An unexpected whirlwind of celebrity, now sadly ended. To fill the void, her attentions turned once more to the quest for love.

When her husband, Edgar, died of lung cancer, Honoraria had no alternative but to shoulder her grief and the burden of widowhood. Friends were wonderful. Colleagues from the King Edward VI Upper School, where she had worked as a history teacher before leaving to look after Edgar, were caring and helpful. People from the village rallied around and ensured she had plenty of company – at least, in the beginning. Everyone led such busy lives, and the support gradually eased off. It was understandable.

Nine years on, she kept herself busy. Two days a week she volunteered at a charity shop in Stowmarket; she hosted regular coffee mornings in aid of Cancer Research; she was involved in several village groups; and the organisation of History Society meetings took up much of her spare time. Mostly, it was enough. But, sometimes, especially on long, solitary evenings, she was lonely. Not that she would ever admit it to anyone. Far better to cover her sadness with cosmetics and show the world a brave face. No one liked a moaner.

Honoraria had anticipated meeting fellow history buff, Marcus Monk, with irrepressible excitement. They had spoken on the phone when he responded to her request, via the History Society network, for information regarding Martha Lightbody. His voice, deep, warm and velvety, had set the blood coursing through her veins. She had conjured a vision of a tall, dark, handsome widower with a thing for redheads. They would walk through the woods together, hand in hand, share hot toddies on her small patio, and romp naked through the night on her satin sheets. The prospect was altogether impossibly thrilling!

However, as was so often the case, reality proved a sad disappointment. When Marcus attended a Wickthorpe History Society meeting, to reveal evidence he had found of Lightbody family members within the old parish registers of Little Horseshoes in Norfolk, the sight of him was woefully less than she had anticipated. Short; rather portly; a large, bulbous nose; heavy jowls. Very underwhelming. He did have nice, brown eyes, Honoraria generously allowed, which crinkled and lit up as he spoke. And at least he still had some hair: grey, neatly-trimmed, although noticeably receding from his wide forehead. As for his voice ... well, if she shut her eyes, his sonorous tone certainly worked magic for her. But she could hardly walk around with her eyes closed! Such a shame the rest of him held so little appeal!

After the History Society meeting, they had spoken often on the phone regarding Marcus' subsequent efforts to discover more about the Wickthorpe Witch. Unfortunately, his further searches had been unsuccessful. Honoraria had promised Marcus she would drive up to the Norfolk coast to the village of Little Horseshoes, perhaps even staying for a few days, so they might continue the quest together. She was aware that he was only an *amateur* historian and would most likely benefit from her professional knowledge and expertise. So far, though, Honoraria had been in no great rush to do so. He appeared flatteringly interested in her but, much as she was eager to follow-up on the Lightbody family ancestry, she had held off from accepting his invitation. It would not be fair to give him any kind of encouragement. Especially as she had a new infatuation. *Gerald.*

Gerald was everything she had ever dreamt of a man in the bedroom and more. His smooth, hard, well-endowed body was every fifty-something woman's fantasy. Just thinking about him caused her heart to dance itself into a frenzy. Other parts of her too. Their first encounter, in a bijou hotel on the outskirts of Cambridge, had been everything she could have desired. A romantic dinner with a handsome, wonderfully attentive, younger man.

Good food, wine and conversation. Lots of flirtation, which continued as they headed upstairs to a room overlooking the River Cam. She gazed out from their balcony at the beautiful, starlit night, and he slid warm hands around her waist. His lips nibbled at her neck, and her legs turned to jelly. Gently, he turned her around and lowered his mouth to hers, caressing, probing. His long fingers stroked her back, snaking upwards to tug at her zip. Her dress slipped from her shoulders, and his hands roved further, tormenting her quivering flesh ...

Honoraria sighed aloud. Gerald had more than exceeded her expectations. After all the trials and disappointments of online dating, and her more recent foray into the world of personal advertising, her new partner had proved most adept at fulfilling her every need. He was intelligent too, currently working towards a post-graduate degree in archaeology, and sharing her interest in all things historical. She had seen him twice so far and was counting the hours to the following weekend, which he had promised to spend with her in Oxford. Yes, Gerald was perfect.

Too bad their affair was costing her an absolute fortune!

An old film, *American Gigolo*, had given her the idea – specifically, its leading man, the gorgeously young and virile Richard Gere. Male escorts! Why had she not thought of it before? With her usual diligence, she had investigated at length – a most enjoyable experience. Who would have thought there were so many escort agencies? And so many mouth-watering men prepared to fulfil her every desire ... for a fee, of course. She had clicked on a vast number of photos, mulling over several possibilities. Finally, she had settled upon Gerald. Very good-looking but not a pretty boy. Good physique. And, more importantly for her relatively limited budget, in the mid-price bracket.

That first time, she had tried to keep her expectations realistic. Although she had been honest about her age, she feared it might prove a stumbling block. Also, whilst he looked perfect on her screen, he might have a particularly annoying habit, such as picking his nose or eating with his mouth open. She would not have been able to tolerate either of those. Having corresponded with him via email – very professional – they had agreed to an initial session of two hours for dinner with an option to continue should both be agreeable. And continue they had – to a most satisfactory conclusion.

When she had embarked on the use of escorts, her plan was to do so only as an occasional treat. With Gerald's fee running at approximately eight hundred pounds per night, plus expenses, she had already spent over two thousand pounds, and next weekend would amount to another two thousand. Yes, she had savings, but they were limited. This craving for him had to stop. Her rational, sensible head knew it, but her heart and body refused to listen. When Gerald bid her adieu, and asked if she would like to book their next date, his amber eyes were so meltingly irresistible she found her lips saying, 'Yes, please,' before she could stop them.

Next weekend would have to be the last time ... at least, for a while. And, until then, she would have a wonderful time daydreaming. She certainly could not spare the time to trot over to Little Horseshoes.

***

Wendy Robinson, the Rector of St Mary's Church, Wickthorpe, fidgeted with her coffee cup. It was difficult to maintain a cheerful front, sitting opposite Jane Holley, part-time pharmacist and wife of Dr Seb Holley, in the latter's gloomy living room. Visiting Jane had become a regular feature of Wendy's busy week and, as months went by, Wendy's concern had escalated. Jane had lost weight, and the grey cardigan she wore drooped on her bony frame as if on a coat hanger. She was just fifty years old but looked a good ten years older, if not more. Her thin face sagged with the weariness of someone exhausted by the pain of living. Wendy tried to provide comfort and support but nothing seemed to help. Unless Jane chose to confide in her, she could do no more.

'How are things at work?' Wendy asked brightly, as a safe opening gambit. 'I bet you're busy, with this latest flu virus going around.'

'Yes, very busy.' Jane took a sip of her coffee and gazed with pensive eyes through the window.

'Have you made plans for Christmas yet? Are the boys coming home?' Wendy tried again. Usually, a mention of her two sons, both away at university studying medicine, helped to perk Jane up.

A listless shrug. 'I don't know. They both have girlfriends so they may choose to spend Christmas with them.'

'Not the whole of Christmas, surely? And miss your legendary Christmas dinner? I don't believe it!'

A tiny hint of a smile. 'Yes, they don't like to miss out.' Jane sighed. 'I expect we'll see them but you know what young people are like. They'll choose what suits them and tell us when they think about it. No point trying to pin them down.'

'I suppose not.' Wendy stared into her coffee cup for inspiration. The frothy surface of the liquid blinked back at her. Jane did make a marvellous cappuccino. 'Delicious coffee,' she offered.

A nod, then silence, apart from the monotonous tick of a black, marble clock, crouched like an ugly toad on a walnut bureau. No wonder the woman was so depressed, Wendy thought, as she cast desperate eyes around the room. The furnishings were so dark and drab. She longed for a splash of colour – anything – to brighten Jane's life. Even her clothes were dull: black trousers; blouse and cardigan in shades of grey; plain, lead–grey slippers. Everything was neat and tasteful, but incredibly boring. Wendy wondered how Seb could stand it. He was such a colourful character. Her lips curved inadvertently as she thought of the handsome, gregarious doctor. He and Jane made for a very mismatched couple, but they had been married for several years now and it was not Wendy's place to judge. Seb was always attentive to Jane when they were out together. He must see something in her which others failed to appreciate.

'Jane, I know something is bothering you,' Wendy began, deciding to bite the bullet. 'Have you spoken to Seb about it?'

An ironic twist to the lips. 'This isn't something I can talk to him about,' came the short reply. Spoken with a whisper of venom.

Oh dear. At least, though, there was the admission that something was amiss. Something to latch onto. 'Is there someone else you can chat to? A friend? Relative? Me? Obviously, you can tell me anything, in complete confidence. Sometimes it helps to get things off your chest.'

'In complete confidence ...' Jane mulled over the words. She shook her head. 'I've done so many awful things. You would despise me.'

Wendy stood and moved to sit next to Jane, placing an arm around the other woman's thin shoulders and giving her a gentle squeeze. 'Jane, we have all done things of which we are ashamed. The Lord knows this, and yet

He loves us anyway. If we are truly sorry for our mistakes, He will forgive us, I can promise you that. And I can also promise, no matter what you tell me, I will not despise you.'

As Wendy carefully removed her arm, Jane leant forward, head in hands. 'I can't,' she wailed. 'It's too terrible.'

'No sin is so terrible you cannot seek forgiveness. You just need to take that first step,' Wendy urged.

A long pause. The clock continued its relentless marking of the passing seconds. At last, Jane lifted her head. 'Alright, I'll tell you what really happened in 1988, the year Ayesha Khan died.' She heaved a long sigh. 'All the things which took place this summer ... Freya Billington ... Deborah Ryecroft ... I can't live with the guilt anymore.' She turned despairing eyes towards the rector. 'But you have to promise, you won't tell another soul.'

'I've already told you anything you say will be in the strictest confidence.' Inside, Wendy trembled with trepidation and said a silent prayer. *Lord, help me say the right things.*

'So be it.' Another heavy sigh. 'In 1988, I was sixteen and best friends with a girl called Melissa Shipman. She was pretty and popular. I was less pretty, and less popular, but Melissa's approval made me one of the cool kids. Without her, I was nothing. This meant I would do anything to make sure she liked me, even things I didn't really want to do. She made fun of some of the other girls so I did too. In fact, I would say I was worse than she was. I had to be, you see, to keep in with her ... or so I thought at the time. We were both very cruel to Ayesha Khan, and to Debbie Ryecroft when she was about, which wasn't that often. Debbie couldn't have cared less, but Ayesha used to get very upset. That made us worse. I suspect we made her life a misery.' Jane exhaled another long, wretched breath. 'I can't help thinking about some of the things we said ... and did.'

She closed her eyes with a shudder and sank back into charcoal velour, as if trying to disappear into the fabric. Wendy said nothing and waited. The story was not yet done.

'Swimming in Dark Water Lake was my idea,' Jane said suddenly. 'Melissa wasn't sure at first. She said it could be dangerous, with the curse and all that. I laughed at her ... told her she was going soft. Anyway, I said, there was no way either Ayesha or Debbie would go for it. That was the plan

... to torment them for being too chicken when they refused. We were both shocked when Ayesha stripped off and got into the water, but even then we thought she wouldn't go far. She would soon turn around and come back. But she didn't. She just kept going. We laughed and taunted Debbie instead ... couldn't lose face you see ...and Ayesha swam further and further away. She had almost reached the far side of the lake when she waved. At the time, I was relieved she'd made it, but also annoyed that my plan had backfired. Then, there was a sudden gust of wind, which was odd because it had been such a still, muggy day. A branch swung across where Ayesha's arm had been and ...' Tears rolled slow tracks down the hollow cheeks. 'We couldn't see her any more. Melissa and I were frozen with shock. Debbie shouted at us to get help and started swimming across the lake. We got out of there as quickly as we could and ran to Melissa's house to raise the alarm. When Melissa's mum asked what had happened, Melissa said that the swimming had been Debbie's idea. She had dared us all to go into the water but we had refused. Melissa's mum hugged us both and cried tears of relief. She said she always thought there was something odd about that girl, meaning Debbie. And that was how the story grew. Melissa told me, when she was interviewed by the police, after we knew Ayesha had died, that she suggested Debbie may have had wicked intentions all along, and hinted that she may have swum across to Ayesha to finish the job. Her mum was present at the interview and insinuated her suspicions that Debbie was an incarnation of the Wickthorpe Witch. Afterwards, she said as much to everyone in the village. And that's what really happened. That's how Deborah Ryecroft became known as the Wickthorpe Witch. The whole thing was a lie, a fabrication constructed by two frightened girls who knew they had Ayesha Khan's death on their consciences.' Jane turned frightened eyes to Wendy. 'Debbie left Wickthorpe for good which should have been the end of it. But Melissa was really messed up after that. Suffered bouts of depression ... and committed suicide in her early twenties. At the funeral, her parents blamed Debbie for her death too. I kept silent. The truth was too awful. And somehow, I managed to live with it all. For a while, I was even happy ... married to Seb ... my two wonderful boys ...' Jane clutched her face with her hands and burst into tears, wracking breaths convulsing her gaunt frame.

Gently, Wendy folded her arms around her, holding her until the sobs ceased. 'You poor girl,' she murmured. 'All this time, you've borne the burden of grief and guilt.'

Jane pulled away, her face an ugly, tear-stained mask of heartache. 'I don't deserve to be happy. And now, I'm being punished. My day of reckoning is upon me, and I don't know what to do. Help me. What should I do?'

Wendy sighed. 'It isn't for me to tell you what to do, Jane.' She paused before continuing. 'What do you mean about being punished? Do you mean what happened to Freya Billington?' A slight nod. 'That was just an unfortunate coincidence. You must put such thoughts from your mind.' Jane opened her mouth as if to argue but snapped it shut. 'As for Deborah Ryecroft ... what happened to her was awful, but you couldn't possibly know what the Hampton-Browns were planning. They were deranged by their own grief. And regarding the village superstition about the Wickthorpe Witch,' Wendy added slowly, her words dropping like lead weights into the room, 'it's never too late to set the record straight.'

A taut silence stretched between them. 'Only three of us know the truth – Debbie, me and now you.' Jane's features were set stony hard once more. 'You say it's never too late but it is. Too much damage has been done already. And there are those who have become too entrenched in their convictions. They made up their minds long ago and they simply wouldn't believe me. Not people like Enid Green, Philip Holder, Brenda Wicks – people like that. I would love to confess all and receive absolution but it would do no good now. It's my cross to bear. And anyway, there are other things ...'

Wendy waited but Jane had turned away from her and the stillness drifted on. 'Other things?' she prompted.

'It doesn't matter now. Another coffee?'

'No, thank you.' Wendy took Jane's hands in hers. They were ice cold. 'You have taken a brave step today, telling me this. Shall we pray together?'

Jane nodded, and lowered her head, letting Wendy's calm voice wash over her as she offered words of supplication to God. *Repentance ... sin ... forgiveness ... love ...* She wished she could absorb the words as real entities, filling her heart. Instead, they fell, meaningless as dust. Whatever platitudes Wendy offered, she knew her fate, and knew too that she deserved it. She was destined for eternal suffering, both in this life and beyond, and there was nothing anyone could do.

CHAPTER 4

It was some while before Deborah felt inclined to return to *The Life & Times of Martha Lightbody*. She had been unable to shake off her feelings of disquiet and the book had disturbed her recent dreams. Somewhat reluctantly, fearing what she was about to read, she turned to Chapter Two:

Roger Holley was a man of some importance in Wickthorpe. His father, Julius, owned several acres of land to the west of the village and employed many to do his bidding. Both Julius and Roger had reputations as harsh, ruthless men who enjoyed the fruits of their wealth.

'Cross them at your peril,' Martha and John were warned. 'Best keep out of their way.' They listened, but considered there was nothing to fear. They saw no reason why their paths should cross.

How wrong they were! Martha was a beautiful woman with long, dark tresses, a clear complexion and comely figure. A young man such as Roger, used to having his pick of the village wenches, was determined to have her. Unbeknownst to Martha, he watched her comings and goings with cunning eyes, plotting his moment. For Roger, the wait was part of the fun, and a sense of anticipation built in his eager loins.

Deborah swallowed. It was worse than she feared. Her fingers gripped the cover as she read of an encounter between Roger and Martha:

'We meet again, Mistress Lightbody,' Roger smiled, bowing slightly.

Martha eyed him warily and failed to return his smile. A quick glance over her shoulder told her they were completely alone. 'So we do,' she replied, pleasantly enough but moving to press past him. 'Excuse me, sir, but I must away home. My child ...'

'Not so fast, my pretty.' He caught hold of her and held her fast, spinning her with ease into his strong arms. 'A kiss ... and more ... before I allow you on your way.' He pressed coarse lips against hers and she struggled in his arms, trying to pull her face away from his marauding mouth. Instead, he moved his head lower, into the smooth curve of her neck.

'Stop! My husband is on his way to meet me. He'll soon upon us.'

Roger chuckled. 'I think not.'

She continued to wrestle against him but soon realised she could not free herself, helpless as she was against his superior strength. A better plan was required. Using guile, she allowed her body to fall limp in his arms, even moaning a little as he loosened his hold to slide his mouth even lower.

'Ah, you like that?' He grinned and held her with one hand as the other slid beneath the neckline of her dress. 'So beautiful,' he moaned.

With all her might, Martha raised her knee between Holley's legs in one hard thrust. As he yelped in pain, he released his grip and she ran, as swiftly as she could, refusing to look back to see if he followed ...

Deborah exhaled a sigh of relief. Martha was clearly a feisty and resourceful woman. But she also knew Martha, in securing her escape, had made an enemy of Roger. She continued through the chapter, her anxiety growing as the two protagonists met once more. However, on this occasion, the outcome was less predictable:

As Prudence recovered from her confinement, Martha was alone by the river, with both families' sets of laundry, when Roger Holley passed by. His appearance gave her quite a start and she braced herself for flight, but need not have worried. The man seemed much preoccupied and made great haste past her. Though he must have seen her, he made no acknowledgement of it. Such incident caused Martha to believe that Holley was as anxious to avoid her as she was him, and she was much relieved.

Deborah frowned. She was less convinced than Martha that the danger from Roger had passed. However, as she continued to read, she realised that Martha was facing problems of a different kind:

Requests for Martha's assistance with the sick and injured in the village continued but, as is the way of things, not all had a happy outcome. A young girl she had been treating for an unknown malady passed away suddenly and, just three days later, there was a second death, another of Martha's patients. This time, the deceased was an older woman who had been coughing up blood. Martha had treated her with the milk of sow thistle, but the cough had worsened and she knew not how to help her. The woman's daughter, in her grief, accused Martha of poisoning her mother. Such wickedness could not have been further from Martha's intent, but whispers of suspicion against her soon spread through the village. It was a most unsettled time, and Martha began to wonder if they should leave Wickthorpe after all.

Yes, Martha, leave while you can, Deborah silently urged. She closed the book and set it on her bedside table, unsure when she would be able to return to it. A busy week lay ahead.

***

Deborah hoped her fiftieth birthday celebrations would be low-key. No fuss. Just her and Tom. The milestone age was just another number. Nothing to get worked up about.

However, others had different ideas.

In the week prior to the big day, Deborah travelled to London twice. The first time was ostensibly for an important work meeting. Although she had taken a step back from her company, Ryecroft Industries, and Paul Williamson, was now the managing director, Deborah remained involved in key decisions. She worked mostly from home, and commutes to the city had become more of a rarity. However, she made a point of attending directors' meetings in person and took the train from Elmswell on the appointed day that week, only to find she had been ambushed.

There was no meeting. Instead, her colleagues had organised a special celebration for her, with champagne, canapes, and many employees and business acquaintances in attendance. Deborah was taken aback, but had no choice other than to embrace the occasion, and was secretly moved by the effort which had gone into it all. She suspected the hand of Agneta Kent, her personal assistant, whose stern demeanour, enhanced by a severe grey hairstyle and steel-rimmed glasses, belied a kind-hearted nature. Although not given to displays of affection in the workplace, Deborah had given Agneta a warm hug. She had changed since spending time in Wickthorpe. She knew it.

Her second day in London had been organised with her birthday specifically in mind by her long-time friend, Josie Lowe, CEO of a cosmetics company. It involved a long, enjoyable lunch at *The Ivy* with two other close friends: her ex, Rupert Smytheson, and Rafe Vincenzi, an art dealer. As the wine flowed, both men grew sentimental.

'We miss you, darling,' Rafe trilled in his falsetto voice. 'When are you coming back to us? I thought you were only meant to be away for a year.'

'Yes, Debs. London just isn't the same without you.' Rupert heaved a theatrical sigh. 'I've been bereft.'

'That's not what I was told.' Deborah raised her eyebrows. 'I heard you were spending your evenings with a blonde model. And holidays. Sounds like you have more than enough company.'

Rupert shrugged. 'That's different. Charisse is a lovely girl, but she's not you, darling.'

Deborah smiled. Josie had told her Rupert seemed madly in love with his latest girlfriend, but he never could resist flirting. 'A year *was* the original plan,' she said, returning to Rafe's question, 'but it's complicated.'

When Deborah's mother died, her will dictated that Deborah had to spend three hundred and sixty-five consecutive nights at Greenways Farm to inherit the house. Having made the decision to move back to Wickthorpe last March, Deborah's intention had been to remain for the year and then sell the house. However, there had been two unforeseen obstacles. After her near-drowning in the summer at the hands of John and Valerie Hampton-Brown, Deborah spent several days in hospital, thereby necessitating the year to begin all over again. The other complication was her relationship with Tom Oldridge which had blossomed into love. It was still early days, and Deborah was tentative about making long-term plans, but she was enjoying life in Wickthorpe and had no immediate thoughts of returning to London.

'I don't know how long I'll stay in Suffolk but, in the meantime, I am selling my London house,' she admitted.

'What?' Josie was aghast. 'I don't believe it! You're a city girl, through and through, like me.'

'I was,' Deborah replied. 'Turns out I love the countryside as much, if not more.' She began to tell them of her passion for gardening but ceased when she noticed their eyes glazing over.

'You'll get bored soon enough,' Rupert said, leaning back in his chair with an affected yawn. 'And anyway, darling, you're not telling us the whole story, are you? Remember, I've met your farmer boyfriend. I saw the sparks flying between you. Admit it, he's the real reason for your country glow.'

Deborah felt three pairs of expectant eyes upon her and squirmed. She was reluctant to talk about Tom. Their relationship felt too private, too divorced from the London lifestyle she had shared with these friends. And she wasn't sure she could explain it either. She didn't understand it herself. 'Rupert is referring to my neighbour, Tom Oldridge, and yes we are seeing each other.' She blushed and reached for her wineglass to conceal her embarrassment. *Honestly!* Where was her cool façade when she needed it?

Josie arched her brows. 'Well, we look forward to meeting him, my darling. He certainly must be quite a man to bring such colour to your cheeks!'

Fortunately, an acquaintance of Rupert happened by their table at that point and, after pleasantries were exchanged, the conversation moved on to safer topics, much to Deborah's relief. Later, she returned home on the train feeling contented and spoilt. The close friends she had in London were great company and unwavering in their care of her. She *did* miss seeing them as frequently as she used to, but she was also eager to get back to Wickthorpe, and to Tom.

***

Deborah's birthday took place on a Saturday and there was much discussion prior to the event about her wishes for the day. It dawned bitingly cold, with a lacy layer of frost, but the clear skies and bright sunshine were perfect for a long, bracing walk with Tom along the beach at Brancaster, followed by an intimate lunch at *The White Horse*. It was perfect. Deborah wanted nothing more. However, she reckoned without Emma, who decided such an auspicious occasion should involve more celebration. They arrived home to find Greenways Farm festooned with balloons and party banners, and preparations for a party in full swing.

'Did you know about this?' Deborah turned accusing eyes on Tom.

'Nothing to do with me.' He held up his hands. 'Em, what's going on?'

'It's just going to be a few friends,' she replied cheerfully. 'Debs, you'll love it. Trust me.'

Dismay was Deborah's first reaction, but she hid it well. Too late to do anything about it and Emma had obviously gone to a lot of trouble. In truth, she was touched. She had never had a party of any description thrown for her birthday before, and this week there had been three. 'I'm sure I will.' She gave a bright smile and crossed her fingers behind her back, trying to dismiss longing thoughts of the cosy evening, cuddling up to Tom with a film and a takeaway, they had previously planned. 'I'm going upstairs for a bath. What time are people coming?'

'Six o'clock,' Emma grinned. 'Plenty of time to glam up.'

A glance at her watch revealed she had barely an hour. 'We fifty-year-olds require a lot more assistance to achieve glamour than you young things,' she replied, her voice dry. 'I may be a little late.'

'No, you won't,' Emma retorted with confidence. 'You're never late for anything. Go on, off you go. You too, Dad. Rick and I have got this.'

Deborah may not have looked forward to her surprise party but she had a wonderful evening with all her favourite people in Wickthorpe. Kai Melandri and Phil Abbott, the couple who lived opposite, guaranteed lots of laughs. The two of them were a veritable double act. Felix and Jules, old friends of Tom who had instantly charmed Deborah with their down-to-earth humour and with whom they had spent many evenings, were also in attendance. Ava Green, from the Post Office, arrived, wearing a shapeless, navy dress and her habitual, anxious expression. Deborah was particularly pleased to see her there. She felt sorry for Ava, forced to look after her dreadful harridan of a mother. Honoraria Simpson-Fairchild was clearly delighted to have been invited and made a jaw-dropping entrance in a long, scarlet sheath and a pearl choker. With a flourish, she presented Deborah with an elaborately wrapped gift, which turned out to be a book, *A History of Suffolk*.

'I thought it would be invaluable in giving you some basic background information for our History Society discussions,' she announced, loud enough for everyone to hear.

Deborah smiled and thanked her. Honoraria could be hard work, but she had a heart of gold and, since Deborah had got to know her a little, she suspected the other woman was lonely. Again, she was glad Emma had thought to invite her.

'I'd like to propose a toast.' Kai Melandri, resplendent in a blue, sequinned jacket, raised his voice and his champagne flute.

'Oh no,' Phil groaned. 'This could take a while.'

'First of all, I'd like to thank the lovely Emma for inviting us all to Debs' fabulous party.'

'The last time we'll ever be invited,' Phil muttered.

Kai gave him a look. 'Speak for yourself. If you will insist on dressing like a boring accountant, I suspect few invites will be heading *your* way.'

The retort received giggles in response and Phil's face took on an affronted look. To stave off a potential upset, Deborah jumped in, 'I think you look very ...'

'Grey,' Kai inserted, without missing a beat. 'I told him not to wear a suit.'

'Handsome,' Deborah supplied. 'Debonair, suave ...' She struggled for a further suitable adjective and gave up. 'I think now is a good time to thank you all for coming and celebrating my fiftieth with me.'

'Fiftieth?' Kai threw up his hands in mock horror. 'I thought you were forty. I'm far too young for a *fiftieth* party.'

'Yes, *you* would be more at home at a *fifth* birthday party,' Phil deadpanned. 'Please raise your glasses everyone and let's drink to the loveliest fifty-year-old we know. Debs.'

'Debs,' everyone echoed and sipped at their champagne.

'I was going to do that,' Kai said indignantly.

'Yes, but you were too slow, as usual,' Phil responded. He gave his partner's shoulders a squeeze. 'Next time.'

'I'm in my fifties too,' Honoraria declared with an expectant glance at the assembled throng.

An awkward silence, before Felix jumped to the rescue. 'You don't look it, Honoraria. None of you ladies do,' he added gallantly.

'That's lucky,' his wife muttered, 'seeing as I'm only forty-eight!'

'Enough about age, you oldies,' Emma called. 'Let's have some music. I've put together a playlist based upon Debs' favourites so if you don't like it, complain to her.'

As the strains of Adele filled the room, Deborah made a beeline for Rick. 'This is why you were quizzing me about my favourite music the other day,' she smiled at him. 'I can't believe you and Emma have gone to all this trouble. Thank you.'

'Em did all the hard work. I was just her designated assistant,' he replied.

'Oh dear, I guess that meant you didn't get a choice. She is one forceful woman.'

'Yeah,' Rick agreed,' A bit like a steamroller.'

'Not at all.' She frowned at him. 'Emma is gorgeous. Absolutely stunning. Certainly not a steamroller.'

He peered at her uncertainly. 'I agree she's a good sort.'

'Good sort!' Deborah snorted. 'Now you're making her sound like a horse! You, Rick Billington, cannot see what is right under your nose.' She stopped abruptly, aware that she was in danger of saying too much. Two glasses of champagne, straight off, had loosened her tongue, and Rick was now looking distinctly bemused. 'Sorry,' she murmured, 'I guess I'm a bit over-protective where Em is concerned.' Deborah bit her lip as an awkward silence ensued. 'How are your parents getting on with their private investigator?' she said, changing the subject. Immediately, she rebuked herself for her choice of topic. *Insensitive.*

Rick grimaced but took no offence. 'Nothing so far. They're still hopeful though.' Rick's parents refused to believe that their daughter had taken her own life and, when the police investigation had ground to a halt, took matters into their own hands. They hoped to discover the identity of Freya's mystery man, spotted with her in Oxford by Honoraria. *Tall. Dark-haired. Wearing black-framed glasses. Much older than Freya.* They were convinced he had something to do with her death.

'Debs, it's time we were dancing.' Tom appeared by her side and slid his arm around her waist. 'Come on. Em has told me we need to get people on the dancefloor. If we lead the way, others will follow.'

'How romantic!' Deborah grinned up at him. 'You know how to make a girl swoon.'

'I only want one girl,' he whispered in her ear, as she drifted into his arms. 'Just you.' He pressed warm lips against the side of her neck, sending delicious ripples along her spine.

Later, once everyone had left, and Tom was in the bathroom, she reflected that it really had been a perfect birthday. And if Tom fulfilled some of the promises he made while they were dancing, it wasn't finished yet.

She glanced at her bedside table where *The Life & Times of Martha Lightbody*, her bequest from Mabel, lay. So far, she had not progressed beyond the opening two chapters.

'Sorry, Martha,' she said, stroking the leather-bound cover, 'but you're going to have to wait.

CHAPTER 5

'Mabel Littlebody's bungalow has been sold.'

A small enclave of villagers was assembled around Enid Green's chair in the Post Office on a cold morning in early December to hear her latest snippets. Enid always knew everything. No matter what the village subject, or how recently the event had occurred, she always seemed to be the first to know. If you wanted information, the Post Office was the place you headed. The semi-retired husband of the rector, Ralph Robinson, old Gretchen Cooper, Philip Holder and Brenda Wicks provided a very satisfactory audience this morning and Enid was in her element.

'Any idea who has bought it?' asked Brenda, a moon-faced woman in her sixties with rigid curls in tones of brown, red and purple. She and Enid had grown closer in recent months, bound together by their entrenched belief in the village curse.

Enid threw a sly glance at her daughter who stood patiently waiting behind the counter. 'An *American* gentleman, or so I heard. Not that those words go together – American and gentleman that is,' she cackled.

'I've always found Americans to be very pleasant,' inserted the ever-genial Ralph. 'Spent some time in Colorado when I was a lad. Beautiful place. I keep trying to persuade Wendy to take a road trip in the States but it will probably have to wait until we're both retired.'

'You need to get to bed earlier,' Gretchen piped up.

'I beg your pardon?'

'If you're tired. Nothing like a good night's sleep.' Gretchen gave him a sage nod.

Enid rolled her eyes. '*Retired*,' she bellowed. 'Ralph was talking about *retirement*, not being tired. Anyway, as I was saying, some American has bought the place and ...' She waited until all eyes were back upon her. 'I've heard he hopes to move in next month.'

'Really? That's quick. I wonder what an American wants in Wickthorpe?' Brenda mused.

'Something to do with Lakenheath, I shouldn't wonder,' Ralph answered. 'The American Air Base. Most Americans living this way seem to be connected to the Air Force in one way or another.' He glanced at his watch. 'I'd best be off. Ladies, Philip, have a good day.'

The small crowd splintered at his departure with Brenda and Gretchen both heading for the counter. Before Philip Holder could follow them, Enid leant forward with surprising agility and gripped him by the arm. 'I haven't seen you about much, Philip,' she remarked, her voice deceptively mild.

The small, wiry man twitched and averted his eyes. 'Been busy,' he muttered, tugging surreptitiously at his arm. 'You know how it is.'

Enid continued to grip his sleeve with the tenacity of a terrier. 'Mm, I think I know only too well. You lack backbone, Philip Holder, you always have. I haven't given up, you know.'

Philip lowered his voice to a whisper. 'Given up what?'

'You know ... Deborah Ryecroft. You're safe to talk here. Brenda's on our side and Gretchen can't hear a word we're saying. What happened in the summer – that woman's miraculous rescue from her trial by drowning – is proof that she really is a witch.' She shuddered. 'I'm just waiting for the next tragedy. There will be one, you realise, unless we stop her.'

'Yes, but what about ... the police? Philip looked furtively over his shoulder. 'We were warned.'

'Pah,' Enid snorted with derision. 'I'm not bothered about them. Remember, we have right on our side. I'm surprised the rector is so enamoured with the woman, given that she does the devil's work! But there, I suppose it's her job to see only good in people. We are the ones who know what she really is, so *we* are the ones who must stop her.'

'But what can we do?' Philip squirmed as the conversation took an even more uncomfortable turn. Whilst he supported Enid's views, his brush with the law in the summer, after it was discovered he, Andrew Green and Enid had been responsible for threatening Deborah Ryecroft with anonymous notes and vandalism to her garden, had put him off further involvement in Enid's schemes.

'I don't know yet. Perhaps *you* can come up with something this time?'

'Perhaps.' At last, Philip managed to detach himself from Enid's claw and shuffled towards the counter where he withdrew some cash, conscious of Enid's eyes still on him.

If he had hoped to escape the Post Office without further interaction, he was disappointed. As he shrank past Enid on his way out, she hissed at his retreating back. 'Don't be a stranger, Philip. Remember, I know things about you.' She tapped her hawk-like nose. 'Things you wouldn't want others to know. Remember that.'

Ava watched the man slip through the door and felt almost sorry for him. There was something about Philip Holder she had never trusted but, seeing the defeated slump of his shoulders and her mother's smug smirk, she wondered if he too was a victim. Was Enid blackmailing him to do her bidding? With a tired shake of her head, Ava wondered where it would all end.

Her relationship with her mother had always been difficult but they had managed to exist in the same house with a degree of civility, so long as she did whatever Enid wanted. However, since she attended Deborah's fiftieth birthday party, her mother's hostility had known no bounds. Enid had warned her, if she went, she would no longer consider Ava her daughter. Emotional blackmail. Ava was used to it and, this time, refused to give in. She had felt honoured to receive an invitation, and was looking forward to a night out, a rarity in her sad life. Enid had never treated her like a daughter anyway, she reasoned, except in her expectation that Ava should look after her, so there would be little difference. She was wrong.

The full force of Enid's vengeance and spite had been unleashed. Since the party, her mother had found countless ways to make her life even more miserable: hiding the toothpaste, Ava's reading glasses, her car keys, her hairbrush ... the list was endless. Trivial things designed to inconvenience and annoy. But she had not stopped there. When her daughter was out, Enid shredded a treasured photograph Ava kept by her bed. It had been the sole remaining picture she had of her dad and she was devastated by its destruction. Also, when she checked in her wardrobe, she found the dress she had worn to Deborah's party covered in ink stains. Subsequent washes had failed to erase them.

Every day brought a new level of torment. Ava was not sure she could stand it much longer.

***

When Emma had suggested a short holiday to Rick, he had been disappointingly lukewarm about the idea. She had hoped to have another go at persuading him that evening but he bounded past her in a flurry of haste. 'I'm off out tonight,' he called over his shoulder. 'Don't worry about me for tea.'

'Brilliant,' Emma muttered to herself as he disappeared upstairs. She gave the bolognese sauce she had made for the two of them an irritated stir. 'Thanks for the notice.'

It was some while before Rick reappeared. When he did, she could see he had made a special effort. He was dressed casually, in jeans and sweatshirt, but she had seen neither before and suspected they were new. His hair was carefully slicked and gelled, and there was a distinct whiff of sandalwood in the air. Her heart plummeted. He was out on a date.

'Going anywhere nice?' she asked, with as much unconcern as she could muster.

'I've booked that new Italian in Bury, *Pasta Perfection*,' he replied. 'Hope it's as good as the reviews say it is.'

Wow! *Pasta Perfection* was all the rage but she had also heard it was quite pricey. 'Who's the lucky lady?'

His cheeks flamed. 'Amelie's back,' he said. 'She texted me this morning and asked if we could meet up. She said she'd missed me.'

Amelie Charles. Emma's insouciant smile slipped. Rick and Amelie had been an item in the summer but Amelie had left Wickthorpe for a job in London, and Rick had taken a while to get over her. Except he hadn't. Clearly. Emma turned back to the bolognese sauce, stirring while she considered her response. Rick was waiting for a reaction but she struggled to think of anything positive to say. *Don't go. Amelie doesn't really care about you. You're just a convenient interlude until she buggers off again. Stay here with me. I'm the one you want.* None of those.

'Well, that's a surprise,' she said carefully. 'I hope you have a nice evening.' She turned to face him.

He gave a grin and a thumbs up. 'Will do. See you later.'

As he headed for the door, she couldn't resist calling after him. 'Rick.' He stopped. 'Be careful. Don't let her hurt you all over again.'

'Don't worry,' he replied with the confidence of a man who believed everything would go right this time. 'Amelie admitted she made a mistake letting me go. It won't happen again. I'll make sure of it.'

And Emma's heart splintered into a thousand pieces.

***

Andrew Green tapped his fingers against his leg and weighed things up. His mother had summoned him to go and see her and, irritatingly, he did not dare turn her down. He wished he knew what she had on him. Without that knowledge, he could not afford to ignore her demands, however much he would prefer to stay out of her schemes. They were bound to feature Deborah Ryecroft. Andrew had no idea why Enid was so obsessed with the woman. It certainly was *not* concern for the spiritual welfare of the village. His mother was the least altruistic person he knew. There was more to it and he would do his darnedest to discover what it was. He was not the only person with secrets. Enid was hiding something.

Would she really blow the whistle on him? He would not put it past her. Yes, at some point, he would have to go and see her, but she could stew for a bit. It would not be in his best interests to appear too keen.

Last time, when he had become embroiled in her plans to drive Deborah Ryecroft from the village, his fingers had got burnt. Julie, his wife, did not know about his visit from the police concerning the notes and vandalism to the businesswoman's garden. More importantly, his father–in–law and boss, Frank Newman, was also unaware. Frank, the owner of a small chain of independent grocery stores, was a wealthy man and Andrew, the husband of the sole heir to the business, was determined nothing should hamper his future prospects.

Julie had given him an ultimatum in the summer when she had suspected him of infidelity yet again. Just as well she didn't know the half of it! Since then, he had been a model husband and father but the role was wearing thin. His old urges were beginning to consume him and, unless he took care of them, he might be tempted into something he would regret.

They had taken on a new girl at the shop he managed for Frank. Fresh out of school. Pretty, blonde-haired, nice figure. Jacquie with a q. A real flirt too. Impossible for him not to flirt back. He sighed. The frustration was unbearable. He was sorely in need of some decent sex. But not with Jacquie. That *would* be playing with fire. He made up his mind. He deserved a night out.

'Love,' he called, picking up his car keys. 'I'm just going out for a while. With Ben. I won't be late.'

'Oh?' Julie appeared from the kitchen. 'I thought we'd start that new box set everyone's talking about. That thriller. Has Ben just called? I didn't hear your phone.'

She was checking up on him, an annoying habit which had curtailed his fun recently. 'He sent me a text.' He held up his phone as if to show her the screen. 'Wants to talk to me about a problem with his boiler.'

She raised her eyebrows. 'Are you suddenly a boiler expert?' she challenged.

He laughed. 'You know I'm not. But Ben knows we've just replaced ours. We were chatting about it. Anyway, he wants to ask me about the new one we had installed.'

'Sounds like an excuse to me.'

He winked at her. 'Probably. You know Ben. Fancies a drink down the pub and a mate to buy him one.'

'Mm.' Her face remained unconvinced. 'Ok. Say hi to Ben for me.'

'Will do.' As an afterthought, he stepped towards her and kissed her lips. 'See you later, love.'

With a jaunty step, he made for his car, a black BMW convertible. Not a family vehicle. The wife had that. This was his baby. And boy, did he deserve it! As the engine roared into life, he slipped off his wedding ring and grinned at himself in the rear-view mirror. *Freedom.* He made a mental note to call Ben who had recently become his cover story of choice. Julie had become suspicious if he cited Mick or Steve, friends who had provided him with alibis in the past. Ben was a single mate. Didn't live too close. No wife or girlfriend to refute his claims. But, tonight, Andrew was flying solo. He was long overdue a treat after the long months of abstinence and he knew exactly where he would receive it.

CHAPTER 6

Deborah set the leather-bound book aside, having read a chapter in which Martha tried to help a young girl struggling to give birth. The girl's mother had spotted Martha's mole, her 'devil's mark,' and accused her of practising the dark arts. The baby subsequently died, raising the woman's suspicions further. Martha had already decided she would have to leave Wickthorpe when, on her way home, she was attacked once again by Roger Holley. Luckily, she was saved by the appearance of another man and his brothers, but worse was to come. Deborah was sure of it. Even though the chapter ended with Martha and John making plans to flee, Deborah knew they would be too late. The 'drowning' lay ahead. She steeled herself to continue reading. Every time Roger was mentioned, a picture of him loomed, vivid and threatening, in her mind, but not an image conjured from the book's description of him. It was the face of *Seb* Holley which hovered between the lines on almost every page ...

Giving herself a mental shake, Deborah checked the time. In less than an hour, she was expected at the studio of the romantically-named Rafaella Van Tryk for her first painting lesson. Whilst she was looking forward to it, she also felt nerves fluttering in her stomach. It was the first time in a long while that she was embarking upon something new. For someone used to being in charge and taking control, something like this was out of her comfort zone. A good thing, she told herself. She would either show signs of talent, or she wouldn't. Either way, she was determined to enjoy it.

Later that evening, she was due to attend the History Society meeting. It was to be just a small gathering, held at Honoraria's cottage.

'Only the regulars will be there,' Honoraria told her. 'We're going to share what we've all found out about the Wickthorpe Witch, Martha Lightbody. I tasked members to try to discover more information about her. I suspect no one will have done anything about it. They leave everything up to me. Luckily, I always have a few things up my sleeve,' she winked.

Deborah pulled a face when informed that Enid Green was one of the regular attendees. 'I'm not sure Enid will take too kindly to my presence,' she cautioned.

Honoraria frowned. 'You're right. I'd better warn her. You will still come though, won't you? You won't let Enid put you off.'

Deborah smiled. 'Of course not. I'll be there.'

She hadn't mentioned the book to Honoraria, thinking it best to read it herself first. Whilst it had claimed, in the foreword, to be a fictional account of events in 1645, based upon Martha's own diary and letters within the family, it felt very real to Deborah. She wondered how such information had fallen into the hands of the book's author, John Littlebody. Was it possible he was a relative? The names were quite similar. Hopefully, all would be revealed later in the book. In the meantime, it would be interesting to see what the History Society meeting turned up.

***

Best get it over with. Honoraria thrust open the door of the Post Office and stepped inside. Enid was in her usual chair, glasses perched on the end of her nose, reading a woman's magazine, which she tossed aside at the appearance of a visitor.

'Oh, it's you,' she muttered, peering in Honoraria's direction, a blanket wrapped around her bulky frame. 'What do you want?'

Honoraria was relieved to see the calm presence of Ava behind the counter. She gave them both a smile. 'Morning ladies. Cold today, isn't it?'

'Yes, I'm afraid winter is well and truly upon us,' Ava returned. 'What can I do for you today?'

Honoraria hesitated. Now the moment was upon her, she baulked at the prospect of Enid's wrath. She took a deep breath. 'Actually, it's about tonight's History Society meeting.' Another bright smile. 'I just wanted to let you know ...'

'Is it cancelled?' Enid interrupted. 'Good. I can watch another episode of *World's Worst*. Tonight, it's all about serial killers.'

Honoraria was unable to prevent a grimace. *How awful! Who on earth would want to watch such a show?* 'No, no,' she said, 'it's nothing like that. It's just ... er ... I wanted to let you know that Deborah Ryecroft will be joining us this evening.'

Enid's reaction was not what she had expected. The old woman cackled loudly, her whole body shaking with mirth. 'That's a good one,' she spluttered at last. 'She'll be able to tell you *exactly* what happened to Martha Lightbody with her inside knowledge.'

'I do hope you'll still want to join us, Enid,' Honoraria said anxiously.

'Don't be stupid!' Enid glared. 'Of course, I'm not coming. Do you honestly think I would choose to spend a whole evening with that woman? You can count me out, Honoraria, and that goes the same for future meetings. Your loss.'

'But Enid ...'

The protest was curtailed by a sneer. 'I didn't enjoy them anyway. Boring. A waste of time.' Enid picked up her magazine once more. The subject was closed.

Honoraria scurried across to the counter. 'Will you still be able to come, Ava?'

'Oh yes, I'll be there.' Ava gave her a reassuring smile.

'I'm so sorry about ...'

'It's fine. It's great that Debs can make it.' An angry snort from the chair. 'I'm really looking forward to it. Especially now,' Ava could not resist adding.

'Lovely. I'll see you later. Bye Enid,' Honoraria offered as she hurried by. No reply. *Oh well, it couldn't be helped.*

***

The History Society meeting attracted a small but friendly group that evening: Wendy and Ralph Robinson, Ava Green, Deborah Ryecroft, Gretchen Cooper (whose attendance could be relied upon as Honoraria always ensured a good supply of quality biscuits) and a surprise visitor, Marcus Monk. He had turned up at Honoraria's door a good thirty minutes before the start of the meeting. Honoraria offered up a silent prayer of thanks that she was fully dressed and well-prepared.

'Marcus,' she cried, upon seeing him on her doorstep, 'I wasn't expecting you. Come in out of the cold.' Goodness, the man had made another long trek from North Norfolk, especially to see her! He must be keen. Too bad she wasn't interested.

As he handed her his coat, Marcus explained how intrigued he was by the story of Martha Lightbody and, whilst he had got no further in his own enquiries, he was fascinated to learn what others had discovered.

Oh, perhaps it *wasn't* her he had come to see after all. Strangely, Honoraria felt a trickle of disappointment. 'This way, Marcus,' she gushed as she showed him through to her cosy living room. A quick mental count. *Yes, there should be enough chairs.* 'I hope you won't find it all a bit of a waste of time. I can't promise that my members will have been very diligent in their research.'

'I'm sure the evening will be most interesting.' His brown eyes twinkled as he smiled and Honoraria experienced an internal quiver. As she left him settled in the best chair beside her wood burner, she loitered in her kitchen, confused by her reaction to Marcus' surprise appearance. It had set her all of a jitter! Must be the unexpectedness of it, that was all, but it was most peculiar.

Fortunately, the arrival of other guests, starting with Gretchen who was always irritatingly early, provided a welcome distraction from her confusion, and the meeting was soon underway.

'Now, a few months ago, I set you all a research task,' Honoraria said with what she hoped was an optimistic smile. 'It's time to share what we've all discovered. Deborah, as you weren't at that meeting, I'm not expecting anything from you. Perhaps Marcus, you would be kind enough to start us off?'

In his deep, hypnotic voice, Marcus recapped the information he had shared with the group previously and his subsequent efforts to discover more. Whilst he had found records of Lightbodys in the old registers from his parish of Little Horseshoes, he had unearthed no information of a

43

Lightbody named Martha in the right timeframe. 'I did find a Martha listed later, in the nineteenth century, but not earlier. Unfortunately, those records are very sketchy. I was fortunate to find some of our parish registers, dating from the seventeenth century, online and that's where I first discovered the recorded death of a Lightbody.' He pulled a piece of paper from his pocket: Matthew Lightbody, buried 1665; Calla Lightbody, buried 1681 ...' He paused. 'Perhaps you don't need to know all the details?' A questioning look at Honoraria.

'They could prove invaluable should we discover more information about Martha herself. Matthew, for example, could turn out to be her husband. Calla could be a child. Whilst your list won't necessarily mean anything to us now, it might in the future. In any case, it's proof of your diligence and excellent work. Thank you, Marcus.' Honoraria beamed her approval. She liked the way he deferred to her in front of the other members of the group. *A man confident in his own masculinity and not feeling the need to posture to others.* She felt her cheeks flushing. 'Has anyone else found anything?'

'I've checked the Wickthorpe registers,' Wendy offered, 'but I'm afraid I couldn't find a Lightbody listed anywhere.'

Honoraria nodded. She already knew that, having checked them herself as a matter of course. 'Thank you, Wendy. Anyone else?' Silence, as she had expected.

'I'm sorry.' Ava's face was full of contrition. 'I'm afraid I forgot all about it until today, when I was working. I am interested though to know where we might look. I wouldn't know where to start.'

'Marcus, would you like to share what you did?' Honoraria could have answered the question, but she liked to delegate the conversation as much as possible. It was important for everyone to feel included. No point asking Gretchen though. In the warm room, the old woman's mouth gaped open and Honoraria suspected she had already fallen asleep. *Honestly! What would Marcus think?* Instantly, she brought that train of thought to a halt. What did she care what Marcus Monk thought?

Marcus explained, in a gratifyingly succinct manner, his trawl of parishregisters.co.uk. That was where his enquiries had ended so it was up to Honoraria to take up the mantle, a role which she was only too happy to assume.

'We are fortunate these days that so many parish registers have been transcribed and are now available online. Unfortunately, you need to know where to look to find the information you require. The website Marcus described is excellent, but records are accessed via the name of the parish, rather than by the name of the person you are researching. Other websites can provide further information. Genealogical websites, for example. But these require a subscription and some can be quite pricey. Apart from that, it comes down to leg work. The Suffolk and Norfolk Records Offices are good places to start. Again, you need to research online and find documents which may be relevant to your search. They all have reference numbers which you need to note down. To arrange a visit, you have to register, and it's advisable to book a table in advance.'

'Is that for dinner?' Gretchen awoke with a start at the prospect of a meal out.

'No, sadly not, Gretchen.' Honoraria treated her to a benign smile. 'I'm talking about a table where you may examine the documents. There are all sorts of requirements for a visit so it is advisable to check online first. But it is a worthwhile experience. I recommend you all try it. Our problem with Martha is that we know so little about her, and what we *think* we know could be the stuff of legend. As far as I'm aware, no concrete evidence of her existence has been discovered. The whole curse may have been a fabrication.' Shocked exclamations and the vigorous shaking of heads greeted that statement. 'I know. I agree with you. I feel sure our village curse is based upon a real event which happened in Wickthorpe but we have no proof. It's up to us to find it. Are you up for the challenge?'

Honoraria's rousing speech induced a few murmurs of 'yes' and 'definitely' and she held back a frustrated sigh. Apart from Marcus, she did not feel anyone present was sufficiently enthusiastic to go the extra mile. Historical research involved a lot of effort. She glanced across at Deborah who had remained silent throughout. 'How about you, Deborah? I know you're a busy woman but are you sufficiently interested to want to find out the truth about Martha Lightbody?'

'I would love to know the truth,' Deborah replied, choosing her words with care. 'It sounds, however, that the process you have described is a bit like searching for a needle in a haystack, with no guarantees the needle is actually there.'

Honoraria frowned, disappointed by Deborah's response. *Very negative.* 'I agree,' she said, in a bit of a huff, 'but the process itself is fascinating. It can throw up some very enlightening surprises and send you off on a new tangent altogether. I would recommend it. Who knows what you may find out? Perhaps, by our next meeting, one of us will have discovered something momentous. Shall we stop now for coffee and biscuits?'

'I'll give you a hand.' To Honoraria's surprise, Deborah stood and followed her to the kitchen.

'Thank you, Deborah,' Honoraria's previous annoyance evaporated with the other woman's willingness to assist. 'Would you be kind enough to go back and ask who would prefer tea and who would like coffee?'

'Yes.' Deborah lowered her voice. 'But first, I wanted to let you know I may have something which will tell us more about Martha Lightbody. I want to check it out first ... but I *will* share it with you when I can.'

'Really?' Honoraria's voice was a shocked explosion of sound and Deborah closed the kitchen door behind them. 'What on earth is it?'

'I'm afraid you'll have to be patient. I would prefer to say no more, but I didn't want you to waste lots of time at the records office if I may have information which could help.'

'Well, how intriguing!' Honoraria's eyes shone at the prospect. 'Please let me know as soon as you can.'

'I will.'

***

As was usual for History Society meetings, enthusiasm for further intellectual discussion waned with the arrival of refreshments. Conversation moved on to Christmas, which was fast approaching, and Wendy took the opportunity to advertise the various church events taking place. Honoraria agreed she might go to the Christingle service and Gretchen said she would be there for everything as a regular attendee.

You had to admire Gretchen, Honoraria mused, as she collected cups after the majority had made their departure. Widowed at forty after her husband was killed in a motorbike accident, alone for the past thirty-five years since her only daughter emigrated to Australia, now in her eighties, getting by on just her state pension, but always out and about, always cheerful, and always on the lookout for a free meal. A survivor, making the best of what was available to her – a bit like herself. Not that, in all other respects, she was anything like Gretchen!

Marcus carried the remainder of the cups into the kitchen behind her. Now the others had left, she felt flustered all over again. 'Thank you. That's very kind,' she smiled. 'And it was so good of you to drive all this way again.'

'Well, I'm still hoping to persuade you to make the trip across the border to Little Horseshoes,' he said in response. His hopeful, brown eyes probed her face

'I've got a lot on at the moment.' Honoraria spun away from him. This obvious attraction he had for her needed nipping in the bud. 'I'm ... er ... seeing someone.' *Well, technically it was true.*

'Oh ... I see. That's nice.' He seemed a shade taken aback rather than disappointed. Had she misinterpreted his intentions? Quite possibly. Risking a quick glance, she decided his smile was one of amusement rather than regret. *How mortifying!*

'Sorry, I thought ... anyway, that said, I *would* still like to come to Little Horseshoes,' she stumbled on. 'Perhaps early next year?'

'That would be lovely. Now, if you're sure you require no further help?' A swift shake of her head. 'I'll be on my way. Take care, Honoraria, and thank you for a most enjoyable evening.'

'Safe trip home.' She closed the door behind his retreating form and heaved a sigh. What a fool she had made of herself! Still, it was fortunate if his interest in her *was* purely academic and based solely upon his fascination with the Wickthorpe legend. She would not want to hurt his feelings as he seemed a thoroughly nice man. Such a pity he wasn't her type.

Strange, then, that his face filled her thoughts as she underwent her habitual, night-time cleansing ritual, and it was his voice she heard as she huddled beneath the satin sheets and closed her eyes.

***

While Ava was at the History Society meeting, Enid lost no time in calling her son, Andrew, and Philip Holder, insisting they pay her a visit. Andrew had promised to pop round but had so far failed to do so. Both he and Philip needed a poke – a reminder of the power she held over them. She felt a little more gratified when both arrived promptly.

'What's this all about, Mother?'

Andrew's tone was quite peremptory and Enid scowled at him. She would make him change his tune. From his reaction to her veiled threats, she was reasonably certain he was the man involved with Freya Billington before her death. Thankfully, he had possessed the sense to cover his tracks. Such a discovery could ruin him.

'I told you before,' she snapped. 'I want Deborah Ryecroft out of this village, and it's up to you and Philip to make it happen.'

'I wish you'd let this whole thing drop!' Andrew retorted. 'You surely don't really think she is a witch?'

'I wouldn't be too sure of that,' Philip chipped in. 'The village curse has existed for hundreds of years. I remember my grandfather talking about it when I was a child, like his father before him. He warned me then as I warn you now. The witch is dangerous. I was told my family have been mixed up in it for years, centuries even. Many have suffered at the witch's hands. Whenever there has been a mysterious death or drowning, there has always been a witch responsible. Many a time in the past, villagers have been forced to drive the witch from Wickthorpe. Isn't that right, Enid?'

'It certainly is,' Enid agreed. 'And this time, the task has fallen to us. The Hampton-Browns tried and failed. We have tried too, with the letters and the damage to the garden, but maybe that approach was a bit heavy-handed. We need to be more subtle.'

'What do you suggest?' Andrew glanced at his watch. He had promised Julie he would be no more than an hour. Currently, he felt under suspicion every time he left the house.

'What do you think, Philip?' Enid asked.

He shrugged. 'Beats me.'

'Any ideas, Andrew?'

'For God's sake, just tell us what you want. You clearly have something up your sleeve.' Andrew's impatience bubbled over and he glared at his mother.

In return, she raised her bushy brows. 'I'd thank you not to take that attitude with me, after all I've done for you ... and everything else.' Her narrow-eyed stare became a warning. She could not resist the opportunity to punish Andrew a little for his recent neglect of her. He needed to know where his best interests lay and they were not all with that mousy wife of his.

To her immense satisfaction, he backed down immediately. 'Sorry, Mother. It's just I'm tired. And I had promised Julie I would spend time with her tonight. I've been out a bit recently.'

Really? The fool was playing around again ... so soon? Enid frowned but let the comment pass. There would be time enough to give him a grilling when they were alone. She made a mental note to ensure that happened sooner rather than later.

'I won't keep you long.' She folded her hands on her lap and checked to see she had both men's full attention. 'I think we will struggle to do anything about Deborah Ryecroft as things stand. Not all the villagers feel as we do. The fools can't see the danger we are in.' She shook her head. 'Even worse, she seems to have attracted a modicum of support.' Instantly, she thought of Ava and her face tightened with anger. 'What we require is information. We need to find out everything there is to know about Deborah Ryecroft. There must be something in her past ... some shady business dealing ... or something in her personal history which she won't want made public. Once we have that information, we can use it against her. Force her out of the village by threatening to expose her.'

'Blackmail, you mean.' Andrew nodded agreement. He could see the sense in what Enid was saying.

'It's what I do best,' she replied with a knowing smile. 'We just need to find the right information. And that's where you two come in. I want you to find it. Dig into Deborah Ryecroft's past; find me something I can use. That's all. I will take care of the rest. I will enjoy it.' She rubbed her gnarled hands together.

'And how are we supposed to do that?' Philip asked.

'That's up to you. By fair means or foul, if you have to. I don't care. Just don't get caught, whatever you do. And it goes without saying, should anyone discover what you're up to, it has nothing to do with me. Agreed?'

They both nodded. Andrew stood up. 'Right, I really must go.' He gave his mother a dutiful peck on the cheek. 'I'll start by looking online. Philip?'

The other man threw him a worried glance. 'I'm not sure. I'll try to think of something.'

'You'd better,' Enid warned. 'I'm counting on you.'

CHAPTER 7

Christmas flew by in a flurry of cards, presents, lights and festive food. Being a part of a family Christmas was a first for Deborah. In the past, she had either spent the festive season alone or with a friend, and often abroad. The sentiment of Christmas had been an anathema and she just wanted it over as soon as possible.

This year was different. Being with people she loved, the magic of Christmas was unveiled, layer by layer, like a Russian doll. Each time she thought she knew what was special about it, she discovered another gift within. Christmas shopping, though, proved a major headache. How do you pick the perfect present? Previously, it had been one of those tasks she assigned to Agneta, her personal assistant, who had also taken care of all the wrapping. Another trial to endure! However, the trouble was well worth it. Seeing the joy on Tom's face, when he opened his gift and found she had bought him the drone he wanted, was something to treasure.

'How on earth did you know?' he asked, his face shining with pleasure. He reminded her of a small boy in a television advertisement upon discovering Santa had, against all odds, delivered the toy he really wanted.

'I had help,' she admitted, glancing across at Emma. She had reached exasperation point before realising she should ask the person who knew him best.

'It wasn't difficult,' Emma said. 'How many times have you talked about buying a good drone so you could take aerial photos of the farm?'

'Once or twice,' Tom replied with a grin. 'This is great. I wanted one with a good quality camera – just like this.'

'I think you may need a licence if you want to fly it anywhere near houses,' Deborah said. 'Emma thought that wouldn't be a problem. You'd prefer a better drone.'

'It's perfect,' Tom pulled her to him for a kiss. 'I love it. I can't wait to give it a go.'

He had bought her an array of painting materials – good quality brushes and watercolours. In her lessons so far, she had been working with acrylics and it was time to try a different medium. She enjoyed her lessons but would be the first to admit she had yet to show any talent.

'Give it time,' her tutor, Rafaella, smiled when Deborah poured out her frustration. 'Baby steps. You've only just started. You can't expect to become Picasso overnight. It takes practice.' And she had improved, applying the techniques taught with careful attention. Rafaella insisted she kept everything she painted so she could see her progress, and both Tom and Emma gave her lots of encouragement.

Emma's own art endeavours had stalled. Deborah wondered if the pressure of her first commission, to create three paintings for the large living space in Greenways Farm, was causing a problem but, when she asked that question, Emma grimaced.

'No, it's not that,' she said. 'It's me and my mood at the moment. I've started a few times but everything I paint ends up looking dark and bleak. Your house has seen lots of sadness. I feel your paintings should be bright, vibrant, full of colour ... and I guess I'm just not feeling it at present.'

Deborah gave her a hug. 'No rush. When you're ready.' She and Tom had been on the receiving end of Emma's dark mood for the past few weeks and knew exactly who was causing it. *Rick Billington*. He and Amelie Charles had been seeing each other daily since Amelie's return to Wickthorpe. To Rick, Emma remained cheerful and supportive, listening to him wax lyrical about Amelie's fabulousness as any good friend would. But it took its toll. The rest of the time she mooched about like a black cloud. It had not helped Emma's festive spirit to discover Rick had been invited to spend Christmas day with Amelie and her family.

'If only Amelie would get another job!' Emma muttered darkly. 'Preferably, in Timbuktu! According to Rick, she's looking for something locally. He's super happy about that, as you can imagine, but I know she'll break his heart all over again. I *have* warned him.'

Tom pulled a face but wisely said nothing. He feared it would be his daughter who ended up with the broken heart.

***

Ava spent much of Christmas on her own. She had hoped to see something of her nieces and sister-in-law but they spent the entire holiday season with Julie's parents. Enid was incensed at the situation and took it out on Ava. Apart from Christmas lunch, where there were complaints – the turkey was dry, the roast potatoes were soggy and the sprouts were too hard – mother and daughter avoided each other. Enid parked in front of the television, ringing a bell when she required anything. Ava stayed in her room most of the time with a book, or switched on the computer to catch up on some accounting. It was a dismal time and she was glad when the Post Office re-opened.

After the pre-Christmas frenzy though, visitors to the Post Office were scarce. Enid found this especially frustrating. Although she sat waiting in her usual chair, only a handful of customers appeared and gossip was hard to come by. One of those customers was Honoraria, needing to return a parcel. Ava was absent from behind the counter and Enid was growing so desperate for company she was even prepared to forgive Honoraria for her treachery regarding Deborah Ryecroft and the latest History Society meeting.

'I've heard someone is going to move into Mabel's bungalow next week,' Honoraria divulged in a stage whisper. 'A single gentleman. American.'

'Oh, yes?' Enid sprang to attention. 'What's his name?'

Honoraria wrinkled her brow. 'I *was* told but I'm afraid I can't remember.' She placed her fingers either side of her temples as if willing the information to return. 'Sorry, Enid.'

'How old is he?' Enid asked abruptly.

'I've really no idea.' Honoraria held up her hands. 'I suppose we will get to know all about him next week when he moves in. I thought I would take a casserole round to welcome him to the neighbourhood.'

'Mm.' Enid was deep in thought, planning whom she could ask for more details. A few months earlier, Brenda Wicks had spotted the buyer looking around the bungalow with an estate agent. A tall, grey-haired man in his forties. She had heard his voice – she was sure he had an American accent – and thought he looked familiar. The rumour mill suggested an American had bought the property and now Honoraria had confirmed it! Enid did not believe in coincidences and was awash with suspicion. Yes, Brenda might be the person to ask.

***

A few days later, having discovered the mystery American's identity at last, Enid hugged the information to herself, planning how best to use it. Initially, she had wondered about saying nothing at all and waiting until the village's newest inhabitant visited the Post Office in person. The opportunity to witness her daughter's shock was enormously tempting. However, she soon realised Ava may find out from someone else first. No, *she* wanted to be the one who broke the news.

She started by dropping a few sly hints. 'Apparently, a *single* man is moving into Mabel Littlebody's bungalow. You're not getting any younger, Ava. This one could be your last chance. Not that anyone would spare *you* a second glance. A wet weekend, that's what you look like.'

Ava ignored the barb, although it stung because she knew it to be true. Her face, pale and lined beyond her years, drooping with world-weariness, devoid of cosmetics, was instantly forgettable. And she really ought to get her hair done. The grey which now peppered her mousy brown locks had aged her. Honoraria said as much the other day but, at least, *she* meant it kindly.

'Anyway, this man is an *American*. You know you're partial to *them*,' Enid cackled into the silence. 'Wouldn't it be funny if it turned out to be someone you knew?'

The rhetorical question was a punch to her solar plexus. Ava gripped the counter and struggled for breath. Her mother delighted in tormenting her but why would she harp on about the man being an American unless ...? She risked a surreptitious glance across. Enid wielded knitting needles with the attention of a woman engrossed in her task, but the smug expression playing on those thin, shrunken lips told a different story. Could it be true? How many thousands of times had she dreamt of Patrick Velaman's return? Every single one of those times, she imagined a glorious, romantic reunion and a happy-ever-after ending. Not that such a thing was likely to happen!

The slow monotony of the clicking and Enid's deliberate silence were driving her mad. In the end, she could bear it no longer. 'Do you know something, Mother?'

'Something about what?' Enid savoured the moment, drawing immense satisfaction from the tortured look on her daughter's face.

'About this American?'

Enid deliberated for malicious seconds. 'I might.'

'Fine. I'll close the shop for a few minutes and pop round to see Honoraria. She's sure to know,' Ava retorted.

Enid set her knitting aside with deliberate care. 'There's no need for that. I can tell you. You only have to ask.'

Ava sucked in a deep breath. 'Mother, do you know the name of the man moving into Mabel's bungalow?'

'I do.'

'And ...'

A martyred sigh. 'I don't understand your attitude, Ava, but I am your mother. It would be cruel to let you find out from someone else.' A pause. Ava was sure her heart stopped beating. 'The man moving in ... the American ... is that faithless, two-timing piece of work who dumped you when you were meant to be married. Patrick Velaman.' When Ava failed to respond, she continued. 'I hope you're not going to throw yourself at him all over again. It was embarrassing enough the first time around. I clearly recall Norma Bishton's glee when I told her the engagement was off. I had never felt so humiliated. Honestly, *my* daughter practically dumped at the altar.' She waited eagerly for Ava's reaction, noting the white knuckles clutching the counter's edge.

Ava held on grimly until the black dots cleared from her vision. A myriad of thoughts and emotions overwhelmed her. And so many questions. She filled her lungs with air and took a step back to escape her mother's prying eyes. Heart still hammering, she stumbled to the bathroom and splashed cold water on her face. Shocked, grey eyes, which Patrick had so admired, stared back from the mirror. How would she cope when she saw him, especially now she resembled an old woman? A low groan rumbled into the tiny space. Instead of a fairy-tale fantasy, meeting Patrick again threatened to be the stuff of nightmares. She needed to do something about how she looked. Quickly, if he was moving in next week. She could not bear the thought of him seeing her and thinking she looked like an old crone. First step, book a hair appointment. Not for *him*, she told herself, but for her own self-esteem.

Enid sat alone in her chair, listening. Often, it suited her to pretend deafness but there was nothing wrong with her hearing. She heard Ava go into the bathroom and then to the phone in the narrow hallway. *Colour, cut and blow-dry.* What an idiot her daughter was! She smiled with grim satisfaction. Her little announcement had sent Ava into a tizzy. The fool still had silly, romantic hopes. No chance of any of them coming to fruition, not if *she* had anything to do with it! Her exaggeration of her own ill health over twenty years ago had scuppered Ava's plans to emigrate with Patrick to Cleveland and nature had eventually taken its course, as she knew it would. No man could be trusted to stay true, as she knew to her cost. And anyway, who would look after *her* if not Ava? Her only other child, Andrew, had his own family and she had never taken to that wife of his. She may be heiress to a healthy fortune but, in Enid's opinion, Julie was not good enough for her handsome son.

Idly, she wondered if either Andrew or Philip had made any attempts to find useful information pertaining to Deborah Ryecroft. Probably not. They would both claim Christmas as an excuse. Well, Christmas was over and she wanted action. She would give them both until the new year, and then they would feel the sharp edge of her tongue. It would not hurt also to remind them of the power she wielded over them. In the meantime, she would head back to her room for another read of that book.

Things were getting interesting in more ways than one.

CHAPTER 8

The Life & Times of Martha Lightbody

Before dawn on 13th August, Martha was seized and dragged from her bed out into the darkness. John, befuddled with slumber, was soon overpowered. He was strong but stood no chance against the three burly men who seized his arms to prevent his escape and punched him unconscious. Josiah, Martha's son, rudely wakened by the commotion, wailed his distress as his mother was bundled roughly from the house. It was fortunate he was too young to comprehend such a violent visitation.

'What is the meaning of this?' she demanded as her hands were tied behind her back.

'Folks say you're a witch,' a voice hissed in her ear.

'You cast spells and practise the dark arts,' said another.

'And you have the devil's mark.'

'Aye.' A chorus of men, convinced of her guilt.

'I am not a witch.' She kept her voice low, fighting for calm. 'I am a Christian. I help people.'

'You will have chance to prove your innocence soon enough,' one of the men growled. She recognised his voice. Tobias Fletcher. She had treated his wife for severe stomach cramps with a brew of mugwort and fennel. On that occasion, he had given her eggs to thank her.

Martha had no chance to say more as a piece of cloth was tied roughly around her head, covering her mouth. With a man at each elbow, marshalling her along, she was led along the dirt track through the village and to the church. They stopped by the door which opened into the south porch, but remained outside.

'Lord, have mercy upon me,' she prayed silently.

The ringleader stood before her, eyes leering. She smelt stale beer on his breath. *Roger Holley.* 'The rest will be here shortly. First light. We knew to act before dawn to thwart your little plan,' he smirked.

Martha stared defiantly back, trying to conceal the fear coursing through her. How did they know what she and John had planned? Had someone seen and betrayed them? No matter now. She would do better to focus on thoughts of escape, but there appeared little hope of that. Bound and gagged as she was, surrounded by men intent upon her death, what could she do? Her thoughts turned instead to prayer. She pictured herself inside the church, kneeling in the chapel, a place where she felt at peace. Commonly, she prayed for others, the sick and the dying. Now, her silent plea was for herself. 'Help me, Lord!' She experienced a rush of warmth, of hope. Was her prayer to be answered? Turning desperate eyes right and left, she checked the streets, searching for succour, but none came.

Patches of purple streaked the sky, heralding the onset of the new day. Martha shivered. She was dressed only in the thin cotton undergarment she wore to bed, scant protection against the early morning chill. Her feet were bare and she could no longer feel her toes. Minor inconveniences compared to the severity of her situation. Seeking a miracle, she raised her head once more.

Someone was coming. Her heart leapt. A grey shape loomed into view, approaching from the left.

'Where is the wench?' A booming voice she knew well. *Jed Finch.* A burst of hope ripped through her chest. Surely, he would help her? Her husband's employer was a fair man and she had healed the soreness of his granddaughter's eyes. He had been most grateful and she had been well rewarded for her trouble.

'Here.' Holley stepped forward as the other men, shielding her from view, stood aside. 'She has the devil's mark, a sure sign she is a witch. And folk have been talking of her mixing potions. There is no doubt of her guilt. We will arrange transportation to the court in Bury St Edmunds where she can be put on trial.'

Jed Finch frowned. 'You have no other proof? No evidence of devil worship? I, for one, know she has used her powers to heal the sick, as any good Christian would do.'

His words produced a murmur of unease from the group. 'Jed is right. Could we have been too hasty, Roger?' Tobias Fletcher cast an anxious glance in Martha's direction as he placed a conciliatory hand on Holley's shoulder.

'No.' Roger glared at him. 'There have been rumours of devil worship, right enough.'

'Rumours?' There was scorn in Jed Finch's retort. 'You know what this village is like for rumours, Roger Holley! Just last month, when you were accused of keeping back some of the village tithes, your defence was the ill-humour of your neighbours, causing malicious trouble. There was no proof you had acted illegally so no action was taken. If there is no proof now, that this woman is a witch, you should release her and allow her and her family to move on from here.'

Holley faced him, hands on hips, defiance writ large in his face. 'This is different. You speak of healing yet, in recent times, two have died after receiving this witch's care. The evil is rife. Young girls in the village could become infected. There is one such, Prudence Harkness, whom she is schooling in her ways. I say if Martha Lightbody is innocent of these charges, trial will prove her so.'

'Aye.' A small man, with a weasel's sharp eyes and pointed chin, arraigned himself alongside Roger. 'Trial by water.' There were mutterings of agreement.

'Good idea, Abel. Tis the best way.' Roger's eyes gleamed with malevolence. 'Take her to the lake.'

Jed Finch frowned. 'I will not be part of this.' He turned eyes full of pity on the struggling woman. 'Trust in the Lord, Martha. He will not let you drown.' To the villagers, he said, 'Do not leave her under too long lest you kill an innocent woman.' He shook his head, heavy of heart at his lack of power against the might of the mob. 'I will pray for you. I will pray for you all.'

As Finch walked away, Roger Holley chuckled. 'We will leave her under long enough, never fear. Tis the only way we will know the truth. If she swims, she is a witch and will be declared so at trial.'

'And if she does not swim?' Tobias Fletcher looked anxiously at the woman.

Holley rolled his eyes. 'Then the Lord will surely save her. You heard what Finch said. Let's get moving.'

The two men holding Martha's arms dragged her further along the street. Beyond lay the woods and the large, shaded lake, commonly known as Dark Water. Martha knew it well, having spent many hours collecting plants and herbs from around there. Today though, the place was one of dread. She had heard of such trials by water. Although a strong swimmer, she would stand little chance of survival tied to a chair. All she could do was trust in the mercy of the Lord, and pray that men would pull her from the water before she drowned.

Within minutes, they reached the wood. When they reached the water's edge, Holley ordered the two men holding Martha's arms to untie her hands. As she tried to rub blood back into numb fingers, her limbs were seized once more and this time secured behind the chair.

Holley stood in front of her. 'Tis your final chance to spare yourself trial by water. Confess you are a witch and this will go no further.' The gag was removed from her mouth for her response.

Martha surveyed the assembled crowd of men with contempt. 'What you plan is a travesty. I am no more a witch than any of your wives and daughters. Your heads have been filled with superstitious nonsense.'

'Are those your final words?' Satisfaction gleamed in Holley's eyes.

'No.' Furtively, she tested the strength of her bonds. They seemed looser than before.

'What do you wish to say?' Holley twitched with impatience.

'I repeat, I am innocent. I am not a witch. But if I were, I would put a spell on you, Roger Holley. I know your true motive for this treachery.'

'What does she mean, Roger?' asked one of the men.

'Talk of spells is proof enough of her guilt,' Holley declared. 'Such utterances can only be those of a witch. We will discover soon enough if she is as innocent as she claims. Lift her into the water.'

'Hear this,' Martha cried, struggling on the chair as the men closed around her. 'Roger Holley is ...' A rough hand swiftly clamped her mouth but she managed to shake her head free. 'If I die, know this. I curse you, Roger Holley, and any man who stands with you.' Martha could say no more. The gag bit into her mouth and was pulled tight. A few men stood back, uneasy now.

'I will have no part in this,' said one.

'Aye, nor me.'

'Cowards. Afraid to do what is right.' Holley's lips curled with disdain. 'We have no need of you. Abel and I will suffice.'

Abel Packer, Holley's right-hand man, nodded and stood on the other side of Martha. With a grunt, the two men hoisted the chair and Martha was carried above the inky depths of the lake.

Silence, apart from the slosh of liquid against thighs and the heavy breathing of the men carrying her. Even the birds ceased their dawn chorus, seemingly hushed by the horror they were about to witness. Soon the water reached the men's chests. 'I reckon here is deep enough,' Holley said. 'On my count of three, throw the chair forward. One, two, three ...'

Martha was launched through the air. She sucked in a deep breath before toppling forwards and hitting the water face down.

A hush descended once more as both woman and chair disappeared. The two men standing closest witnessed bubbles of air dimpling the surface and then all was calm.

'Roger,' Tobias Fletcher called from the bank, 'for God's sake, tis time. The lass will drown.'

'Best to be sure,' came the response.

'Tis time enough. Pull her out!' Fletcher plunged forward from the bank, followed by other villagers, ducking beneath the water, searching. Within seconds, one of the men held the empty chair aloft.

'She is gone,' he cried.

'Then find her, fools. Do not let her escape!' yelled Holley. He turned to Tobias Fletcher. 'I told you she was a witch. Now we have the proof.' He turned back to scan the surrounding trees. The far side of the lake was hidden beneath two enormous willows. 'She will have made for the trees over there.' He pointed towards them. 'Split up. You three go this way.' He gestured to his left. 'The rest go t'other way. I will wait here in case she doubles back on us. You four keep checking the water. She will not get far.'

'But how did she get free in the first place?' Fletcher mused. 'Tis a mystery.'

'The woman is a witch. She practises the black arts, tis how.' Holley turned his gaze upon his companion. 'For pity's sake, man, what is the matter with you? You are white as a sheet.'

'If she is really a witch, then you heard her curse. Both you and Abel are doomed forever.'

Holley eyed him with contempt. 'You all played your part. If I am cursed, then so are you, and all the villagers who accused her. The witch has cursed the whole village. You had best find her.'

CHAPTER 9

The legend of the Wickthorpe curse had lasted through the centuries and, over the previous summer, Martha Lightbody's story had been reported in various guises across the nation. The curse uttered by the supposed witch, condemning the village, had given Wickthorpe a notoriety of its own. Some believed it, especially those who had lived in the village all their lives and witnessed tragedies blamed on the curse. Others scoffed and pronounced it superstitious nonsense. No one really knew the truth. No one had produced evidence to prove either claim. No one knew what had really happened to Martha Lightbody in 1645.

Until now.

If what was written in the book was true.

Deborah read the excerpt describing events leading up to the drowning with fingers numb from gripping the pages so tightly. When she reached the end of the chapter, she paused, sensing she was missing something important but unsure what it was. If the book were to be believed, it would seem Martha cursed only two men – Roger Holley and Abel Packer – not the rest of the village. The other men present, cowards though they were, had no hand in the drowning. Deborah reread the moment of the curse. It was prefaced, '*If I die ...*'

If Martha survived, surely the curse was invalid? Given the belief in it, almost four hundred years later, did this mean she was about to learn Martha had drowned after all? And how much of it could she believe anyway?

Deborah flicked back to the book's *Foreword* to check its claims of authenticity:

My writings are taken with the utmost attention to accuracy from letters passed down within the family and a diary kept by Martha herself. That diary has since been lost but her great granddaughter, Elizabeth Croft most diligently recorded information in a series of letters to her own granddaughters, as repeated to her by her grandfather, Josiah Lightbody, Martha's son. Many of these fascinating epistles remain and have, after more than a century, fallen into my unworthy hands. It is a true account, to the best of my knowledge ...

A diary and letters. If only she had those too. As it was, she had to rely upon the honesty of the author, John Littlebody. Again, she wondered upon the nature of his relationship to the Lightbody family. Had the name changed to Littlebody over time? If so ...

Her mind veered off into territory she had previously avoided. Mabel Littlebody had possessed the book and wanted her to have it. If Mabel was a descendant of John Littlebody, and John was somehow related to Martha, then it was possible Martha Lightbody was her *own* ancestor.

Her thoughts wandered further. Two women had been found dead in Dark Water Lake whilst she resided in Wickthorpe. Last summer, she had been forced to endure her own trial by drowning. The ghostly, dark-haired woman – her saviour in the lake – still appeared in her dreams. Then, there was that nightmare she had – the premonition of Freya Billington's death. How could she have known? Cynical as she was about all things mystical, her life had been affected by Martha's story and its consequences were now threatening her sanity. She had to read on, and find out what had happened next.

Just as she turned the page, the doorbell sounded an unwelcome intrusion. Setting the book aside, she sprung to her feet. Most likely it was a delivery and she would have time to get back to Martha's next instalment before her scheduled, online work meeting. Swiftly, she unlocked the front door, threw it open and managed to hold back the shocked gasp which formed in her throat. On her doorstep stood the last person she expected to see. *Jane Holley!*

'I'm sorry to bother you, Deborah. May I come in?'

Wordlessly, she opened the door wider and stepped back. She had encountered her old enemy just once since her return to Wickthorpe, at the social gathering Tom had organised to welcome her to the neighbourhood.

Thankfully, their paths had not crossed since ... until now. *What on earth did she want?*

Deborah watched as the other woman made a production of wiping her feet on the mat. Jane was nervous, she realised. There was a noticeable tremor of the hands and gnawing of her lower lip. And she looked terrible. As Jane shrugged off her long, woollen coat, Deborah saw just how wraith-like she had become. The Jane she had met at Tom's party had been slim and haughtily elegant. Now, she was rail-thin and her clothes hung off her. Was she ill?

Deborah forced a smile. 'Come through this way. Can I get you a drink? Tea, coffee?'

'Nothing, thank you.'

Deborah led her through to the living room and gestured to the three fat sofas. 'Take your pick.' Jane perched stiffly on the edge of the nearest one to the exit. Deborah sat facing her, waiting to find out what she wanted. As a taut silence ensued, and Jane continued to fidget with her fingers, she felt she had to say something, however inane. 'How are you?' she asked.

Jane seemed confused by the question and searched Deborah's face. 'Fine, thank you,' she said at last. Another pause. 'How are you? I hear you had quite an ordeal in the summer.' Her voice had lost its imperious tone and was anxious, slightly hesitant.

Deborah gave her a rueful look. 'Yes, *another* awful experience of Dark Water Lake.' At the immediate distress on Jane's face, she wished she had avoided a reference to the incident which had blighted her teenage life. 'I'm quite recovered, thank you.'

There was another long silence while she waited for Jane to state her business. When nothing was forthcoming, she asked bluntly, 'Jane, why are you here?' Again, that look of panic. Despite the animosity she felt towards her, Deborah's pity for the other woman grew.

Jane drew in a breath and lowered her eyes. 'I've come to ask for your forgiveness.'

Deborah was unable to hide her shock and it was a struggle to know how to respond. *Forgiveness? Really?* The bald statement provoked a welter of emotions. How *did* she feel about it? Eventually, she shrugged, pretending a nonchalance she did not feel. 'It was a long time ago. We were little more than kids.'

'We were, and we are the only ones who know the truth. Oh,' she clamped a hand over her mouth. 'I recently confessed everything to Wendy Robinson, the rector. I feel so terrible about it all, you see. But she won't tell anyone.' She shook her head. 'None of it was meant to happen. It was supposed to be a joke. Neither of us believed you or Ayesha would *swim* in Dark Water Lake. But I know it was a mean thing to do.'

'More than mean. It was cruel,' Deborah replied, her tone flat.

Jane sighed. 'Yes, cruel,' she agreed.

'And, if you and Melissa didn't want us to go into the water, why didn't you try to stop Ayesha?' Deborah felt the old anger returning and fought to keep her voice calm. 'You did the opposite; you both egged her on. You told her she had to swim to the far bank and back and then she could hang out with you. When she got into trouble, you did nothing. She died, Jane, because of what you and Melissa did. Nothing you now say or do will bring her back. It's not up to *me* to dispense forgiveness; it's Ayesha's parents, her brother, the rest of her family.' Her dam of self-control burst and the accusations flooded out, a tidal wave of rage and resentment. 'Afterwards, did you spare one thought for them? Oh no, you and Melissa were both too busy trying to cover up your lousy guilt!'

Her words exploded like bullets, cracking the tension in the room. A leaden stillness followed, and Deborah glanced across. Fat, silent tears glistened on Jane's gaunt cheeks.

Deborah exhaled, anger spent, her heart heavy. For years she had mentally rehearsed that speech, thinking she would never have the chance to say it. Now she had, but it had not helped. The time for such words was long past.

'You're right.' Jane fumbled in her bag for tissues. 'You're right about all of it. We were cruel and selfish. When Ayesha died, we were only worried about ourselves. That was why we directed the blame at you. I'm sorry.'

Deborah raised her eyebrows. 'Sorry enough to tell everyone the truth?'

Jane's grey eyes met hers. 'I will if that is what you want,' she said quietly.

Silence strained like a tightrope between them. Was that what she wanted? Jane to confess all? Subconsciously, she shook her head. It would do no good and cause only more heartache – to Jane and her family, if no one else. There was a time when she would have taken her chance for vengeance. Not anymore.

'That's not what I want,' she said, her voice stiff. 'It would only bring it all back and there is no point. Not now. People have already made up their minds about me, and nothing you nor I say will change their opinions.'

'I *am* truly sorry, Deborah. For all of it.'

'I can see that.' Another pause. Jane shuffled forward as if to rise but Deborah had more questions. 'What happened to Melissa?' she asked. Melissa Shipman. Jane's partner-in-crime.

'Apparently, she suffered from depression,' Jane replied. 'She and I never spoke again of what had happened that day and we drifted apart. When she was at university, she started self-harming. It was a while before anyone noticed. Her parents ensured she got the best medical help but mental illness was not regarded then as sympathetically as it is now. She took her first overdose when she was twenty-one, the day after her birthday, and tried at least twice more before she succeeded in killing herself when she was twenty-seven. No one could understand it at the time, including me. Now, I can.'

'What a waste! Melissa was always so full of life, a girl who had everything. Looks, money, popularity ...' Deborah shook her head. 'When Ayesha died, I hated her ... and you. Now, I just feel sad.'

'I'm sad too. I don't think I'll ever be happy again, but I know that's what I deserve.' Jane reached for her bag. 'I'd better go. I know I'm years too late but I wanted you to know how sorry I am. None of it was your fault but you must have suffered terribly.' She sighed heavily. 'We were so young and foolish. Little did we know there would be repercussions, years down the line.' She stood, wavering, unsteady on her feet, and Deborah leapt to support her arm.

'Are you sure you're alright, Jane? You don't look very well.'

A shrug. 'Just my past misdeeds coming back to haunt me. The irony is, the mistake I made in 1988 may not have been my worst error of judgement.'

She looked Deborah straight in the eye. 'Please don't feel sorry for me. I don't deserve anyone's pity, least of all yours.'

Deborah felt herself growing increasingly anxious about her uninvited guest as she walked her to the door and retrieved her coat. 'You say you've spoken to Wendy about all of this. That's good. But what about your family? Have you spoken to Seb about how you're feeling?'

Jane snorted, the vehemence of it taking Deborah by surprise. 'Seb is the *last* person I would talk to. My *husband* is not the man everyone thinks he is. If I can do anything for you, let me give you a warning. Stay well clear of Seb. He seems quite attracted to you but inviting his attention would not be in *your* best interests. Let me put it like that.'

'I can assure you I have absolutely no designs on your husband,' Deborah retorted, annoyed at the implication.

Jane sighed again. 'Sorry if I've offended you. I've said too much about Seb but I had to warn you. I'd never forgive myself if another ...' She stepped through the doorway. 'Goodbye, Deborah. Thank you for giving me your time.'

'If another what?' Deborah called but Jane continued along the drive without turning back. As she closed the door, she heard the ping of the computer in her office, reminding her of her online meeting. *Damn.* There was no time to process any of what had just happened. Jane Holley's visit had left her reeling, and with more questions than answers, but they would have to wait.

CHAPTER 10

Amelie Charles flicked back her shiny, black hair and cast a casual glance around the pub. How Rick could love a place like this was beyond her! *The Olde Kings Head.* The old people's home, more like! Two men, who looked to be in their eighties or nineties, were playing dominoes by the large, log-filled, open fire; a mixed group of middle-aged somethings were eating at a round table in the corner; four older men sat drinking pints by the bar; and there were two empty tables. That was it. This was the 'wonderful pub full of charm' Rick could not wait to share with her. And she had been bounced and jolted for miles along awful country roads in his beaten-up Land Rover to get here. She was not impressed.

'What do you think? Isn't it great?' Rick's enthusiasm bubbled like a kid at a party.

She licked her shimmer-pink lips and reached for her glass. 'It's certainly ... different,' she replied, taking a sip. *At least the wine was halfway decent.*

'I know,' he beamed. 'Emma and I came here once. We loved it. Check out that tiny nook over there. Can you see it?'

He pointed to the left of the fireplace and she peered to see. 'What?'

'I'll show you.' He took her hand and guided her to the spot. 'There.'

She wrinkled her nose. There was a small recess between the bricks and a couple of old paperbacks were strewn across it. 'So?'

'This inn was built in the early sixteenth century. Apparently, there is a cavity behind it, large enough for a person to hide. In those days, the bricks were loose and could be removed and replaced quickly if necessary. There used to be a monastery nearby. When Henry VIII ordered the dissolution of the monasteries, the monks hid gold and precious artefacts here to protect them from the king's men. Isn't that great?'

'Mm.'

'And then, two hundred years or so later, Bonnie Prince Charlie came here. He slept in one of the bedrooms.'

'Really?' she murmured. Did he think this was interesting her? He would be dragging her upstairs next to show her!

'Yes, can you believe it? Anyway, that's not the best bit. The story goes that Charlie boy had been putting himself about with some of the local wives and daughters. A posse of angry husbands and fathers came here looking for him ... but he had completely disappeared. They couldn't understand it. The innkeeper pretended to be just as bemused as they were, but he knew the truth. Just seconds earlier, he had finished replacing bricks to hide Charlie boy behind the wall.'

'Amazing,' she drawled.

'Isn't it?' He grinned, missing the sarcasm in her tone, and gazed appreciatively around him. 'I bet these walls could tell a few tales. When Em and I were here, we made up a few ourselves. She came up with a brilliant one about ...'

'Are you going to talk about Emma Oldridge all night?' she interrupted, with a forced smile to take the sting from the barb.

'Of course not.' With an apologetic look, he leant forward to plant a lingering kiss on her lips. 'You're looking gorgeous tonight, Ammy, as usual.'

'Amelie,' she returned sharply. 'And thank you. The dress is new. I couldn't resist it. Half price in the new year sale but still expensive.' She sighed. 'I really hope I get this job. My tastes don't suit an unemployed budget.'

Rick's face fell. 'But the job is in London again, isn't it? I thought you were done with the city.'

She shrugged. 'Needs must. Pay in London is so much better and, to tell you the truth, I'm bored stiff back in Suffolk.'

'Oh.'

'Present company excepted,' she added belatedly. 'You've been great, Rick – ferrying me around, entertaining me.' Her manicured hand patted his.

'That sounds like you've already made up your mind about going back. What about us?' Rick's hopeful, blue eyes implored her to reconsider.

'We're friends, Rick. We've always been friends. No more than that. I thought you felt the same.'

'Friends don't sleep together,' he huffed.

She shot him an amused glance. 'Don't they? Whyever not?'

He frowned, 'They just don't. Sleeping together means you are in a relationship.'

'Really? Who told you that?' Amelie teased. 'Are you saying you don't have the occasional bunk-up with the lovely Emma, the one you can't stop talking about?'

'Don't be daft. Of course not.'

'Well ...' Another shrug of her slim shoulders. 'I bet she would be willing.'

'No, she wouldn't,' Rick glared. 'Em's not like that!'

Amelie smirked. 'You might be surprised! You know she likes you, don't you?'

'I know. We're best friends.'

She sighed. 'No, I mean, she *really* likes you.'

His cheeks flamed. 'Who told you that? Did *she* say she did?'

'No. She doesn't like me much and I can guess why. She has designs on you herself. Why don't you ask her?'

'You're being ridiculous, Amelie, but I know what you're doing. You're deflecting the conversation away from us.' He lowered his voice and took her hands in his. 'I'm in love with you. I don't want you to leave. I want us to be together.'

Never going to happen, mate. She smiled gently. 'That's very flattering, Rick. I care about you too ... a great deal.'

'Could it be enough?' he asked, his voice low and urgent.

Her smile grew. 'Maybe. I'm not sure. Let's give it a bit more time, shall we, before we get too serious about anything?' *After all, I haven't actually got the job in London yet.*

He grinned back, relieved. 'Take all the time you want, my darling.'

My darling? Yuck! He really was beginning to get on her nerves. With a flutter of her long, black lashes, Amelie reached for the menu, propped up by the wall by their table. 'Shall we order? I'm starving, and you did promise me supper.'

***

Honoraria's visit to Little Horseshoes proved an unexpected delight. The small village, perched on the easternmost edge of the North Norfolk coast, was a quaint mix of eclectic houses, a small church, and scattered farmhouses and farmland stretching inland. She arrived late morning and Marcus offered her freshly-brewed coffee in his smart, modern kitchen. Unfailingly nosy, she hinted at a tour of his renovated home – previously two semi-detached, fisherman's cottages converted to one house – and he duly obliged. Her opinion of her host grew as she oohed and aahed her way through each room.

'Truly wonderful,' she exclaimed as they returned to the kitchen. 'You've done a super job of retaining the old cottages' character. I love it.' He gave her his smile, the one which lit up his face and brought sparkles to his warm, brown eyes, and she felt a trembly feeling spread from her chest to her limbs. For once, she was rendered speechless and had to feign sudden interest in a parish magazine which lay on the worktop.

'Right, shall we get on? I've got lots to show you.'

'Yes, please!' Honoraria slapped the pamphlet down with a jolt, her internal confusion lending a rosy hue to her cheeks. She was *not* interested in Marcus, not in *that* way. Again, she reminded herself of his shortcomings: short, chubby, balding ... Quite a brief list. She taxed her brain to remember all the other things which had put her off him in the first place but no undesirable traits were forthcoming. *Oh dear. This really wouldn't do.* She had already rebuffed Marcus when he made a tentative advance. *Think of Gerald!*

These feelings lasted throughout the tour of the churchyard, where two crumbling headstones of latter-day members of the Lightbody family remained, and the delicious pub lunch at a nearby village. It was hard for Honoraria to concentrate on the reason for her visit – the quest to find a record of Martha Lightbody.

'If you remember,' Marcus was saying, as she lost herself in his deep, velvety voice, 'I didn't find any information for a Martha Lightbody in the right time period. I did find a few listed in the parish register from the nineteenth century but the early records are not all available.'

With effort, Honoraria pulled herself together, 'I recall you managed to find some seventeenth century Lightbodys though. They may well have been Martha's relatives.'

'That's right.' Marcus had his sheet of paper ready. 'Matthew Lightbody, buried 1665; Calla Lightbody, buried 1681; Luke Lightbody, 1683; Robert Lightbody, 1690. Then a gap. Missing records, I'm afraid. The next was a John Lightbody, 1729.'

'May I have a copy of that?' Honoraria asked. 'I'll see what I can find out, using some of the resources available to me.'

'With pleasure. It's such an intriguing mystery. I would love to discover what really happened to the famous witch of Wickthorpe.'

'I'll certainly keep you in the loop, Marcus. Should I find anything, you will be the first person I'll call.'

He looked pleased at that and she left shortly afterwards, anxious to return to Wickthorpe before the predicted fog descended. Seeing Marcus had given her spirits a boost after a long and lonely Christmas. As she drove home, she found herself scheming another opportunity to spend time with Marcus ... in a purely platonic sense, of course.

***

Enid's lip curled as she hobbled through to her chair in the Post Office. Another new dress – the third this week. What a waste of money! Ava had spared no expense to impress Patrick Velaman, a man who had thrown her over when they were engaged to be married. As Enid had pointed out, promises meant nothing to that man. Not that Ava listened to her. Well, she was setting herself up for another fall and serve her right. She had been warned.

'Do you need any help, Mother?' Ava appeared beside her, ready to take the stick and get Enid comfortably settled.

'I see you've been frittering even more of our money away,' came the sour reply.

'My money, Mother,' Ava replied firmly. Enid had her own savings and pension, and didn't offer a penny of either towards the household expenses. 'Money I earn by working here every day.'

'Hmph.'

Ava smiled to herself. The new clothes and honey-coloured hairstyle had given her confidence a real boost. Some of the Post Office customers had noticed and complimented her, telling her she looked years younger. The money spent had been well worth it. It had started at the hair stylist. After some consideration, she had cancelled her appointment with Glenda Hill, the hairdresser who had cut both her and her mother's hair for years, and decided to risk a trendy salon in Bury St Edmunds. The stylist, a young girl called Gina who appeared to have more piercings than Ava had had birthdays, coloured her hair and cut it into a soft, becoming style which suited her fine bone structure.

'You have fantastic skin,' Gina, enthused, as she revealed the finished result to a stunned Ava, 'and beautiful eyes. With a touch of mascara to enhance your eyes, and blusher to highlight your cheek bones, you would look even more amazing. My sister's a make-up artist. Would you like to make an appointment with her?'

Ava had declined the offer, but thanked her and added a generous tip to her payment. She was thrilled with her new hair, but the thought of using make-up for the first time in her life was a step too far. However, she *did* need some new clothes. She hadn't bothered buying anything for years, and everything she owned was dowdy and old-fashioned. Updating her wardrobe was long overdue.

As she headed to the carpark, she bumped into Deborah Ryecroft, who commented on the hairdo. 'Wow, wow, wow! That new style really suits you, Ava,' she said. 'The colour too.'

Somehow, after that, the conversation turned to clothes-buying and Ava's lack of confidence selecting the kind of outfits which would complement her looks. Immediately, Deborah offered her assistance, and Ava found herself whisked through boutiques and department stores she had never previously visited. It was like being caught up in a whirlwind. By the time they had finished, she had spent a fortune but had several different ensembles and even a whole new set of underwear. Her favourite item from the entire collection was also the most expensive – a beautiful, wraparound dress in a gorgeous deep turquoise. When she baulked at the cost, Deborah insisted upon buying it for her.

'Please allow me,' she urged. 'It would give me so much pleasure. And the dress is made for you. It would be criminal not to buy it.' It went against all of Ava's principles, but Deborah would not take no for an answer and, somehow, it ended up in one of her bags. 'Just promise me that you'll get rid of all your old clothes,' Deborah said when they finally parted ways. 'After this, I don't want to see you in a grey shift dress ever again.'

Ava smiled, 'I promise,' she said.

True to her word, she returned home, removed every item from her wardrobe and sorted the stack into two piles – one suitable for a charity shop; one for the clothing bank. With the confidence she felt from wearing the new items, she was now ready to face Patrick Velaman, should he appear in the Post Office.

She had heard plenty about him, in dribs and drabs, as different villagers passed on snippets of information. He had moved in on January 4th; he was tall, very polite, single, divorced. Honoraria had already had him round for coffee – *of course she had* – and was, as ever, a good source of information. In fact, she appeared to be quite taken with him. *Typical.* Mild-mannered Ava seethed inwardly at the thought of Patrick being seduced by the older woman's ample charms, but she managed to present a calm façade as she quizzed Honoraria. It wouldn't do to reveal what she was really feeling.

'Do you know, he was stationed at Lakenheath before, several years ago, when he was just a young man? And now he's back, this time at Mildenhall, still working for the US Air Force. An engineer.'

Ava looked interested but revealed nothing of her past relationship with Patrick. The fewer people aware of it, the better. 'Did he ... er ... mention anything from when he was here before?'

Honoraria shook her red curls. 'No. Why?'

'Just wondered. If he lived around here ... oh, look at the time! I still haven't finished doing the order. Sorry, Honoraria.' With a look of apology, Ava beat a hasty retreat. Just talking about Patrick had sent her into a spin.

Ever since she had heard about his return, she had been on tenterhooks, waiting for him to appear every time the door bell sounded. Surely, he would come to see her soon?

It would be an awkward meeting, especially if her spiteful mother was there to witness it. Enid had spent every day in the shop since imparting the news of Patrick's return, probably waiting for that very event to happen. The more Ava thought about it, the more she realised it would be better to pay *him* a visit. Not yet, but at some point over the next few days. She needed time to consider what she would say and to pluck up the courage. The prospect of knocking on his door filled her with dread, but the alternative was worse. And at least she would have the advantage of being prepared.

CHAPTER 11

The Life & Times of Martha Lightbody

Weights had been tied to the base of the chair and it sunk directly to the bottom of the lake. The water was indigo black and impenetrable. Martha fought against the panic which consumed her and struggled desperately against her bonds. She felt them loosen and continued to wriggle her wrists. A deathly silence surrounded her as she battled on.

When one hand slipped through the knot, she felt a jolt of hope. A few precious seconds more to release the other, and she was free. Her feet remained tied but her arms were enough to pull her away from the men who stood waiting. Her senses were sorely disorientated and she swam sightlessly, knowing that, at all costs, she must remain below the surface of the water. Should one of the men spot her, all her efforts would be in vain. Lungs bursting, she continued, thankful for the strength in her arms which pulled her along. Still, she dared not take a breath. If only she could reach the shadows of the trees, on the far side of the lake, she might maintain her concealment. Her hands bumped against something rough – a dead branch, floating on the water. It was shallower here. Had she managed to find the far bank? Not before time! Her chest burned; only a few seconds more ...

Cautiously, she tilted her head back as she broke the surface and gasped for air, careful to reveal as little of her body as possible. Above her, shafts of sunlight danced through gaps in a canopy of branches. Gratefully, she sucked in breaths and waited for shouts heralding her discovery. They were not forthcoming. Clutching the branch with one hand, she tugged the gag away from her mouth. Never had taking an unencumbered breath of air felt so good!

Now she faced a dilemma. Should she stay hidden beneath the water, risking detection every time she surfaced for air, or should she attempt to pull herself from the lake and flee? Both options were fraught with danger, but her ankles were still bound, so running would not be possible. Decision made. She would remain in the water. It was bitterly cold though, and she wondered if she would die from the chill. Despite the heat of the previous months, the lake was well shaded and had resisted the sun's efforts to warm its icy depths.

The air had been eerily silent but now, in the distance, she heard men's shouts. They had discovered she was missing but knew not where she was. Their voices travelled across the lake and she could hear anger from some, fear from others. The thought pleased her. Her escape had convinced them of the veracity of her curse and struck terror into their hearts. However, her satisfaction was short-lived. They would leave no stone unturned in seeking her out. She remained in mortal danger.

The voices fractured as the men headed in different directions. They were scouring the banks, looking for signs of her exit. She had lost her chance to escape the water, and had no choice but to remain where she was. Shivering with cold and fear, she moved deeper into the shadows.

Conscious thought faded in and out as she remembered happier times – childhood memories of playing with her siblings and trying to help her father load the carts. Her mind spun forward to her first encounter with John Lightbody who had been heading for Kings Lynn market but had been strangely drawn towards the water. His kind, grey eyes had met hers and she was lost. He was the one; she knew it instantly.

A call from nearby jerked her back to the present. Someone was coming. Noiselessly, she took a deep breath and slipped into the bowels of the lake. Her heart thudded painfully as she waited long moments, praying no one would see the tiny air bubbles breaking its surface. Perilously close to her hiding place, feet thrashed through the undergrowth and men talked of the way Martha Lightbody had contrived to disappear into thin air. There were also grumbles. Voices complained of losing pay if they were late for work and of the fine weather they were missing. This year's harvest awaited. Much was to be done in the fields and there was no time to waste on a fool's errand. The woman was a proven witch and thus would evade capture, no matter how long they searched. The sounds drifted away and Martha rose once more.

Shrinking beneath the low-hanging branches of a large oak, she risked a first look around. The banks of the lake were empty; the men had gone. Shuddering with relief, she dragged her frozen body from the clutches of the water and sagged onto the earth, all energy spent. Yet she knew she could not rest. Somehow, she must contrive to flee the village without being seen and find refuge somewhere. The small cottage where she lived with John and Josiah would be watched, and she knew not where else to go. How she ached for the comfort of her husband and son but, for now, she must manage alone. Although she had survived the drowning, her prospects remained dubious. And first, she needed to free herself from the ropes cutting cruelly into her legs. Numb fingers picked and pulled at the knots but they were set fast, drawn tighter by her exploits in the water. It was hopeless.

She was casting around for a stone or flint with which to saw through her bindings when she heard a rustle in the trees behind. Sucking in her breath, she crawled back to her hiding place, praying it was a deer or a rabbit.

It was not.

Heavy boots appeared on the ground in front of her. She looked up to find a bearded face peering at her through the foliage. She was done for!

A low whistle. 'So, this is where you've been holed up, Martha Lightbody. Come out of there. No one is with me.'

Martha had no choice. Mutely, she shuffled forwards. It was Tobias Fletcher. She had treated his wife for stomach cramps and would pray for his mercy. When he drew out a knife, she gasped.

'Hush there, I mean you no harm,' he murmured and reached forward to slice through the ropes. 'I am sorry for what passed today and sorely regret my part in it. I was ignorant of what was intended and was fooled by another. But tis no excuse. Twas an ill deed.' He shook his head. 'Now, you must leave this place. Tis not safe. Roger Holley will not rest until you are found.'

'But where should I go?'

'My cousin lives north of here, on t'other side of the woods. He will shelter you ... or his wife, Ruth, will. Daniel will be in the fields. Here.' He pulled a silver cross suspended on a thin strip of leather over his head. 'Give her this, and tell her I sent you.'

Martha clasped the cross to her chest. 'You trust me to return this?' He nodded. 'Thank you. I shall take good care of it.'

Tobias smiled, his weathered face creasing with compassion. 'You have been sorely treated, Mistress Lightbody, and many in the village are sorry for it. I shall try to get word to your husband you are safe, but that may prove difficult. I fear Roger Holley has issued an order for him to be watched.' He scratched his beard, regarding Martha with a solemn expression. 'To be sure, you should trust no one, although you can rely 'pon me to conceal your whereabouts. There are many who would wish to curry favour with Roger Holley and such folk would know well the value of information about you. Go quickly now, but take care. Follow the path through the woods to the north, past the dead oak with the cleft in its trunk. You know it?' She nodded. 'Continue in the same direction til you reach a clearing. Ruth and Daniel live beyond, in a thatched cottage. You'll see goats grazing in a small enclosure. No others live nearby so it should be safe enough.'

'I don't want to cause your cousin trouble,' she said.

Tobias laughed, a rich, throaty sound. 'Worry not about Daniel! He's the size of an ox and guards his land with a gun where necessary. None will bother him. Even Roger Holley knows to stay away. You will be safe there for a day or two but you will need to move on, perhaps to somewhere your husband will find you.'

On impulse, Martha threw her arms around Tobias' broad shoulders and hugged him. 'Thank you,' she said again. 'I won't forget your kindness.'

She found the path Tobias had mentioned but chose not to walk along it. A chance encounter with another villager might not have such happy consequences. Instead, she crept through the trees, crouching low and taking no chances. The cross hung from her neck and bounced against her chest. The feel of it was reassuring, a talisman of good fortune.

The journey proved tortuous. Every crack of a twig, every rustle of a leaf sent her heart skidding into panic and her eyes seeking out a hiding-place. Hours were spent crouching in the undergrowth, waiting, watching, before summoning the courage to move on once more. She spared no thought for her own physical discomfort. The skin on her feet was torn and bleeding and her whole body ached with exhaustion, yet she barely noticed – so focused was she upon remaining undiscovered. At last, she happened upon the dead oak tree she had visited many times before. The soil nearby was a fruitful source of mushrooms and she gathered a few now, collecting them in the fold of her nightdress, still damp from the lake. It would not do to arrive empty-handed.

She travelled on, her vigilance waning as a spell of dizziness overcame her. Mushrooms fell unheeded from her grasp, and, sitting down to rest, she sighed in dismay when she saw only a few remained. By now, she was feeling most unwell and it took enormous effort to rise once again and stumble onwards. Fortunately, it was not long before she reached the furthest edge of the wood and saw the thatched cottage, just as Tobias had described. It was tucked in a hollow, surrounded by roughly-fenced enclosures and small patches of grazing. Beyond lay a golden field of corn and she saw male figures working to cut and sheaf the stems. Flashes of sunlight caught the rhythmic strokes of a scythe wielded by the largest figure. The sight filled her with dread. What if these men were to spot her before she reached the safety of the small abode?

Clutching the cross tightly in one fist, she kept to the sanctuary of the trees and crept as close as she could. There was nothing for it. She must trust in the Lord to keep her safe, as He had done until this moment. Taking a deep breath and keeping her head bowed, she broke cover and walked as briskly as she dared. She was sorely tempted to run, but knew such exertion would draw more attention to her appearance. And very strange it was too! Her nightdress had dried but was ripped in places and barely covered her modesty. Her dark locks hung in a wild, tangled mess. In other circumstances, she would have been mortified, approaching a stranger's home in such state of dishevelment but, after today's proceedings, her pride was of little consequence. The danger to her life was a much greater preoccupation.

Good fortune continued to smile upon her. The men in the field, busy with their tasks, did not once glance her way. As the cottage loomed closer, she saw young children scrabbling in the dirt amongst goats, pigs and chickens. The door to the cottage hung open but there was no sign of Ruth, Daniel's wife.

Then she heard a shout …

CHAPTER 12

Enid tossed the book aside with a grunt. Of course, Martha Lightbody survived, just as Deborah Ryecroft had! She was a witch. There was the proof. Anger and resentment bubbled as she hid the tome at the back of her bedside cabinet. Martha Lightbody and her ancestors had much to answer for, and Enid would make them pay. It was up to her, the village's sole avenger. Her family had suffered at the hands of the curse, and she had her own grievance against the Ryecroft woman. A day of reckoning was long overdue.

The clock by her bedside table showed almost eight o'clock. Ava would soon bustle in to get her up, dressed and breakfasted before the post office opened. With a sigh, she pulled the covers higher over her decrepit, failing body. If only she was thirty years younger and able to sort the problem of Deborah Ryecroft herself! Instead, she was forced to rely upon men she did not trust. She had heard not one word from her son, nor Philip Holder, since she had issued her directive. Time to summon them for a progress report and, perhaps, to remind them of her power over them.

Philip was a nasty, little cheat of a man. Should he fail to discover incriminating evidence against Ryecroft, he was the type to fabricate something, purely to save his own skin. Enid had no problem with that. Needs must. She was not above a little deception herself, when circumstances called for it. After all, her daughter would have been long gone into the sunset with that American had Enid not exaggerated her illness when she needed to. Another glance at the clock. Ava was late this morning. Probably busy tarting herself up in case the American came calling. Stupid girl! She of all people should know by now that men could not be trusted.

Philip Holder – a case in point. His mother, Betty, lived in Wickthorpe all her life. She attended the village school, married a local lad, Ken, a blacksmith, and had the one son. Enid had counted her amongst her circle of close friends. Before she died, Betty and son, Philip, had a falling out. At the time, Enid did her best to wheedle details out of her friend but Betty remained adamantly tight-lipped about the whole affair. However, whatever it was, it was sufficient for Betty to change her will, just before her death. Enid and another friend, Norma Wilson, witnessed an amendment, handwritten by Betty who was concerned she did not have time or sufficient health to visit a solicitor. Enid had pointed out that a solicitor could come to her but Betty insisted it was too late. Death was fast approaching.

It turned out she was right. Betty died two days later, was buried in St Mary's churchyard, and Enid waited eagerly to see what would happen when Philip realised he had lost his inheritance. In the amendment she had witnessed, Betty had expressed the wish that her house should be sold and the proceeds given to Cancer Research. However, weeks went by, the house was not put up for sale and Philip continued to live there. Eventually, Enid phoned Betty's solicitor, a man named Quentin Bullit, and informed him of the amendment. Bullit said he would look into it. When she phoned again six weeks later, having heard nothing, she was told there was no evidence of any such document. Betty's original will stood. That was when she realised Philip must have discovered the amendment amongst Betty's personal belongings and destroyed it. Norma Wilson, the other witness to the document, had died from a heart attack shortly afterwards, leaving Enid the only person, apart from Philip, who knew the truth. And Enid had no compunction about using this knowledge to her own advantage. She even hinted to Philip that Betty had given her a photocopy of the amendment. He said he didn't believe her – especially when she refused to produce it – but he couldn't be sure. It was in his interests to keep her sweet, a fact she intended to use to her full advantage.

Andrew was another story. Her son was a man after her own heart. No silly romanticism for him. He took what he wanted and damn the consequences. But at least age was teaching him caution. Enid admired the fact that nothing had been discovered about Andrew's affair with Freya Billington, despite the efforts of the police and the Billington's own investigator. Thank heavens he had covered his tracks well or he could be facing a murder charge! Not that Enid thought he had actually *killed* the girl. Her boy was too lily-livered to commit murder. But he *had* been stupid enough to embroil himself with a local girl and he was fortunate that only his mother had guessed the truth. And it must be the truth. Why else, when she had dropped a few hints, would he agree so readily to do her bidding? When she had asked Andrew the previous summer to help scare Ryecroft away from Wickthorpe by trashing her garden, he had initially refused. It was only when she told him she knew what he had done that he became more obedient. She recalled how the colour had drained from his face ...

'What do you know?' he demanded.

She tapped the side of her nose with her twisted finger. 'I know you've been a bad boy and your wife would like to know what I know. More to the point, her *father* would be most interested. Let's be clear, Andrew. I have information which could be very damaging for you.'

'You wouldn't say anything!' His voice shook.

She responded with a sad grimace. 'I'm not asking for much, Andrew. And I know I can trust you to help me, can't I?'

He stared at her then, with such hatred she was worried she had gone too far. But she had not backed down and he had relented ...

Her mother's instinct had proven correct. If only Ava was as compliant. *Where was that girl?* At this rate, she would barely have time for breakfast before the post office opened! And she fully intended to be there, on the dot of nine o'clock, just in case Patrick Velaman appeared. She had no intention of missing that.

***

That evening, Rick returned home with a friend in tow, a man Emma had never seen before. Tall; well-built; early thirties; sandy-haired; pleasant, genial face; wide grin and even, white teeth.

Emma couldn't help smiling back. 'You must be Max, the new vet. I'm Emma.' She held out her hand which he clasped firmly.

'Good to meet you, Emma. I hope you don't mind me dropping by like this. Rick kindly invited me for something to eat, and then we're going out for a beer.'

'I know. He rang ahead. Mind you, it's his turn to cook. What are we having, Rick?'

He held up the bag he was carrying. 'Bangers and mash. Won't be long. Just need to peel some spuds and stick the sausages in the oven.'

'And make gravy.' Emma winked at Max. 'Onion gravy would be nice. We've got loads of onions. I'll just get Max a drink and we'll leave you to it.'

'Cheers, mate!'

'I don't mind helping out,' Max said.

'No, Max, you're a guest. And Rick can manage a few potatoes and onions.' Emma steered him through to the snug, giving Rick a cheery pat on the back as she passed. 'Call when it's ready.'

By the time Rick did give them a shout, forty-five minutes later, she had ascertained that Max had a brother, two sisters, and was originally from Cheltenham. After qualifying as a vet, he had worked in rural Yorkshire, mostly large animals – horses, cows, sheep and pigs. Having come to Suffolk, specifically to Stowmarket where the practice was situated, he was looking forward to seeing more dogs, cats, rabbits and other, more exotic pets.

'We had an iguana in last week with a broken leg,' he enthused. 'Easy enough to fix but this was the second time it had happened. Tests revealed the poor thing has metabolic bone disease. When we checked, we discovered the underlying cause was insufficient calcium in its diet. Sorry, I'm talking shop.'

'No, carry on. I'm interested. I'm the same talking about farming operations or machinery. Once I get started, I get carried away. It's great that you love your work.'

He beamed. 'I really do. Now, tell me all about you. I've gone on about myself long enough.'

The chat between them flowed easily and, by the time the meal was finished, it was as if they had known each other forever. Rick was amused by their instant rapport. 'I feel a bit like a spare part with the two of you,' he joked. 'Perhaps *you* ought to take Max to the pub, Em, instead of me.'

Max's grey eyes instantly lit up. 'Yes, can you come, Em? Er ...' he glanced across at Rick, 'and you too, Rick, obviously.'

'Sorry boys, but you'll have to manage without my scintillating company.' She pulled a face. 'I've promised to drive over to see Mum tonight. She rang earlier. In fact, I ought to be on my way. I said I'd be there by half seven.' She grabbed her keys and coat. 'Good to meet you, Max.'

'You too,' he returned warmly, casting a lingering look after Emma as she departed.

'Never mind. Just us lads, eh Max?' Rick grinned.

'Disappointing, but I guess we'll manage. Er, is Emma seeing anyone, do you know? I didn't get around to finding out.'

Rick thumped him on the arm. 'Schoolboy error! Luckily, I can help. No, she's single. Why? Are you interested?'

'Definitely.'

'Well, she's a great girl. You couldn't do better.'

Max nodded. 'Agreed. And a complete stunner.' He regarded Rick anxiously. 'If I ask her out, do you reckon I stand a chance?'

Rick shrugged. 'You never know with women, but I would say so, judging by how well the two of you were getting on.'

'Great.'

As Max helped him clear the plates from the table and load the dishwasher, Rick smiled to himself. Max was a fast worker! He wondered if, in time, they would go out as couples, he and Amelie, and Emma with Max. A double date. Probably not. Amelie had said Emma didn't like her much. Shame! Then he pictured Max with his arm around Emma, kissing her ... For some obscure reason, the image bothered him. Best forget the whole idea.

***

Deborah lay wide awake in the darkness, Tom peacefully asleep beside her. Her mind churned like a tumble drier, refusing to switch off. *A lump. In her breast. Pea-sized. Painless. Cancer?* The same thoughts – a relentless cycle of impending doom.

She had felt the lump whilst showering that morning. Disbelief was quickly followed by dismay. It had been difficult to think of anything else all day. Tom had noticed her distraction.

'Anything wrong?' he asked, his kind, handsome face full of concern.

'No,' she answered, as brightly as she could manage. 'Sorry, I've just got a few things on my mind, that's all.'

He continued to regard her anxiously throughout the evening, so much so that she feigned tiredness and went to bed early. When he came up, some while later, she pretended to be already asleep.

Perhaps it will be gone in the morning. She tossed and turned, willing the worry away. How could she have survived a near-drowning experience, only to have her life claimed by cancer? She was strong and healthy. It would not be that dreaded disease. It would all be fine.

If it's still there tomorrow, I'll make an appointment with the doctor. Not Seb Holley, though. She shuddered at the thought. Someone else. When she had registered at the practice, her nominated GP was Dr Singh. She would ask for her, or another female doctor.

Decision made, sleep still eluded her. Distraction. That was what she needed. Switching on her bedside lamp, she reached for her book. Time to find out if Martha managed to escape from Wickthorpe and the clutches of Roger Holley ...

CHAPTER 13

The Life & Times of Martha Lightbody

'Ma, Ma, someone's coming!' It was a child's voice, high-pitched and shrill, slicing through air now stuffy with summer heat.

Martha glanced around nervously but the men in the fields remained oblivious to the cries. By the time her gaze returned to the cottage, a stout woman was striding towards her, a fat plait streaked with grey swinging in time to her step. As she grew closer, Martha observed heavy jowls in an unsmiling face but eyes which were curious rather than angry. She knew she must look a sight and tugged the cross over her head.

'Tobias Fletcher sent me to you,' she said breathlessly as she handed the talisman to the woman. 'Are you Ruth?' At the woman's nod, she rushed on. 'The men of Wickthorpe have falsely accused me of witchcraft and near drowned me in the lake this morn. Tobias aided my escape and has sent me to you, to beg for refuge til I can flee this place for good.'

Ruth's puzzlement turned to horror as Martha recounted her sorry tale. 'Oh, my dear! Come inside. You are most welcome to shelter here. I will fetch you bread and water while you rest and recover your strength. Come this way.'

Ruth ushered her into the dark confines of the small cottage and Martha's heart sank. She could not impose on this family. There was not space for her here. The cottage was cramped enough as it was: just a single room with mattresses pushed into a pile in one corner, a laundry tub, broom and roughly-hewn wooden table in another. A black pot bubbled on a stove on the other side of the room where Ruth had been cleaning and gutting a small chicken.

Wiping her hands on her apron, Ruth poured Martha a beaker of water and tore off a chunk of bread from a half-eaten loaf. 'Here, get this inside you,' she said kindly, steering her guest to a nearby stool. 'You look near to collapse, you poor thing.'

Martha was feeling quite light-headed and took the offering gratefully. However, as she bit into the bread, bile rose in her throat and she struggled to swallow the small mouthful she had taken. A sip of water helped but the thought of eating more made her feel quite nauseous.

'You will return the cross to Tobias for me?' she asked to hide her discomfort. 'I promised him faithfully he would receive it.'

'Most surely, I will. Worry not about that.' Ruth had moved closer and was peering at her with concern. 'Are you alright, my dear? You've gone white as a sheet.'

Martha barely had time to nod before leaping to her feet, stepping outside and retching vile pondwater into the earth. Ruth placed a comforting arm around her shoulders as she remained doubled over for some while, ridding herself of liquid she had swallowed.

'There, there,' the woman murmured, smoothing Martha's hair away from her fevered brow.

As Martha stood, stomach emptied of its meagre contents, she became aware of a ring of small faces, staring at her. She gave one of them a weak smile but, try as she might, she could not get the child's features into focus. Blinking, she looked at another but, if anything, this was even worse. Blurry colours swam before her eyes and Martha leaned heavily on Ruth's arm, thankful of its stout support.

'She looks awful pale, Ma.'

'Come on lass, let's get you back inside.' Ruth's voice sounded strangely distant, competing with a sudden roaring in her ears. A dark grey mist descended and Martha fell to the ground.

***

When Martha woke, she was soon aware of the strangeness of her surroundings. She tried to raise her head but the effort was too great and she sank back down. A raging thirst consumed her.

'Water,' she moaned through cracked lips.

'Ma, she's awake. The lady's awake!'

A child's voice penetrated her bleary consciousness and a strong arm helped to lift her head and shoulders. A beaker was pressed against her mouth.

'Try to drink,' a woman soothed. She sipped at the water gratefully, again and again. 'Good girl,' the woman encouraged. 'That's better. You've had us worried but the worst is over. Now rest.'

Martha was only too happy to do as instructed. The mere effort of drinking had exhausted her. With a sigh, she sank back onto the mattress and closed her eyes.

The next time she woke, she felt better. Memories flooded back and she knew where she was. Ruth and Daniel, cousin of Tobias Fletcher. Fear also returned. How long had she been here? With every hour, she risked discovery. She tried to rise but soon realised her weakness. Her limbs would not obey her brain's direction. Wearily, she lay back. However perilous, she would have to stay a little longer.

'How are you feeling?' Ruth's round face hovered above hers and a cool, rough hand rested lightly on her forehead.

It was wearisome to speak but she owed the woman her life and Martha knew her obligation. 'Better,' she croaked. 'Thank you. Have I been here many hours?'

'Hours! Days more like! Three to be exact. You had a raging fever but you're through the worst now.'

Three days! Martha reeled anew. What had happened in those missing hours? Were men still looking for her? And what about John and baby Josiah? Did they know she still lived?

'But ...'

'Hush now,' Ruth interrupted. 'You're safe here. Time enough for questions when you're stronger.'

Two more days passed before Martha knew the full story and had regained sufficient strength to be on her way. She learned there had been much talk in Wickthorpe of her disappearance and her curse. Many were fearful she would wreak vengeance upon them, even those who had not been involved in the drowning. This fear had been whipped into a frenzy by Roger Holley who had thereby managed to drum up support for a full-scale search. So far, the hunt had drawn a blank and people had grown disgruntled at being kept from more pressing tasks. The search party had grown smaller and was losing impetus.

'Did they come here?' Martha asked.

'They did. Luckily, it was late. We covered you in a blanket and used the children to feign sleep and conceal you from view.'

Martha shuddered. A narrow escape. 'Thank you all. You saved me!' she smiled at the young children. There were three, two girls and a boy, but also two older boys who helped their father in the fields. She had barely seen them, nor Daniel, such long hours they worked.

'Is there news of John, my husband, or Josiah, my son?

Ruth took hold of her hand. 'They have left the village,' she replied. 'They left the day after, in fear of their own lives, tis said. No one knows whence they have fled. Tis dangerous to ask, given the mood of folk at present. And we have seen none but the search party and cousin Tobias, who visited on the pretext of bringing Daniel a flagon of ale. I have returned his cross,' she added before Martha could ask.

Martha digested the information. She wondered if, despite their differences, John would head for his father's farm in Norfolk to seek respite. But would he be safe there? Eventually, would not Roger Holley follow him to seek revenge upon her family for both her escape and the curse? Concern clutched at her heart. Somehow, she needed to find her husband and son before Roger Holley did. She feared Holley would not rest until someone had paid the price for her perceived sins.

Her other more immediate problem was the manner of her own departure. She was a stranger to the wider area and would risk detection until some distance from Wickthorpe. Roger Holley was a man of means and would have paid spies to report any sighting. She could trust no one except the Fletchers but she knew she could not stay longer in their small cottage. The family had risked so much to protect her and they could ill-afford to provide further food and lodging for her.

Ruth, once again, proved herself a resourceful woman and came up with a solution. Disguise. Martha possessed nothing of her own beyond the torn nightdress which she had repaired as best she could. In Ruth's clothes though, with lots of padding and a scarf over her head, she looked most unlike herself. A stooped gait and a face darkened with a madder root completed the illusion of a much older woman.

Ruth agreed to accompany her for the first and most dangerous part of the journey. They would walk together to visit Ruth's sister, Anne, in Elmswell. Anne's husband would be asked to give her safe passage to Bury St Edmunds and secure the services of someone to take her to her family in King's Lynn where she would hope for news of John and Josiah. Martha argued against these plans, worried at putting others to so much trouble, not to say danger, but Ruth refused to be thwarted, such was this fine woman's compassion and generosity.

'Tis not safe for you to travel alone,' she argued. 'Are you not forgetting the bounty on your head?' She was referring to Roger Holley's reward of ten shillings to anyone who captured the Wickthorpe Witch.

'But how will I ever repay you?' Martha cried.

'Your thanks are all I need, and a thought in your prayers.'

With everything agreed, it was decided to leave at first light the following morning. Daniel and the older boys would be stacking sheaves of corn into stooks nearby, and the eldest girl, Hannah, would keep an eye on the younger children. And so, after bidding farewell to the rest of the family, Martha took her first trepidatious steps away from Wickthorpe, wondering what adventures lay ahead.

CHAPTER 14

The morning dawned crisp and bright. There was a lightness to the air which heralded good things following the dank, dark days of early January. Deborah padded through to the shower, her worries fading as a faint shaft of winter sun peeked through the blinds. Her fearful imagination had run riot through the night but daytime brought a welcome dose of practicality. She would confront any medical issue in the same calm, pragmatic manner she used to deal with business problems. She would take control.

The lump was still there. Her cautious, probing fingers located it almost immediately on the side of her left breast, towards her armpit. With deliberate thoroughness, she checked each breast, finding nothing else. She returned to the lump: small; pea-sized; painless when she pinched it between her fingers; no bigger nor smaller than when she discovered it yesterday.

After towelling herself dry, she dressed, went downstairs and switched on her coffee machine. There was work to do in preparation for a meeting in London the following day so she took her coffee into the office and sat in front of her computer. When her watch showed half past eight, she picked up her phone to make a doctor's appointment. Pointless to waste time and energy fretting over something which could be nothing. A pre-recorded voice told her she was thirteenth in the queue. *Thirteen, unlucky for some.* Cross with herself for the silly, superstitious thought, she set the phone on to speaker mode and settled down for a wait.

Twenty minutes later she finally got through and explained her situation to the receptionist on the line. 'I'm terribly sorry but the earliest appointment I have with Dr Singh is 10.30 tomorrow,' came the response.

Tomorrow! Deborah ended the call, disappointed. Another day of waiting. And now she would have to cancel her meeting in London. At least, though, her appointment was with Dr Singh, a female doctor. It could have been worse.

***

Emma was up a ladder cleaning out gutters when her phone rung. It was buttoned up in her trouser pocket and not easily accessible. Whoever it was would have to wait. Or leave a message. She was keen to get the job finished before she went in for breakfast. Humming to herself, her mind wandered back to the previous evening. Belinda, her mum, had seemed in a better frame of mind. She had heard from Lewis, Emma's brother, currently back–packing in Australia. Except he wasn't. He had settled in Sydney with his partner. And Belinda was planning on going out there just as soon as she could get a ticket.

'I didn't know he had a partner!' Emma exclaimed. 'I thought he'd hooked up with some chap he had met, and was doing some bar work to earn a bit of money before he moved on.'

Belinda gave her a knowing smile. 'You don't know your brother like I do. Lewis is gay. The chap you mentioned is his partner, Ray.'

Emma's eyes widened. 'Lewis? Gay? But he was always hanging around with some girl or another!'

'That's true,' Belinda nodded. 'It took him a while to work it out for himself. But I always knew.'

'I'd never have thought it but, actually, it makes sense,' Emma said. 'Gosh, Australia! That's a long way away. Is he planning on staying there permanently?'

'Yes, he's already applied for residency. Ray works in advertising and has put in a word for Lewis at his agency. Graphic design.'

'Does Dad know?'

Belinda grimaced. 'Not yet. I was rather hoping you would tell him ...'

And that was how things had been left. Her dad would be cool about it all, she knew, but it would come as a bit of a shock. She was just debating how best to broach the subject when her mobile rang again. Someone was persistent. Having completed that section of guttering, she descended the ladder and answered.

'Hi Emma. It's Max. We met last night.'

She smiled. 'Yes. Hi, Max.'

There was a slight pause. 'Er … I just wondered if you fancied going out for a drink this evening … or a meal … or anything really?'

Her smile turned to a frown. Was he asking her on a *date*? 'Um, I'm afraid I'm busy this evening. Some other time?'

'How about tomorrow night?'

Oh Lordy! She relented a little as she remembered the poor guy was new to the area and probably at a loose end when not working. 'Tomorrow night is good for me. How about bowling?' *That should be safe enough!*

'Brilliant! Shall I pick you up at half seven?'

She could hear the grin in his voice. It was infectious and her smile returned. 'Great.'

He sounded keen. Emma felt flattered to receive attention from such a good-looking, likeable man. 'Let's face it,' she muttered to herself, 'it's not what I'm used to!' The only trouble was it was coming from the wrong person. And the man she had adored for so long was all loved-up with someone else. She sighed as she moved the ladder. What a mess!

***

Hands clenched deep in the pockets of her new, double-breasted, taupe, woollen coat, Ava marched up to the door of the bungalow, until recently the home of Mabel Littlebody, and rang the bell. Too late to turn back now. She had rehearsed her lines and was prepared. Patrick Velaman no longer had the power to upset her. For once, she would have the upper hand.

The door opened and his eyes lit up. 'Ava!' he exclaimed, throwing out his arms as if to embrace her.

She took a swift step backwards. 'Hello, Patrick,' she returned coolly. 'May I come in?'

'Sure.' He stood aside and gestured her forwards, his head slightly stooped to avoid the door frame. Tall, a little broader than he had been twenty-two years ago, but still lean. He wore an old college sweatshirt, faded jeans and black slippers with Snoopy on the front. 'Sorry, I'm not really ready for visitors. I'm unpacking, and still waiting for furniture shipped from the States.' There were boxes everywhere and she picked her way carefully through to the small room which had been Mabel's sitting room. 'Here, let me take your coat.'

'Thanks, but I'll keep it on. It's a bit chilly in here.'

'Sorry.' He gave her a rueful grin. 'I guess I don't feel the cold, and I've been plenty warm unpacking these darn boxes. Anyway, take a seat.' He waved at an old, green leather sofa which lined most of one wall. 'At least that arrived safely. And my coffee machine. Can I get you a cup? I'm afraid I haven't gotten round to buying tea.'

'Yes, thank you. A coffee would be nice,' she answered primly as she perched on the edge of the sofa, sitting her smart, new handbag beside her and feeling rather like a maiden aunt. A coffee would give her time to recollect her equilibrium. Inside, long-suppressed emotions seethed like secrets threatening to burst forth. Just seeing his dear, kind face had made her want to throw herself into his arms. And those eyes! Beautiful, cornflower blue; gentle; guileless; faithful ... *No! Deceitful; unkind; faithless.* Those eyes alone could make her weep as she reminded herself of his duplicity.

His mop of unruly, light brown hair, now peppered with grey, appeared once more in the doorway. 'Do you still take milk, one sugar?'

He remembered how she liked her coffee! Swallowing the lump which clogged her throat, she replied, 'Milk but no sugar, thank you.' To her ears, her voice no longer sounded calm and in control, but weak and quavery. *Get a grip, Ava! Deep breaths.*

He reappeared, carrying two plain, white mugs. 'There you go.' Smiling broadly, he set one on a box beside her and sat on another box, facing her. 'Gee, it's good to see you, Ava. You look well.'

'I am well, thank you.' She reached for her coffee with a trembling hand. 'How have you been, Patrick?'

'Good, thanks.' His grin widened. 'All the better for seeing you. I wasn't sure you'd give me the time of day.'

She pursed her lips. 'No. Well, that would have been no more than you deserved. But it was a long time ago. I'm sure we've both moved on.'

'I guess so.' His face became serious and he regarded her sadly. 'I'm truly sorry, Ava. I know I must have hurt you badly.' He shrugged. 'If I could have that time again, I promise you things would have turned out very differently. But I blew it.'

'Yes, you did.'

'And I ended up hurting myself too. More than you could ever know. The biggest regret of my life by far is letting you go.'

'Letting me go?' She would not allow him to get away with that. 'Cheating on me with another woman, you mean.' The anger she detected in her tone stopped her from saying more. She had promised herself she would not come across as a victim. Rather, she wanted to portray herself as a strong woman who had learned from past mistakes. And prove to him that he had made a mistake in giving up on her. *Except he had already admitted that!* Ava shook her head, trying to rid herself of her confusion.

'You're right.' He picked up his mug and gazed at its contents as if to find answers. There was a long pause before he took a sip. Still, she waited, willing him to say more ... to explain. When he looked up, he fixed her with eyes brimming with sorrow. 'What I did was unforgivable. I'm so sorry, Ava. I say that from the bottom of my heart.'

She sighed, determined not to be swayed by his apology. 'Why have you come back, Patrick? Why here, in Wickthorpe?'

A sad smile. 'It's a long story ...' he began.

'I suggest you get started then,' she retorted. Did he think she was going to let him off the hook?

He nodded. 'Sure, I guess I owe you an explanation, at the very least.' He averted his gaze from her and stared out of the window. 'I understood why you felt you couldn't leave your mother when I moved to Cleveland. She was ill. You were a dutiful daughter. I got it. But, as the months went past and you showed no signs of joining me, I began to wonder if you would ever come. I guess I began to feel you were choosing her over me. If you really loved me, you would organise alternative care for Enid. That's what I thought. To tell the truth, I felt pretty sorry for myself.'

'But I wrote to you,' she interrupted. 'I explained how difficult it was. I told you over and over, in my letters, how much I loved you and wanted to be with you. You should have trusted me.'

'I should have,' he agreed, 'but I was lonely. I missed you ... so much. We were so far apart and every one of your letters broke my heart a tiny bit more.' His chest heaved. 'And then I met Candice.' He grimaced. 'We were work colleagues and I guess I was flattered by her attention. As you know, I wasn't the kind of chap who had pretty girls throwing themselves at him. Anyway, to cut a long story short, she kinda dazzled me. When I was with her, I didn't feel lonely ...'

'I bet you didn't!' Her voice dripped with bitterness and she bit her lip.

'One thing led to another ... I broke things off with you and married her. We got divorced six years later. It didn't work out.' He shrugged. 'I've been single, more or less, ever since.' The cornflower eyes turned back to her. 'But I never forgot my first love ... my true love. I guess when I got posted back to Britain, to Mildenhall, I took it as a sign. I flew over a few months back to do a bit of recon. I discovered you still lived at the Post Office with your mother and that you had never married. Then I saw this bungalow on the market and decided to buy it. If I was to have any chance with you, I knew I had to convince you I was here to stay. This is my final posting and I'm going to live in Wickthorpe. I didn't want to see my time out living on the base, or renting somewhere. I wanted to prove to you I was here for good.'

She stared at him in disbelief. Her wildest imaginings were unfolding in front of her and yet her feelings were very mixed. A part of her wanted to believe the sincerity of his words and drown herself in those blue eyes; but another part felt anger that he thought he could just rock up in the village and expect her to swoon at his feet. She wanted to rage and rail at him for the way he had carelessly destroyed all her hopes and dreams. Instead, she raised her eyebrows. 'This is very ... unexpected,' she said carefully.

He gave her a lopsided smile. 'I'm sorry. All my well-laid plans went out of the window as soon as I saw you again. I meant to invite you out to dinner somewhere fancy. Take you to lots of places. Treat you real good. Get to know each other again. Hope that, maybe someday, you would forgive me. I love you, Ava.' He stood and extended a hand towards her. 'I always have and I always will.'

She stood to face him, ignoring the outstretched arm. Her legs felt wobbly. She needed to get out of there. All her thoughts and emotions tangled together, constricting her voice.

'Are you OK, Ava?' Patrick's concerned face swam before her and she felt strong hands grip her elbows. 'You look very pale.'

'I need ... air,' she muttered.

He snaked an arm around her waist and steered her to the rear garden. 'There's a bench out here,' he explained. 'You can sit and catch your breath. I guess this has all been a bit of a shock.'

He sat beside her, still holding her, as she took long, trembling breaths. Gradually, the dizziness subsided and embarrassment surfaced. Pulling away from him, she remained seated, not quite trusting herself yet to stand. 'It has been a shock,' she said. Thankfully, strength had returned to her voice. 'I was not expecting ... you know. I'm not sure what you expect me to say.'

'Don't say anything.' His hand closed over hers, long, elegant fingers squeezing her short, stubby ones. 'I'm scared right now I've blown my chances by blurting out my feelings in that unconsidered manner. Best you take some time. Here, I'll walk you home. Just give me another chance. That's all I ask.'

Once again, she pulled away. 'You're asking a lot,' she answered, 'and I can walk myself home.' She stood and took a step towards the rear gate to prove her point.

'If you're sure ...'

'Goodbye, Patrick,' she said firmly.

'Bye, Ava. I'll be in touch ...'

CHAPTER 15

Seb Holley liked his poached eggs cooked through but still runny in the middle. It was not much to ask; usually it was something his wife did well. This morning, he had sliced into the first egg and a pool of yolk and liquid albumen seeped over his carefully buttered toast. Wrinkling his nose in disgust, he had tried the second. Same.

'Ugh!' He pushed the plate aside with a snort of displeasure, expecting Jane to apologise and make him another breakfast but she appeared not to notice. Even when he scraped his chair back and muttered something about having to make do with toast, she said nothing. She was eating nothing too, he saw. No wonder she was skin and bone. He frowned. She had been like a wet weekend ever since the body of Freya Billington had been discovered in Dark Water Lake. People had noticed. Several had spoken to him about it. It was time she pulled herself together. He made a mental note to have another word with her that evening.

With a huff of annoyance, he threw the offensive eggs in the bin and made fresh toast, eating it in giant mouthfuls as he stood by the kitchen worktop. The mere act of looking at Jane these days was enough to irritate him. Perhaps the stupid woman would starve herself to death and do them all a favour.

'Time to go. Are you ready?' he snapped.

His wife stood wordlessly and walked to the front door where she slipped on ugly, black shoes and the grey coat which sagged on her skinny frame. She waited there, as she always did, as he unlocked the garage and reversed his Lexus. As she slid into the passenger seat and buckled her seatbelt, he watched with an expression of distaste, scarcely able to believe his wife had become such an old crone. She was once a very different woman.

When they first met, he was an undergraduate at Edinburgh university and she was a post grad. Her maturity and confidence had immediately appealed. Older than him, she was slim and beautiful in an understated way, with a kudos not evident in the younger bevy of girls seeking his attention. His peers, many of whom had tried and failed to attract her notice, had tagged her 'the ice maiden.' Seb had always relished a challenge, and had deliberately set out to seduce her, confident she would be unable to resist him. No woman could. It was a gift. He prided himself in his ability to bed even the most unavailable of women. Jane had initially been deterred by his reputation but succumbed eventually, as he knew she would. And, after that, she had proved very useful.

At twenty-five minutes past eight, he parked in his designated space at the rear of the building. Although he lived only half a mile away, he drove to work in case he needed to make an emergency house call, although that was a rarity these days. If a patient required a home visit, the task was usually designated to one of his less senior colleagues. Jane stepped out of the car and through the back entrance to the practice without a word. It irritated him. Usually, they were at least civil to each other, especially at work. Not that he was the least bothered whether she spoke to him or not, but they both cared about appearances and it was disquieting to see her so … unbalanced? Yes, that was the word. She was unbalanced and that did not bode well. He would have to deal with it, one way or another.

Having stopped for a brief chat with the receptionist – a pretty, young thing who always batted her eyelashes at him – he headed for his consulting room. Annoyingly, Indira Singh, one of the other GPs, had suffered an emergency at home and was not in. His workload had increased accordingly, although young Hannah had sorted things so his other colleague, Paul Sawyer, was bearing the brunt of the list. He smiled to himself when he saw what she had done. One of Dr Singh's appointments today was with Anya Harrison. That woman was a nightmare! She had been transferred to Dr Sawyer's list. His morning chats with Hannah and enquiries about her young son were paying off. And he was the senior GP after all, now old Tony Evans had retired. He *should* get the easier patients.

His eyes skimmed down his list and stopped abruptly at 10:30 – *Deborah Ryecroft*. Excellent! Perhaps he could use the appointment to his advantage. He had very definite plans for Ms Ryecroft but she had kept her distance since she had moved into Greenways Farm.

He knew Jane disliked her, and had heard the story of the girl who died in Dark Water Lake in the late eighties. Jane had explained how Deborah Ryecroft had taunted the girl until she went in the water. There was something in his wife's tone, though, which caused him to suspect that was not the whole truth. He would love to hear Deborah's account of the incident. Perhaps, today, he could begin his charm offensive in earnest. Rubbing his hands together, he called for his first patient. 10:30 could not come soon enough.

***

It was ridiculous to be so nervous. Women had breast lumps checked all the time. Most were harmless, Deborah knew. Hers would be too.

Having entered Wickthorpe Health Centre, she keyed in her personal details on a tablet, as directed, and received a message to report to Reception. So much for technology! The young girl behind the desk gave her a reassuring smile.

'We're terribly sorry, Ms Ryecroft, but Dr Singh has been called away on an emergency. Fortunately, we *have* been able to fit you in with Dr Holley. Would that be OK for you?'

Deborah stared at the girl, unable to formulate a response. *Dr Holley?* Every part of her recoiled at the thought. But she had already waited a day for her appointment. The thought of a further delay was untenable. 'Is there anyone else I could see?' she asked.

The girl's brow furrowed as she scrutinised her screen. 'Not today, I'm afraid. We could do 5:30 tomorrow with Dr Sawyer. If you particularly wanted to see Dr Singh, that won't be possible until next week. I'm very sorry.' She looked up. 'Dr Holley is our senior partner and very highly regarded,' she added with enthusiastic warmth. 'You'd be in *very* good hands.'

Deborah shuddered – an instinctive reaction and one she was at a loss to explain. The receptionist was watching her expectantly and she needed to decide. 'Alright,' she agreed with a tight smile. 'Dr Holley it is.'

She took a seat in the waiting room and tried to rationalise her antipathy to Seb Holley. She had felt it from their very first meeting. He was a disturbingly attractive man, and yet he set all her senses tingling with alarm. Then, since reading the account of Martha Lightbody's fateful interactions with Roger Holley, Seb's namesake, she had subconsciously drawn parallels between them. In her mind, Seb had taken on Roger's villainous persona. She was empathetic to Martha and, therefore, antagonistic towards Roger, aka Seb. No wonder she was so on edge at the thought of seeing him instead of Dr Singh! But Roger and Seb were different people, living in different times. Seb was a medical professional. She had nothing to fear.

'Deborah Ryecroft.' She stood at the sound of her name. 'Along the corridor and second on the right.'

Deborah straightened her shoulders and marched to the designated door, giving it a sharp knock.

'Come in.' Seb was by a large, walnut deck, his fingers skimming over a keyboard. 'Take a seat.' He looked up and gave her his shark smile. 'Deborah. Good to see you, but perhaps not in the best circumstances. What can I do for you?' His voice oozed warm concern.

Succinctly, she told him of the lump she had found in her breast. After she had answered a few more questions, he asked, 'Are you happy for me to examine you?'

'Of course.' She knew it would happen but the thought made her feel sick.

He gave her a sympathetic smile, acknowledging her anxiety, and gestured to the examination table at one side of the room. 'Remove your top garments and lie down for me. Pop the sheet over you when you're ready. I will call for a nurse to be present.'

He pulled a curtain around her and left her alone to follow his instructions. She covered her exposed breasts with the sheet and lay shivering, feeling like a victim about to be sacrificed upon an altar. Seconds ticked by and still she waited. Her fists clenched by her side. *Just get it over with!*

After what seemed like an eternity, she heard a door open and someone else enter the room. The curtain was pulled aside and Seb appeared beside her. She turned her head, focusing instead on the dark-haired woman who had joined them.

''This is Angela,' Seb said, inclining his head towards the newcomer. 'Now then, let's take a look. Left breast, you said.' Gently, he tugged the sheet aside and she gritted her teeth as his fingers probed the lump. 'Mm, have you noticed anything untoward in the other breast? Any abnormalities?'

'No.'

'Do you mind if I take a look?'

'No.' Of course she minded! But he was being thorough. It was his job. All her senses screamed at the invasion as he pressed his hands over both breasts. She squeezed both eyes shut.

At last, the hands lifted and the sheet was pulled over her. 'I don't think it's anything to worry about but get yourself dressed and we'll have a chat,' he said.

Nothing to worry about. Relief flooded her body. The humiliation was nothing if everything was fine. Feeling considerably happier, she scooted off the examination table and pulled on her clothes.

Seb was back by his desk, typing with dexterity, as she sat on the patient's chair. His white teeth flashed. 'All done. As I said, I don't think the lump is anything sinister. Most likely, it's a sebaceous cyst. These are very common and quite harmless. However, just to err on the side of caution, I'm going to refer you to the hospital for a mammogram and, possibly, an ultrasound. Best to be on the safe side. You should receive an appointment within the next two weeks.'

'Thank you.' She stood, keen to escape.

'You're very welcome.' The smile widened. 'We must get together sometime soon.'

'Mm.' Her lips framed a non-committal response and she closed the door behind her before he could say anything else. As she walked away, she felt her body relax. *A cyst. Harmless.* All the pent-up worry dissolved away and, for the first time in three days, the spring in her step returned. *Nothing to worry about.* The best news.

***

Rick Billington felt strangely out of sorts all evening. He had no idea why. Amelie was away with friends for a few days but that was not the reason. Things were cooling once more between him and his enigmatic girlfriend, and he had accepted Amelie did not see him as a long-term partner. That was fine by him. He had come to realise she was not the woman for him either. When she returned, he would break things off between them.

Tonight, he was on his own. Emma had gone out on a date with the new vet, Max Benson. Max seemed a nice enough chap and Rick wished him well. Emma too. It was about time she found someone special. She was a great girl. His best friend. She made him laugh and was fun to be around. More than that, he didn't know what he would have done without her these past six months since Freya's death. She had been unfailingly kind and caring. Attractive too. He wondered why he had failed to notice that before. When she had appeared, earlier that evening, in a dress and heels, he had been blown away by just how stunning she looked. Max had showered her with compliments, whilst he had made some throwaway remark like, 'Yeah, she scrubs up OK.' She had blushed, as she always did when someone complimented her, and he had felt his heart squeeze, just a little bit. Max was a lucky man.

He yawned and checked his watch. 11:35 p.m. Time for bed, yet he was reluctant to go up. He wanted to see Emma and share one of their late-night chats. And see her all dressed up again. She had looked good.

A car pulled up outside. It occurred to him she might invite Max in. Maybe he should beat a hasty retreat after all? *Too late.* The key rattled in the lock. He grabbed a farming magazine and pretended to be engrossed when Emma sailed through the door, flushed and glowing, looking gorgeous. She was alone.

'Still up?' she chuckled. 'And reading an old *Farmer's Weekly*! Have you turned into my dad?'

He tossed the magazine aside. 'It was very interesting,' he answered, his tone lofty. 'And I hadn't realised the time. Did you have a good time?'

'Yeah, brilliant,' she enthused. 'Max took me to this great place for dinner. It was in Eye. Posh but friendly. The food was fabulous. And he wouldn't let me pay for a thing.'

'He was obviously trying to impress you.' He looked pointedly at his watch. 'Were you there all this time?'

'No, we stopped at *The Olde King's Head* on the way home. I know you said Amelie wasn't too keen but I love it and I wanted to see Max's reaction.'

'And ...?'

'He loved it too,' she beamed. 'He's really interested in history so he was fascinated by the place. He's keen to go back there ... said we should think of it as our place.'

Rick's eyebrows shot up. 'I thought it was *our* place!' He wanted to grab back the words even as they slipped out of his mouth. They made him sound jealous.

Emma laughed. 'Don't be daft, Rick. *We* don't have a place. We're just friends. Anyway ...' she said, stifling a yawn, 'I'm bushed. Night.'

'Night, Em,' Rick called after her as she headed upstairs. With a sigh, he set about the task of switching off all the downstairs lights and checking the doors were locked. He was glad his best friend had enjoyed herself. Of course, he was.

***

It was late but Deborah felt wide awake. Tom lay silently beside her, already sound asleep. She had told him about the lump that evening and he had shared her relief at Dr Holley's assessment.

'I knew something was up,' he murmured, holding her close, 'but you didn't want to talk about it.'

'I didn't want to worry you,' she returned.

'I know.' He hugged her tighter. 'But I wish you would. You don't have to cope with stuff like that on your own. Not anymore.'

She slid her arms around his neck and kissed him. 'I guess old habits die hard.'

There was not much talking after that, but now he was asleep and she was not. Carefully, so as not to wake him, she reached across to her bedside table and curled her fingers around the green, leather-bound book. Time to return to Martha's world ...

CHAPTER 16

The Life & Times of Martha Lightbody

The first part of the journey was completed without mishap. Menfolk at work in the fields or on the road heading to market paid little heed to two middle-aged women, deep in chatter and bearing baskets of vegetables. They walked cross country where they could, skirting Wickthorpe and heading uphill towards Elmswell. The weather was cooler than of late and the sun was mostly obscured by cloud. Martha was glad of this as her extra clothing, her disguise, was warm enough as it was. Her recent illness also took its toll and Ruth, upon noticing her companion's breathlessness, slowed her pace. Even so, Martha felt quite weary by the time they reached their destination. They found Ruth's sister, Anne, spinning yarn on a wheel. A girl of around ten years of age stood with her hands in a large tub, washing a fleece.

There were many happy exclamations at their appearance, the two sisters not having seen each other for many months. Martha drew curious glances but was introduced as Ruth's close friend and was willingly included in the offer of refreshments, of which they were happy to partake. Ruth's sister, Anne, shared a likeness with her sibling, both being large of frame and plump of cheek. Anne was two years younger and had been blessed with just the one living child, having endured the birthing of seven more babies, sadly stillborn. This information Ruth had shared with Martha on their trek up the hill. Anne's husband, Gideon, worked as a trader, taking goods to market on his cart and buying goods in return to sell to villagers. As such, Ruth had hoped he would be willing to take Martha for the next part of her journey.

However, when Ruth suggested this to Anne, without confessing any details of Martha's circumstances, an unexpected problem presented itself. Gideon's horse was lame and needed rest. He had no plans for travel until the horse was fully fit. Martha's face fell at such news. Her hopes of reaching King's Lynn where her mother and father lived, before another week was out, were dealt a severe blow.

For a while, Ruth was silent before once again proving her resourcefulness. Surely another horse could be hired from a neighbour? Gideon was losing valuable income while he waited for his horse to heal, she argued. Anne was doubtful. It transpired Gideon was a lazy man at heart and content to take the opportunity to be idle for a few days. He made a good living from his trade and he, his wife and child wanted for nothing.

When Gideon returned, several hours later, after supposedly helping his infirm father but also wearing a suspicious aroma of ale, Ruth employed her persuasive tongue to good effect and the next phase of Martha's journey was agreed. She would travel with Gideon to Bury St Edmunds the following day and Anne's harassed husband was charged with finding a safe means of onward transport for her. Martha was verily filled with gratitude to the strangers so willing to assist her. Tears welled in her eyes at her parting with Ruth. Anne insisted Ruth take some money back with her, being blessed with a generous spirit like her sister. Martha was glad of this, being in receipt herself of coins for her travel which she knew Ruth could ill afford. Although she had vowed to pay the family back, she knew not how or when that would be.

After Ruth had bid them farewell and headed back to Wickthorpe, Martha set about making herself useful, skinning and gutting two rabbits for the pot and setting them to cook on the stove. She would have liked a choice of herbs with which to flavour the meal but made do with some parsley she found drying in the parlour. Anne's house was spacious and comfortable after the confines of Ruth's cottage and she considered herself most fortunate. Both Anne and her daughter, Hannah, were kind souls with a ready smile and friendly conversation. Martha was less sure about Gideon. At first, he had seemed a genial, good-natured man, happy to oblige when his sister-in-law had begged a favour. However, as the day wore on, the cheering effects of the alcohol he had consumed wore off and he became more belligerent, arguing it was a great inconvenience to borrow a horse. Anne remained calm in the face of his dour mood and told him she had already acquired the use of a horse from Benjamin Harrow who lived but two doors away. The matter was settled. Gideon complained for some while after but eventually settled to sleep in a chair, an occurrence for which Martha was much relieved. She was not looking forward to being alone in the company of this dark, surly man, and hoped that the next part of her journey would not prove too unpleasant.

They set out shortly after dawn after she had helped Gideon load rolls of cloth and sacks of grain on his cart. The weather remained clement although the sky was heavy with cloud, and rain was expected. Martha was quite warm with all her padding and would have welcomed a cooling drizzle but Gideon complained bitterly at the prospect. He wished to complete the trip there and back in dry conditions. The horse Anne had hired was willing enough and they set out at a brisk trot. Martha attempted to engage the man beside her in pleasant conversation but, having elicited little or no response, was quite content to lapse into silence.

Bury St Edmunds was a bustling place and there were many on the rough road leading into the town. Martha kept her scarf pulled down over her head and her face lowered. There was every chance folk from Wickthorpe would be amongst them. When they reached the market, Gideon helped her down from the cart and, much to her surprise, bid her a curt farewell. She opened her mouth to remind him of his obligation to find her the means of onward travel, but he had already turned his back on her and was laughing with a portly man of his own age who had seen their approach. Shrugging her shoulders, she walked away. She was on her own.

Head bowed, Martha headed away from the busy market place. On another occasion, she would have been interested to see the smart town houses and the finery of dress worn by some of the gentlemen and ladies, but she dared not risk a look. At any moment, she expected to hear a shout heralding her discovery, so conscious was she of the peril facing her.

The expected rain had not come. Instead, the clouds had cleared and the sun was fiery hot. Martha's immediate preoccupation was thirst. Anne had kindly given her a chunk of bread and cheese for her sustenance but she was not hungry. Indeed, she felt quite parched and had no means to assuage the dryness in her mouth. Whilst Anne had provided liquid refreshment for the journey, such had not been offered to her by Gideon, and Martha's pride prevented her from returning to find him and request a drink. Casting around, she realised she would be forced to buy a small ale from an inn. Such an undertaking filled her with dread but, as the sun approached its zenith, it burnt with unrelenting ferocity. Sweat beaded her brow and her thirst made her feel quite faint. Keeping to the shade of the buildings, she hustled along, ignoring bawdy establishments peopled only by men and searching for a more genteel place. After almost an hour of walking, she was about to give up on such an ideal when she happened upon a place also frequented by women, albeit these were coarse, loud creatures, not much better than their male companions.

Cautiously, she surveyed the scene. It was less populated than other inns, being further from the heart of the town, and therefore more likely to be used by locals rather than visiting travellers. And the sight of flagons of cool ale made her swoon with thirst. Without further ado, she ventured inside, finding immediate respite from the heat, and ordered a small ale. Shyly, she handed over the payment from the purse she kept tied to her wrist. It was but a few coins and so delicious she was tempted to have another, but she was also conscious of narrow-eyed glances from two rough-looking types standing by the doorway and thought it better to move on. She still faced the task of securing passage northwards and knew not how best to go about it.

Resolutely, she headed back onto the streets and took a left turn, followed by another left, to take her back to the more populous area. How she regretted her decision to walk away from Gideon when he had unceremoniously abandoned her! She had let pride overrule common sense and should have demanded he fulfil the obligation he had promised to her, his wife and his sister-in-law. Doubtless, both Ruth and Anne would be aghast if they knew how she had been treated. As she walked, she noticed a younger woman, well-dressed, hurrying along in front of her. This lady stood out amongst others. She looked as if she should be in a carriage, accompanied by servants, but she was quite alone and clearly on some mission. The street, which ran parallel to the main throughfare, was empty and, despite the difficulty of her own situation, Martha was intrigued. When the woman cast an anxious glance over her shoulder, Martha could not help herself from shrinking behind the corner of a terrace. She wanted to see what would transpire.

The woman's intent soon became clear. A young man walked from the other direction, his face lighting up as he beheld the vision before him. As they met, the couple clasped each other's hands. The man was less well-dressed and clearly not as nobly-bred as the lady. Martha smiled as she stood watching from her hiding place. A case of star-crossed lovers, no doubt. Saying a quick prayer for the lovelorn couple, she turned away, reluctant to pry further.

The flash of an arm alerted her to danger, but too late. Rough hands gripped her elbow, pulled the purse free of her wrist, and pushed her to the ground. She fell with a loud cry, banging her head first against the wall before crashing to the earth.

'Stop, thief!' she cried but the two scoundrels responsible for the attack had already disappeared. How foolish she had been to let her curiosity blind her to danger!

'Here, let us help you!' The young man she had observed seconds before was by her side, helping her to her feet. 'I'm afraid the ruffians have flown,' he added.

'Is she much injured?' The young woman had the voice and face of an angel, and viewed Martha with much compassion. 'Oh, my poor dear, are you greatly hurt? Oh, Bertie, she is bleeding.'

At the same moment, Martha became aware of a sticky warmth trickling down the side of her face and inwardly cursed her idiocy. Her tribulations were growing by the second! 'To be sure, I am fine,' she said. 'Tis but a scratch. Howe'er …' her voice faltered, 'those men have stolen my money.'

'Is there a companion we can find to assist you?' the man asked.

'No, I am travelling alone, having sadly lost my husband. I was hoping to find a family or such with whom to continue onwards, but now I have not the means to pay for my passage.' The despairing words tumbled out before she could stop them.

The young lady looked at the man with troubled eyes before turning to Martha. 'I am Cecile and this is Bertie. Please allow us to help you. I can assure you, twill be no trouble,' she continued as Martha began to protest. 'First, let us find a physician to stop the bleeding and then we will see to the problem of transportation.'

'No doctor,' Martha said quickly. 'I assure you tis not necessary.' She withdrew a handkerchief from her apron pocket and pressed it against the wound. 'See, tis stopped.'

Two sets of eyes viewed her with consternation. 'But a doctor will …' Cecile argued.

'Let her be,' Bertie interrupted. 'Tis but a surface wound and will soon heal right enough. What is your name, madam?'

'Ruth,' Martha answered, saying the first name which came to her head.

'And whence are you headed, Ruth?'

'King's Lynn.'

Cecile frowned. 'King's Lynn?' she queried. 'I have ne'er heard of such a place. Mind you, I am so little travelled. Where is King's Lynn?'

A good question. Martha knew only that she must journey in a northwards direction but could not precisely describe its location. 'Tis by the river which leads to the sea,' she replied. 'I know not how to get there exactly. My family live there.'

'Tis on the northern coast,' Bertie came to her rescue. 'I could accompany you as far as Thetford, where I reside, but I am on horseback. I do not possess a carriage.'

'Fret not, Bertie, I have the very thing!' Cecile exclaimed. 'Ruth will return home with me in my carriage to ensure she is recovered, and then I will dispatch one of the servants to take her the rest of the way. Mind you,' she added with a nervous glance about her, 'you must promise to say nothing of my meeting with Bertie, Ruth. That must remain a secret, you understand?'

'You have my word,' Martha promised, 'but I could not possibly impose 'pon you and your family.'

'Fear not,' Cecile chuckled. 'Mama and Papa are used to me acquiring waifs and strays. They are quite resigned to it.'

'Cecile, I fear I must take my leave of you,' Bertie sighed, longing in his eyes. He caught hold of her gloved hand. 'I know not when I will see you again.'

'Oh, Bertie, I cannot bear it. How am I to persuade Papa ...?'

Martha moved discreetly away, allowing the two lovebirds some privacy. Guilt rested upon her shoulders at her unplanned intrusion to their tryst but she also felt some measure of relief that Cecile had offered her protection away from this town. The sooner she left Bury St Edmunds the better as far as she was concerned. However, she felt honour-bound to renew her protestations when the young lady returned to her side.

'Please Cecile, I do not wish to inconvenience you further but I would be much obliged for your assistance. I assure you I will see you repaid for your kindness. If you, or perhaps your servants, could find someone of good reputation who will take me in the right direction, I would be sorely grateful.'

'Please do not distress yourself, Ruth.' Cecile companionably linked her arm with Martha's and led her along the street. 'All will be well. First though, I need to locate my servants, Fred and Honour, and prepare myself for a terrible scolding. I gave them the slip, you see, so I could contrive a meeting with Bertie.' Her china blue eyes pooled with tears which she brushed irritably away. 'I must not appear sad or they will suspect something. Please leave everything to me. Go along with whate'er I say and I will be in your debt.'

Martha nodded and allowed herself to be swept along, back towards the busiest part of town. Fortunately, her head wound had ceased bleeding and, apart from feeling a little sore, she had incurred no other injuries. As they turned a corner, they beheld a red-cheeked, middle-aged woman and a thin, bald man heading towards them.

'There you are, Honour ... Fred. I am most relieved to find you at last,' Cecile cried.

'Miss Cecile, where have you been? Fred and I have been tearing our hair out with worry for you,' the woman exclaimed.

Cecile snorted at the statement as Fred was possessed with not a single hair on his shiny, bald pate, but she quickly assembled her features into a visage of contrite decorum. 'I am so very sorry, Honour. Please forgive me. You know how flighty I can be. Tis a great failing and, in future, I swear I will try harder to overcome it.'

Cecile's pretty apology took the wind out of her maidservant's sails and that harassed lady found herself unable to deliver the tirade she had planned when she caught up with her charge. 'But I don't understand how it could have happened, Miss. Fred and I were beside you whilst you were admiring the hats in the milliner's window and then, without one word to us, you hared off across the street and disappeared. What on God's earth could have possessed you to do such a thing?'

Cecile's rosebud mouth drooped. 'You will think me so stupid but I was sure I glimpsed my brother, Edward. The fellow strode away from me before I could reach him and I followed, trying to catch up. Before I knew it, I was well and truly lost. Imagine my consternation when the man stopped to greet an acquaintance and I discovered twas not Edward after all! I found myself in a horrible predicament and not the first clue how to find you both. I confess I burst into tears which is when, luckily for me, Ruth happened by. She was most kind to me, even though she had also suffered, having lost her purse to a pair of thieves.' Cecile pulled Martha forward and gave her servants a smile. 'Honestly, I know not what might have happened perchance Ruth had not so kindly helped me. First, I thought to reimburse her so she could continue with her journey but then I had a better idea. I wish to take her home with us so my parents can thank her properly. After that, perhaps Tom could take her to her own family in King's Lynn? I fear there are many rogues on the road and poor Ruth is forced to travel alone after the tragic loss of her husband. I would hate to think of her being accosted yet again before she reaches the safety of her family.'

'Mm, King's Lynn be a fair step from here,' Fred said, his weathered face frowning at Cecile's speech. 'I'm not sure your father will ...'

'Leave Papa to me,' Cecile interrupted, before taking Honour's hands in hers. 'Please, Honour, say you forgive my foolishness or my heart will be quite broken!'

'Well, Miss …' The long-suffering maid shook her head, grey curls wobbling under her bonnet, but her face had softened as she regarded her charge's penitence.

'Oh, thank you, Honour. And Fred. I am much afeared I do not deserve your kindness. Perhaps I shall buy you something pretty, Honour, and something for your wife, Fred.'

'There is no need …' Honour began but Cecile was not to be thwarted. Martha watched in amazement at her saviour's artfulness, so easily she won back the favour of her servants. They watched with worshipful eyes as she insisted upon purchasing two fine, embroidered shawls, fringed with lace. 'Mistress, tis too much,' Honour protested but Cecile merely smiled and parted with the money as if it were nothing.

Such a pretty face hid a resourceful brain, Martha thought. Whilst she could not approve of Cecile's deception, she could understand it, and wondered anew at the relationship between such a lady and Bertie. Cecile was clearly from a wealthy family and well-used to getting her own way. Although Bertie was from a poorer background, surely that was no obstacle if the young lady's heart was set upon him? Martha had not come across such a problem before and did not understand it. She herself had been allowed to marry for love and had refused other, wealthier suitors before John. She could not comprehend how it could be different for those from the highest echelons of society. Perhaps she would learn were she to spend more time in the young lady's company.

As they ambled in and out of small shops at Cecile's whim, Martha concentrated upon keeping her head bowed and saying little. She still feared meeting someone from Wickthorpe who knew her well enough to see through her disguise. Certainly, she would be thankful to see the back of Bury St Edmunds. Still weak from her illness, the heat, along with the thickness of her attire, combined to make her feel quite dizzy. When, swaying in a most alarming manner, she was forced to grasp Fred's arm for support, the kind manservant called for Cecile's attention.

'I fear Mistress Ruth is unwell, Miss,' he said.

Cecile was most contrite. 'Oh, you poor dear. Let's get you home at once. I was forgetting your earlier fall when you were beset by scoundrels. Fred, fetch the cart. We will rest here til you arrive.' To the shopkeeper, she commanded, 'Some refreshment, please. My friend is quite overcome by the heat.'

Black spots swam before Martha's eyes but she was aware of others scurrying to do Cecile's bidding. She was helped to a seat and a goblet of cool cider was pressed into her hand. After that, she remembered little. Strong arms settled her onto a cart and she was made as comfortable as possible until the jerky, rocking rhythm sent her fast asleep.

***

Martha awoke much refreshed in a large bed with freshly scented linen. For one moment, she was convinced she must have died and gone to heaven, so sumptuous was her bedchamber, but then she remembered ... Cecile. She pushed herself upright from the gloriously soft pillow and realised she was dressed in a beautiful cotton nightgown which did not belong to her. Her own clothes were nowhere to be seen. How was she to dress? Awareness dawned, a sickening spread of concern in her belly. Someone had disrobed her and found the layers of padding wedged around her middle giving her proportions of an entirely different dimension. They would know she had deceived them and was not as she had seemed.

Martha was still pondering her dilemma when a young girl entered the room, carrying a tray. 'Good morning, Miss. I hope you slept well.' The maid deposited the tray on a table and pulled back the heavy drapes guarding the windows. 'The mistress asked me to bring you some vittles. I trust you are feeling much refreshed this morning?' The girl was fresh-faced and prettily dressed in a plain dress, apron and linen cap. Tendrils of dark hair peeked beneath the cap, and large, brown eyes regarded her without guile.

'Yes, thank you,' she replied.

The tray was carefully placed upon Martha's lap. 'There you go, Miss. Please ring the bell if there is anything else you require.' The girl indicated its position on a bedside table. 'I believe the mistress intends to visit you shortly.' She bobbed a curtsey and left the room, leaving Martha feeling flummoxed. Servants waiting upon her! Whatever next? She could barely contain her chuckles at such an unlikely turn of events! But then she thought once more of the reckoning doubtless to come and her stomach churned anew.

Before her lay a plate of eggs and a thick hunk of ham. Such a feast! Truly, she did not warrant such kindness. Martha's feelings of guilt disappeared as she tucked into the tasty morsels and she realised how little she had consumed the previous day – nothing, in fact, since she broke her fast with Anne at first light. Already that meeting seemed a lifetime ago. Her thoughts turned, as they so often did, to her beloved husband and child. She did not expect to find them with her family in King's Lynn but hoped they might have sent word as to their whereabouts. Originally, she had thought to try to find John's family holding in Norfolk but, after some thought, considered that to be an unlikely place of refuge following John's rift with his father. Martha had hoped time would heal the conflict between them but John remained adamant it would not. His elder brother, Matthew, whom she had met at her wedding, had left the family nest a few years earlier because of their father's domineering behaviour and now lived with his wife and children somewhere near the coast. He too had not returned to the home of his childhood.

The door burst open and Cecile hastened into the room, a vision in pink, her blonde curls dressed in a most becoming fashion. Martha thought she had never seen anyone so beautiful.

'Good morning, Ruth. Pray tell me you are feeling greatly recovered. I have such plans for us today.' Without ceremony and before Martha could respond, she removed the tray from her guest's knees and rang the bell in a most imperious manner. The same servant girl appeared almost immediately. 'Return this to the kitchen, Fairlie.'

'Yes, Miss.' The girl bobbed once more and did as she was bid.

Cecile seated herself on the bed and china blue eyes assessed her guest's face. 'Now, Ruth, how are you feeling? Your cheeks have quite the blush about them this morning so I am persuaded you are returned to good health.'

'I am, thank you, and much indebted to you for all your kindness.'

'Oh, think nothing of it.' Cecile waved a careless hand. 'But I do want to know the truth. I sensed straight away there was something of the mystery about you. You had a secret lurking in your eyes, and Honour and I were much intrigued by the thick clothing you chose to wore on such a warm day. We discussed the matter on the journey home while you slept and decided she should attend to you last night. Together, with Fred's help, we ensured that few of the household set eyes 'pon you, and I told Papa and Mama we had a house guest once you were safely in bed. As I said yesterday, they are used to me bringing companions home. I have long done so. I have no sisters, you see, and my only brother, Edward, Lord Horley, has his own estate and rarely visits. I confess, though, that Honour and I were most surprised to find such a slim, young figure beneath that stout, matronly appearance!' She raised her eyebrows. 'Now, I insist you tell me everything. What secrets are you hiding, Mistress Ruth?'

Although she could not but like Cecile, Martha wondered how much she could trust her. 'Tis true I am travelling in disguise,' she admitted slowly. 'There is a man who wishes me dead and I seek only to avoid capture by him.'

'Goodness!' Cecile's eyes widened and she leaned in closer. 'Why does he wish you harm? What could you possibly have done to incur such wrath?'

'I rejected his advances.'

'Ah ... I see ...' Cecile mulled the information over. 'And, being a widow, you had no husband to defend your honour. You poor thing.'

'Well ...' Martha's cheeks blushed as she remembered saying she had lost her husband.

'Ruth?' Cecile waggled a long, elegant finger at her. 'You are telling me the truth?'

Martha gave up. She had nought of which to be ashamed and she was a poor liar. 'My husband still lives. We have a baby son. But a powerful man in the village of Wickthorpe took against me when I refused to submit to his will. I was known for mixing herbs into potions to heal the sick, and the man used this knowledge against me, accusing me of witchcraft.' In a low voice, she continued the rest of her tale, sparing no details but also protesting her innocence of the vile charges, and begging Cecile's forgiveness for her duplicity. 'I am so sorry,' she said, her face contrite, 'but I knew not who to trust and my life depends 'pon my concealment.'

'Oh, Ruth, tis I who am sorry for all you have endured. Fear not, I will keep your secret and do my utmost to reunite you with your husband and son.'

'Martha.' She hung her head in shame. 'My name is Martha, not Ruth.'

Cecile gave a tinkling laugh. 'My, you are almost as skilled in the art of deception as me! Martha is a most pretty name but the household believes we have a Mistress Ruth staying with us, so Ruth you must remain. Pray, should I be asked, what is your family name?'

'Lightbody,' Martha replied.

'That is your true name?'

'Yes.'

'Mm, Lightbody is a most unusual name. I suggest you change that also. Ruth Littlebody. Close to the truth but not enough to arouse suspicion. Littlebody is a much more common name in these parts. Now ...' She stood and clapped her hands. 'We need to get you dressed, disguise and all. I will speak to Honour and she will help you. Stay here until I return.'

Cecile left in a veritable whirlwind, leaving Martha considering how matters had been taken out of her hands. She was most grateful for the assistance but still fretted that someone might betray her. Not Cecile. She now trusted that young lady implicitly. But this was a large household. Someone might catch a snippet of strange conversation and be alerted. Such musings caused her skin to prickle anew with anxiety and she waited impatiently for Cecile's return, resolved to stating her intention to leave the house as soon as possible.

She did not have to wait long. Cecile flounced back into the room, closely followed by Honour, bearing swathes of material which she set down with a 'Morning, Miss,' before disappearing again.

'I've instructed Honour to bring you a bath,' Cecile said, regarding Martha's face with a discerning eye. 'I know not what strange concoction you have applied to your face but you now have brown streaks which give you a most peculiar appearance. Such stains will attract attention, to be sure.'

'Oh!' Martha clasped her hands to her face in embarrassment. ''Twas madder ... to give my pale cheeks some ruddy colour.'

'Mm ...' Cecile shook her head. 'I thought you had a skin complaint yesterday. I felt quite sorry for you. No matter, twill soon wash off. Stay beneath the covers til the maids have filled the bath and venture out only when Honour tells you tis safe to do so. When you are washed and dressed, I shall return and together we will concoct an excellent scheme.' She rubbed her small hands together. 'This is so exciting!'

Martha did as she was bid. She really had no choice in the matter. Cecile was a young lady used to having her commands obeyed and, before long, Martha found her freshly washed body encased in swathes of linen, skilfully bound about her person to give her a bulky shape. Over that, she wore a simple cotton dress, plain in appearance befitting a woman of more mature years. Her long hair was plaited, coiled around her head and covered by a cap. She resembled the trusted, older servant of a wealthy family.

When Cecile reappeared, she exclaimed in delight. 'That is perfect, Honour. Ruth looks most unlike her natural appearance. That will be all.' Once they were alone, she clasped Martha's hands in hers and spun her around. 'Oh, we shall have such an adventure, you and I!'

'We?' Martha queried, with some alarm.

'Oh yes. Tis quite decided. I shall go with you to King's ... wherever you are going ... to ensure you are safely restored to your family.'

'But ...'

Cecile held up an imperious hand. 'No buts, Ruth, I pray you. I wish to do this. We will leave tomorrow. Tis most fortunate my godparents live not far from there, it appears, and we will be made most welcome. I have already sent a missive informing them of my visit. They have long begged my family to venture north but none have yet made the journey so they will be quite delighted, I am sure. I will rest there awhile so will be on hand should you need further assistance. Oh, isn't this the most ingenious plan?'

Martha's eyes were wide with shock at such an unexpected turn of events and her mind mulled over potential problems, finding none. 'Tis indeed,' she said at last, 'but I cannot allow you to go to such trouble for me. What do your parents say? Surely, they are against such a jaunt? It cannot be safe for a lady such as yourself to be abroad. Mr Cromwell's soldiers ...'

'Are currently far from here,' Cecile interrupted. 'You are correct. They did make that objection and I gave them the same response. I dare say they are relieved to be shot of me for a while. I fear I give them both quite the headache. And they know I will be perfectly safe with the servants. As to it being a trouble, I confess tis quite the opposite. Life in the countryside can be most dull, I assure you. You have no idea how much I crave some excitement!' Her blue eyes shone and Martha realised she spoke the truth. How different their lives were! She could not begin to imagine having the time to be bored, so busy with chores were her own days.

And so it was that Martha embarked on the next part of her journey as part of an entourage and, for the first time in a while, feeling hopeful about her future.

CHAPTER 17

Enid Green allowed the book to fall into her lap. Martha had changed her name to Ruth Littlebody! *Littlebody.* Elijah Ryecroft, Deborah's father, had Littlebody blood. His mother had been born a Littlebody. *There* was the connection she had been seeking, the first piece of evidence that Deborah Ryecroft was a descendant of the infamous Wickthorpe Witch. For once, she wanted to read on. Ploughing through the tedious text no longer felt such an onerous task. But there was no time. Her son, Andrew, and Philp Holder would arrive at any moment.

Enid had summoned them earlier in the day, feeling she had waited long enough. It gave her satisfaction to have two men at her beck and call, ready to do her bidding, because they feared the information she possessed. Quite right. She would have no hesitation in using it, if they crossed her, although Andrew had less to fear. Certainly, she could give him a scare but even *she* would stop short of throwing her own son into penury. That would hardly be to her own advantage, after all. Philip Holder, though, was another matter. To see *him* squirming before a judge, having to answer for the crime of destroying his mother's amended will, would be a pleasure. She rubbed her gnarled hands together, relishing the prospect of making the horrible, little man grovel.

Voices. Snatching up the book, she hid it beneath her cushions, ready to continue reading later. She heard both Andrew and Philip, talking to Ava, and then a polite knock at her door.

'Enter,' she croaked.

'Mother!' Andrew appeared first, arms outstretched, stubbly chin grazing the side of her face. 'Good to see you.' He was dressed smartly in a suit and carrying a briefcase. Doubtless, he had come straight from work.

'Hello Enid.' Philip stood back, eyes downcast, mumbling as usual. The smaller man, by contrast, was wearing a baggy, green, woollen sweater with a hole in one of the sleeves, and brown, corduroy trousers splattered with old oil stains.

'I'm pleased to see you both,' Enid said graciously. 'Take a seat.' There was no option for them to sit anywhere other than squashed together on the small sofa opposite her. From her position in her comfortable chair, she prepared for her role as interrogator. 'Now then, please tell me what information you have managed to find out about Deborah Ryecroft.'

While Philip looked uncomfortable, Andrew's face wore an expression of smugness. He hefted his briefcase on to his knees and pulled out a typewritten file. 'This is all the data available about Deborah's company, Ryecroft Industries, and there's a section at the end detailing her personal record.' He reached across to hand it to Enid.

'Very impressive.' Enid stared at the slick folder on her lap without opening it. 'What does it say?'

'Basically, it gives you all the facts and figures for Ryecroft Industries, yearly accounts and so forth.'

'Yes, but what does it *say?*' Enid repeated. 'I said I wanted the dirt on Deborah Ryecroft. Where is it?'

'Well ...' Andrew was squirming now. 'To tell the truth, I haven't had much chance to go through it ...' He had picked the file up from a private investigator only that afternoon. 'Oh!'

The folder was flung back at him with some force. 'Then I suggest you go through it with a fine toothcomb until you find something useful. If I had wanted that woman's accounts, I'd have asked for them! Not good enough, Andrew.'

'Sorry, Mother. I have been busy but I will do as you suggest. If there's something to find, you can rely on me to find it.'

'Hmph, you'd better! And you, Philip? Are you going to produce some bits of paper, thinking to bamboozle an old woman with facts and figures?' Enid steepled her fingers as she looked expectantly across at him.

There was a pause as Philip wriggled in his seat. 'I ain't one for figures or computers and such, you know that, Enid.' His accent bordered on surly and Enid shot him a fierce glare. 'But I've been doing what I can. I've talked to some of the older folk in the village, them that would've been around when the woman was a kid ... and even earlier.' Another silence. When no one responded, he continued, tugging at a loose thread on his sweater with a grimy hand. 'Some knew Elijah when he was still a young man, before he upped and got 'imself married to some outsider.'

'I knew him then. I lived here too,' Enid reminded him sharply.

'I know that.' Philip met her eyes for the first time, his face assuming a slyness which had not been there before. 'Some said you and he were stepping out a while, before Hannah appeared on the scene, if you catch my drift.'

Enid flushed angrily. 'That's none of your business.'

He shrugged. 'Just suthin' I found out, that's all.'

'I'm looking for *useful* information, Philip,' Enid retorted, her voice icy. 'Do you have any?'

He nodded. 'Way back in the day, there were rumours about the Littlebody family being descendants of the Wickthorpe Witch. People said there was a book what proved it ... said your pa had told 'em of it.' When Enid chose neither to confirm nor deny it, he continued. 'No one 'ad seen it, mind you, but they believed 'im. That's why they were so quick to believe that Elijah's daughter was a witch when that young kid drowned. That would be sometime in the eighties.'

'Hang on a minute, you've lost me,' Andrew interrupted. 'You said the Littlebody family were descendants of the witch, not the Ryecrofts. I don't follow.'

'Ah, well now, that's because Elijah Ryecroft's ma was a Littlebody before she wed. Then, she became a Ryecroft, so Elijah and his daughter have Littlebody blood,' Philip replied.

'Did you know this, Mother?' Andrew asked.

It was Enid's turn to look shady. 'Some of it,' she admitted. 'But most of it is gossip or hearsay. We need hard proof.'

'Surely the book, if it exists, would give you that. Did Grandpa ever mention it to you?'

Enid hesitated. 'I seem to remember something about it ...' she hedged. 'In fact, that's why I asked you to get those old boxes down from the loft. They were your Grandpa's things. If he had a book, it will be there.'

'Have you had a chance to look?'

'I've made a start. I'll get back to it.'

'Would you like me to look?'

Andrew's offer took Enid by surprise. 'Er, no ... you've enough to be getting on with.' She pointed at the folder. 'I'll take care of it. If the book's there, I'll find it. Did you discover anything else, Philip?'

He hunched his shoulders. 'Bits and pieces. Nuthin' I s'pose you'd think was important.'

'Right. Well, you'd best be off then. Keep your ear to the ground. I'll be in touch.' Enid fidgeted in her chair, conscious of the book hidden behind the cushion.

Philip almost leapt to his feet and shot through the door without a word, happy to be off Enid's hook, at least temporarily. Andrew was slower to move. 'You and old Elijah Ryecroft, hey?' he said with a wink. 'Who'd have thought it?'

'Don't believe everything you hear,' Enid snapped. 'You'd better get going too. You don't want your wife becoming suspicious, do you?'

The crafty smile on Andrew's face slipped. 'Stop making threats you have no intention of following through, Mother. I've done what you asked of me.'

'Don't be too sure of what I will and won't do, Andrew. Remember you have a lot to lose, and if things *do* go badly for you with your in-laws, you'll have brought it all on yourself.'

Andrew's handsome face contorted into an ugly sneer. 'I'm not the only one around here with secrets, am I, Mummy dearest?'

Enid paled. 'I don't know what you mean.'

He tapped the side of his nose. 'Night, Mother. Have a good evening.'

***

Andrew slammed his car door in annoyance. He was sick of his mother's threats. Even when he did as she asked, paying good money for a private investigator, she still wasn't satisfied. He slapped the folder on the seat beside him and started the engine. Not for the first time, he wondered what she knew – what she was holding over his head like a guillotine. When she had first blackmailed him into helping her, she had hinted that she knew something which would finish him for good with *Newman's Stores*. His first thought was it had to be something to do with the business. Had she found out about the time he skimmed money from the till? It was in his early days and, when the losses were discovered, he managed to find a scapegoat to take all the blame. Luckily, he himself was never considered a suspect. Frank took him into his confidence, telling him how concerned he was that the accounts didn't add up, and of his suspicion that someone was stealing from him. It was easy, after that, to plant some evidence against a hapless employee and then take the credit for finding the culprit. If Enid knew this, and told Frank, it would indeed finish him. But how would she have come by such information? The employee had left the area shortly afterwards and he had mentioned nothing of the incident to anyone at home. The more he thought about it, the more he suspected she knew something else. And that possibility had him clammy with fear. Perhaps, she had learnt, somehow, of his darkest secret. *Impossible, surely?* He had been so careful. There was no way she could know about that. No, he reassured himself, if it wasn't the money thing, she had to be referring to his previous, extra-marital affairs – the least of his concerns. Since Frank Newman's ultimatum, he had become obsessively cautious. Or Enid could be making empty threats. He would not put it past her.

Still, he could not risk thwarting his mother. He would dance to her tune, much as it irritated him. And he would continue to go overboard to keep things sweet at home, if it kept his father-in-law off his back.

Damping down his black thoughts, he drove home and announced to his delighted family he was taking them all away the following weekend. Nothing was going to come between him and the Newman fortune, and certainly not his interfering mother.

***

Enid sat, staring into space, long after he had left, dismayed by the revelation of her relationship with Elijah Ryecroft. It was so long ago but the memory of the whole affair and its humiliating end still stung like vinegar on an open wound.

In her early twenties, she and Elijah had stepped out for more than two years. Her father had been furious that she was consorting with a Littlebody, but she had ignored his objections. The curse of the Wickthorpe Witch meant little to her then. At that time, she had fully expected Elijah to propose but he was dragging his heels, despite the hints she had dropped. She had even confided to other girls in the village that a wedding was imminent. Then, out of the blue, Elijah announced he had met another girl he wanted to marry. Some tart from a travelling fair, no less! The humiliation had cut deep into her soul. To spare herself from pitying looks, she had been forced to accept an offer from Freddie Green, the postmaster, a poor second-best.

She had never forgiven Elijah, nor Hannah Ryecroft, for robbing her of the destiny she had expected. As the years passed, her father's words, and his hatred of Littlebodys and their offspring, took on a whole new dimension. She came to the realisation that she was yet another innocent victim of the witch's curse. It had to be the reason Elijah had rejected her. And her hatred of the Ryecrofts had intensified.

Still deep in thought, she pulled her copy of the book from its place of concealment and found the next excerpt. The quicker she discovered all its secrets, the sooner she could plan the witch's downfall.

CHAPTER 18

The Life & Times of Martha Lightbody

Martha Lightbody returned to the hustle and bustle of King's Lynn, seated beside a finely-dressed young lady and surrounded by servants. It had been a long journey, taking all of three days, as Cecile soon tired of travelling and insisted upon many rest breaks. Each one felt hazardous to Martha – more chance of someone recognising her – but she also felt safer the further they ventured northwards.

During their enforced proximity in the carriage, Cecile had confided her own secrets regarding Bertie, and Martha had listened with mounting sympathy for the young woman who seemed to have everything except the thing she most desired.

Martha learned that Bertie and Cecile had grown up together on the family estate, albeit from very different backgrounds. He was the son of the blacksmith and just a year older than she. With only one sibling, a much older brother, Cecile craved the company of her peers and frequently sought out the boy with dark, curly hair and serious, brown eyes. This relationship was enabled by the indulgence of Cecile's parents who saw no harm in it. In fact, when Cecile showed a marked disinclination for her studies, they suggested young Bertie join her lessons. His eagerness to learn prompted a veritable change in Cecile's attitude as her competitive, young spirit could not bear to be bested by her friend, and Lord and Lady Gage congratulated themselves upon their progressive foresight. Their spoilt, pretty, wild daughter would hopefully grow up to be a well-educated lady after all.

They reckoned without the closeness between the two friends which grew more romantic as the years passed. Cecile was barely thirteen when she began to weave fantasies about Bertie and, being the sort of person she was, she soon declared her feelings. Bertie held back. He knew no good could come of such a love affair and, although he felt the same sentiments as she, refused to acknowledge them to her until the night before he left. Cecile recounted the moment with tears in her eyes.

'Twas seven years ago and how I railed at him for leaving me! But he explained how he desired to make his own way in the world. He was fifteen and to be apprenticed to a smith in Thetford. That was when he told me he had always loved me.' She gulped back a sob. 'He said he would work hard, prove himself worthy of me and then, maybe, my father would consider him as a prospective suitor for my hand in marriage. We have met so rarely since that time and yet our devotion to each other has only increased. And he has done well for himself. The smith to whom he was apprenticed has since died and Bertie has taken over the smithy. He has developed the art of making jewellery from silver and his work has become most popular.'

Martha was forced to wait for the next instalment which was delayed by their arrival at the manor house belonging to Cecile's godparents. She was despatched to the servants' quarters to maintain her persona as Ruth Littlebody, Cecile's maid. The story Cecile had concocted was that Ruth was to travel further northwards to Kings Lynn to look after her allegedly ailing mother. Cecile's godmother was most dismayed that Cecile planned to accompany her the following day but, as usual, that young lady had little trouble in attaining her stated desire.

'I worry about you travelling to such a town,' her godmother entreated. 'Mr Cromwell's army lies not far from there, I'm told. Soldiers such as they cannot be trusted to allow a young lady safe passage. These are dangerous times.'

'Nonsense, Aunt Bea,' Cecile had scoffed. 'Papa received a letter from my dearest brother just a few days ago. Tis true that the Royalists have suffered some heavy defeats, but those were at Naseby and Carlisle, many miles from here. We are quite safe in our small neck of the woods, I assure you. I will be there and back in less than a day, I promise, and I did give my parents my assurances that I would personally ensure Ruth is delivered into the bosom of her family. My mother is especially fond of her.'

Martha had stood by, in awe of the innocent look in Cecile's blue eyes, against which her godparents were helpless.

'Well, if that is what your dear Mama wishes ...' Aunt Bea had murmured doubtfully.

'It is,' Cecile replied, and that was the end of the matter.

It was mid-morning when Cecile and her entourage were ready to leave, and Martha could scarcely contain her excitement. How she longed to be back within the safety of her beloved family, and how she hoped they would have received news by now of John and little Josiah! Maybe, she might even find her husband and son waiting there for her.

The remainder of Cecile's story provided a welcome distraction as they embarked upon the final seven miles of their journey. The young lady herself had quite forgotten that her tale remained unfinished and Martha had to prompt her with a gentle statement.

'Tis wonderful that your Bertie has done so well for himself,' she said.

'Yes,' Cecile exclaimed, eyes bright. 'I am so very proud of him. He is well on the way to making his fortune.'

'And do you think your father will receive his proposal favourably?'

Her beautiful, young face clouded immediately. ''Tis complicated,' she replied quietly. 'Papa has set his heart on a match with the eldest son of his dearest friend. Henry is a fine man, to be sure, but I do not love him. 'Tis quite convenient that he is away fighting alongside my brother for the Royalist cause at present or I swear Papa would have contrived the marriage somehow. I have told him I have no feelings for Henry but he only replies that I am a goose to concern myself with such things and he is sure I shall be perfectly happy as a duchess.'

'A duchess? Goodness me!' Martha exclaimed, thinking privately that poor Bertie stood no chance against such a lofty match.

Cecile shrugged. 'I have no wish for a title. I want only Bertie.' Her mouth remained set in a mutinous line for some while after that and Martha found herself revising her opinion. Even a duke may find his ambitions thwarted at the hands of such an obstinate, young miss!

'Does your father know of your feelings for Bertie?' she asked.

'Not as yet. We thought it best to wait until ...' Cecile's voice tailed off and a long pause ensued before she spoke again. 'I fear telling him may cause severe consequences. He will never consent.' A heavy sigh and then a hushed whisper. 'We are planning to elope.'

Martha's eyes widened. 'Surely not? You could lose everything – your fortune, your family, your reputation! That would be a most foolhardy course.'

The stubborn look returned to Cecile's perfect features. ''Twould be most exciting ... and romantic ...'

Martha shook her head. 'I beg you both to reconsider. If Bertie truly loves you, I cannot believe he has suggested such a thing.'

'He did not. Twas my idea.' Cecile frowned. 'He is still to be persuaded but I will have my way. Tis the only solution.' She folded her arms and turned away in a sulk, annoyed by her travelling companion's objections.

Martha held her tongue. She did not want to upset Cecile further, especially as the girl had been so kind to her, but she remained convinced that an elopement in such circumstances would be a disaster. However, as they approached King's Lynn and she recognised familiar landmarks, her thoughts turned to her own affairs.

'There's the water,' she cried in excitement, seeing a grey strip upon the horizon.

'Oh, where?' Cecile immediately forgot her dudgeon and peered in the direction of Martha's arm. 'I see it. And boats!'

Martha felt almost overwhelmed by a wave of homesickness and could not speak for the lump in her throat. The emotion of the past weeks rushed upon her and she felt tears spring to her eyes. At last, she could relax.

***

Having bid Cecile a tearful farewell and promising to write with news, Martha hurried to the quayside abode she had shared with her family. So much was familiar to her: the tumbledown shacks lining the streets; the curses of men loading or unloading boats; the skinny, poorly-dressed urchins with hungry eyes and hands ready to filch whate'er they could. Seeing them, Martha realised how much she had changed. What had seemed dull and humdrum before, now felt safe and familiar, although she still wore her disguise and took care to keep her head down, skirting those areas where she would be most likely recognised. The salty air filled her senses and the stench of fish did not make her nostrils wrinkle in distaste as it had before. Excursions with her mother, Mary, to gather plants and herbs from the nearby countryside and woodland, had previously been her salvation, so eager was she to escape such surroundings. Now, she found comfort in the scenes of her childhood. Surely nothing bad could happen to her here?

Martha's family lived in one of the larger houses, built of brick, at the corner of the street. The small warehouse beside it also belonged to her father, Solomon. He had prospered in his occupation of wool merchant. All four of her brothers worked with him in the family business, and the eldest, Seth, was the first to spy his sister heading towards him. He was tall man, much like his father, dark and swarthy. His eyes widened and he stopped dead in his tracks.

'Lord above, can it really be our Martha?' He stepped with caution towards her, doubting the evidence of his eyes. 'Yet looking much changed. I knew it! I knew ye lived still!'

She grinned and held out her arms. 'Very much alive, my dear brother.'

His face lit with joy and he pulled her into his arms. 'But how? We were told you had likely drowned. John sent word to Ma and Pa. Poor Ma. She's been beside herself with grief. Come! We must tell her, tell everyone!'

Fear flashed through her and she kept a grip of her brother's arm. 'Tell only the family. I'll see them in the house later. There is danger in the news of my survival. The fewer folk aware of it, the better.'

His face darkened and he looked about him, menace clear in the set of his shoulders. 'I am not surprised. Strangers have been sniffing around here just last week, asking for you. Well, if they come back, they will have me to deal with.'

'Strangers?' Martha glanced about her nervously but saw nothing untoward. 'I had best get inside. Is Ma there? How I long to see her!'

He nodded and, without further ado, she hurried indoors, knowing she would see her father and the rest of her brothers later. Sadly, she would not see her sisters. They were all married now and had homes of their own.

She found her mother, Mary, in the kitchen, stirring a large pot on the stove. Martha's stomach rumbled at the delicious aroma. No one made a stew like her ma. Mary turned at the sound of footsteps and her face paled. 'Is this a ghost I'm now seeing?' she muttered, the Irish lilt of her heritage warming her daughter's heart.

'Nay, Ma, tis I, Martha. I'm alive.'

'Oh, the Lord be praised! My daughter!' She clasped Martha to her bosom. 'I declare, you have put on a deal of weight!'

Martha laughed. 'Tis my disguise, Ma! Much needed to keep me safe.'

At last Mary pulled away, searching her daughter's face with confused eyes. 'John wrote to us, saying you had likely been drowned as a witch. What happened?'

Mary had aged since Martha had last seen her mother. Her features were the same: a slightly pointed, upturned nose; wide, generous mouth much given to smiling; hazel eyes identical to Martha's. However, those eyes now drooped in skin worn and shrivelled. Mary's whole demeanour appeared stooped and shrunken, causing Martha to wonder about her mother's health. Certainly, her pallor was tinged with grey and her left hand kept straying to her hip, as if to stem a pain which lurked there. A stab of anxiety pierced Martha's heart as she recalled treating a person in Wickthorpe who bore the same look. Despite her best efforts, the woman had died.

Swiftly, holding her mother's hand, Martha recounted her recent history, all the time trying to ignore the fear that her beloved Ma was dying. Mary gripped Martha's fingers tightly, shaking her head as she listened. 'This man,' she said, 'Roger Holley. He is evil.'

Martha sucked in her breath. 'Maybe,' she shrugged. 'Vengeful certainly, and powerful. It seems he will stop at nothing to find me.'

'Aye. Men were here, just last week, looking for you,' Mary told her. 'It had not been long since we received John's letter. I sent them on their way with sharp words, I can tell you, but they were unwilling to believe you had died and tried to search the house. Fortunately, Sol and your brothers were on hand but I fear they may return.' She squeezed tighter. 'You are not safe here.'

Martha's heart sank. Where was she to find sanctuary if not with her family? 'Do you have John's letter? Did he say where he and Josiah were staying?'

Mary hobbled over to a small, wooden box, kept on a shelf. 'Tis here. You can read it for yourself.' She handed the missive to Martha who opened it with trembling fingers, her pulse quickening at the sight of John's writing. It began formally:

I regret to inform you of the likely tragic death of your dear daughter and my beloved wife, Martha. Men from the village of Wickthorpe saw fit to take it upon themselves to drown her as a witch in the lake. Her body was not recovered so there remains a tiny vestige of hope of her survival but, in all conscience, I cannot swear to you that such is likely. Josiah and I left that place shortly after, for our own safety, and have made our way to my brother and his wife where I am seeking work.

I will endeavour to bring your grandson to visit when he is older, so that he may know his mother's family.

My condolences.

Your loyal son-in-law,

John Lightbody.

'When we received that letter,' Mary said when her daughter had ceased reading, 'we prayed you were alive but feared the worst. We have grieved ever since. Those men turning up last week reignited our hopes, although we insisted most strenuously to them that you were dead. Seth saw them talking to the men loading the boats after that.' Her tired face creased further. 'Did anyone see your approach?'

Martha sighed. 'I cannot be sure. I kept my head down and spoke to no one. My disguised form would have fooled most. But Seth exclaimed most loudly when he recognised me. 'Tis possible someone heard him.' She sank into the chair by the fireplace. 'John said he has taken Josiah to his brother and wife but I cannot recall where they live. I know John's brother, Matthew, who is some years older than John, left his father's house when he was just a young man.' She shook her head. ''Tis a sad tale. John never knew his mother as she died giving birth to him. His father, Gabriel, soon married again. By all accounts, Gabriel's new wife was a young, docile woman, fond of her stepsons but unable to protect them from their father's bullying nature. Nothing either of his sons did was ever good enough for Gabriel and he beat them often. Things worsened as the years went by. As I said, Matthew left long ago and, before we wed, John also departed to make his own way – at that time, in Grimston. He said, if we stayed, we would all be subjected to his father's tyranny and he refused to countenance that.' Her brow furrowed. 'Matthew purchased a small piece of land somewhere a little away from here. I am sure John told me the name of the place but I cannot recall it. Oh, Ma!' She wrung her hands. 'What am I to do? If only he had written the address!'

'I feel sure 'twill come to you when you are not trying so hard to remember.' Mary patted her daughter's hand. 'Rest awhile. Some good food will help.'

Martha sat fidgeting while her mother served up a bowl of stew. Whilst it was wonderful to see her family, her worries remained. Unless she could remember the place where John's brother resided, she might never see her husband and son again.

CHAPTER 19

Since the day of her appointment with Seb Holley, Deborah had been kept busy with work. Lainey Lewis, the strategic director of Ryecroft Industries plc, was off sick, and her absence had left loose ends. Deborah had no option but to fill the breach. Whilst managing director, Paul Williamson, was a steady hand at the helm, he lacked Lainey's flair and drive. Plus, he was already stretched to the limit of his capacity and unable to take on Lainey's additional workload. Recently, Lainey had orchestrated two great deals for the company but was now unavailable to follow them through. The potential clients had been left dangling and Deborah had stepped in to pick up the pieces. The past week, she had travelled to London every day, returning late and falling exhausted into bed.

There had been little time to continue Martha's tale, yet the story continued to hover at the fringes of Deborah's mind. The feeling lingered that she was herself involved somehow. It had begun with her dreams of the woman in the nightdress who had guided her to safety from her trial by drowning. Then, disturbingly, she had dreamt of Freya Billington's death, before it had happened. Finally, there was the Littlebody connection, mentioned in the last episode from the book. Having discovered that Mabel Littlebody was her father's cousin, it was possible she really *was* a descendant of Martha Lightbody, the alleged Wickthorpe Witch.

Deborah was keen to continue the story and, hopefully, find some answers but work held her in its thrall. It soon became clear that, even with Lainey back in post, the company was currently understaffed. In his efforts to maximise profits, Paul had been remiss in filling vacancies which had arisen. Potentially, there were three opportunities for junior positions and

Gill Leatherstock, her trusted personnel director, had been tasked by Deborah to fill them without delay. Amelie Charles, Rick Billington's girlfriend, had been discussed as a potential candidate. Upon Deborah's advice, the ambitious, young woman had sent her CV to Gill the previous year. At the time, there had been no vacancies, but Gill had been sufficiently impressed to ask Deborah about interviewing her this time around, and Deborah had agreed. Amelie deserved every chance in her career path, and it was up to her to decide if a move back to London was what she wanted. Young Rick might be devastated but, Deborah thought, another young woman would be delighted.

However, Emma did seem quite taken by the new vet, Max Benson, and had been out with him on a few occasions. This was a first. Emma had previously turned down dates because of her unrequited passion for Rick, and Deborah and Tom both hoped Max might help her move on. Bravely, Tom had asked how the relationship was going.

'Absolutely none of your business, Dad,' Emma retorted hotly, but the glow on her cheeks told its own story.

Yesterday, a letter had arrived from the hospital with an appointment at the breast clinic the following week. She had told Tom who had offered to accompany her but she told him there was no need. 'I'm sure there's nothing to worry about. It's just a precaution,' she assured him. 'Dr Holley has put my mind at rest on that score.'

Dr Holley. Every time she thought of the man, she felt the shadow of premonition. It was unfair of her to link him with Roger Holley, and yet her subconscious mind refused to let go of the connection. Just as she felt *she* was involved in Martha's story, she sensed Seb was too. It was more than the fact that Seb and Roger shared the same surname. That perception of both men being predators, a threat to the women around them, would not be shaken off. Jane Holley's strange visit, and her hints about Seb, had supplemented that feeling of danger. Jane had appeared frightened of her husband. In fact, as Deborah recalled the conversation, she had almost suggested any woman involved with Seb would come to harm.

Thinking of Jane, Deborah felt a stab of guilt. Should she have done something to follow up the visit? Jane had clearly been very distressed and, afterwards, Deborah had felt oddly concerned for her welfare. But, then again, she had been busy with other priorities. And she owed the other woman, who had caused such tragedy when they were teenagers, absolutely nothing. Jane Holley was not her problem and she had enough of those with work.

A phone call wouldn't hurt, though. The kinder voice in her head was insistent. Lights twinkled in the darkness outside as she sat on the train, heading back to Wickthorpe – little sparks of brightness pricking at her conscience. With a sigh, she reached for her phone. She couldn't bear to think of the other woman, disturbed and alone. If anything happened to Jane Holley and she had done nothing, she would forever feel guilty. She had no contact details for Jane so she rang the rector, Wendy Robinson, to pass on her concerns.

Wendy, it appeared, was equally worried. 'I've been meaning to call round to check on her more frequently but haven't got around to it. I'll go and see her tomorrow. Thank you for prodding me.'

Deborah hesitated. She wanted to add her fears about Seb Holley but the words stuck in her throat. Her gut instinct, and the warning Jane had issued, were insufficient to start making accusations against him. Tentatively, she began, 'I'm not sure all is well in her marriage ...'

Wendy sighed. 'It's not my place to comment but Jane is certainly very unhappy. Suffice it to say, we have had some very long chats recently but I don't seem to have helped her much. I think many of her troubles stem from the past.'

'Yes.' Deborah remembered Jane had confided her part in Ayesha's drowning to Wendy, and she told the rector that Jane had asked her forgiveness. 'I'm afraid, at the time, I wasn't able to give her the comfort she wanted,' she admitted.

There was a brief silence before the rector's kind voice spoke once more. 'That was to be expected. She took you by surprise and you, no doubt, had many years of anger and bitterness stored up against her. Perhaps, in time ... I'm happy to discuss it with you further if you feel that would help.'

'I ... I don't know,' Deborah said honestly. 'I'm not sure I can ever truly forgive Jane for what she did. And, at the moment, I'm back working full–time so it would be difficult. I know that sounds as if I'm making excuses ...'

'Not at all,' Wendy interrupted. 'You were concerned enough about Jane's state of mind and that speaks volumes. I'll make it a priority to visit tomorrow. I know she doesn't work at the pharmacy on a Tuesday so I should catch her. If you have no objections, I'll tell her you called me. That is the act of a good Christian and I'm sure Jane will be comforted by your concern. She needs friends like you at the moment.'

Deborah wriggled in her seat. The last thing she wanted to become was Jane Holley's friend. It felt churlish to say that to Wendy though, so instead she said, 'That's fine with me. And tell her I hope she's soon feeling better.'

'I will. Thank you, Deborah. Have a lovely evening.'

'You too.' Deborah ended the call, Wendy's words mulling in her head. Whilst she genuinely pitied Jane, it was a massive step to talk about forgiveness and friendship. Jane and Melissa's actions had cost Ayesha Khan her life and, because of the subsequent accusations that Deborah was a reincarnation of the Wickthorpe Witch, had almost cost her own. The idea of granting Jane an easy escape from her guilt left a sour taste in her mouth.

But *she* was happy. The love she had found with Tom Oldridge had done much to dissolve away many of her long-held resentments, as had the discovery that her mother, Hannah, whilst too weak to defy her father, had loved her after all. Her company was successful and she was considered a role model for women in business. Also, her recent cancer scare was just that – a scare and nothing more. She could consider herself very fortunate whilst Jane Holley was clearly suffering. It would not hurt to try to help, so long as her path did not cross Seb Holley's. Deborah shivered. That would be going too far!

***

The following evening, the same Dr Holley was boiling with frustration and bracing for a showdown. His efforts to talk to his wife over the past week had fallen on deaf ears. Neither cajoling nor anger had worked. She just looked straight through him as if he did not exist. Tonight, would be different. He *would* get the answers he was seeking, whatever it took. The situation was intolerable and could not continue. Whilst he attempted to avoid her at work, others had noticed his wife's hostility towards him. It had to stop.

He squared his broad shoulders, preparing for a fight, but she surprised him, appearing docile and compliant. When he issued his curt command, 'We need to talk,' she meekly agreed.

'Yes,' she said, head bent. 'It's time to get everything out in the open.'

'Good,' he concurred, mixing himself a strong gin and tonic. 'Would you like one?'

'No, thank you.' Her face was serene. 'I've spoken to Wendy today and she feels I should be honest with you. It will be the first step in my healing process and my path to forgiveness.'

'Good,' he said aloud, giving her an encouraging smile, concealing his annoyance. *What had she been saying to the interfering rector?* 'I've been very worried about you, darling. You haven't been yourself at all.'

'Oh, please!' A scathing look and a flash of the old Jane. 'Don't pretend to be the caring husband, not after all this time! Remember, I know you too well. The only person you care about is yourself!'

'That's not true,' he countered. 'I do care about you. We've been married a lot of years, you and I. We have history.'

She laughed at that, a harsh, sarcastic sound. 'Oh, don't I know it!' Then, she took a deep breath. 'Wendy said to stay calm. Don't let you upset me. She offered to act as a counsellor for us both but I knew you would never agree to that.'

'Too right!' He struggled to contain the explosion of rage inside him. *Who did that Robinson woman think she was?* 'What have you been telling her?' he demanded.

'The truth.' She shot him a look of triumph.

He wanted to throttle her. It was as much as he could do to keep his hands from her skinny neck and squeeze the life out of her. Instead, he raised his eyebrows. 'The truth?' His voice was dangerously quiet.

She sighed, suddenly deflated, spirit extinguished. 'Nothing that concerns you. Not yet.'

He let that slide. 'What *did* you tell her?'

'About the past – my past. What happened all those years ago, when I was an arrogant, self-obsessed teenager.' He waited. Her head was bent and her slate-grey hair hung like a lank dishcloth, obscuring her face. 'She said I should tell you.' Another rasping laugh. 'Might as well. I don't care anymore. I'd rather the truth was out, but Deborah Ryecroft wants to leave well alone. Says it's too late. I suppose it is really.'

'Deborah Ryecroft?' His shoulders jerked to attention.

'Yes. I told you we were all there when Ayesha Khan drowned – Debbie Ryecroft, Melissa Shipman and me. Melissa was my best friend. You perhaps remember she took her own life when she was just twenty-seven?' She looked up and he nodded. 'I suspect she couldn't live with the guilt. It plagued her, just as it haunts me now.' She stood and began pacing the room, up and down, talking as she walked, avoiding his eyes. 'Anyway, I didn't tell you the truth about that time in my life. No one knew ... except Melissa, Debbie and me.' She shuddered and took a deep breath. 'Debbie didn't challenge *us* to swim across Dark Water Lake. It was the other way round. We taunted Ayesha and Debbie to go in. We knew it was dangerous but we didn't think they'd do it.'

'But they did?'

'Ayesha did. Debbie refused, point blank. She always looked down on Melissa and me. Went to boarding school. Thought she was better than us. We tried to burst her bubble of superiority, but we could never touch her. Ayesha was different, though. Her parents had come from Pakistan and the family wasn't exactly welcomed in the village. There was a lot of racism here in the eighties. It was a very different time ... pretty awful, thinking back. Some of the names we called them! Ayesha was a quiet girl. She wanted to fit in but, of course, she didn't. Kids at school gave her a rough time. Weirdly though, she and Debbie were friends.' She shrugged. 'Both misfits, I suppose. The two of them hung out together when Debbie was back from school in the holidays. Debbie tried to persuade Ayesha not to swim in the lake but Melissa and I egged her on. And Ayesha was so desperate to be accepted that she did it.'

'And she drowned.'

'Yes.' Jane's thin face was haggard with grief. 'We didn't mean for that to happen ... of course, we didn't ... and afterwards, I suppose we were in shock. Anyway, while we went to get help, Debbie swam across the lake to try to save her. But she was too late. We were all too late.' She sat again, slumped on a sofa, far away from her husband.

Seb's blue eyes remained glued to his wife. 'And Deborah was blamed. I assume that was when people began to call her the Wickthorpe Witch?'

'Yes.' A long pause. 'As I said, Melissa and I were scared. We told everyone it was Debbie who dared *us* to swim. One thing led to another. When our account was brought into question, we even suggested Debbie swam across to make sure she was dead, rather than to save her. It was awful.' She covered her face with bony hands. 'We were terrified people would believe Debbie and not us. But we needn't have worried. Everyone believed us. Debbie was questioned at the police station, and people drew their own conclusions. Meanwhile, our story soon filtered through the village. Everyone hated Debbie after that, except for Ayesha's parents who continued to accuse us. Not that their opinion counted for anything. There was an inquest and the whole thing was recorded as a tragic accident. Ayesha's parents sold up and left, and Debbie disappeared, never to be seen in the village again, not even when her parents died. Until last year.' She drew in a shuddering breath. 'Actually, I will have a gin.'

Seb rose to make her one. *How interesting! So that was how Deborah Ryecroft acquired the tag, the Wickthorpe Witch! Sometimes Fate had a strange way of working.* The machinations of his wife and her friend had played a crucial part. Not that he blamed them – not at all. They were just doing what they needed to protect themselves. If anything, he wished Jane still had that same kind of spunk. She had become a pathetic shadow of the woman he had married.

Jane accepted the glass with trembling fingers and took a long, deep sip. 'Thank you,' she added belatedly, eyes downcast once more.

'What happens now?' he asked. The last thing he wanted was for Jane to start broadcasting her confession to all and sundry. It suited him for village opinion about Deborah Ryecroft to remain unchanged.

Jane shrugged. 'Nothing.'

'Probably for the best. Try to put it behind you,' he said, concealing his relief with a show of compassion. He set his drink on the coffee table and moved to sit beside her, intending to give her a hug and mend the rift between them.

Instantly, she shrank away. 'Did you have an affair with Freya Billington?' she asked with sudden vehemence.

'Of course not,' he snorted. 'Whatever gave you that idea?'

Suspicion spread across her face. 'I think you did. In fact, I think *you* were the man who got her pregnant, the one who was with her in Oxford when Honoraria spotted her. I even think you may have been involved in her death.'

'What a vile thing to say!' He stood, anger turning his face into an ugly mask. 'So much for loyalty!'

'Oh, I've been loyal alright.' She stood too, confronting him. 'All those alibis. Starting before we were married, when that girl fell to her death in Edinburgh and the police were sniffing around. You were very keen for an alibi then, I recall. In fact, you were desperate. So much so, you were prepared to marry me! Not that I could see it at the time. I was so stupidly in love with you, I would have done anything you asked. Did you kill her too?'

'You're raving! I suggest you take some tablets and sleep it off,' Seb replied, his voice glacial.

'Back then, I was willing to pay any price to have you as my husband. But I'm telling you now, the price was too high. And I'm done with paying!'

'What do you mean?'

He towered over her. For one moment, she feared he would strike her but he kept his fists clenched by his side. She stuck out her chin. 'I mean, I'm not going to lie for you anymore. Too many things don't add up about that weekend when Freya died. I think you may have been responsible. And I'm no longer prepared to stay silent … about anything.'

He paled. 'Jane, you're upset. You're not yourself. Go and have a lie down. I'm sure you'll feel differently in the morning.'

'I won't.' She stared back defiantly. 'I've had enough, Seb. The guilt is making me ill. I need to make my peace with God.'

'God?' he spat back at her. 'Is that what all this is about? *God*? You've told lies in the past and now you feel you have to confess. Damn the consequences for everyone else! What about your boys … our sons? Don't you care that dragging us both through the mud will destroy the two of them?'

'The boys will be fine and you know it. They have their own lives now. They don't need us anymore.' She turned away from him. 'But you're right. I *am* tired. I'm going up to bed.' Straightening her back, she walked away.

'Stop! We're not done yet.'

She looked back over her shoulder. 'Oh yes, Seb, I think we are.'

CHAPTER 20

The Life & Times of Martha Lightbody

Martha continued to fret. If she could not recall the name of the village where John's brother and wife lived, she would not find her husband and son. However, when she revealed the cause of her distress to her brother, Seth, much later that same day, she discovered he was in possession of that vital information! Seth and John had spent time together prior to the latter's marriage to Martha. Whilst John had always worked the land, such was not his natural calling. He had therefore shadowed Seth whenever he could, learning the merchant trade, thinking to start his own venture sometime in the future.

'Twas Little Horseshoes, a small village further along the north coast,' Seth said. 'I remember John telling me.'

'Seth, you're a marvel. Little Horseshoes! I remember now. Such a peculiar name.' Martha turned excitedly to her father. 'Pa, if it be on the coast, is it possible to go by boat?'

Solomon turned benevolent, brown eyes upon his daughter. 'Weather is set fair,' he smiled. 'I know Little Horseshoes. I'll take you myself. Twill be good to give the boat a sail.' He was referring to the boat one of his sons regularly used to transport wool to other parts of the nearby coast. 'We'll head out at first light.'

Mary's face fell. 'So soon? Oh Martha, but you've only just returned!'

'Tis safer for the lass to be on her way, much as we'd all like her to stay.' Solomon patted his wife's hand. 'And she'll be wanting to see her husband and bairn.'

Martha felt torn. On one hand, she would have liked nothing more than to spend time with her beloved family. Seeing them again made her realise how much she had missed them and she remained greatly concerned for her mother's health. But the opportunity to be soon reunited with John and Josiah could not be denied. How she longed to see them!

'Pa is right,' she said slowly, her hazel eyes brimming with regret. 'Tis best to leave as soon as possible. But I promise to return as soon as we are able. I cannot wait for you to see how bonny Josiah is and for him to meet his grandparents.'

Mary said little after that, already resigned to losing the company of her daughter. Guilt burned in Martha's kind heart, knowing that, however soon she returned, it might well prove too late for her mother. Their final moments that evening held a special poignancy and the two women remained close to each other. When the moment came for them to say farewell, each hugged the other as if she would never let go. For Martha, it was one of the hardest things she had ever done, leaving her stricken mother in such circumstances.

***

Her father was right. The cerulean sky heralded fine weather and wind conditions too were favourable. The early morning sun warmed Martha's skin and the breeze fanned her cheeks. In the distance, she spotted larger vessels, heading out across the sea to faraway lands, and remembered how, as a child, she had dreamt of embarking upon such an adventure.

Her father's boat was small with a single mast, used only for short journeys. Most of his trade still took place by horse and cart to local towns. There had been talk of expansion, as demand for a variety of goods grew. Trade in wool was declining and grain was now the biggest commodity. However, Solomon had resisted his sons' persuasions to change. War still raged between Parliamentarians and Royalists, he argued, and they all remembered how difficult life had been when King's Lynn had been besieged for three weeks in 1642. Such an occurrence could happen again. Now was not the time to risk expanding their business.

They made good headway, skirting the coastline, adjusting the sail as necessary, and rowing a while when the wind dropped. Seth and Amos, Martha's youngest brother, were also aboard. Martha kept out of their way except to supply them with the food and drink provided by Mary. Rations had to last for the return trip, most likely the following day, so Martha was forced

143

to endure the men's good-natured moaning about the small portions allotted to them. She herself ate very little. Her stomach was taut with nerves. What would she do if she failed to find her husband in Little Horseshoes? To distract herself from such thoughts, she asked her father how he could be so precise in knowing their location upon the water.

'When I was a boy,' he answered, 'I spent many a day out on a boat on this sea. Pa was a fisherman, like his father before him. My family lived none too far from Little Horseshoes. There were six of us lads though. Too many mouths to feed. I was apprenticed to a sheep farmer and then to a wool merchant. Twas a good living and, when I met your Ma, I decided to strike out on my own. She was raised not far from King's Lynn and it seemed as good a place as any to settle. I've never regretted it but I miss being out on the waves, especially in weather as good as this.'

Martha nodded. 'I had forgotten you came from these parts. Do you know Little Horseshoes well?'

'Well enough. There's nowt much to say 'bout it. Tis a small place. Just a few boats and a few houses. Shouldn't be too hard to find John and the bairn if they're still there.'

'They will be,' she replied confidently.

When he turned to speak to Seth, she crossed her fingers. 'Please let them be there,' she whispered to the breeze.

***

Dusk was shrouding the sky as they moored up by the tiny, wooden quayside. In silence, they stepped onto dry land and looked about them. Martha's legs felt somewhat strange after so many hours on the water and she gripped her father's arm. He gestured towards the nearest house.

'Old Ned Sander used to live yonder,' he said. 'There's as good a place as any to ask where your family might be.'

As they approached, a younger man stepped outside, eying them with a mix of curiosity and suspicion. 'You're not from around these parts,' he said by way of greeting.

'We're looking for Matthew Lightbody. Can you tell us where he lives?' Martha asked.

'What's he to you?' the man demanded, his voice harsh.

'My husband's brother.'

The man's face cleared. 'Right enough. I heard he had family staying with him. He lives just beyond yon copse, along the track here. Be sure to give him my best.'

'We will.' Martha gave the man a dazzling smile, her heart beating fast at his talk of family. 'Your name is?'

'Tench. Phineas Tench.'

They bid Tench a good evening, and hurried along the path, Martha leading the way, anxious to reach their destination before Matthew and Calla retired for the night. As they rounded the copse, she glimpsed a lamp burning through one of the windows and she increased her pace further. Through the gloom, she heard animals, restless at the intrusion. Then, a door opened.

'Who goes there?'

Two men stood framed in the doorway. One was a tall, bearded man she recognised as Matthew. The other was her husband.

With a squeal of delight, Martha broke into a run. 'John,' she cried and hurtled straight into his warm embrace.

CHAPTER 21

The dark days of January resumed their usual pattern for Honoraria Simpson-Fairchild. On Tuesdays and Thursdays, she volunteered at a charity shop in nearby Stowmarket. *Save the Children* – a charity close to her heart. Having longed for children but never blessed with them, she and her late husband, Edgar, held regular fundraising events for worthy children's causes. It gave them comfort to feel they were supporting young people in need of help. After Edgar died, and having retired from her position as a secondary school history teacher, Honoraria spotted a plea for help in the *Save the Children* shop window. She had never regretted her decision to sign up and enjoyed the social aspect of working in retail, although it had occurred to her recently that perhaps she ought to consider paid employment. Her finances, although comfortable, were insufficient for a regular arrangement with Gerald.

That thought gave her pause. It was a shock to realise she had not missed the company of Gerald so much recently. In fact, her current fantasies scarcely featured him. Rather, the unprepossessing, portly figure of Marcus Monk seemed to have taken a starring role, much as she willed it otherwise. The man seemed to have become something of an obsession and she now regretted telling him she was involved with someone else. Since then, he had not contacted her at all and it had been a disappointment to discover he was unable to attend the next meeting of the Wickthorpe History Society. The guest speaker was giving a talk on the history of farming in East Anglia and Honoraria had gone to considerable trouble to arrange the loan of artefacts from local museums. As usual, she was hoping for a good turnout and the chance to recruit some new members. Secretly though, she had also been hoping to impress Marcus. But there, he wasn't coming and it couldn't be helped. She had asked Deborah Ryecroft to help her spread the word amongst the farming community so her fingers were firmly crossed.

As for finding out more of the elusive Martha Lightbody, she was still waiting on Deborah. It seemed to be taking a frustratingly long time. Apparently, Deborah had been busy with work but had revealed, when prodded by an impatient Honoraria, that she was reading a book based upon a diary and letters allegedly written by Martha herself. Honoraria itched to get her hands on the book and had hinted as much to Deborah.

'If you're too tied up with work, I would be happy to ...'

She had been given a polite but definite 'no' in response. Deborah, understandably, wanted to finish it first. In the meantime, Honoraria was left kicking her heels, a most annoying situation but – she uttered a long–suffering sigh – there was nothing more she could do.

Edgar's voice sounded in her ear, as it so often did. 'Be patient, my dear. All good things come to those who wait.'

'That might be case,' she would answer crossly, 'but patience has never been my strong suit.'

'Indeed,' Edgar would smile back at her. 'Luckily, you have ample, other qualities to compensate.' He would slide his hands around her middle, tug her to him and, just like that, whatever was currently annoying her would swiftly be forgotten.

Nowadays, without the benefit of such distractions, the hours spent alone at home seemed to drag like a reluctant, old dog on its daily constitutional. Every now and then, she almost weakened and contacted Gerald but the thought of a night's sweaty wrestling with his firm, young form did not excite her as much as it should so she resisted the temptation. If only she could see Marcus and make it clear she was available, such glorious grappling may be hers. Furthermore, the pragmatic side of her acknowledged, she would not have to part with a fortune to acquire it.

***

Since her visit to see Patrick Velaman, Ava had found herself often distracted. After the busy month of December, January was quiet in the Post

Office and it was all too easy to lapse into silly daydreams. Not that anything was going to happen between them, she told herself firmly. Despite his protestations and apology, Patrick was not to be trusted. Seeing him had cleared the air, that was all. Any future meetings between them could now take place without embarrassment.

Except, she remained on tenterhooks, waiting for his tall frame to appear in the doorway. And Enid was still very much in attendance, watching her with knowing, spiteful eyes. Seeing him under those conditions would be truly horrible, and she prayed fervently that, should he require stamps or to post a parcel, he would go to an establishment elsewhere.

Stupidly though, she longed to see him again, even whilst she chided herself for her weakness. When they had parted, he had promised to contact her and, despite telling herself that she was unwilling to pick up where they had left off more than twenty years ago, she waited breathlessly for his call. As days drifted by, with no communication from him, that thrilling sense of anticipation slowly deflated. There really was no hope for her!

Staring miserably through the window at the drab, grey day beyond, she wondered where her spark had gone. Hers was not a life. It was a pitiful existence: waiting on a woman who despised her; doing a dead-end job which bored her; every day the same. Where was the stimulation, the challenge, the interest? She had become a pathetic creature who cowered in corners and watched the world go by without engagement. In fact – she allowed herself a wry smile – she would make an ideal spy. No one ever noticed her. Even with her new clothes and hair, most customers had not seemed to discern the difference. Only a few had made a kind comment. The renewed confidence her transformation had afforded her gradually ebbed away. Change, she realised, needed to come from within. *She* had to start behaving differently. She should be taking risks and trying new challenges. Maybe, she could look for a different job ... move out, away from her domineering mother ... go on a cruise and flirt with handsome strangers ...

The harsh shrill of the Post Office phone jerked her from her reverie. 'Wickthorpe Post Office, Ava Green speaking.'

'Hi, Ava. So good to hear your voice.'

And there he was! Patrick's unmistakeable drawl sent her heart skidding out of her chest. 'Good afternoon. How may I help you?' Conscious of her mother's vigilant stare, she half turned away from the prying eyes. It felt so intimate, hearing him breathing on the other end of the line. She felt dizzy with longing.

'Er, I was calling ... you remember, I said I'd be in touch?'

'I do.' His obvious nervousness squeezed at her heart, yet her voice sounded ridiculously formal.

'Er ... well, I guess I was wondering if you would do me the honour of accompanying me to dinner?'

She swallowed. 'When?' she said.

'Well ... I guess ... tonight is good for me ... but I expect that may be too short notice ...'

'Tonight is fine.' *Where had that come from?* Even as her brain had been formulating a polite but firm refusal.

'Great!' His tone was noticeably lighter. 'Wow, that's just ... great.' She couldn't help smiling as she waited for him to say more. 'I'll pick you up at six ... unless you'd prefer to meet me somewhere?'

'No, six o'clock. I'll come outside ... so don't be late!' she added tartly.

'I won't. You can rely on me.'

An acerbic rejoinder sprang to her lips but she bit it back and ended the call. Without a word, she headed for the sanctuary of her room, joy spreading as she sped up the stairs. He had called to ask her for a date and she had said yes! All rational thought, all that determination to keep her head and maintain a distance from him, had fled at the sound of his voice. Despite everything, she still loved him. She had always loved him and always would. That would never change, whatever the future held, so she would grasp a chance of happiness while she could and blow the consequences.

Having composed herself, she headed back downstairs, knowing she could do nothing about the secret smile curving her lips.

'Who was on the phone?' Enid's question snapped as she reappeared behind the counter.

For a moment, she thought about lying but what the heck! 'It was Patrick,' she replied serenely. 'Patrick Velaman. He's invited me for dinner tonight. I'm out at six so I'll reheat something from the freezer for you before I go.'

A short silence. Her statement was a shock, she could tell. Even Enid could not control the immediate play of emotions across her embittered face – surprise, dismay, contempt, in that order. 'You're even more of a fool than I thought you were!' she spat.

Ava did not respond. Instead, she stared once more through the window. Flickers of afternoon sunshine filtered through the dull cloud. The forecast had predicted things might brighten up later. They had.

CHAPTER 22

The Life & Times of Martha Lightbody

Martha, John and baby Josiah settled into life on the Norfolk coast in Little Horseshoes. The night of Martha's arrival, there was great rejoicing. Matthew and his wife, Calla, fussed around the tired travellers and they talked long into the night. Early the following morning, Martha's father woke her with the news it was time for him and her brothers to leave. Their departure was a wrench and Martha prayed it would not be too long before she and her family would travel to King's Lynn.

Little Josiah had grown and was thriving. Those first few days, Martha was content to spend hours cuddling and playing with her son. Such moments were precious after facing the likelihood of her death.

Calla and Matthew, she discovered, were kind and generous folk. They had three children of their own and another on the way but made no complaint at the prospect of housing and feeding yet another body. On the contrary, they went out of their way to make Martha feel welcome and, in turn, John and Martha were keen to prove useful additions to the household. The harvest had been safely gathered but the hot, dry spell continued and John worked long hours in the fields alongside his brother. It had proved a bumper year for the barley and wheat crops. The land was light, sandy soil but an abundance of rain in the spring had resulted in good yields.

The two men had been making plans. With the money received at market for his grain, Matthew planned to purchase more land to the south, whilst John proposed to set up as a grain merchant to capitalise upon the growing demand for corn. Martha was content to help where she was needed and, as Calla's confinement drew near, proved a blessing in keeping the household running smoothly. At times, she fretted that she, John and Josiah had no house of their own but at least she felt safe. Little Horseshoes was a small hamlet, situated some way off the busier byways, and passing strangers were rare.

Martha spent the little spare time she had writing letters. She dared not write to her dear friend, Prudence Harkness, for fear such correspondence might fall into the wrong hands. Instead, she penned a letter to Ruth Fletcher who had aided her escape from Wickthorpe. In it, she asked politely about Ruth's husband, Daniel, and the family before requesting information regarding the situation in Wickthorpe, and particularly about Roger Holley and his search for her. She did not tell John she had written lest he forbade her to send the letter. He had expressed the opinion that the past was best forgotten; it was the future which mattered. Whilst she agreed in some part, she was eager for reassurance that the witch hunt had been called off. She also asked that they secretly get word of her survival to Prudence. It was unbearable to think of her dear friend grieving in ignorance.

Her other letter was penned to Cecile who had, when they parted company, begged for news of her situation. This was a much lighter missive, full of small anecdotes to amuse the young lady and asking briefly about Cecile's own romantic dilemma. How she hoped her friend would think better of her silly elopement notion! As someone with little in the way of possessions, she could not understand how anyone could so blithely throw away a life of such wealth and entitlement. The child was a hopeless romantic, to be sure, and naïve to the realities of life in the lesser echelons of society. She could only pray Cecile had heeded the fervency of her warnings or that Bertie's own good sense had held sway.

A reply was received from Cecile less than two months later. She was at home, bored and bemoaning the fact that she had seen nothing of Bertie. However, she had been forced to spend time with her other suitor, Lord Henry, son and heir to her father's friend and neighbour, the Duke of Suffolk. That young man had been injured in the Battle of Naseby when Parliamentarian forces, under the command of Lord Fairfax and Oliver Cromwell, had inflicted a serious defeat upon the Royalist army. Cecile had been despatched by her father to aid Henry's recuperation. Doubtless, he had hopes that enforced proximity would awaken feelings of tenderness in his daughter's bosom. Martha was amused to read Cecile's grudging description of Henry as 'tolerably handsome, witty and amusing' and the fact that 'he must have been fearfully brave in confronting the enemy when his troops were so terribly outnumbered' in amongst declarations of her continued passion for Bertie. She wondered if her friend's protestations were a little forced and if her attitude towards the wounded man was softening. Time would tell. It would be best for Cecile, to be sure, but she did feel sorry for poor Bertie should that happen.

Further weeks passed and John began building a house for his family, a short distance away from his brother's. The year reached its end and it was February 1646 when word finally arrived from Ruth Fletcher. Martha wrapped herself in the warm cloak she had made and took the missive outside into the cold, winter sunshine to read without interruption.

Dear Martha,

We were so happy to hear news of your happy reacquaintance with your beloved family.

I have much news but also great sadness in informing you that our much loved, youngest child, Alice were took from us with consumption and cough. I remember dear Alice was a favourite with you and I am sorry to send such sad tidings.

Martha set aside the letter with a choked sob. Poor Alice and poor Ruth. She remembered the little girl as clearly as if she were right in front of her. A cherub, not yet two years old, with dark curls, liquid brown eyes and a gap-toothed grin. Such a mischief and so full of life. Ruth was correct that young Alice had burrowed a special place in Martha's heart and she prayed for her now, tears burning her eyelids. At length, she turned to the rest of the letter.

Daniel has done as you asked and spoken to your friend, Prudence Harkness. She was overjoyed at the news and passed on her best wishes to you. She fares well and once again is with child but says she misses you sorely.

Dearest Prudence. Martha wondered if she would ever see her friend again. Given her current situation, the prospect seemed unlikely and the thought made her sad. Perhaps, when they were settled in their own house, she could invite her to stay awhile. The travel would be difficult though ...

Roger Holley has been much frustrated in his search for you and I believe he has now ceased his efforts. The word in Wickthorpe is that the witch is dead but that her curse lives on. Indeed, such has been the talk on everyone's lips as there has been a drowning in the very same lake where they took you – that folk call Dark Water. All are now much afeared and refuse to go near it. The drowned woman was the recently-wed wife of Roger Holley no less. You will have known her as Jane Finch, elder daughter of Jed.

Martha gasped. Jane had been a tall, thin woman, meek and most unprepossessing in appearance, with a birthmark disfiguring the left side of her face. There had been but few words spoken between them but Martha found her nature sweet and kind. The poor girl was painfully shy. How did someone like that manage to ensnare tall, blond, handsome Roger Holley? Martha was cynical enough to believe it was not a love match on his side. There must have been some arrangement with her father ... and now she was drowned, her own curse cited as the cause. How ridiculous! She would not be surprised if Roger had a hand in it himself ...

No sooner had the thought popped into her head than it took hold and sprouted. Of course! Holley was not above using the curse for his own ends. This way, he could enjoy the financial benefits of the match with none of the encumbrance. Her heart bled for Jane and raged anew at the instrument of her own attempted murder. Her mother was right; the man was evil. He needed to be stopped. But how? She returned to the letter to see what else Ruth had to say ...

Some in the village have their suspicions that Holley had a hand in the unfortunate woman's drowning but he has been publicly much distraught. Father David was called to cast out the lake's evil spirits but most believe the curse lives on. For that reason, dear Martha, I beg you to remain cautious. Roger Holley would like nothing better than to drag you back to Wickthorpe where most in the village now believe in your guilt. Please take care.
Your faithful friend,
Ruth.

Martha remained outside for some while, unfeeling of the chill wind whipping her tear-stained cheeks. Ruth's letter had borne most tragic news and she mourned the deaths of little Alice and gentle Jane, praying most fervently for their souls in heaven. But, as she headed to the river to splash cold water on her face, her thoughts were once again of Roger Holley. Despite Ruth's claims, she knew such a man would not rest until she was discovered.

How Martha wished that curse unsaid! Had she not uttered those vengeful words, poor Jane Finch would most likely still be alive. And how many more innocent women would find themselves victims because of it?

***

Thursday night. 11:30 p.m. Deborah set the book aside with some reluctance. With an early start the following day, she needed sleep. Her eyelids had been drooping, but when she read that Roger Holley's wife, another Jane Holley, had drowned in Dark Water Lake, an ominous sense of dread settled in the pit of her stomach. Parallels between Roger and *Seb* Holley taunted her mind. Could the current Jane Holley be at risk of a similar end?

Deborah turned off her bedside lamp and brooded in the darkness. The strangeness of Jane's recent visit, her ill health and disturbed mental state, her fear of her own husband – all these were reasons to be concerned for Jane. However, her premonition that Jane may be in danger of suffering the same fate as Roger Holley's wife, almost four hundred years earlier, was nothing short of irrational. The author of the book admitted it was a work of fiction, albeit based upon fact. The drowning of Roger's wife might have been a fabrication, designed to paint Roger in an even more villainous light. The first Jane Holley might have lived a long and happy life ....

No, she did not believe that. Poor Jane Finch was doomed as soon as she became Jane Holley. Awful images continued to plague her: Jane's unconscious form, carried to the water's edge; her lifeless body, face down, bobbing in the water; *Seb* Holley's face, harsh with murderous intent ...

Stop! It was late. Her imagination was running away with her. She was allowing Martha's story, and her emotional involvement in it, to play havoc with commonsense. Tomorrow, in the clear light of day, she would realise how ridiculous this all was.

She forced herself to concentrate on business details. The following day would see her in discussions with the CEO of an electrical wholesaler. It was a company Lainey Lewis had highlighted as having lucrative potential. Deborah was not so sure. To her mind, the numbers did not quite stack up and there were niggles she wanted to address. She had always been a details person, working methodically through the figures, looking for gaps and spotting any loopholes. It was her accountant brain. She knew how statistics could be presented to tell more than one story and enjoyed the challenge of analysing data in depth, thereby being one step ahead in subsequent meetings. *Know more than your opponent.* Lainey was an excellent strategic director with vision and the ability to see the bigger picture. Her ideas were often brilliant in their scope. But, in the end, it all came down to the small print and that was Deborah's forte. Having run through the figures she had memorised, she repeated the process, again and again, trying to block out all other thoughts.

But the haunting image of a floating, bedraggled figure continued to plague her and sleep proved elusive, long into the depths of the night.

CHAPTER 23

Four days later, on Monday afternoon, DI Beth Honeysuckle exited Ipswich Crown Court where she had been called as a witness for the prosecution in a case against two men on trial for fraud. When she switched on her phone, she saw she had three missed calls. Instantly, it rang again.

'The body of a woman has been found in Dark Water Lake.'

The stark words reverberated like the shockwaves of an explosion. Her synapses fired into action and her first thought was the obvious one. *Deborah Ryecroft. Drowned as a witch after all.*

'I'll be right there,' she assured her boss, Detective Superintendent, Allison Pallister.

It was a relief, thirty minutes later, to discover she was wrong. The body was not that of Deborah Ryecroft after all. As she looked down at the bloated grimace of a woman's face, she knew she recognised the victim. It was someone she had previously interviewed.

'We think this is Jane Holley,' DS Jack Everard told her, his voice sombre. 'Wife of the doctor, Sebastian Holley, resident of Wickthorpe.'

'I agree, but she is yet to be formally identified?'

'Correct.'

'Who found the body?' she asked.

Everard consulted his notes. 'Heather Manning. Out walking her dogs. Weimaraners. Three of them. One of the dogs started sniffing at something tangled by the edge of the water. Ms Manning saw it was a woman and dragged her out in case she was still alive. She recognised Mrs Holley from the pharmacy at the village health centre.'

Beth nodded. 'Where is Ms Manning now?'

'With paramedics. Being treated for shock.' A woman with a blanket draped around her shoulders was surrounded by emergency medical personnel.

'I'd like to ask her a few questions,' Beth said, 'while things are still fresh in her mind.' She surveyed the scene. Police officers had cordoned off the area whilst awaiting a forensics team. The pathologist had completed his preliminary examination of the body in situ and Jane Holley was currently being carefully transferred to another ambulance.

'Initial observations?' she asked.

'Suicide,' Jack replied. 'An empty gin bottle and a box of prescription anti-depressants were found near where the body was discovered.'

'Mm,' Beth frowned. The similarities with Freya Billington's case seemed too much of a coincidence. Both female; both apparent suicides; alcohol and medication found at the scene; both bodies found on a Monday; the same gut feeling things were not as they seemed. Could they have a serial killer on their hands? Too soon to say but her throat was dry with suspicion. 'Was there a note?' she asked.

'Not so far.'

'And has the next of kin been informed and asked to confirm identity?'

'Not yet.'

As Beth turned, she noticed a large, middle-aged man sporting a grey beard arguing with a young police officer barring his way. 'Who is that?' she asked.

'Ms Manning's husband,' Jack answered. 'She called him to collect the dogs while she was being treated. He only lives a few minutes away and said he would return to take her home.'

Beth nodded. 'In that case, best we talk to Ms Manning sooner rather than later.'

***

Seb Holley was at work at Wickthorpe Health Centre when he was told that the body of a woman, probably his wife, had been found in Dark Water Lake. DI Honeysuckle, accompanied by DS Everard, studied his reaction carefully as they broke the news. Shock and disbelief. When they mentioned the possibility of suicide, his horror slowly turned to sad acceptance.

'My wife was prescribed anti-depressants some while ago,' Seb admitted. 'Her mental state has declined recently.'

'Which anti-depressants?' Beth Honeysuckle asked.

'Sertraline. My wife is ... *was* under the care of Dr Singh. You can ask her about my wife's medical history and the treatment she was prescribed.'

Beth nodded. The empty medication pack found discarded near the scene was sertraline. 'You say your wife's mental condition deteriorated only recently. Was there something which, in your opinion, might have triggered this?'

Dr Holley hunched his shoulders, his countenance troubled. 'I suppose it started almost a year ago. It's difficult to remember exactly. I know Jane was very upset to learn that Deborah Ryecroft was returning to Wickthorpe. She was the same age as Deborah and both were present when a young girl drowned, some time ago now.' He furrowed his brow. 'It must have been very traumatic for Jane, having it dredged up again, along with all the village talk of the Wickthorpe Witch. And then Freya Billington drowned last summer. She worked in the pharmacy with Jane so it was an awful shock. Jane's condition took a nosedive after that. Obviously, you know about the curse?' Beth nodded again. 'I suspect Jane believed the curse was happening all over again.' He sank his face into his hands with a sob. 'Sorry.' A shuddering breath. 'I tried to talk to her about it but ...' He gave a helpless shrug.

'Take all the time you need.' Beth glanced across at Jack, sitting placidly on a hard plastic chair and chewing on a thumbnail. 'We understand this is very difficult for you.' She tried to inject a note of sympathy in her tone but still managed to sound brusque. There was something off about the charismatic doctor and she wondered if her colleague felt it too. 'Can you tell us what you and your wife were doing this past weekend?'

Seb looked surprised at the question. 'Jane was away, visiting a school friend who had just received a cancer diagnosis. She was due back today. I don't understand how she could have ended up in the lake.' He turned to the officers in bewilderment. 'Are you absolutely certain it is her?'

'I'm afraid so. However, we would like you to make a formal identification when you feel up to it.'

'Of course. I need to know for sure ...' his voice tailed off.

After a respectful moment of silence, Beth prompted, 'And your whereabouts, this past weekend?'

'I was enjoying a rare few days to myself. I played golf with a couple of old friends on Saturday. Sunday, I was at home on my own ... pottering ... doing a few jobs ... reading. I don't know what else I can tell you.'

'Do you have a name and number for the school friend your wife was visiting?'

'Her name is Davina Locksmith. I'm afraid I don't have her number. She lives in Norwich, Taverham way, I believe.'

'And the names and contact details of your golf buddies?'

He frowned. 'Am I under suspicion here, Inspector?'

Her face remained bland as she gave him the stock answer. 'We are simply trying to ascertain all the facts surrounding your and your wife's activities before she died. A forensics team are gathering evidence at the scene and the pathologist will be able to tell us more when she has examined your wife's body. Until then, we are treating her death as suspicious, Dr Holley. These are just routine questions. I apologise if they are causing you distress.'

'Not at all.' The charm was back. 'Whatever it takes to find out what happened. I'm only too happy to help. Let me just get my phone.' They waited while he scrolled through his contacts to give them the information they wanted.

'Thank you, Dr Holley.' Beth stood and handed him her card. 'Should you think of anything else, anything at all, however trivial, please don't hesitate to give me a call. Do you have family or friends you would like us to contact for you?'

'Yes ... no ... that is, I'll let them know. My sons ...' His shoulders shuddered as he sat. 'I still can't believe it.'

'Once again, we are very sorry for your loss, Dr Holley.'

They left, closing the door gently behind them and striding through a packed waiting room of curious stares in silence. Neither spoke until they were back inside the car.

'What did you think?' Beth asked.

Jack shrugged. 'Seemed genuine. Looks like suicide to me. The victim was disturbed and suffering from mental health issues. I'll check that with Dr Singh. The medication too.' He shrugged. 'When we interviewed the Holleys concerning the Freya Billington case, they seemed like a devoted, married couple. Why would he have killed her?'

'That's for us to find out,' she replied.

***

The news spread through the village like flames licking through paper. There was nothing like a tragedy to bring all the gossip-mongers from their homes and into communal spaces. *The Pastry Parlour*, Wickthorpe's small café, became a hive of activity as people assembled to ask questions, shake heads, share what they had heard and hypothesize about what had happened.

'She hadn't been well for a while,' Honoraria confided to the group of matrons squeezed around her table. 'I've been quite concerned for her.'

'The police think it's suicide,' someone announced in a loud voice from across the room. All heads turned in that direction. It was Brenda Wicks, a round-faced, red-cheeked widow, known to be a crony of Enid Green. 'But I wouldn't mind betting that it's murder, pure and simple. The same as Freya Billington.'

'What makes you think it's murder?' someone asked.

'Don't you think it's too much of a coincidence – two women, both drowned in the same, cursed lake, barely six months apart? In my book, that would be suspicious in *any* circumstances but the Wickthorpe Witch has returned ...' She left the statement hanging.

'That's a good point, Brenda.'

'Murder! Well, I never!'

'She's right. There are evil forces at work here.'

Mutterings of assent rumbled around the café. Likewise, similar statements were being vociferously aired in the Post Office.

'I warned you,' Enid pronounced to anyone who entered. 'I warned everyone that Freya Billington would not be the last victim. The sooner Deborah Ryecroft is arrested and removed from the village the better.'

'The police are useless,' grumbled Naomi Clover, a sharp-featured woman in green leggings and a padded jacket. 'Don't expect them to get anything right.'

'I hope you're wrong, Naomi, I really do.' Enid's chins wobbled earnestly. 'None of us will be safe until that woman is locked away. They ought to bring back hanging, that's what I say.'

'Mother!' protested Ava.

'What?' Enid shot her a defiant look. 'I can speak as I please.'

Ava did not respond, knowing her mother was relishing this opportunity to fire up a witch hunt. For someone like Enid, who detested Deborah Ryecroft with a passion, Jane Holley's awful end was nothing short of a gift from the heavens.

Privately though, Ava was also worried. First Freya Billington. Now Jane Holley. Both very similar circumstances. It *did* seem too much of a coincidence. Not that she believed in superstitious village folklore – not at all – but she was worried for Deborah. The chances were that some other 'do-gooders' would take matters into their own hands, just like the Hampton-Browns had done the previous year. And, even more concerning, she could not help but wonder if they had a murderer in their midst …

CHAPTER 24

The Life & Times of Martha Lightbody

As days passed, Martha's anger against Roger Holley grew. If Holley was using her curse for his own ends, others could surely do the same, confident that the blame would be ascribed to the Wickthorpe Witch. She fretted that other innocent victims would follow. Something had to be done.

But what? She vented her indignation in another letter to Ruth Fletcher. A brief note of condolence had been sent as soon as she felt able but she followed it up, a few weeks later, with an expression of her strong belief of Holley's hand in his wife's untimely death. Having scribed the missive, she felt a little happier and her attention was pulled in other directions as they moved into their own house. John had worked tirelessly, his brother oft beside him, and they were now blessed with a timber-framed house built in the modern style with brick walls and a thatched roof. It was not as big as Matthew's house but had a kitchen and a sitting room downstairs and three small rooms upstairs. Compared to their tiny, tied cottage in Wickthorpe, it was a veritable mansion and Martha was thrilled. She had recently discovered she was expecting another child and, it seemed, the future was bright for the Lightbody family. Both John and Martha were most grateful to Matthew and Calla for, without their considerable assistance, they would never have accomplished so much in such a short time.

In early summer, she received an excited letter from Cecile announcing that young lady's betrothal to Lord Henry, eldest son of the Duke of Suffolk:

Isn't it thrilling? I do hope you will be happy that I have so dutifully followed your wise advice. Henry was quite the hero at Naseby, I am reliably informed. So dashing and brave! Am I not the luckiest girl alive?

Martha read the words with an amused smile. Oh, the fickleness of youth! Of poor Bertie there was no mention. Despite knowing the hopelessness of that liaison, Martha could not but feel sorry for him. She prayed that the kind, handsome, young man would also be blessed with a suitable match. And she was very pleased for Cecile. The girl had a sweet, generous soul and deserved every happiness.

It was the middle of August before she received further news from Ruth. Roger Holley had continued to prosper and was once again betrothed, this time to the sole daughter of Lord Busby, a man who owned extensive lands in east Suffolk. There had been no more drownings, thankfully, but other events had been blamed on the witch's curse. Longstanding feuds in the village had escalated with perpetrators of such foul deeds, as the poisoning of a cat and the burning of a barn filled with straw, protesting their innocence and calling for Martha Lightbody to answer for her sins. Such information filled Martha with dismay. She feared for the safety of Holley's new bride, barely more than a child by all accounts. Doubtless, the man would stop at nothing to add to his wealth and power, and the curse would provide him with the perfect exculpation should the worst once more befall his wife. Ruth wrote that some in the village shared Martha's conviction that Holley was responsible for Jane's death. However, none dared speak out against him, too few were they in number and too afraid of incurring his enmity.

Such information heaped fuel upon Martha's distress and her sense of helplessness grew also. For her own safety, and that of her family, she could not speak out against the vile injustices occurring in her name. She could only rely upon the bravery of others to properly investigate these crimes and that would never happen unless …

Once the idea popped into her head, it quickly took root. She would write to Lord Busby and tell him of her suspicions regarding Holley. Her letter would be anonymous, of course, but hopefully it would be enough for him to check further and, perhaps, halt preparations for his daughter's wedding. Having satisfied herself that such a plan might thwart Holley's latest intention, she decided to write several such epistles, addressing them to inhabitants of Wickthorpe and beyond. The more she wrote, the more questions would be raised against Holley, even if many dismissed her claims as malicious gossip.

It was better than doing nothing. With determination, she gathered paper, pen and ink and began to write. After several false starts and discarded attempts, she had a version with which she was satisfied:

Beware the machinations of that ambitious devil, Roger Holley! Doubtless, Jane Finch, a woman in whom he had shown no previous interest, brought an advantageous dowry to the marriage. How convenient that, shortly after, she should be found drowned in the very same lake Holley sought to drown Martha Lightbody, falsely claiming that poor innocent to be a witch! And how convenient also to blame his wife's death on the powerless curse of a condemned woman.
Holley is an evil man. Stop him before others become victims.

Without further ado, she set about copying the letter several times. Roger Holley may consider himself untouchable. She would do her utmost to cause his undoing.

***

It did not take Roger Holley long to discover that something was afoot. He found himself summoned to the home of Lord Busby, barely a week prior to his upcoming nuptials. A servant showed him into the living room where he was kept waiting more than an hour. His patience was running thin by the time his prospective father-in-law made an appearance.

Lord Busby was a squat, balding man of some sixty years. Previously, he had always proved a most affable host. Upon this occasion, however, his face was solemn and there was no apology for his tardiness. He carried a piece of paper in his right hand and brandished it in Holley's direction, as if swatting an unwelcome insect from his path.

'What's all this about, Roger?' he scowled. 'I have only agreed to this match with Matilda as she has her heart set 'pon it. If I find out that you rid yourself of your first wife and are planning harm to my daughter, I'll ...' Busby's round face was near apoplectic with rage and Holley was most taken aback.

'My Lord ...' He offered an obsequious bow. 'I can only assure you most ardently of my love and devotion to your beautiful daughter. Anyone who claims otherwise is guilty of the most heinous slander. If I may be permitted to see the contents of the letter ...'

With a growl most alarming, Lord Busby handed over the parchment and stalked to a side table to pour himself a brandy. He offered none to his guest.

Holley read the neat script with increasing rage but took care to conceal this from his host. Instead, he schooled his countenance into one of dismayed innocence. 'My Lord, I can only think this has been written by someone jealous of my union with Matilda – a less fortunate suitor, perhaps? Tis untrue, all of it.' He tossed the letter aside with a contemptuous sneer and shrugged. 'A man as successful as myself has made a few enemies along the way, I cannot deny it, but I swear to you, my Lord, as God is my witness, I had no hand in the tragic death of my dear Jane. I am sure you are aware of the curse placed 'pon me by Martha Lightbody, the Wickthorpe Witch. Doubtless, twas her evil which caused poor Jane to take her own life in such a way. At the time, I was unfortunately detained on business or I might have been able to prevent the tragedy. Since then, I have had men searching day and night for the woman responsible. We are closing in and hope soon to bring her to justice. Then, the curse will be laid to rest.'

Lord Busby frowned. 'I had heard some such tale ... are you now telling me tis true? If so, surely my Matilda will be at risk if she becomes your wife?'

Damn. Holley swore under his breath as he struggled for a response. He had underestimated the man he had previously considered an abject fool and overplayed the curse element. 'I will protect Matilda with my life, my Lord. As I said, we are near to capturing the wench and freeing ourselves of her evil, once and for all. You need have no fears for your daughter.'

Busby shook his head. 'I am not so sure.' He took a long swig of his brandy before turning back to Holley. 'In fact, I think the wedding should be postponed until I can be completely assured of my daughter's safety. Find the witch; get the curse lifted. Only then will I allow the marriage to go ahead.'

'But, my Lord ...'

'That will be all.' Busby raised an imperious hand. 'No contact with Matilda until these conditions are met. Do you understand?'

'Yes, my Lord.' Holley gave a small bow and walked stiffly from the room, inwardly seething. There was nothing for it. He had to find Martha Lightbody. Fast.

***

Over the next days and weeks, more such correspondence, accusing Holley of the murder of his first wife, arrived in Wickthorpe, causing much hushed discussion within those environs. Holley became aware of strange looks as he passed, long before he knew the cause. When he found out, he raged anew. By this time, he had no doubt as to the identity of his anonymous accuser. It could be none other than Martha Lightbody. He had, at first, suspected one of Jane's family had written them but investigations in that quarter proved such was not the case. To Lord Busby, he had mooted the possibility of a jealous suitor but did not believe that himself. Such an insipid chit as Matilda Busby was unlikely to inspire such strong feelings, after all. He himself, despite his protestations to the contrary, had no affection for the plump, doe-eyed maid but her dowry – lands to the east of his current holdings – would prove most valuable. Fortunately, she had proved easy pickings for a man of his experience. If necessary, he would seduce her so the match was forced to go ahead despite Lord Busby's ultimatum. However, he was pragmatic enough to realise that an amicable alliance with such a man as his father-in-law-to-be would be far more favourable. Martha Lightbody had to be found ... and soon.

The worst thing was he had been so very close to catching the witch. At no time, after the trial by drowning, had he thought she was dead, even though an extensive search of the area had failed to find her and no one claimed to have seen her, despite the incentive of a large reward. He discovered she had family living in King's Lynn and sent men there, to no avail. However, they had found informants who were paid to alert them should she appear. And lo and behold, just a few days later, there she was! His men had returned post haste but too late; she had already gone, no one knew whence. All anyone could tell them was that she had left by boat with her father and two brothers. The men had returned late next day without her. An attempt to seize one of them, to beat the necessary information out of him, had been a disaster. The brothers had combined to administer their own beating and his men had returned with their tails between their legs. It had been the talk of Wickthorpe and Roger was aware he had become the butt of jokes bandied in the village.

Despite his claims to Lord Busby that he was close to capturing the witch, he was as ignorant of her current whereabouts as he had ever been. Unwilling to expose himself to further embarrassment, he decided more stealth was required. Secretly, he continued to employ the services of a weaselly-faced man by the name of Ralph Holder who claimed to specialise in bounty-hunting. Given the information Roger was able to provide, Holder was convinced he would be able to pick up Martha's trail somewhere along the north/north-east Norfolk coast, within a day's sail from King's Lynn, and was currently despatched to investigate those claims. So far, there had been no news. As each day passed, his irritation grew. One thing was certain; when Martha Lightbody was discovered and brought back to Wickthorpe, she would pay. He would see to it personally. At night, he lay awake thinking of the worst ways the wench could be punished. Such thoughts filled him with pleasurable anticipation. How she would regret thwarting him so!

CHAPTER 25

Another drowning. *And Jane Holley.*

Deborah was devastated. Since reading of the suspicious death of Roger Holley's wife, her sleep had been disturbed by fears for the present Jane Holley. And previously, before Freya Billington drowned, she had also dreamt of that poor girl's death. There was no way to explain such premonitions, unless she herself was somehow connected to the curse. But how could she tell anyone? Who would believe her? No one in their right mind.

Rumours suggested that Jane had taken her own life but Deborah was not so sure. Although she remained silent on the subject, she instinctively believed Seb Holley was involved? She paced about the house, more disturbed than she could ever have thought possible at the news of Jane Holley's death.

Other concerns filtered in. She would be blamed, especially when people remembered the circumstances of Ayesha Khan's death. Four sixteen-year-old girls were there that fateful day. Now, she was the only one remaining. *The witch.* She fancied she could hear the whisper of voices in the air, accusing, condemning. Would she never be free of Martha's legacy?

Doubtless, the police would call sometime soon and the questioning would start all over again. Did she have an alibi? She cast her mind back over the weekend. On Saturday, she and Tom had gone to Fakenham in Norfolk for the horse racing. It had been a fantastic day out, doing something she had never done before, and she had even backed two winners! On the way home, they had stopped for a drink at a pub in a small village near the pretty market town of Swaffham. The drink had developed into a bar meal and they had returned home at approximately 8:30 p.m. On Sunday, Tom had travelled to a farm in Lincolnshire, to pick up a machinery part he had bought, and she spent most of the day alone, catching up on paperwork. In the morning, she had called briefly on Kai and Phil to see if they, or their spaniel, Jez, wanted to join her for a walk, but they were out so she had gone on her own, circling the outskirts of the village. She tried to recall if she had seen anyone on the way. If she had, she could not remember. Tom had not returned until about 7 p.m. No alibi for most of Sunday then. She hunched her shoulders. So be it. Nothing she could do about it. She had nothing to hide. But would they believe her?

There would be many in the village certain of her guilt, led, no doubt, by Enid Green. Would she receive more unwelcome visitors – vigilantes like the Hampton-Browns – who decided to take matters into their own hands? The sensation of black water, closing over her, flooded her senses and she fought back the urge to be sick.

Fresh air. A brisk walk to clear her head. That would help. Wrapping up warmly in a thick coat, hat, scarf and sturdy boots, she headed from her back door and through the bolted gate at the rear of the house. From there she could skirt around the margins of Tom's fields and steer clear of the village itself. She did not want to risk coming across any accusers, or anyone wishing her harm.

She had not gone far when she spotted Tom's truck, parked up at the entrance to one of the fields. As she was walked towards it, she pasted a cheery grin on her face. No point bothering Tom with her worries. However, the figure down in a ditch belonged to Emma.

'What on earth are you doing down there?' she asked.

Emma's expression was rueful. 'Dad has got me rodding drains. Rotten, old job but it needs doing. As you're here, though, I guess I could take a coffee break. Will you join me? There's something I want to run past you.'

'What, here?'

'Yep. I've a flask in the truck. This is thirsty work and I've come prepared.' Without giving Deborah a chance to refuse, she clambered out of the ditch and pulled a large thermos from the passenger seat.

'What's up?' Deborah asked, her hands wrapped around a steaming mug.

'It's Rick.' Emma came straight to the point. 'He's been weird recently.'

'In what way?'

She pulled a face. 'Just ... you know ... not like Rick. Grumpy; out of sorts; weird.'

'Have you asked him if anything is wrong?'

'Yes, of course. He just denies it and says everything's fine. Except it's not. If anything, I'd say he's avoiding me.'

And ...' Deborah grimaced, reluctant to bring up the subject, 'how are things between him and Amelie?'

Emma was unable to conceal a quick smile. 'It's all over between them.'

'Ah well, perhaps that's why he's unhappy?'

'No, he says not. In fact, *he* was the one who finished things. He said he realised they had too many differences to be happy together long-term. If anything, he was relieved, he told me.'

Deborah took a sip of her coffee. It was strong and scalding hot. 'Changing the subject,' she said, her tongue still stinging, 'how are things between you and the other young vet?'

'Max?' Emma grinned. 'Cool. He's a good guy and fun to be with, not like some other people.' Her face darkened. 'Honestly, I don't know why I bother with Rick at all these days. He might as well move out.'

'Do you mean that?' Deborah furtively crossed the fingers of her free hand. Perhaps Emma had moved on from Rick at last.

'No.' The reply was accompanied by a loud huff. 'It's just he's making us both miserable and I don't know what to do about it.'

Deborah reached across to give the girl she now considered a daughter a one-armed hug. 'I'm afraid I can't help you. I suggest you talk to Rick again. It could be something at work that's bothering him or ...' she remembered her own recent scare, 'a medical issue.'

Emma nodded. 'That would make sense.' Her face paled. 'Oh God, I hope there's nothing seriously wrong with him. Poor Rick.'

'It was just a thought,' Deborah hastily reassured her. 'Let's not jump to conclusions. I just meant it could be something we haven't thought of. And obviously, the news of another drowning is bound to affect him ... bring back what happened to his sister.'

'Yes of course. You're right. I should be a kind, patient, caring friend, rather than demanding answers as to why he's being such a misery guts. I'll make him a special dinner tonight, just the two of us, and do my best to cheer him up.'

'That sounds like a plan.' Deborah drained the remainder of her coffee and handed Emma the cup. 'I'll leave you to your ditch. Rather you than me. Thanks for the coffee.'

'No problem. Thanks for listening.'

Deborah moved on, feeling better for the chat, even though Emma had instigated it. Focusing on someone else had helped her get things into perspective. Perhaps Jane Holley had committed suicide, after all. It was entirely plausible, given her mental state when she visited Deborah last week. And, when she had spoken to Wendy, the rector had shared her concerns. Suicide *was* most the likely explanation. Deliberately, she discarded her suspicion that Seb Holley had murdered his wife. It was because she had become too immersed in Martha's story, and too ready to identify the doctor with the villainous Roger Holley, his namesake and lookalike. Honestly! She was no better than the superstitious village crones who thought she was a witch!

As she strode along, she shook her arms, chiding herself for her foolishness. The crunch of frosty ground beneath her feet was reassuringly normal and the sight of a hare scampering across a field made her smile.

Yet the chill in her heart remained, as did the sensation that the past was returning to haunt the present ...

***

The news of Jane Holley's death set Enid pondering. Jane *Holley*! *There* was the Holley connection. She wondered why she had not considered it before. Holley was a reasonably common surname and the fact that Seb came from down south somewhere had thrown her off the scent. But now her nose was well and truly to the ground. Seb was yet another victim of the curse – or rather, his wife was – but he would be unaware of it. It was her responsibility to tell him. He could be the answer to ridding them of the Wickthorpe Witch. A man like him was bound to find a solution.

But how to contrive a meeting? She could not summon him to see her, like she could her son or Philip Holder, especially given what had happened.

The easiest way would be to feign a medical issue and make an appointment to see him, but he was currently off work following his bereavement. More than one customer had complained in the Post Office about the difficulty in getting an appointment with a doctor at present, with both Dr Holley and Dr Singh out of action.

'My poor back is playing up something chronic but I was told no appointments were available until a week Friday!' moaned Naomi Clover, just that morning. 'It's a disgrace! I've a good mind to write to my MP.'

'It is difficult,' Ava had sympathised. 'Have you tried ibuprofen?'

'Doesn't touch it. I need something stronger. Dr Holley knows. He always sorts me out.'

'Well, I don't expect Dr Holley will be back at work anytime soon, poor man,' Ava replied. 'It must have been such a shock for him.'

'Apparently, Jane had been away for the weekend, visiting a sick friend,' Enid chipped in, irritated at having been side-lined from the conversation. 'She was always looking out for others. Did you know that she only returned to Wickthorpe to care for her sick mother? A saint, that's what she was, and now her life has been snuffed out, just like that, by that evil woman.'

'Mother, you should be careful what you say. Deborah Ryecroft could sue you for slander,' Ava warned.

Enid snorted. 'She could try but she wouldn't get very far, especially as I'm telling the truth. I've said from the very beginning, when she crawled back to Greenways Farm after her mother died, that she would bring death to the village and look what's happened since then!'

'You're right, Enid,' Naomi Clover nodded sagely. 'You warned people to stay away from her, but poor Jane Holley didn't listen. Did you know that she went to see Deborah Ryecroft just last week? Brenda saw her going up the drive as she drove past.'

'Brenda? Brenda Wicks?' At Naomi's nod, Enid drew herself up. 'I'd better give her a ring. She didn't say anything about that to me.'

'She'd probably forgotten, or didn't think it was important at the time. Anyway, I'd best be off. With this back, it will take me ages to get home and I've made a pasta bake that needs to go in the oven.'

After she had gone, Enid demanded Ava's assistance in getting through to her sitting room. She immediately phoned Brenda Wicks who confirmed what Naomi had said. Surely Dr Holley would see the connection? But first she had to scheme a way to speak to him.

***

Left alone in the Post Office, Ava was able to return to her own, deliciously private thoughts. It seemed wrong to be so happy when poor Jane Holley was lying cold in the morgue but she couldn't help it. That first 'bite to eat' with Patrick had been a wonderfully extravagant, fine dining experience at *Gastronomique*, an upmarket French restaurant in Newmarket. She was so glad she had worn her best dress, the one Deborah had bought for her. Patrick had showered her with compliments and it had been a magical evening. No talk this time of love, but an intimate conversation between two friends. Her angst about the way Patrick had treated her previously just melted away, somewhere between the entrees and the wickedly indulgent dessert. Since then, she had been out with Patrick twice more. He was courteously attentive, as he always had been – a proper gentleman, like her dad. But he also made her laugh. She felt she had laughed more in the past five days than she had over the entire twenty years they had been apart. Shyly, she admitted that fact to him and had been surprised at his response.

'Me too.' He had taken hold of her hand at that point. 'I feel I can relax and be myself with you, Ava. I've never felt that way with anyone else.'

There was a slightly awkward pause as she floundered for a witty rejoinder but nothing was forthcoming and, gently, she withdrew her hand, even though she wanted to leave it where it was. Yes, she was being cautious. She had been hurt so badly before; she could not let it happen again. The disappointment in Patrick's eyes almost made her replace her hand but she held firm. She had promised herself, when she found herself agreeing to that first date, she would take things slowly and that was just what she was doing.

Tonight, he was taking her to the cinema. She had no idea what film they would be seeing and, quite frankly, she didn't care. Just being with him was enough. A smile played on her lips as she wondered if he would hold her hand. Perhaps she should suggest they watch something scary so she could cuddle up to him. Or she could surprise him and slip her fingers around his … or even along his thigh …

Stop, she told herself sternly. That would be far too forward. She didn't want to give him the wrong impression. And she did not want to lose her heart too readily.

Too late, whispered the voice inside her head.

CHAPTER 26

The Life & Times of Martha Lightbody

'There's been a man about asking after a wench named Lightbody.' The words of their neighbour, Phineas Tench, struck terror into Martha's heart.

'Who?' she asked sharply, looking about her in fear.

Tench shrugged. 'Ne'er seen him afore. Small man, dark hair. Said he'd been along the tip o' Norfolk from King's Lynn. Offered a reward for information.'

'What did you tell him?'

He gave her a kindly smile. 'Nowt. Folks round these parts are suspicious of strangers and look after their own. No need to fret, lass.'

Martha clasped her hands protectively around her swollen belly and took a deep breath, trying to control her mounting panic. 'Thank you, Phineas. You know I appreciate it,' she responded politely and then burst into tears. 'But not everyone may prove as loyal as you,' she wailed. 'And the name Lightbody is becoming known around here. Tis Matthew's name too.'

At her distress, Tench wriggled uncomfortably. As a confirmed bachelor, he was unused to the vagaries of females and unsure how to proceed. 'There is that,' he ruminated. 'But don't ye worry. Forewarned is forearmed. I'm sure your husband is man enough to send the likes of him packing.' Martha shook her head as she wiped her eyes, and her neighbour took the respite offered by her silence to mutter, 'Twill be fine, Martha. Best not to worry. John will know what to do,' before heading back down the path, thanking the Lord for his own blissful state of unweddedness.

'What are we to do?' she cried when her husband appeared later that evening and she had apprised him of the nature of Tench's visit. 'This stranger is one of Holley's spies, I know it is. He mentioned King's Lynn. Ma told me there had been men asking for me there. Oh, John, we are done for!'

He held her close and calmed her trembling body. 'We have no choice. We'll leave tonight. I nearly lost you once, Martha. We'll not chance it again.'

'But the house ... all your work ... Matthew and Calla! How can you bear to leave the life we have here?'

She felt him shrug against her as he stroked her hair. 'None of that is important. Not really. We'll make a new life somewhere else. As long as we're together ... you, me, Josiah, the babe.' His hand moved to caress her stomach.

'Yes, the baby! We must protect her. I care not about myself.'

'Don't be daft! I care about you both. There's no way I'll let them take you again.'

Martha listened to the calm tenor of John's voice and the steady beat of his heart and was soothed. He was right. They would escape, this time where no one would find them. Another terrifying thought struck her. 'This man – the one who spoke to Phineas – he might be, even now, watching the house. He could follow us.'

John frowned. ''Tis possible but unlikely. We don't know yet if he's found out where we are. Phineas said he was asking. Chances are he's already moved on.'

Martha's amber eyes widened with hope. In her terror, she had ignored that possibility. 'If that's the case, we're safe here. We just don't know. Maybe we should wait.' She pulled away from John and paced around their small kitchen, her mind frenzied, before turning back to face him. 'Let's not do anything until we know for sure.'

John watched his wife with worried eyes, trying to keep the fear churning within from showing. She knew nothing of his desperation, when he saw her dragged away, and his horror, upon learning she had been drowned as a witch. The sense of failure and hopelessness at losing the woman he loved beyond life itself, in such circumstances, threatened to destroy his sanity. The need to care for Josiah had been the only thing which kept him going. He knew Martha would never forgive him if he also failed to protect their son. 'I still think it best to leave,' he said at last. 'This stranger will attempt nothing on his own. If he has discovered us, he will send word to Holley. We have time to get away now. Best not leave things to chance.'

'But I don't want to leave!' She flung herself against him once more. 'Oh John, this is all my fault!'

'Don't even think that! You cannot help being the most beautiful woman in the whole of England. Little wonder Holley wanted you for himself.' He slid a finger under her chin and pressed warm lips against hers. 'I love you so much, Martha. I lost you once and I'm not about to let it happen again. We leave tonight.'

'But Josiah is sound asleep and we need to get everything together ... and let Matthew know. We can't leave without saying goodbye. Tis already late. We haven't eaten and we're both exhausted. It would make sense to wait until tomorrow night. You're right – we have time. Please, John.'

He sighed, helpless to refuse her. 'Alright. Tomorrow night. Say nothing to anyone and stay in the house. I will let Matthew know and maybe make a few enquiries myself. See if this stranger is still about.'

'Thank you,' she breathed, hugging him tightly.

He held her to him for just a few more precious seconds before turning away. His capitulation was sensible, he told himself. It was practical to give themselves time to make plans before uprooting once more and venturing into the night.

But he could not eat the food she had prepared and he could not sleep. Uneasiness at that decision wormed through his body, suffocating all attempts to thwart it.

***

It was with some urgency that John steered his family and possessions onto the waiting cart the following evening. Martha had packed only necessary items, upon his strict instruction, but their speed would be hampered by their slow method of travel. Easy for men on horseback to catch them up. He pushed the thought aside as he helped Martha into the corner of the cart he had fashioned into a makeshift bed. He had not told her of the worrying news he had learned that day. When he had visited Phineas Tench, he was most disturbed to learn that the stranger had first appeared in the vicinity more than a week ago, not yesterday, as he and Martha had believed. More than enough time to send word to Holley. Phineas had not seen the man again but others had and informed John that he had sought lodging with a neighbour only two miles away. They thought he was still there. This knowledge sent John dizzy with alarm and he had hastened home immediately, half expecting to find Martha had already been taken. It had been such a relief to find her singing to herself as she loaded their belongings into the wooden boxes Matthew had given them!

Matthew had been an enormous help and had even provided John with a purse full of silver to smooth the path ahead. It was most generous and John had tears in his eyes as he hugged his brother. Who knew when or if they would ever see him, Calla and the children again? Parting with them all brought further tears and John vowed, there and then, that whatever happened, he would do his utmost to repay their kindness.

With his family and possessions safely loaded into the cart, John stepped up onto the seat and picked up the reins. The horse in front of him had also been provided by Matthew, a sturdy chestnut with a calm temperament. The beast stood passively waiting for a command and moved forward obediently at a steady walk once instructed to do so. The silver moon lit their path and the horse proved sure-footed, picking its way carefully along the track.

For the first five minutes, John held his breath, waiting for a yell from someone behind determined to halt their flight. When such did not occur, he relaxed and tried to get comfortable upon his hard bench seat. It was to be a long night ahead for him but he hoped Martha would manage to get some sleep. Josiah was already slumbering soundly, snuggled up against his mother.

When they reached the coastal track by Tench's house, they turned left, heading east and away from the other scattered abodes in Little Horseshoes. More importantly, they were now heading away from the cottage in which the stranger was lodging. John tensed as a horse whinnied in the distance and their own horse, known as Red, snickered in response. 'Hush, boy!' he whispered. 'We're not away from danger yet.'

'How very true!' drawled another man's voice. *Holley!*

Sure enough, a figure on horseback loomed ahead of them, blocking their path. Desperately, John tugged on the reins and looked over his shoulder, searching for escape. There was none. Two more men on horseback stood behind them. John's heart plummeted. He had no weapon with which to defend his family but he would fight to the death to prevent Martha from being taken. Bunching his muscles, he prepared to launch his attack.

At the same time, the man ahead raised his musket ....

CHAPTER 27

The investigation into Jane Holley's death continued. Murder could not be ruled out and DI Beth Honeysuckle was determined to conduct a thorough review. Officers were currently searching the deceased's house, with her husband's permission, and Detective Sergeant Jack Everard had been tasked with tracing Jane's movements prior to her death.

Forensic evidence from the scene showed no sign of a struggle but the pathologist's report revealed Mrs Holley had consumed sufficient alcohol and sertraline, a commonly-prescribed anti-depressant, to be comatose and incapable of resistance. That fact rang alarm bells for Beth. The levels of the substances involved were sufficient to floor a young, healthy male, according to Dr Andrews, the pathologist. Yet they were meant to believe a woman who weighed barely fifty kilograms was able to walk into the water unaided.

There were also sufficient parallels in the manner of the two recent deaths in Wickthorpe, Jane Holley's and Freya Billington's, to re-open the Billington case. Once the news of Jane's death was made public, Mr and Mrs Billington had contacted the Police and Crime Commissioner for Suffolk Constabulary demanding it. And members of the press were having a field day. When they discovered that yet another drowning had taken place in Dark Water Lake, reporters had been out in force, interviewing villagers, inferring all sorts of nonsense, and questioning the competence of the police. Beth had been told, in no uncertain terms, to ensure the investigation ran smoothly. Failure was not an option. A quick result would be even better. Her superiors made it clear they were hoping for proof of suicide. The last thing they wanted was the whiff of a serial killer at large.

Jane had left no note. When they had contacted Davina Locksmith, the friend with whom she was ostensibly staying over the weekend, they discovered that no such plans had ever been made. In fact, Ms Locksmith had not heard from the deceased for over six months – not even the usual Christmas card. She was devastated by the news of Jane's death.

'I should have contacted her sooner,' she sobbed, her husband's arm around her. 'I knew something was wrong but we were busy and I kept putting it off. If only I'd done something, she might still have been alive.'

'How would you describe Mrs Holley's relationship with her husband?' DS Everard asked.

'Seb?' Her face took on an inner glow. 'Such a gorgeous man. Jane was so lucky to have him. I mean ...' She faltered and tears filled her eyes once more, 'They were lucky to have found each other. They always seemed happy, wouldn't you say?' She turned to her husband.

'As far as we could tell, at any rate,' he agreed, 'but who knows what goes on behind closed doors?'

Who, indeed? Beth took a sip of her coffee and yawned. Late nights and early starts were the current norm and she wondered if tiredness was affecting her judgement. She remained convinced there was something off about Seb Holley and had looked back at the notes taken when he was interviewed in the Billington case. Then, he had spent the entire weekend at home with his wife who had confirmed his alibi. This time, he was alone at home all day Sunday. Time of death was estimated at between 4 p.m. and 11 p.m. on the Sunday evening. That gave him the opportunity ... but, as yet, they had discovered no motive. The doctor was loved and revered by all he knew.

So why did he make the hairs on the back of her neck rise? Tiredness. That was probably all it was.

Jack Everard popped his head around her door, carrying a small sheaf of papers. 'A word, Ma'am?'

'I know we're in the office, Jack, but there's no need for the formality. I've told you before!'

'Sorry, Ma'am, I mean, Beth. Just habit. I can't help it. Anyway, we've found emails on Jane Holley's phone.' He sunk his heavy frame onto the chair nearest her desk. 'Between Mrs Holley and ...' he looked down at his notes, 'Stuart Bickerstaff. Looks like they were having an affair. They communicated solely via a separate email account Jane had set up. These emails go back six weeks. The last was on Friday, finalising the arrangements for a weekend together.'

Beth straightened in her chair. 'Stuart Bickerstaff,' she said. 'Do we know anything about him?'

'Not yet. There were no concrete details we could check in the emails either, other than they were going to meet in a lay-by off the A1075 between Thetford and Watton in Norfolk. He seems a bit of a mystery man, this Stuart Bickerstaff. We haven't yet managed to trace his email address. The tech guys are working on it so hopefully we'll have details for him soon.'

'Another mystery man,' Beth mused. 'I wonder if he's the same one who was with Freya Billington in Oxford?'

'Could be.' Jack gave her a grin. 'If so, we've a lot more to go on this time.'

'I hope so but I've a horrible feeling he may prove just as elusive. If he is our man, Stuart Bickerstaff is likely to be an alias. He would hardly be careless enough to name himself in an email.'

Jack's face fell. 'You're right. Let's hope the tech guys find something useful soon.'

She gave him an encouraging smile. 'It's a lead. I'll have a read through the emails before I interview the husband. He's coming in this afternoon for an update. It will be interesting to see how he reacts to this latest development. If he was aware of his wife's affair,' she mused, 'that gives him a motive ...'

***

Seb leaned back in his chair looking composed and relaxed. He wore a tan leather jacket over a cable-knit, charcoal sweater and black jeans. Aged forty-five, he could easily pass for mid-thirties, Beth decided, as she surveyed him, casually sipping coffee, through the viewing glass of the interview room. She turned to her sergeant, waiting beside her.

'Let's go,' she said, her voice terse. This was an informal chat. Seb Holley was not being interviewed under caution. They had no reason to suspect him of anything but Beth found herself unexpectedly on edge. There was just something about this man – this *paragon*, if the majority of those interviewed were to be believed – which did not feel right.

He stood as she entered, a respectful smile on his lips, his hand outstretched. 'Detective Inspector Honeysuckle,' he greeted her politely, 'and Detective Sergeant Everard. Good to see you both.'

'Thank you for coming in, Dr Holley. Please take a seat.' Her smile in return felt forced, her tone clipped and cool. Swiftly, she updated him regarding their investigation, focusing on what they had learned from the forensics team and the pathologist's examination of the body.

He nodded sadly. 'Suicide,' he murmured. 'I knew Jane was severely troubled and I tried to get her to discuss what was on her mind but she seemed to have retreated deep inside herself. Dr Singh had prescribed drugs for her depression and I know she had strongly urged counselling but ...' He shrugged and chewed on his lower lip. A brief silence ensued as he pulled a linen handkerchief from his jacket pocket and blew his nose. 'Excuse me. As I was saying, Jane declined counselling and preferred to talk to Wendy Robinson, the rector of St Mary's Church. Jane was quite religious. That's why I find it so strange she would take her own life ... and she hasn't left a note. I've searched everywhere I could think of, as have your detectives, with my permission of course. I'm prepared to do whatever it takes to find answers.'

'Do you know of anyone who might wish your wife harm, Dr Holley?'

'Please, call me Seb. No.' His brow furrowed in puzzlement. '*Harm?* Are you suggesting someone might have ...?' His voice tailed off, his startlingly blue eyes wide with shock.

'We can't rule anything out at this point, Dr Holley ... Seb.' Beth replied briskly.

'No ... I suppose not.' He thought for a moment and pulled a face. 'I know villagers are talking about Deborah Ryecroft ...'

'Do you know Ms Ryecroft well?'

'No. I've met her on a few occasions and I've seen her professionally as a patient.'

'Do you subscribe to the opinion of some in the village that Ms Ryecroft is a witch?'

A wry smile and a shrug. 'I would not claim to know anything about it. I know there is some deep-seated resentment towards Deborah but it would be wrong of me to offer an opinion.'

Beth nodded thoughtfully. 'So that's not a denial?'

'Nor an agreement,' Seb countered.

'Do you know a man called Stuart Bickerstaff?' Beth asked, changing the subject.

'No. Should I?'

'We found emails between Stuart Bickerstaff and your wife on her phone. For these emails, she used a different email address.'

'Really?' A look of puzzlement. 'What kind of emails?'

Beth hesitated before responding. 'Were you aware of your wife's affair, Dr Holley?'

'Affair? Don't be ridiculous. Jane wasn't having an affair. I would have known.' He paused, shaking his head, mulling it over. 'Was *that* where she was last weekend? I already know she wasn't with Davina because she told me. She and her husband called round after they had heard the news. It was a bit of a shock at the time. Then, I suspected Jane must have holed up in a hotel somewhere, planning what she was going to do. I didn't think for one minute ... no, I still don't believe it. We were happily married for twenty-three years. She had no reason to ...'

'I'm sorry this is difficult, Seb.' Beth tried and failed to inject some warmth into her voice. 'Take your time.'

'Do you have proof?' he asked. 'Do you know for a fact that she *was* having an affair?'

'No. We just have the emails. They were of an intimate nature which would suggest the two were lovers. As yet, we've been unable to trace Mr Bickerstaff. We wondered if you would be able to help with that?'

'Obviously not.' He exhaled an angry sigh. 'Do you think this man might have been involved in her death?'

'We are keeping an open mind about that. We will know more once we've spoken to him.'

Seb thought for a moment. 'There was talk of a mystery man being involved in Freya Billington's death ...' His eyes widened. 'Do you think this could be the same man?'

'I'm afraid we cannot as yet answer that question. But we will.' Beth stood. 'Thank you again for your time. We will keep you informed of any developments.'

Seb grimaced. 'Interview terminated, I guess you would say.' He rose and made a point of shaking the hands of both detectives. 'Drop the bomb and observe the fallout.'

'We are not in the explosives business, Dr Holley,' Beth replied in a tight voice. 'We're just trying to find out what happened to your wife.'

'And everyone's a suspect until proven otherwise, especially the husband, isn't that right, Inspector?' When there was no response, he sighed and walked to the door, before spinning on his heel and facing them both, his indignant face proclaiming his innocence. 'I will tell you both this. I loved my wife. Whatever she has done, I will always love her. And I did *not* kill her.'

His departure left Beth feeling drained. Gathering up her papers, she too headed for the door.

'Wait up,' Jack called. 'What did you think? I would have said the affair came as a complete shock. How about you?'

She shrugged. 'Maybe, but methinks he doth protest too much.'

CHAPTER 28

The Life & Times of Martha Lightbody

Martha gasped as the man's face was revealed by the moonlight. 'Tis him ... Roger Holley!' she exclaimed. Furtively, she lifted the blanket higher to conceal her sleeping son.

'The very same.' The man's smug satisfaction resonated through the cool night air. He urged his horse a step closer and waved the musket towards John. 'Release the reins, place your hands above your head where I can see them and step down from your perch. Packer!' he called to one of his men. 'Take a hold of this horse. We don't want anyone having ideas of escape.'

John did not obey the instruction. Instead, he held Holley's arrogant stare with a glare of his own and edged closer to him, ready to fling himself at the mounted man and disarm him. Unfortunately, Holley deciphered his intent and countered by aiming his musket at Martha's head. 'Try anything and I shoot,' he snarled.

'Stop!' Martha's voice rang out in the darkness. 'Leave my husband be. This is nothing to do with him. I will come with you.'

'Don't move,' Holley commanded as she rose, a ghostly figure in her grey cloak. 'Stay where you are. I give the orders.'

'No.' Martha took a step forward. 'This is between you and me. Or are you afraid I'll put a spell on you?' Her voice taunted him.

'I said, stay still. Move again and I'll fire.' Holley urged his horse close enough to the cart to reach out a gloved hand, intending to push Martha to the floor.

At the same time, John launched himself from his seat. He had hoped to grab Holley but misjudged the distance, cannoning instead into the horse's flanks and tumbling to the ground. Martha screamed. The horse reared up, hooves flailing. Holley tried desperately to control his mount and stay in the saddle but failed on both counts. The horse reared a second time, even more violently. Holley fell hard, hitting his head upon a rock and, simultaneously, his musket fired. A blossom of blood quickly spread across the chest of Abel Packer and he too slid from his horse. The riderless mare galloped away into the night and Martha had to fling herself forward to catch the reins of their carthorse, Red, to prevent it from following and trampling the prone figure of her husband. The remaining horseman took one shocked look at the dead bodies of his master and accomplice, and fled in the opposite direction, muttering that the witch's curse had indeed come true.

'John?' Having secured Red's reins, Martha jumped from the cart to assist her husband. His groans told her he was at least alive and, much to her relief, he staggered to his feet.

'What happened?' he asked groggily, gazing in disbelief at the two dead men.

'Fortune smiled 'pon us,' she answered helping him onto the cart. 'Or God was watching over us. One of the two. But we must hasten away from here. Other men will question what has occurred and will be quick to blame a woman who has survived a witch's trial by drowning.'

'You are right, my love.' John's face was pale and anxious. 'But I fear my head is not recovered. I feel most dizzy.'

Martha took one look at the sheen of sweat glistening upon her husband's forehead and the glazed nature of his eyes and urged him to lie in the cart. 'You must rest and recover. You fell badly and tis a miracle you were not slain,' she said. 'I will drive us. We need to get as far away from here as we can before the bodies are discovered.'

John mumbled a protest but his wife had already taken up the position and was clicking at Red to break into an uncomfortable trot. Clouds had parted to leave a starlit sky, illuminated by the full moon. Given such conditions, they could make good progress.

They travelled such for the next twelve hours until both Red and Martha were near collapse with exhaustion. Again, Fate was on their side, providing them with the cover of woodland, plentiful grass for Red and a freshwater stream. There they rested, eating some of the supplies Calla had packed for them, before moving onwards once more. The further they travelled, the safer Martha felt, but she knew they could afford to take nothing for granted.

When they had been on the move for more than a week, keeping themselves to themselves and sleeping in the cart in places of concealment, they agreed it should be safe to approach a village and restock. By this time, they had exhausted their supplies of food and were drooping with fatigue. Fortunately, John was, by now, recovered from his fall and he, Martha and little Josiah sat side by side as they trundled towards a scattered collection of cottages.

'Good day to you folks.' A squat, middle-aged man ceased his task loading bundles of rushes onto a cart to hail them as they passed.

'Good day. Whoa, boy.' John smiled a greeting and tugged on the reins to halt alongside. 'We are looking to replenish our food supplies. Would you be so kind as to tell us where best we might enquire?'

The man scratched his chin. 'Well now, that would depend ... are you bartering or paying with coin? I know Saul Makepeace be looking for labour. He farms down by the river. Poor chap broke his leg a few weeks back and is struggling to cut his wheat. He'd be most grateful of the help, I'm sure.'

John nodded. 'We're not planning on settling but some work would be welcome. It would give my family a chance to rest a while. They are weary of travelling.'

Having obtained further directions, they made their way to Saul Makepeace's house. His wife, a small, harried-looking woman holding a baby in her arms, pointed them towards a strip of land yonder, where a man was fighting a losing battle, wielding a scythe whilst leaning heavily on a crutch. John left Martha and Josiah in the cart whilst he went to talk to him.

Saul Makepeace was a young man worn down by his current circumstances. His holding of land, which he rented from the local manor, was small, merely ten acres, and he had a herd of dairy cows, grazing in a meadow by the river. He had a wife and three young children to support and no labourers to assist him.

'Folk in the village have helped out where they could,' he explained, 'but they have their own work and tis a busy time of year. I cannot afford to pay you but you are welcome to stay with us and share our food. In return for your help, when you leave, you can take as much bread and cheese as you wish, and any other supplies you need.'

One look at Saul's anxious face was enough to persuade John. The man was in sore need of aid and he could not turn away. With a cheery grin, he agreed to the man's terms and together they walked back to the house where Martha was now chatting in the kitchen. Josiah played at her feet with an older girl. Saul explained the situation and they all shook hands.

'What be your names?' asked Saul as his wife, who was called Elizabeth, ladled stew into bowls.

'Ruth.' Martha jumped in before her husband could speak. 'Ruth Littlebody and my husband is John.' She ignored her spouse's questioning look.

'Littlebody ...' mused Saul. 'There was a Herbert Littlebody lived here a few years back. Had a fall, leg got infected and died. Sad.' He rubbed his own splinted leg thoughtfully. 'Any relation?'

'My father had a cousin Herbert,' Martha improvised. 'I'm not sure but it could have been the same man.'

'Well, you're most welcome, to be sure. Maybe you'll settle in these parts?'

'Maybe ...'

***

And that, dear Reader, is exactly what happened and where the story ends.

Martha and John settled happily in Tocklewood, near the east Suffolk coast, for such was the village where Saul and Elizabeth Makepeace made them welcome. There they were known, for the rest of their lives, as John and Ruth Littlebody. Their five children and descendants thereafter also bore the Littlebody name.

After many years, Martha wrote to Ruth Fletcher, enquiring as to life in Wickthorpe, and was most dismayed to learn that the curse had become legendary. There had been more drownings in the lake known as Dark Water and all had been blamed upon Martha Lightbody, the witch who had blighted the village. In the light of this information, Martha never dared return to Wickthorpe to clear her name, but instead wrote her story in a diary, hoping that one day her reputation would be restored.

Sadly, this did not happen in her lifetime, nor in the years since. Hence, I have written this tome so the truth will be told and trusting that you, dear Reader, will ensure justice is done.

May the Lord smile upon your endeavours, as I hope He will also favour mine.

CHAPTER 29

Deborah set the book aside. So that was how the story ended. She felt – well, she wasn't sure how she felt exactly. Relieved, of course. Martha was reunited with her husband and son, and escaped the nefarious intentions of Roger Holley who had met with his comeuppance. But she also felt slightly cheated. The simple epilogue, glossing over the remainder of Martha's life, seemed an anticlimax. It all seemed so easy yet it could not have been. She could not shake off the sense that something was missing. It was like staring at a picture, knowing something was wrong with it, but being unable to pinpoint the fault.

She pushed back the duvet and headed for the shower. Outside, mist hung like a shroud over the fields and she paused at the window to absorb the scene. Tiny shafts of light were beginning to filter through the dense greyness, allowing flickering glimpses of countryside. Beautiful, but elusive.

Deborah's mind turned inwards once more. She would like to believe John Littlebody's account of Martha's life was true, but still she wondered. Was it the whole story? Martha's curse should have ended with the deaths of Roger Holley and Abel Packer, and yet, almost four hundred years later, it lived on. Villagers now claimed *she* was the Wickthorpe Witch. And women were dying, drowning in Dark Water Lake, the site of Martha's barbaric trial. Meanwhile, another Holley, physically the likeness of Roger, loomed at the periphery of the story, his own wife one of the victims. It felt as though the threads of fate were being pulled inexorably together by some unknown weaver.

Invigorating jets of hot water did little to soothe her troubled mind. It had been a strange week. The shock of Jane Holley's death; her visit to the hospital where she had thankfully been given the all-clear; her interview by the police. The latter had been conducted sympathetically at Greenways Farm by DI Honeysuckle and DS Everard, for which Deborah was thankful, but she was left in no doubt that some very serious allegations had been made against her.

The evidence: she had a motive. As a sixteen-year-old accused of the drowning of Ayesha Khan, she had claimed fault lay with Jane and her friend Melissa Shipman, but had not been believed. And Jane and Melissa were responsible for the subsequent hate campaign against her. Revenge was a plausible motivation. Corroborating evidence also conspired against her, albeit some of it based upon old superstition. Deborah had seen the victim in the week prior to her death; she had no alibi for the time in which the drowning happened; two suspicious deaths had occurred since her return to the village; she was known as the Wickthorpe Witch, allegedly wreaking vengeance under the mantra of Martha Lightbody's curse.

Deborah answered the questions as best she could. DI Honeysuckle was especially interested in Jane's unexpected visit to Greenways Farm. Deborah carefully recounted Jane's admission of guilt regarding Ayesha Khan's drowning, adding that this could be verified by Wendy Robinson, in whom Jane had also confided. The officer seemed satisfied with her responses. The interview was short and to the point.

As Honeysuckle and her colleague prepared to leave, Deborah asked, 'Some people are saying Jane took her own life. Is that a possibility?'

'I'm afraid we are unable to share any details of our investigation at this time.'

A stock response. She tried again. 'If she was murdered, have you considered her husband as a possible suspect?' As soon as the words were out, Deborah regretted them. What had possessed her? She could not explain her suspicion without losing all credibility.

Beth raised her eyebrows, clearly taken aback. 'Why do you say that?'

Deborah pulled a face. 'You would think me mad if I told you. Let's just say, it's a feeling I have I can't shake off. And Jane did warn me away from her husband for my own safety.'

'How so?'

Deborah outlined that part of the conversation in more detail.

'Don't you think she was just doing what many wives would do, warning another woman off her territory?'

'It didn't come across like that. I don't think she cared much for her husband. Rather, she seemed fearful of him. I know Jane wasn't herself but her attitude towards him seemed odd. Previously, I had assumed they were a happily married couple.' She shrugged. 'As I said, though, it's just a feeling.'

Beth nodded. 'You can rest assured we are pursuing every avenue, Ms Ryecroft. Please remain in the area as we may have further questions. Thank you for your time.'

Since then, Deborah had wondered how seriously the detectives were considering her as a suspect. She had been half expecting their return to arrest her but, much to her relief, had heard nothing more.

Wrapped in a towel, she padded through to her bedroom. *The Life & Times of Martha Lightbody* lay on the bed where she had left it. Reading it had left her with some answers but more questions. How much of it was true? Could details in John Littlebody's account be checked to confirm their veracity? And, most importantly, could she really be a descendant of Martha Lightbody?

She needed help, and she knew exactly whom to ask.

***

There were no biscuits or cakes in the house! How mortifying!

Deborah Ryecroft had turned up unexpectedly and Honoraria had *nothing* to offer her with her coffee. She fussed about her small kitchen, arranging her best china cups on a tray and pouring milk into a matching jug. *Milk, no cream!* If only she had known Deborah was visiting, she would have been prepared.

'Please don't go to any trouble on my account,' Deborah called through from the sitting room where she had been ushered.

'No trouble at all,' Honoraria called back gaily. She surveyed the tray with a sigh. It would have to do. Her shortcomings as a hostess would be sadly exposed but there was nothing for it. Thank heavens, at least, she had some decent coffee. Imagine having to serve Deborah Ryecroft a cup of the instant variety!

'This is really kind of you,' Deborah smiled as Honoraria set down the tray and carefully poured two cups of coffee from a silver cafetiere.

'Milk?'

'No thank you.'

'Please help yourself to sugar.' Honoraria poured a generous dollop of milk into her own cup and perched on her sofa, ready to spring into action should her guest require anything else.

'I'm so sorry to turn up like this, Honoraria, but I have something I wanted to share with you.'

'Oh, is it what I think it is?' Honoraria watched agog as Deborah reached for her bag and withdrew a book. It looked old. She licked her lips and waited, although she was aching to get her hands on it.

'I told you after the last History Society meeting I had access to information about Martha Lightbody. I think I later told you it was a book.' Honoraria nodded. 'This book was a bequest to me from Mabel Littlebody. It was written by someone called John Littlebody in 1845 and, allegedly, is an accurate account of what happened to Martha.'

'Oh, my goodness!' Honoraria sucked in a shocked breath. 'That's incredible! I have so many questions, I don't know where to start.'

Deborah smiled. 'I can imagine. It tells her story – her arrival at Wickthorpe and what happened after that.'

Honoraria's fingers twitched. 'May I ...?'

'Of course. I'll leave the book with you. I'd like you to read it and let me know what you think. Most of all, I would really appreciate it if, using your expertise and knowledge, you would be able to check the information in the book. It was written two hundred years after Martha was accused of witchcraft and, although the author claims many of the details are true, that they come from a diary written by Martha and some letters, those sources are sadly lost.'

'This is quite incredible!' Honoraria breathed. 'I would be honoured to read it and to check the information within. How very exciting!' Her face glowed with anticipation. 'Was there anything specific you doubted, or anywhere particular you would like me to start? Oh dear, I'm jumping ahead of myself! I need to read the book first.'

'No, they are good questions, and there *is* something I would particularly like to know ...'

As Deborah's hesitated, Honoraria leant forward in eager readiness to receive what she suspected might be a confidence. 'Of course. You can rely upon my utmost discretion.'

'Thank you. It's a delicate situation because of my circumstances in the village,' Deborah smiled, 'but I know I can trust you. The reason I received this bequest from Mabel Littlebody was because she and I were related. I have no idea if anyone else in the village knows. I only found out after I returned to Wickthorpe. Mabel's father and my paternal grandmother were siblings. Apparently, there was a falling-out and the families became estranged. When I was a child, I used to visit Mabel secretly, as my father had forbidden it, and she never breathed a word about our relationship through deference to my father's wishes. So, what I'm coming to is this ... I know I'm descended from the *Littlebody* family but does that make me a direct descendant of Martha Lightbody? Once you have read the book, you'll see why I think it could be possible.' Her face became serious. 'I'm sure you appreciate why that information could prove ... problematic?'

Honoraria's blue eyes sparkled but she tried to look suitably solemn. 'Of course, of course.' Her red curls bounced in vigorous agreement. 'I'll read the book straight away. I can't wait.' At last, Deborah handed it over, and she clutched it with due reverence upon her lap, her thumb stroking the title indented in its leather-clad spine. Now, she just needed Deborah to leave so she could get on with it.

Her guest reached, finally, for her cup and sipped at the coffee. A silence ensued as Honoraria stared, mesmerised, at the book in her hands, guessing at the secrets she was about to uncover. *Martha must have survived! Or maybe she didn't; Deborah hadn't said. And could Deborah really be Martha's descendant? Was the village legend true after all?*

With a start, she looked up to find Deborah watching her with an amused smile. 'Er, will you and Tom be coming to the History Society meeting on Wednesday?' she asked in a fluster. 'You remember we have a speaker coming to the Institute to give a talk on the history of farming in East Anglia. I'm sure it will be right up Tom's street.'

'I'm sure it would but, given the current circumstances, and with the ongoing police investigation regarding Jane Holley's death, I'm keeping a low profile in the village. I'm sure you understand.' Deborah's tone was full of regret.

Honoraria gave what she hoped was a sympathetic sigh. 'That's a shame, but yes, I understand.'

Deborah set the dainty cup back on its saucer and stood. 'Thank you so much, Honoraria. I really appreciate your help. And thank you also for the delicious coffee.'

'Not at all,' Honoraria replied graciously. 'I'm so happy you came to me. Let me show you out.'

As Deborah negotiated her way into her coat – beautifully soft cashmere, Honoraria noticed, as she handed it over – another question occurred.

'Oh, I've just had a thought. I wonder if, when I've read the book, you would consider allowing me to share its contents with Marcus Monk? You remember he came to the meeting in December? He lives in Little Horseshoes and found evidence of Lightbody burials in the parish registers. We've since done further research together and I would value his input. I'm sure I can vouch for his discretion.'

Deborah thought for a moment. 'Yes, I do remember him. He was very impressive and had discovered a lot of information. In fact, some of the names he mentioned are in the book so yes, by all means. I'm sure he will be a great help.'

Honoraria almost broke into a dance of delight. 'Excellent,' she beamed.

Closing the door behind her guest, she shot back to her living room, desperate to make a start. She could not decide which thrilled her the most – the thought of finding out what really happened to Martha Lightbody, or the pulsating prospect of seeing Marcus Monk again.

***

Enid Green leaned back in her favourite chair in the small sitting room and deliberated upon the best way to handle things. Blackmailing her son into helping her had been a mistake, she realised. It had set him against her when she needed him as an ally. Time to use a little persuasive guile.

Andrew currently sat opposite, tapping his toe with impatience, and she summoned up her fondest smile 'Has Ava offered you some tea or coffee?' she asked.

'Just get to the point, Mother. I'm in a hurry.' Andrew checked his wrist to enhance his comment.

Enid sighed. 'You're still cross with me. I can't say I blame you. I was wrong to try to coerce you into finding dirt on Deborah Ryecroft.'

Andrew's sapphire eyes widened. 'You were *wrong*? Good grief, Mother, that's a first! Are you feeling well?' Sarcasm dripped from his words.

She dredged up all the contrition she could muster. 'Yes, I was wrong. It doesn't happen very often.' He smiled at that. 'But I should not have threatened to make public what I knew about you. It was an empty threat. I would never do anything to harm you, you know that. And I was very thankful you went to so much trouble to discover what you could about the Ryecroft woman. Did you have a chance to look at those figures, by the way.'

'I did. I'm not an accountant but everything looked above board.' He shrugged. 'Obviously, that doesn't mean there's nothing shady going on. Someone like her would have the resources to be able to hide anything suspicious. You would need to dig much deeper and that would cost money.'

She nodded. 'That's what I expected and I don't think the answer lies there, although I really appreciate your efforts so far. Obviously, with Jane Holley's murder, things have moved beyond that.'

'Murder? I thought it looked like a suicide?'

'Trust me. I know it was murder.' Enid pulled out her copy of John Littlebody's book from its hiding place behind her cushion. 'You remember that book of your grandfather's? I've found it! I've been through it and now I'd like you to read it too. You recall I told you about it last time you visited?' He nodded. 'Well, it *was* in amongst your grandfather's things, in one of those boxes I asked you to get out of the loft. I remember my father wanted me to read it but, I'm ashamed to say, when I was younger, I didn't realise its importance. It was only after recent events that my father's words came back to me. I remembered how he talked about the danger to our family and how the book proved it.' She gestured to Andrew to take it from her. 'It's an account of how it all started – the curse … and the feud between the Lightbodys and the Holleys.'

Andrew leant forward to grasp it, puzzlement creasing his brow. 'I know about the curse but … a feud? Lightbodys and Holleys? What do you mean, Mother?'

'The whole thing started between Martha Lightbody and a man called Roger Holley. You will see when you read the book. But a word of warning. It's written by someone on the witch's side so it's full of lies.'

Andrew frowned. 'In that case, there doesn't seem much point reading it!'

'No, it's important, Andrew. I'm sure you will be able to see beyond the lies. The book will tell you how it all begun and why it's vital, for our family's sake, that this woman be stopped.'

'Who? Deborah Ryecroft? I'm confused.' Andrew thought for a moment and then said slowly, 'Are you saying that *we* are involved in all of this? That *we* are in danger?'

'That's *exactly* what I'm saying. You remember that I was a Holley before I married. Because of what happened to Roger Holley, our family has been blighted by that curse throughout the centuries.'

'Ah yes, I'd forgotten you were a Holley. That makes a bit more sense … but who is Roger Holley, and what about Deborah Ryecroft? How does she fit into all of this?'

'Roger Holley was our ancestor and the person who suffered most from the curse. He was just trying to save the innocent people of Wickthorpe from Martha Lightbody's witchcraft after she tried to seduce him and he rejected her advances. Of course, that is not what it says in the book but, believe me, I'm sure that's what happened. As for Deborah Ryecroft …' Enid gave a huff of disgust. '*She* is a Littlebody, a descendant of John Littlebody who wrote the book … about *his* ancestor, Martha Lightbody. That makes *Ryecroft* a direct descendant of the witch.' She sat back in triumph.

Andrew stared at the book in his hands and shook his head. 'All that you've just said … I have to tell you Mother, I can't say I believe any of it. This whole Wickthorpe Witch business is a load of nonsense, in my humble opinion.'

Enid bit back her annoyance and bestowed a sad smile on her son. 'I agree it sounds a little far-fetched but I have more proof. Trust me when I say that our family has suffered over the years because of the curse. It is time for the Holleys to finish the feud, and the curse, once and for all. But ... no matter if you don't believe me. Just read the book, that's all I ask, and then warn Dr Holley. Persuade him to read it too. We need to work together as a team. Only together will we be strong enough to break the curse.'

'Dr Holley?' Andrew's mouth dropped open. 'Are you saying he's involved too? Are we somehow related?'

'We must be. I didn't realise it until his wife was killed. Then I knew. It's too much of a coincidence otherwise. He *has* to be a part of this. And you and the doctor look so similar ... you could almost be brothers.'

Andrew emitted a low whistle. 'Wow, you're expecting a lot, Mother, but you *have* intrigued me. I will read the book.'

'Thank you.' Enid's shoulders sagged with relief. 'One more thing, my dear ... back to Deborah Ryecroft. I assume you employed someone to find that information about her?'

He flushed. 'Yes. I was busy so ...'

'Would you be kind enough to send him my way? I have a little job for him regarding a certain American who has moved into the village.'

'Patrick Velaman? He was the one who dumped Ava after he went back to America, wasn't he? I heard he had moved into Mabel Littlebody's bungalow ... *Littlebody*. Was old *Mabel* involved too?'

'Read the book first. Then it will be easier to explain the rest.'

'Curiouser and curiouser ... and Patrick Velaman? Does Ava know he's back?'

Enid pursed her thin lips. 'Your sister is a fool. It falls to me once again to point out the error of her ways.'

Andrew grinned. 'I'll take that as a yes. Has Ava taken up with him again?' At Enid's cold silence, he chuckled. 'Oh dear. Poor Ava.'

'Exactly. I have to protect her.'

Andrew raised his eyebrows at that but thought it best to stay quiet on the subject. He was all too aware his mother's concern stemmed from pure self-interest. Perhaps, now he had agreed to do as she asked and put her in a genial mood, it would be a good time to discover what she claimed to know about him. 'Just one thing before I go,' he began. 'When you were blackmailing me before, what *did* you think you knew about me? I've been wondering.'

'Blackmail is too strong a ...'

'Let's not argue semantics, Mother.'

Enid snorted and folded her arms. 'Alright, if you must know ...' Another long-suffering sigh as she wondered how best to phrase it to cause the least offence. Now she had Andrew back on track, it wouldn't do to upset him. 'You've always been a good-looking boy,' she began, 'and I know the girls have always flocked around you.'

He grinned. 'True enough.'

'I don't blame you at all. You're a red-blooded male and your wife is ... well, let's just say that I know you've sometimes found it hard to resist the ladies.'

His heart lightened at her answer. A promising start. 'That was a while ago, Mother. You must have heard from Julie that I'm a changed man.'

'Mm ...' She shot him a disbelieving look. 'A leopard never changes its spots and you never could resist a pretty face.'

He pretended to look confused. 'You'll have to explain, Mother. I don't know what you're talking about.'

'I'm talking specifically about a pretty, *young* girl.' His chest constricted with horror. *Bloody hell! She did know.* Still, he maintained poker face and waited. Silence stretched between them, until Enid huffed once more. 'Do I have to spell it out? I *know*, Andrew. I know *you* were the mystery man everyone was gossiping about. I'm talking about *Freya Billington*.'

'Freya Billington?' He managed to find his voice.

'Yes, but I don't believe you killed her. The two of you had an affair, she got pregnant – stupid girl – and wanted you to leave Julie. You said no, of course, and she committed suicide. As I said, I don't blame you. And thank goodness you were sensible enough to cover your tracks. You could be in a lot of trouble if anyone else discovered your identity.'

'I see.' Andrew nodded slowly. He stood, his fingers gripping the green-covered book, and walked across to Enid. A sly smirk spread across his face, although, inside, his heart still hammered against his ribs. 'I have to tell you, Mother,' he said, 'you couldn't be more wrong.'

CHAPTER 30

It had been a frustrating week for DI Beth Honeysuckle. The forensic evidence regarding Jane Holley's death had been inconclusive. Suicide remained the most likely verdict but the possibility of murder remained. Beth had hoped for a single, irrefutable piece of information which would steer them one way or the other. There was none.

Meanwhile, her team had focused on the victim. Interviews with those who knew her suggested she was deeply troubled, and had been for the past six months – since Freya Billington's death. Her medical records revealed she had been prescribed anti-depressants since August last year. All interviewees had expressed their concern at Jane's physical deterioration prior to her death. Her sons claimed to have been shocked when they saw her at Christmas. Both felt she was severely anxious but their efforts to find the cause had proved unsuccessful. Jane did not want to talk about whatever was worrying her. Almost all of those asked, including her sons, were adamant that Jane shared a loving and supportive relationship with her husband. However, both Wendy Robinson and Deborah Ryecroft, who had been party to the victim's most recent confidences, suggested all was not well between the couple. When interviewed, Reverend Robinson admitted she had urged Jane to speak to her husband but that Jane had expressed reluctance to do so. Deborah Ryecroft had stated the opinion that Jane was fearful of Seb, and had even urged them to look at him as a potential suspect. However, when challenged for reasons for her suspicion, she had shrugged it off as just 'a feeling' she had. And Ms Ryecroft herself could not be ruled out as a suspect. She had no alibi for the time of death and her history with Jane Holley gave her a motive. Meanwhile, some villagers in Wickthorpe were baying for Ms Ryecroft's blood, just as they had after Freya Billington's death. They claimed she was a witch, continuing the ancient curse which had supposedly blighted Wickthorpe's past. While Beth remained sceptical, it was hard to ignore the fact that two deaths had occurred since Deborah's return to the village.

There was a further link between the Billington and Holley drownings; both women had worked together in the pharmacy at Wickthorpe's Health Centre. Wary of such a coincidence, Beth had reviewed the Billington case and efforts had been redoubled to discover the identity of Freya's 'mystery man' – the possible father of her unborn child. So far, nothing further had come to light. She had interviewed a private investigator, Liam Hatton, whom the Billingtons had employed to find answers for their daughter's death. It appeared they had wasted their money. Mr Hatton's exertions in the case had been minimal, to say the least, and she had dismissed him with a flea in his ear.

Following her own hunch about Seb Holley, and in the absence of any other leads, Beth had delegated resources towards digging into his past, finding out what they could about the relationship between the couple. Yesterday, there had been a small breakthrough. Whilst pursuing inquiries in Surrey, in Jacob's Well, where the Holleys had lived prior to settling in Wickthorpe, they made a discovery. In 2014, an accusation had been made against Dr Holley by the parents of an eighteen-year-old girl, one of his patients. They alleged Dr Holley had conducted an inappropriate relationship with their daughter. On one occasion, she had visited Dr Holley's home, a secluded house on the outskirts of the village. Seb claimed she had turned up unexpectedly, distraught and needing advice about a personal matter. He had permitted her entry, safe in the knowledge his wife was also at home and fearing the girl was suicidal. His account suggested that, once inside, the girl had 'thrown herself at him.' He described her as a 'fantasist' who, much to his dismay, had developed an unrequited obsession over him. With Jane's help, he had tried to let her down gently and, when she was calm and appeared stable, sent her home. Concerned about a possible breach of medical ethics, he had immediately contacted a colleague from the surgery where he worked, to tell him what had happened. The whole incident had been managed professionally and with sensitivity, Holley claimed, and his wife had corroborated his account.

The girl's story was very different. She insisted that she and Seb were 'in love' and had enjoyed a sexual relationship for the past month. On that occasion, she had thought to 'surprise' him at home, knowing his wife was away. He had been angry and told her it was over between them, which was why she had been so upset and, eventually, admitted everything to her parents. It was a case of her word against the combined weight of the Holleys' account. After a short investigation, the matter had been dropped and the Holleys had moved away soon after, to Wickthorpe, so Jane could look after her ailing mother.

The discovery of the episode had deepened Beth's distrust of the esteemed doctor. His reputation appeared untarnished but this incident in his past, concerning a teenage girl, sounded alarm bells. The case was dismissed with reasonable speed because of Jane Holley's adamance that the girl was lying. Personally though, Beth felt investigating officers had done little to disprove this claim. What if Jane had been lying and the girl's statement had been accurate? It then cast Seb in the role of a sexual predator. Could he also have been having an affair with Freya Billington? Was Seb their mystery man? Looking back through her notes, Beth noted he was 'at home with his wife' for the entire weekend prior to the discovery of Freya's body. Again, Jane Holley was staunch in her support of Seb's account. But if she had lied before, she may have lied again. A lot of 'ifs' and 'buts' – but no hard evidence; just pure supposition. And the cold fact remained that Seb's DNA, checked as part of the Billington investigation, did not match that of Freya's unborn child.

Meanwhile, Beth was under increasing pressure to wrap up the Holley case. Without clear indication of murder, she was told, it was a waste of police resources to continue the investigation. Most likely, Jane Holley had taken her own life whilst the balance of her mind was disturbed. Beth had argued against this but time was running out. They needed to find something soon, or the decision would be taken out of her hands.

***

Lainey Lewis had returned to her desk at Ryecroft Industries plc and Deborah was able to draw a breath. It had been a hectic month but work had also provided a welcome distraction from events at home. With less to occupy her mind, her distress at Jane Holley's death and concern for her own safety returned. Night terrors – the legacy of her near-drowning experience – were back with a vengeance. During the day, she kept doors and windows locked whilst she was in the house, and used security cameras to check out visitors in advance of answering her doorbell. Resolutely, she continued with walks whenever she could but took varied routes across the countryside to avoid the notice of anyone wishing her harm.

The day had dawned clear but cold and, wrapped up in coat, hat, boots and gloves, she skirted along one of Tom's fields, picking her way over the uneven ground. The icy wind stung her cheeks and she pulled her scarf a little higher to protect her face.

As the rear of Tom's house came into view, Deborah pulled up short. Two strange men were making their way towards the back entrance of the farmhouse. The glare from the low winter sun made it difficult to see and she raised a gloved hand to shield her eyes. As she watched, the smaller of the men opened the door, which must have been unlocked, and stepped inside, closely followed by the second man.

She willed herself not to panic. There was surely a simple explanation, a reason for two men to be there. Plumbers, perhaps, or electricians? But Tom would have mentioned if he was having some work done, and the men were not dressed like workmen.

And there was no sign of Emma. Deborah's heart drummed against her ribs as she remembered Emma was alone at the farm. Tom was at a meeting that morning. Why would two unknown men let themselves in like that unless they were up to no good? There was definitely something furtive about the smaller one, she decided. He had looked around before he stepped into the house.

Where was Emma? She would be somewhere in the farmyard, or could be inside, having a coffee or doing some paperwork in the office. Deborah fumbled for her phone and, with trembling fingers, located Emma's name in her contacts. *Please pick up!*

Emma answered on the fourth ring. 'Hi Debs, what's up?'

'Where are you?'

'Just in the workshop. Why?'

'I don't want to alarm you, but two men have just gone into your house. I'm round the back and I saw them.' She tried to keep her voice calm.

'Are you sure it wasn't Rick, or Max?'

'Yes. I've never seen either of these men before.'

'Oh hell, I'd better go and investigate.'

'Don't you dare!' Deborah's panic shot into overdrive. 'I'm ringing the police.'

'Hold fire. Just wait a sec, Debs. The men might have a perfectly good reason for being there. I need to check it out.'

'Please don't. It could be dangerous. Two women have died recently in suspicious circumstances. There could be a killer on the loose.' Deborah started walking again, much faster this time, anxious to reach the cut-through which would bring her out around the other side of the Oldridge farm. 'Wait for me. Hold on, one of the men has come out again. Oh heck, it looks like he's heading your way.' She broke into a stumbling run. 'Stay on the line. I'm coming.'

Silence. The man disappeared from view. Then she heard a male voice calling, 'Dad? Emma?'

'Lewis?' A delighted laugh. 'You idiot! You scared me silly. Debs, are you still there?' Emma was chuckling. 'No need to worry – it's just my brother, over from Australia, doing his best to give me a heart attack. Come round and meet him.'

The line went dead and Deborah pocketed her phone with a relieved smile. *Lewis!* Tom would be so pleased to see him. But who was the second man? She would find out soon enough.

Both men were sitting in the kitchen when she arrived. Emma was making coffee, chattering excitedly. 'You must be exhausted after such a long journey. How long are you staying? Have you seen Mum yet? Did she know you were coming?'

'Yes, to your last question, but I haven't seen her yet. She's a bit peeved with me as she was meant to be coming over to us. Our trip back here instead has meant she's had to postpone her holiday for a bit. Hi, you must be Debs.'

Lewis gave her a casual wave of the hand. 'Good to meet you at last. This is Scott, my friend.'

'Hi Lewis ... Scott. Good to meet you too. Tom will be thrilled.'

Lewis pulled a face. 'We'll have to see about that.' He glanced across at Scott, and then over to Emma.

Deborah's smile faltered and she looked at the three now-serious faces. *What was going on?* 'Have I missed something?' she asked.

Lewis sighed. 'You'll find out soon enough. Scott's my partner. I'm gay. We've flown over especially to break the news, as Em didn't feel it was her place to tell Dad.'

'Well, it wasn't,' Emma replied hotly. 'You know it. It has to come from you. Dad will be fine about it, I told you.'

'I hope so,' Lewis said grimly, 'or it could be a very short stay. Where is the old man anyway?'

'At a breakfast meeting in Stowmarket.' She glanced at her watch. 'He'll be back shortly. Do you want me to ring him or would you prefer it to be a surprise?'

Lewis shrugged. 'Whatever you think. I just want to get it over with.'

He looked so glum Scott reached across and squeezed his hand. 'It'll be alright, mate. Your sister says so.' He had a rich baritone voice and a tanned, open face. Whilst Lewis was slight with dark curls, Scott was broad-shouldered, muscular and bald. Tattoos lined both forearms and he looked relaxed and calm, a foil for Lewis' nervous, pent-up energy.

'For what it's worth, I'm sure Emma is right. Your dad has said often enough that he hoped you would find your way and be happy. If you have and you are, he will be happy too. I guarantee it.'

'There you go!' Emma grinned. 'Debs always knows what she's talking about. She's a top businesswoman, you know. Always right.'

'I wish!' Deborah demurred, taking a mug of coffee from Emma's outstretched hand. 'Thanks. I feel we should be cracking open the champagne.'

'Better wait and see if we have something to celebrate first,' Lewis said.

They did not have to wait long. After chatting for ten more minutes, Tom's dark red Land Rover swung into the driveway. Lewis went to the door to meet him.

'Lewis!' Tom's voice exploded with raw emotion as he pulled his son in for a hug. 'This is amazing! When did you get here?'

'About thirty minutes ago. I thought I'd surprise you!'

'You've certainly done that! How long are you staying? Or are you back for good?'

'No, I am going back. I love Sydney. I'm going to settle there.'

Tom's face fell. 'Obviously, I'm gutted we won't get to see you as often as we'd like.' He shrugged and gave his son a resigned smile. 'But if that's what makes you happy, Son, that's all that matters.'

'There is something else, Dad,' Lewis said slowly as they made their way inside. 'I've met someone there.'

Tom grinned. 'I knew it. There had to be a girl involved. Is she here too? Am I going to meet her?'

There was a pause and Lewis came to a standstill, pulling away to stand opposite his father, his grey eyes brimming with uncertainty. 'You are, but Dad, it's not a girl. It's a guy. I'm gay.'

Tom's mouth dropped open and his eyes widened. 'Gay?' he croaked. He cleared his throat and spoke again. 'Are you sure?'

Lewis tensed. 'I'm sure. His name is Scott. He's waiting in the kitchen to meet you.'

'Scott, wow!' Tom shook his head. 'I'd never have guessed.' He smiled at his son. 'Right, lead on. I guess I'd better meet him.'

Lewis hesitated. 'Are you sure you're OK with it, Dad? I know it's probably been a bit of a shock ...'

Tom gave him a wry smile. 'To say the least!' His arm returned to his son's shoulders. 'But if you're happy, I'm happy. I've always been proud of you, Lewis. You're so talented, not to mention the fact that you inherited my good looks.' He gave him a hard squeeze. 'But you never seemed settled. You were always struggling to find your way in life. If discovering you're gay has given you peace of mind, I honestly could not be more delighted.' He cleared his throat. 'You know I love you, Lewis.'

Lewis folded himself against his father's chest. 'I love you too, Dad.'

***

Honoraria shimmied to her front door, quivering with excitement in a figure-hugging, emerald green day dress which set off her auburn curls. She knew she could do with shedding the extra pounds which had crept on during the winter but, today, she wasn't going to worry about that. As always, she had a plan. Marcus Monk would not know what had hit him.

'Marcus!' she cried as she threw open the door. 'How lovely to see you!' She leant into him for a warm hug, allowing the irresistible scent of *L'Amore* to wash over his senses. 'Come in, come in.'

'Honoraria,' Marcus replied, somewhat taken aback by the enthusiasm of the greeting. 'Good to see you too. I'm most excited to learn what you have in store for me.'

If only you knew! She smiled as she led him into the sitting room. Having seated herself next to him on her cosy sofa, so their bodies were pressed together in delicious contact, she said, 'I have something you are going to want to see!'

'You said as much on the phone. Information about Martha Lightbody. I can't wait to discover what it is.' His deep voice sent shivers tingling down her spine. It was difficult to concentrate, so close to him.

'Yes.' She paused, looking deep into his eyes, a secretive smile on her lips. Her natural sense of theatre could not resist prolonging the moment of revelation, until she could wait no longer. 'It's a book, Marcus! Can you believe it? All about Martha's life.' As succinctly as she could, she filled him in on everything she had learnt before producing, with a flourish, the tome itself.

Marcus' reaction was all she could have hoped for. His liquid brown eyes remained upon her with almost hypnotic attention, right up until the moment he took the book into his hands. He held it carefully, reverently. 'That's incredible,' he murmured. 'I'm so pleased you chose to share it with me. May I ... would I be allowed ... to read it?'

'You may,' Honoraria beamed, 'but Deborah is concerned that its content is quite sensitive and should remain confidential. I'm sure that won't be a problem.'

'Certainly. You can trust me, Honoraria.'

'I know that,' she purred huskily, sliding her hand across to pat him on his corduroy-clad knee.

He reacted like a scalded cat. 'Oh, sorry, you startled me,' he squeaked, reddening with embarrassment.

How she longed to comfort him against her bosom! *Not yet.* Instead, she merely smiled, before continuing with her habitual brisk efficiency. 'Marcus, you and I have a great deal to do, if you are up for the challenge?' She outlined the initial research required to find some of the answers to questions Deborah had raised.

He arched his rather unfortunate, bushy eyebrows. 'Gosh,' he said, 'that *is* a lot of work. Very time-consuming, but I'd love to help. In fact, I can't wait to get started. What did you have in mind?'

She leant closer to him, holding his arm so he was unable to withdraw as before. 'I think we should get started straight away. And then I propose dinner here, just the two of us.' She pressed still closer to whisper in his ear. 'After that, I would very much like it if you would stay over with me.' She slid her free hand along his thigh. 'I know we're going to make a great team.'

He stiffened, facing her like a cornered deer, a mix of confusion and uneasiness on his face. 'But you said you were seeing someone,' he mumbled.

'Not anymore.' She brushed her lips against his cheek. 'Would you be interested?'

He pulled away from her. 'I'm not sure,' he frowned. 'This is all a bit sudden and, I'm afraid, I'm an all-or-nothing type of chap. I'm sorry, Honoraria, but if you're thinking of a brief fling, that would *not* be for me.'

She ran her tongue against her highly-glossed lower lip, her previously-hopeful heart settling to a more despondent beat. This was not going the way she had hoped and, feeling somewhat mortified, she eased her hand away from his leg. 'I'll be honest, Marcus, I can't make any promises,' she said. 'Who knows where anything between us might lead? I was married to Edgar for twenty-seven years and I loved him every second of the time we spent together. I yearn for that kind of love again, but there are no guarantees. With you, I think I just might find it. I *do* know I haven't been able to keep you out of my head, or out of my dreams, lately.' She drew in a deep breath. It was time to risk everything. At this point, she had nothing to lose. 'Anyway,' she continued, her voice husky with pent-up emotion, 'I'm willing to take a chance. The question is ... are you?'

Anxiously, she watched the play of emotions across his face as her words sank in. He was staring at her intently, his brown eyes searching. The ensuing silence seemed to last a horribly long while.

At last, his face relaxed into a smile. 'Well, let's try, shall we?' He placed his hands either side of her cheeks and lowered his lips to hers, gently caressing her mouth.

She closed her eyes, wanting more, *so much more*, but not daring to spoil the moment. Tentatively, his hands slid down, feathering the sides of her breasts and slipping behind her back to pull her closer. The kiss deepened. She could hold back no longer and dared to allow her hands to roam over his body, becoming more brazen as his enjoyment became obvious.

After some while, he pulled away. 'I think that was a good start, wouldn't you say?' he twinkled.

She was breathless with desire. 'I know we've got lots of work to do,' she gasped, 'but Marcus ... I honestly think that first we should finish what we've just started.' With a question in her eyes, her fingers toyed with the top button on her dress.

His smile widened. 'If you insist, my dear.'

CHAPTER 31

The dining room of *The Lamb Inn* was filled with raucous laughter. Rick Billington leaned back in his chair, enjoying the company of the people around him. He should not feel so happy, he mused. The renewed investigation into his sister's death had, yet again, brought no satisfactory answers. How could he be content when Freya's death remained unexplained? Yet, right at this moment, sitting around a table with Emma, Lewis, Scott, Tom and Deborah, being included in their special family time, he felt good. Guilt may come later and the grief was always there, an ache in his heart, but, in that moment, his spirits were high.

The preceding weeks had been difficult. The discovery of Jane Holley's body had brought everything back: the anguish he felt when Freya died; the anger; the need for answers. His parents felt it too. Both were working tonight – smiling hosts as always – but he knew how much they were hurting.

At first, there had been some optimism. The police were re-opening Freya's case and investigating a possible link between the two drownings. Jane's death, awful as it was, could bring answers to explain his sister's tragedy. As the days went by, though, that hope had dwindled. The police seemed no further forward than they were before, offering platitudes rather than explanations. Personally, he now believed they would never know why Freya ended up in Dark Water Lake, although he remained convinced it was not suicide. She just wasn't the type. Freya was a sunny, outgoing, glass-half-full person. Determined too, to the point of stubbornness. Definitely *not* the sort to succumb to the level of hopelessness which would make her take her own life. Also, they had always been very close as a family. Freya may have kept secrets from them but, if really troubled, Rick was sure she would have turned to them. No, the suicide theory made no sense.

A tragic accident? He did not believe that either. Murder was the only explanation. He should be down at the police station, demanding they do more to find the person responsible.

Instead, he was having a good time, next to Emma, enjoying the lively interactions around the table. They had all had a bit too much to eat and drink; everyone was relaxed and determined to make the most of this final evening together. Lewis and Scott were leaving tomorrow. Their stay at the farmhouse had done much to lighten his mood. They were irrepressible company and there had been plenty of laughs. Rick had not known Lewis very well but remembered him as a sullen, withdrawn type – very different from his sister. Now, with Scott by his side, he was a changed person. Rick supposed that was what love could do.

'You must promise me that you *will* take up painting again,' Deborah was telling Lewis. 'Your portfolio shows incredible talent. Emma's work is amazing but I now see why she says you are the artist in the family. No offence, Em.'

'None taken,' Emma responded good-naturedly. 'My paintings are OK, but Lewis is on another level. He always has been. It would be travesty to the art world if he did not use that talent.'

Lewis turned a flushed face upon them all. 'Give it a rest! I stopped painting because the pressure of success got too much. It wasn't fun anymore. I *will* paint but I have to enjoy it and I can't do that if I feel people are constantly expecting a masterpiece.'

'Fair enough.' Deborah held up her hands. 'I won't mention it again, although I would love a painting for Greenways Farm. And I *am* still waiting on my first family commission.'

'I know.' Emma shook her head. 'I will get around to it, I promise. And soon, before we get busy with spring land work.' She shrugged, 'I guess, like Lewis, I haven't been in the mood. But no more excuses. I'll make a start next week. Take a few days off work.'

Rick's ears pricked at that announcement. He was due some holiday. If next week's work roster allowed him to scheme at least one day off, he could suggest to Emma that they go to the coast for a walk, followed by fish and chips. It had been ages since they had done that. His fault. He had been preoccupied with keeping Amelie happy. And, recently, she had been busy traipsing about with Max Benson, although not since Lewis and Scott's arrival.

That too had lifted Rick's mood. Whilst he had been included in the recent family gatherings, Max had not. Rick wondered how his colleague felt about that, but the young vet seemed as cheerful as ever and did not appear fazed by his exclusion from Emma's family circle. When Rick mentioned, casually in passing, that Emma's brother was staying with them, Max replied that he knew.

'Emma mentioned it when I rang to see if she was up for some bowling. I went with Jo instead.'

Jo Bingham – another colleague. All this made Rick wonder if things were as serious between Max and Emma as he had believed. He had admitted to himself that their closeness bothered him. In fact, he was as jealous as hell. Given these latest developments, he wondered if Max was just a friend, like himself, no more than that. The thought was like a rainbow after a downpour. Even better, *he* was the one sitting by Emma's side as she enjoyed a farewell meal with her brother and Rick was determined to make the most of it.

***

It was a beautiful evening, clear, bright with stars. Patrick stopped the car on their way back after yet another sumptuous meal out. Ava looked across at him, puzzled.

'Is anything wrong?'

He turned that delicious, slow smile upon her. 'Nothing's wrong. In fact, everything's right when I'm with you.' He took her hand.

'Now Patrick ...' she began.

'No, listen. Just hear me out, Ava, please.'

She swallowed, knowing instinctively what he was about to say. Everything about this man was so perfect ... except he had broken her heart before. And things were happening so quickly. Since that first date, they had been riding a whirlwind of romantic evenings together. It was hard to keep her core of self-preservation intact. But, so far, she had stood firm. It was too soon.

'Ava, you know I've always loved you. Getting to know you again has made me realise I love you more than ever. I know you don't trust me yet so I'm not expecting an answer but ... hold on a minute, I guess we need to get out of the car.'

'Patrick ...' she protested but he had already unfolded his lanky frame, swung out of his seat and was striding around to open the passenger door.

'Out you hop.'

She found herself obeying, dizzy with longing but terrified to admit it to herself. 'Patrick, it's freezing ... oh!'

He had gone down on one knee before her. 'Sorry. It is cold. I'll be quick. Ava Green, I love you with all my heart and promise to remain faithful to you as long as I live. Will you do me the incredible honour of becoming my wife?'

'I ...'

'Shush.' He stood and placed a finger against her lips. 'I don't want you to answer ... not until you can say yes and know all your doubts about me have gone. I just couldn't wait any longer to ask you. But I've learnt from my mistake. This time, I'm prepared to wait forever if you want me to.' His face split into a grin. 'I just hope I don't have to! Now, back into the car with you. It's freezing out here!'

She laughed. 'It really is. Patrick Velaman, you choose your moments!'

As he slid in beside her and started the engine, he chuckled. 'I know. I didn't exactly set the bar high last time I proposed, did I?' He was referring to the fact that his declaration had been marred by his cry of pain as a drawing pin pierced his kneecap. He had knelt to propose in an old barn as they sheltered from the rain during a countryside ramble.

''At least you didn't scream this time!'

'I didn't scream then! I might have uttered a manly moan but it darned well hurt!'

'I bet it did, and you *did* scream. I was all set to rush you off to hospital!'

He grinned. 'Well, I remember it differently ... and at least this time was better. By the time I ask you for the seventeenth time, it will be perfect.'

He was infectious. She couldn't help smiling at him. And that warm, fuzzy feeling that being with him always brought, remained with her as she let herself in through the back door, crept past her mother's room and scurried up the stairs to a guaranteed night of sweet dreams.

***

Alone downstairs, across the other side of the village, her brother Andrew sat deep in thought. Julie had long gone to bed and he had taken the opportunity to finish reading the slim, leather-bound tome given to him by his mother. It had not been a comfortable experience. He could see why Enid saw parallels between him and Roger Holley. And she didn't know the half of it.

The story had been written from Martha's point of view – Martha the victim, the wrongly accused, the innocent. Good versus evil. How simplistic it was! Life was not drawn in such black and white lines. It was a messy jumble of assorted hues, each scrambling for ascendancy. Another, similarly-naïve account would see Roger as a strong, God-fearing man, trying to protect his family and his community. After all, fear of witchcraft was rife in the seventeenth century. Roger was only doing what he thought was right and, in the end, had paid with his life, a victim of the Lightbody curse. And that was another thing – *the curse*. What was *that* if not a tool used by witches to wreak vengeance?

Roger's death had struck fear in his own heart. Enid believed they were in danger themselves and he now felt more inclined to believe her. The curse remained a watchword in the village. The recent drownings, so reminiscent of Martha Lightbody's experience in 1645, were warnings. He had been dismissive of such claims in the past. Now he was not so sure. His mother had hinted at a continuing feud between the Holleys and Lightbodys ... or Littlebodys. He needed to know more.

The book had struck a chord within him for another reason, one he would never admit to another living soul. He recognised Roger Holley's predatory instincts; the same stirrings coursed through his own body. Whilst he loathed them, he could not deny them and could not stop himself acting upon them. He tried to keep it to a minimum, he really did. Such behaviour disgusted him. And yet it excited him as nothing else could. He could not stop, even if he wanted to ...

Was that his curse? Was his destructive nature the legacy bequeathed upon him by the Wickthorpe Witch? And would it, in the end, destroy him? Such dark questions the book had raised! He wished he had never known about it. Yet his mother had hinted there was a way to end the curse and that it would need the involvement of another Holley – Dr Seb. Personally, Andrew could not see that the charming doctor would want to be a part of whatever Enid was scheming, but there was no denying the fact that the death of his wife may well be a part of it all. Maybe they were both descendants of Roger Holley, and both victims of Martha's curse?

Much as it pained him to admit it, his mother was right. There was only one way to find out. Tomorrow, he would go and see Dr Holley.

CHAPTER 32

Beth Honeysuckle punched the air. Her team had worked their socks off over the past few weeks and maybe – just maybe – they were getting somewhere at last.

Dr Seb Holley. The grieving widower. His suave manner and effortless charm may have enslaved the majority of Wickthorpe's residents but it grated on Beth. *Too good to be true.* Her natural cynicism regarding men such as Seb Holley had made her suspicious of him from the start. She still bore the scars of her ex-husband's betrayal and was instinctively wary of any good-looking charmer. However, she had to set her own prejudices aside and follow the evidence. Her natural antipathy towards Seb did not make him a killer, she knew that. But the lack of any other leads had enabled her to take a closer look at him. When they discovered the incident in Surrey with the teenage patient, her suspicion had hardened into conviction of his guilt. Seb had killed his wife. He may have also killed Freya Billington. They were a long way from proving anything but they were closing in, she was sure of it.

Today there had been another breakthrough, a further question mark over Dr Holley's past. One of the youngest in the team, DC Alina Antonova, a young Ukrainian, had made the discovery.

The year was 2000. Seb was a twenty-two-year-old medical student at Edinburgh university. Popular, good-looking, charismatic, excelling on his course. In May of that year, a young student, twenty-year-old Maxine Darkin, fell to her death from the roof of a house where Seb and three other male students lodged together. A skylight provided access from inside the house and the roof provided a spectacular view of the city. The boys took girls up there regularly to impress them. All four lads were questioned at length but particularly Seb Holley, who was known to be the victim's boyfriend at the time. However, all four had alibis, claiming they were not in the house that evening. Eventually, the police investigation had concluded that Maxine had let herself into the house, looking for Seb. The boys often forgot their keys and were in the habit of leaving a spare under a pot by the rear entrance – something which Maxine, a regular visitor, knew. When she found the house empty, she decided to wait. At some point after that, she decided to climb onto the roof alone. It had been a warm, clear evening and it was something she had done many times in the past. Then, tragically, she had fallen. The coroner recorded a verdict of accidental death; the skylight was bolted down to prevent further roof misadventures; and the four young men resumed their lives. End of story.

Except, in the news coverage of that time, DC Antonova had discovered a few anomalies. Maxine was known to be fearful of heights. Friends and family insisted she would never have ventured onto the roof alone. Someone must have been with her, they claimed. Another of Maxine's close friends said that Maxine had told her she was meeting Seb that night to discuss their future. She had recently discovered she was pregnant and, as a Catholic, was not prepared to have an abortion.

With Beth's permission, DC Antonova travelled to Edinburgh to investigate further. She was able to talk to an officer who had worked on the case, Sergeant Baines, a stern-faced man in his early fifties. He had been born in the city and lived there all his life. When Alina told him they were investigating the recent death of Seb Holley's wife and that the doctor was a person of interest, Baines gave a gruff snort.

'Slippery as an eel, that lad was,' he muttered. 'It would never surprise me to learn he was somehow involved in the wee girl's death, but he had an alibi tighter than a duck's arse. With another lass, he was. She was a bit older than he was, I remember. Holley claimed they had been out for a pizza and then were together the whole night. Other witnesses saw them at the pizza place so his statement checked out.'

Alina Antonova sat up straighter. 'Do you remember the woman's name?'

Baines shook his head. 'Too long ago, but I remember him alright. Smooth as silk, he was. Claimed he was sorry about what had happened to the lass but it was nowt to do with him. Said she'd never told him she was pregnant and the bairn wasnae his. The lassie's friends disagreed but we couldnae prove owt. Then Holley volunteered a DNA test and that clinched it. His DNA didnae match that of Maxine Darkin's baby and he was off the hook.' He shrugged.

'Could I see the file?' Alina asked.

'Dinnae see why not. If it's still here. I remember it was kept open, in case further evidence came up.'

Alina was in luck. The file was soon unearthed and she studied it carefully. The evidence was just as Sergeant Baines had described but there was one fact which jumped out at her. The older woman, who had provided Seb Holley with his alibi, was twenty-eight-year-old Jane Hodrick, a post-graduate student at the university – the same woman he married soon afterwards.

Coincidence after coincidence. Beth's heart beat faster as she listened to Alina's findings. They had to be on to something ... but there remained one big stumbling block. The DNA evidence. Seb's story was believed once a DNA test proved he was not the father of Maxine's unborn child. Similarly, the absence of a DNA match meant he had not been considered in relation to Freya Billington's death. Beth frowned and made a mental note to take another look at that evidence. Could Seb have fiddled the test somehow? Procedures may have been less rigorous than they currently were. Beth knew she was clutching at straws but – and it was a very big 'but' – *if* there were any anomalies, it would give them a reason to question Seb again.

Less than thirty minutes later, Beth's excitement was mounting. She had checked the Billington file for the report on the DNA results. All men known to have been acquainted with Freya had been routinely tested under the supervision of Detective Constable, Neil Dent, an experienced member of the team. All except one ... Dr Seb Holley. In his case, there was no need for a test as his DNA data was already on file, collected in Edinburgh in 2000 by PC Keira Campbell.

Beth reached for the phone. 'Alina, I want you to track down a PC Keira Campbell. She was the officer who took the DNA sample from Seb Holley in Edinburgh in 2000. I want you to ask her about the testing. Find out if there was anything untoward about it.' She listened impatiently to the response.

'Yes, I know it was a long time ago and she may have left the force. You're an excellent detective, Alina. I have every confidence you will find her. ASAP.'

***

The call from Alina came later that same day. PC Campbell was now Keira Williams – no longer working for the police but married to someone who was. She still lived in Edinburgh and Alina had spoken to her personally.

'Keira remembered the Maxine Darkin case and had no trouble recalling Seb Holley, Ma'am,' Alina said drily. 'In fact, she blushed when I mentioned his name. And again, when I mentioned the DNA test. Then, she became a bit cagey. In the end, though, she admitted that she had allowed Holley to take the test into the bathroom and administer it himself. He had a phobia about having his mouth swabbed, she told me, and persuaded her to go against procedure. She felt guilty about it but didn't think it would do any harm.'

'That means the sample was compromised! Sterling work, Alina. Well done.' Beth ended the call and leapt to her feet, pulses racing. It was time to talk to Seb Holley again and she would take great pleasure in bringing him to the station herself.

***

Accompanied by his solicitor, Alistair Featherington, a boar-like man with small, round eyes and a large nose, Seb remained as unruffled and untroubled by Beth's questions as ever. Several times, his solicitor advised him not to answer. Each time, he waived away that right.

'It's fine, Alistair, I'd like to clear that up, if you don't mind. Anything I can do to help the detectives, I will. I have nothing to hide.'

Beth conducted the interview alongside DS Jack Everard. She took the lead, hoping to surprise Dr Holley with revelations of his murky past and prompt, at the very least, a revealing reaction. After some initial, routine questions, she brought up the subject of the girl in Edinburgh.

'Poor Maxine. I still can't understand why she went up on to the roof on her own.' Holley shook his head, recalling old grief. 'We were close for a while but not exclusive, if you know what I mean.'

'Did you know she was pregnant with your child?'

A flash of annoyance. Once again, he ignored his solicitor's shake of the head. 'There are two questions there but I am prepared to answer both, as I did before. No, I did *not* know she was pregnant, and no, it was *not* with my child.'

'How can you be so sure?'

Holley sighed. 'How can anyone be sure of such things, detective? Because we had not had that kind of relationship for a few months, not since I'd met Jane. And if you took the trouble to investigate a little further, you would discover I provided a DNA sample. That proved the baby was not mine. In fact, I was the one who suggested a DNA test.' He shrugged and gave Beth a resigned smile. 'You see, I had nothing to hide.'

'Yes ... the DNA sample. We will come to that in a moment.' Beth pretended to consult her notes. 'You were with Jane Hodrick at the time Maxine Darkins fell to her death?'

'I was. I wished it had been different. If I'd been at home when Maxine turned up, the tragedy would never have happened.'

'How so?'

'Maxine was a troubled soul, Inspector. I always suspected that her death was no accident, that she meant to fall.'

'Suicide? There was no mention of that in the police reports. Did you say this to detectives at the time?'

'I'm afraid not.' Again, he dismissed his solicitor's warning to ignore the question. 'I was very young, very upset, and scared. For a while, it appeared I was under suspicion. I wanted to keep Jane out of it, to protect her, but I was forced to tell everyone where I was, to prove I wasn't involved in whatever had happened to Maxine. Also, it didn't occur to me until much later that Maxine may have *intentionally* fallen from the roof. By then, the furore had died down and things had gone back to normal. There didn't seem any point in coming forward with an alternative theory. Besides, I'm sure the police would have considered the possibility anyway. Presumably, it was something they ruled out.'

Beth stared into his face, trying to work him out. It was impossible. She was certain there was another man behind the bland, genial mask but she was unable to lure him into the open. The interview was being conducted to his tune rather than hers. She decided it was time to play her ace. 'To return to the matter of your DNA sample, can you tell me when you submitted it?'

'It would have been sometime in 2000 after I had been accused of being the father of Maxine's baby.'

'Can you explain why the sample was not taken in line with police procedures at the time?'

Seb looked surprised. 'I'm afraid I have no knowledge of police procedures, Inspector Honeysuckle. You will have to enlighten me further.'

Beth's brown eyes lasered across the desk. 'You refused to allow PC Keira Campbell to take a buccal swab and persuaded her to allow you to do the test yourself in a separate room.'

Seb shook his head and took his time in answering. 'I'm afraid I don't recall how the test was taken, Inspector. You'll have to forgive me. It was a long time ago.'

Beth ploughed on. 'This means the sample was compromised. You cannot use it as a defence.'

'I have no intention of using it as a defence,' Seb retorted. 'I have done nothing wrong and have no need of a defence ... unless I am mistaken and you are charging me with something?' He gave the detectives a challenging stare.

'We would like you to agree to give another sample, Dr Holley.'

'Is that really necessary?' Seb shook his head and glanced at his solicitor.

Alistair Featherington puffed himself up. 'My client has been extremely tolerant of your line of questioning, Detective Inspector Honeysuckle, but none of it appears relevant to the tragic death of this poor man's wife. I would advise you to say nothing more, Seb.'

'Will you agree to give another sample of DNA, Dr Holley?' Beth persisted.

'I would advise against it,' Featherington intervened, 'unless, of course, my client is being charged with something?'

'Not at this time,' Beth said through gritted teeth. She decided to try another tack. 'Tell me about the incident in Surrey, in 2014, when you were again questioned by the police.'

A pause. A frown furrowed the tousled brow. Seb ran a hand through his hair, thinking. '2014 ... oh, you mean the ridiculous allegation about me by that young girl. That was all cleared up very quickly. No case to answer. Another troubled soul.' He hunched his shoulders. 'Doctors, teachers, any professionals in positions of trust are always vulnerable to spurious allegations. I remember it was very unpleasant at the time but, in the end, no harm was done. I was exonerated from all accusations of wrongdoing and you will find my professional record remains, to this day, completely untarnished.'

Beth raised her eyebrows. 'Yet again, it was the word of your wife which got you off the hook, wasn't it, Dr Holley?'

For the first time, there was a small chink of exasperation in his answer. 'Because it was the truth! I'm sorry but I can't see how raking over my past misfortunes is going to help. I appreciate that you consider me a suspect in my wife's death. It's the old cliché, isn't it? The husband must have done it. But I didn't, I promise you that. I loved my wife. I had no idea that, for Jane, life had become so unbearable she had to end it. I wish I had. I would have tried to stop her.' He brought his hands to his face.

His solicitor patted him awkwardly on the back. 'Do you have any questions relevant to Mrs Holley's death, Detective Inspector Honeysuckle? If not, I suggest it would be a good idea to terminate this interview,' Alistair Featherington declared, his piggy eyes cold with disdain.

Beth did not respond. The optimism she had felt beforehand had evaporated. Seb had an answer for everything and she was getting nowhere. Rather desperately, she ploughed on. 'Did you know your wife was having an affair, Dr Holley?'

Seb allowed his exasperation to show. 'You've asked me this before. It's nonsense. Something about emails. I trust you've traced this man, the one who sent the emails? I'm afraid I can't recall his name.'

'Stuart Bickerstaff.' Beth was not about to reveal that they had come to a dead end with the emails. They had questioned two potential matches but had been unable to find a link between either of them and Jane Holley. The email address had, as yet, proved untraceable. Beth jerked back to attention as Seb spoke again.

'That's right. Stuart Bickerstaff. Have you questioned him? I did wonder if he may have been an old school acquaintance ... someone she knew before we met. You suggested the emails were of a personal nature but I refuse to believe Jane would have an affair. Until recently, when she became depressed, ours had been a very happy marriage.' When Beth did not respond, he repeated. 'You *have* questioned this man?' Another beat of silence. 'No?' Seb exhaled with a frustrated shake of his head. 'In which case, unless there is anything else ...?' He raised his eyebrows at Beth and his solicitor began purposefully collecting up the papers in front of him.

It was hopeless. Beth felt her case disintegrating around her but was determined not to show it. 'Thank you for your time, Dr Holley,' she said coolly. 'Please remain in the area as we will need to speak to you again. Interview terminated at ... 18:10.' Head held high, she rose and swept from the room, leaving DS Everard floundering in her wake.

***

Afterwards, after a short debrief with her team and an awkward meeting with Detective Superintendent, Allison Pallister, Beth closeted herself in her office. Her mood was at an all-time low. She had no means of forcing Dr Holley to submit another DNA sample and he was not prepared to co-operate. His refusal, Beth felt, could almost be construed as an admission of guilt but her superiors did not see it that way. Pallister had been adamant that, whilst mildly suspicious, it proved nothing. The investigation into the drowning of Jane Holley was providing no definitive answers. Likewise, the reopening of Freya Billington's case had yielded nothing further. Hunches and feelings were of no consequence. Successful prosecutions needed concrete evidence. Beth had failed, and she had run out of time. Jane Holley's death would be assigned a verdict of suicide. Beth had been told, in no uncertain terms, that her superiors were disappointed with her performance. It was time to let both cases go.

But it was so frustrating! Beth was sure she was on the right track regarding Jane Holley's death and it would be impossible to forget about it. It remained an itch she had to scratch, no matter that it made things worse. The Bickerstaff emails, for example, made no sense. Not one of Jane's acquaintances had believed she might be having an affair. Most had laughed at the idea. But, if it was true, and Seb had found out, a case could be made against him that, in a jealous rage, he killed his wife. Once again, though, there was no proof.

Another theory: the emails were a deliberate fabrication, written to throw them off the scent. The untraceable email address was a definite red flag. It belonged to someone covering his tracks. Could it have been Seb? If so, why, when the emails gave him a motive for murder? Looking at it logically, it was more likely the emails were written by a third party, someone attempting to deflect suspicion onto Seb. *Deborah Ryecroft?* Was there more to the Wickthorpe Witch theory than she had given credence?

Wearily, Beth pulled on her coat. Her team had already left and she was shattered. The sense of defeat was overwhelming but she had to be pragmatic. Win some, lose some. It was the nature of the job.

Driving home, though, her brain refused to switch off. Coincidences, for example. There were just too many to dismiss. Freya Billington was pregnant; so was Maxine Darkins. Both knew Seb Holley; both were then found dead; both possible suicides. His wife's death made a third 'suicide' of women known to him – all suspicious.

Beth sighed with frustration. No proof; in fact, no evidence to suggest Holley was involved in the Billington case at all. She was merely a colleague and someone who lived in the same village. But Holley's alibi for the time of Freya's death was, yet again, his wife. Very convenient. If you counted the girl in Surrey, Holley had a proven connection to three incidents where the alibi was always the same. *Jane Holley.* She was the key. If only she was still alive to question, and how convenient for her husband she was no longer available for interrogation! A dead end ... literally.

Beth allowed herself a grim smile as she parked on the road outside her small, terraced house in Ipswich, locked her car and opened her front door. She headed straight for the fridge and pulled out a bottle of wine. After the day she'd had, she needed it! She poured herself a large glass, carried it through to her sitting room and sank into her favourite chair. Her stomach rumbled, reminding her she had skipped lunch, but she couldn't be bothered to cook. Not tonight. She would order a takeaway later.

Pensively, she sipped at her wine. Had she missed something? Was there some crucial piece of evidence, right under her nose, that she had forgotten, or rejected as insignificant? The possibility tormented her and her mind skimmed back over trivial details. She paused when her thoughts turned to the description of Freya Billington's 'mystery man.' Not much to go on, and she had thought at the time, probably unfairly, that the excitable Mrs Simpson-Fairchild might not be the most reliable of witnesses. As Beth took another sip of cold wine, she recalled the final sentence in that witness statement. In it, Simpson-Fairchild had suggested there was something about the man which was familiar, and the possibility of it being a local man was investigated. That line of inquiry terminated once DNA samples had been taken and all were negative. But now they knew Seb Holley's sample was questionable. It *could* have been him, perhaps wearing a disguise.

Beth knew she was clutching at straws. She had been told to drop the case and, if she was sensible, she would forget all about it. But that wasn't possible and being sensible, in her opinion, was overrated. Tomorrow, she decided, it would not hurt to have another, 'unofficial' word with Mrs Simpson-Fairchild.

***

Much later that same night, Seb Holley poured himself a strong gin. It had been quite a day. First, the police grilling. He smiled as he recalled how easily he had deflected their questions – child's play for a man like him. His smile slipped, however, as he remembered the issue of the DNA test. That was serious and could become a problem. He would have to give some thought as to how to proceed.

Having arrived home after the police interview, he had been surprised by a visit from Andrew Green. That had proved *very* interesting. Green had produced a copy of the book, *The Life and Times of Martha Lightbody*, and given Seb a convoluted summary of its contents. There then followed an astounding series of revelations. He claimed his mother's maiden name was Holley, and that both he and Seb were descendants of Roger Holley, Martha's accuser in the book. Green then linked the curse to Jane's death, and informed Seb of his mother's certainty that members of his family were in danger from Deborah Ryecroft, the current Wickthorpe Witch. He intimated that his mother, Enid, would like to see him to discuss it further, once he had read the book. Apparently, she had a plan to put an end to the curse.

Seb had listened, expressing surprise, interest, disbelief and grudging agreement, in that order, as Green's story unfolded. With practised solemnity, he had promised to read *The Life and Times of Martha Lightbody*, and to contact Andrew when he had done so.

Green's visit may have been unexpected but it could prove extremely fortuitous, Seb decided. After the younger man had gone, he had pondered for some while. Of course, he had no intention of reading the book. He did not need to. A similar copy graced a bookshelf in his father's study.

He had been fifteen when he was summoned to that hallowed sanctuary and told his destiny. At the time, he had been teenage-cynical and dismissive, although he would never have dared express such sentiments to his strict disciplinarian of a father. He had taken the copy and read it carefully, as instructed. Subsequently, there had been many 'man-to-man' discussions on the subject in his father's study.

'There will be a day of reckoning,' his father had prophesied with sonorous portent. 'It may come in your lifetime so it is best to be prepared.'

A load of rubbish, he had thought.

But, later in life, his opinion had changed. His father's premonition was coming true. And now Seb was making sure of it. The day of reckoning *was* coming and the Green family could prove most useful ...

CHAPTER 33

Honoraria could not deny, after the exhilarating discovery of *The Life and Times of Martha Lightbody*, that progress thereafter had proved disappointing. She and Marcus had both read the book and had been excited to learn of the Martha's settlement in the Norfolk village of Tocklewood. A real lead! However, despite extensive searches through the archives of Tocklewood and its surrounding area, she and Marcus had been unable to find any trace of Martha Lightbody or her alias Ruth Littlebody. It was most frustrating. Despite John Littlebody's assertion that the family saw out their lives in Tocklewood, Honoraria suspected they may have moved on at some point. But if so, where? And why? It seemed the book only told half of the story. Honoraria remained bullish about their prospects of finding Martha but it was going to take some time.

She and Marcus had managed to find some of the people mentioned in the book. In 1646, Cecile, daughter of Lord and Lady Gage, married Henry, the heir to the Duke of Suffolk, and later became the Duchess of Suffolk. They had four children, and she was buried in the family crypt in St Andrew's church. Prudence Harkness remained in Wickthorpe all her life and died in 1663, aged thirty-eight. The burial of Roger Holley in St Mary's church, Wickthorpe was recorded in 1646. It was a good start.

Meanwhile, Marcus had changed tack, wondering at the longevity of belief in the Wickthorpe curse. 'There must be a reason it still resonates, even after four hundred years have passed. It's beyond credibility to believe nothing has happened to keep it going,' he mused. He began searching the British newspaper archive website which contained news stories across the regions from the 1700s. So far, he had focused on 1700 to 1749 and found three matches. The first, reported in the *Ipswich Journal* in 1707, featured the hanging of Jonathan Littlebody, following his conviction for the murder of George Oldman. The second, in 1714, was of more interest and detailed the accidental drowning of Mary Bell in Dark Water Lake, Wickthorpe. It mentioned the curse, and accusations made that a Letitia Clarke was responsible. Mrs Clarke was also described in the report as the Wickthorpe Witch. Marcus became most animated when he read this and Honoraria flung her arms around him.

'How thrilling!' she declared. 'I do believe you have earned yourself a reward, you clever man.' Her eyes shone with promise. 'But perhaps later. I wouldn't want to stop you whilst in the very throes of discovery. Who knows what else you might find?'

Marcus duly returned to his research and trawled diligently through the years, finding nothing of interest until he reached February 23rd, 1749. A brief paragraph, again in the *Ipswich Journal*, stated that Nicholas Holley had been convicted of robbing Sarah Littlebody at her home in Aldeburgh, Suffolk, and had been sentenced to transportation. Marcus investigated further and discovered that, after the trial, a disturbance was reported in Aldeburgh. Several men had been arrested, all later released without charge. Although possessions belonging to Mrs Littlebody had been recovered from Holley's home, thereby proving his guilt, there had been an angry protest by members of his family declaring his innocence and claiming he had been framed. There was even a passing reference to Martha Lightbody's trial by drowning in 1645 and the legend of the Wickthorpe curse. Marcus spent some while on the website after that, trying to find out more about the incident and the people involved, but had drawn a blank.

'What it does suggest,' he said to Honoraria, 'is that some sort of feud continued between the two families, the Holleys and the Littlebodys. This was the only match I found for both names, but descendants will also have changed their names through marriage. It is possible there are many such incidents involving the two families, thereby perpetuating the legend of the curse.'

Honoraria pulled a face. 'As you say, it is possible ... but very hard to prove. Exciting though,' she continued when she saw how Marcus' face had drooped. 'Excellent work, Marcus. I'm very impressed.'

His brown eyes twinkled with pleasure. 'Does that mean I deserve my reward now?' he murmured, sliding his arms around her waist and nuzzling her neck.

'Well, you have worked hard ...' she muttered breathlessly. 'Probably a good idea to take a short break.'

'Mm, the problem is, what I have in mind could take a while.' His lips travelled lower.

'In which case,' she gasped, 'perhaps you should wait until later.'

'I can't wait.'

And that was another reason progress had been slow. At first, Marcus had been a shy, slightly tentative lover but, with Honoraria's encouragement, he had become more adventurous and now he took her breath away. It was impossible to resist him and, quite frankly, she had no desire to do so. The curtains of her cottage were drawn at all hours of the day and it was the same when she stayed over at his house in Little Horseshoes. Since that first time he had taken her in his surprisingly powerful arms, they had been inseparable.

This had resulted in moments of embarrassment. A delivery driver requiring a signature had to be confronted by Honoraria in her silk dressing gown in the middle of the afternoon. She felt she had to explain she had been taking a bath for the benefit of her aching joints, although the delivery driver, a young man who spoke with an East European accent, was clearly anxious to get away.

It had been worse when Deborah Ryecroft knocked at the door. The lovers had been indulging in some delightful role play at the time which had resulted in Honoraria emitting a mock squeal.

'Are you alright, Honoraria?' Deborah called through the letter box. 'I heard a scream.'

'I'll be right with you, Deborah. Hold on a moment. I'm fine. I ... er ... just stubbed my toe as I was ... er ... getting out of the bath. Giving my joints a soak, you know.' The same lie as before, equally unconvincing.

When, five minutes later, Deborah was admitted entrance, she took one look at Honoraria's flushed cheeks and Marcus' studied insouciance and smiled to herself. Honoraria launched into a long-winded explanation for the delay, embellishing the brief details she had already given in a vain attempt to make the story seem more believable. Deborah continued to smile and make polite noises until Honoraria recovered her composure sufficiently to offer her a cup of tea.

'Only if I'm not interrupting anything,' Deborah could not resist saying. 'I was just wondering how you were both getting on with your research into Martha and her descendants?'

They told her what they had discovered so far, anxious that she would be disappointed. Instead, she was delighted. 'That's amazing. I can't believe you've found all that in such a short space of time. I've joined an ancestry site and am trying to trace backwards. It's made me very aware how difficult it is, and what slow going!'

Honoraria nodded. 'At least, we've managed to corroborate some of the details in the book. Prudence Harkness was living in Wickthorpe in 1645, and did bear her first child in that year. And Cecile did become the Duchess of Suffolk. Her title made her easy to find. Poor, old Bertie. I wonder what became of him.' She sighed, 'Love was more complicated in those days, I suppose. In the end, she chose the sensible option.'

'It seems to me that love is complicated enough, no matter when you live,' Deborah responded, 'but I agree – poor Bertie. It would be nice to think he got over Cecile and found love elsewhere.' She smiled. 'Anyway, I won't keep you from your ... er, research. I'm excited to find out what else you discover.'

As she stood, Marcus spoke. 'I've been looking through old newspaper archives, concentrating on events possibly linked to the curse. It's early days as yet but I have found some evidence which suggests the enmity between the Holleys and the Lightbodys – or Littlebodys – did not end with Roger's death. Rather, it's looking as if descendants on both sides continued a feud between the families. I've found bits and pieces which support that theory. To prove it, though, we would need to trace the protagonists back to Roger and Martha and, as we've not yet found Martha, that's going to be tricky. Just hypothesis and supposition at present, I'm afraid.'

'A feud?' Deborah sat down again. 'Really?' Something within her resonated with his words. Holleys and Littlebodys. It rang true. From the first, she had experienced an antagonistic reaction to Seb Holley without knowing why. Was she part of a private war between families, waged for four hundred years? The idea did not seem far-fetched. It even made sense.

'As I said, early days.' Marcus rubbed his hands. 'Lots more work to be done. Will you ...?'

A knock at the door interrupted his question. 'I wonder who that is,' Honoraria pondered, peering through the window. 'Oh, my goodness, it's the police. Whatever can they want?' Her face turned pink.

'I'd best be going. Thank you so much for your time, both of you.' Deborah allowed Honoraria to open the door and smiled a greeting at Beth Honeysuckle and Jack Everard. 'Detectives, I was just leaving.'

'Good day, Ms Ryecroft. Mrs Simpson-Fairchild, may we have a word?'

'Of course, of course. Do come in. Goodbye Deborah.' In a fluster, Honoraria ushered the two detectives inside. 'This is my friend, Marcus Monk. He's staying with me at the moment. Please, take a seat. Can I get you tea or coffee or something?' Her mind was whirring. What was this about? *Oh no!* Her face flushed beetroot as she wondered if someone had made a complaint about her and Marcus and their vigorous sexual activities. Surely not? They had been discreet ... hadn't they?

'Nothing, thank you.' Beth answered for them both. 'Mr Monk, would you mind if we had a word with Mrs Simpson-Fairchild in private? It concerns a case we are working on.'

As Honoraria heaved a sigh of relief, Marcus stood. 'Certainly. I could do with some fresh air. I'll go and take a walk.'

'Thank you.'

The remaining three sat in awkward silence as he laced up his shoes, zipped up a large Barbour jacket, wound a scarf around his neck and found his hat. Once the door had finally closed behind him, Beth shifted her weight towards Honoraria. 'Mrs Simpson-Fairchild, I've recently been reviewing your statement in which you described the man you saw in Oxford with Freya Billington. Would you mind repeating that again for us?'

'Oh gosh, it was a long time ago.' Honoraria had not been expecting that. 'He was tall and dark-haired. Had a dark moustache. Wore glasses. It was so quick. I'm afraid I didn't really get a good look. I wish I could tell you more.'

They waited. When nothing was forthcoming, Beth tried again. 'Take your time. Cast your mind back and picture the scene again. This time, concentrate on other details. What he was wearing, for example? His build. How he walked.'

Honoraria closed her eyes. 'I was sitting in a restaurant just off the High Street in Oxford where I'd met a friend for lunch. Not someone from around here,' she added hastily, fearful they would want her disastrous date's name and contact details. 'He didn't know Freya and I didn't say anything about it to him. There would be no point questioning him. None whatsoever. Anyway, back to Freya's mystery man. He was tall. Sorry, I've said that. Well-built. Muscular. Broad shoulders. He was wearing a short-sleeved, checked shirt and a green gilet over the top. It was a relatively warm day. Freya was in a pink, long-sleeved, loose-fitting top and jeans.'

'How did you know they were together?'

'Oh, that's easy. They were arm in arm. Sorry, I should have mentioned that. She had her head turned, talking to him. He was smiling. A nice smile. Even teeth. It reminded me of someone ...' She shook her head. 'I wish I could think who it was.'

'Take your time,' Beth repeated softly. 'You're doing very well. You mentioned in your original statement that the man was older. What made you think that?'

'Oh yes, definitely older. Not a young man.' She wrinkled her nose, trying to pin down the description. 'His face was older, and he didn't have the build or walk of a younger man.'

'Tell me about his walk.'

'Long strides. A bit of a swagger, maybe. He gave me the impression of confidence ... and power. Freya was definitely looking up to him.'

'This is really good, Mrs Simpson-Fairchild.'

'Oh, please call me Honoraria. Simpson-Fairchild is such a mouthful.' Honoraria preened at the compliment. 'Are you sure you wouldn't like something to drink?'

'Quite sure, thank you,' Beth said firmly. 'Now, we have reason to believe the man may have disguised his appearance. Take away the glasses and the moustache. The hair could be different too. Can you picture him now?'

Honoraria frowned. 'It's difficult. Can't you do some mock-ups based upon my description? You know, like they do in books and films?'

'That is a possibility down the line. Just do your best for now. I'd like you to return to your comment that he reminded you of someone you knew. If that were the case, it could be someone you know locally, someone who was also acquainted with Freya Billington. Start by thinking about possible men from the village. We could give you a list to help you, if you like.'

'No, I'm sure that won't be necessary. I have excellent recall. Always have had. Something of a prodigy, my teachers always said,' Honoraria beamed. She was about to embark on one of her favourite childhood stories when she realised, in the current circumstances, it was probably inappropriate. Instead, she took a deep breath and did as she had been asked.

Tom Oldridge? He often wore that kind of clothing; he was tall and good-looking. Not Tom though. Everything else was wrong. She shook her head unconsciously. *His friend, Felix Goode? Definitely not. Too short. The American who moved into Mabel's bungalow. Don't be silly! He wasn't here last year. And not those two nice boys living next door to him either.* Her mind travelled along Green Road and stopped at Andrew Green. *Now, he was a possibility. The right kind of physique, and he was certainly a charmer!* She could see Freya Billington falling for someone like him.

She opened her eyes and blinked. 'I'm not sure, but it could have been Andrew Green. Lives further along this road with his wife and two children.'

'Oh, what makes you think that?'

Was it her imagination or did DI Honeysuckle look a bit disappointed? 'I'm not sure.' Honoraria frowned. 'He's the right sort of build and, well ... I don't know if I should say this but ... Andrew has a bit of a reputation,' she admitted in a stage whisper.'

Beth nodded. 'Anyone else?' she prompted.

Honoraria closed her eyes once more, letting her mind meander through the village, crossing off men as she thought of them. *Too old; too young; too short; not the right build.*

'Oh, goodness me!' She spluttered aloud as realisation struck.

'What is it?' DS Everard almost leapt from his chair.

'Good heavens! But it can't be ... surely?' Honoraria continued muttering to herself as she toyed with the possibility. It was the teeth, she realised – that killer smile – and the arrogance. Both men carried themselves with the exact same confident saunter. It *was* him ... or it could have been.

'Mrs Simpson-Fairchild ... Honoraria ... do you have a name for us?' Beth urged.

'I do, but I can't believe it. I must be mistaken.' Honoraria clasped her hands together.

'Let us be the judge of that. Who is it?'

Her china-blue eyes wide with obvious dismay, Honoraria looked straight at Beth. 'It can't be right,' she said, 'but the person I'm thinking of is Dr Holley.'

CHAPTER 34

Julie Green was most distressed to receive a visit from two detectives early that same afternoon.

'We're so sorry to trouble you, Mrs Green, but we would like to ask you a few questions about your husband. May we come in?' said the man who identified himself as DS Jack Everard and his colleague as DI Beth Honeysuckle.

Her heart plunged to the pit of her chest. What had Andy done now? 'Yes, of course,' she murmured, standing aside to allow them entrance. 'Through there. I'm afraid I don't have long. I'll need to pick my daughters up from school.'

'We'll try not to take up too much of your time,' Everard said with a winning smile. 'Nice place you have here.' He glanced around in appreciation.

'Yes.' Julie sat opposite them, in the chair nearest the door, and waited. She felt sick.

'Mrs Green, I'd like you to cast your mind back to last summer – June, in fact – when a young female was found drowned in Dark Water Lake.'

'Yes.' Her voice was barely audible and she cleared her throat.

'Do you recall that both your husband and yourself were interviewed as to your whereabouts on the weekend of ...' He consulted a notebook, 'June 22nd and 23rd.' She nodded. 'On that occasion, your husband claimed he was in Basildon with friends ... er, Mick Davis and Steve Hobbs ... all weekend. You, along with Mr Davis and Mr Hobbs, corroborated that statement. Is that correct?'

She bit her lip. Yes, Andrew was away all weekend but he had originally told her he was going to a stag do. Clearly a lie as he had a different story for the police. Conveniently, it featured his mates, Mick and Steve, who had covered for her errant husband on other occasions in their marriage. At the time, she felt she had no choice other than to support Andrew's statement. How could she do otherwise? The police had seemed satisfied and Andrew had been grateful. It had been a dreadful time but they had got through it. So why were they now back here, asking questions? Fiddling nervously with her fingers, she nodded.

'Mrs Green.' The detective sergeant was regarding her sternly. 'May I remind you that it is an offence to give false information to the police. Are you sure your husband was in Basildon? Could he, in fact, have been in Oxford ... with Freya Billington?'

Julie's eyes darted anxiously between the two officers. 'That is what he said,' she murmured. 'I have no reason to believe otherwise but I'm not my husband's keeper. Do you think he was in Oxford?' Her fears from the previous summer rose like a tidal wave, swamping her with dismay.

There was a pause and Jack glanced across at Beth. 'How well would you say you and your husband knew Freya Billington?'

Julie wriggled in her seat, sensing her answers were proving unsatisfactory. 'I knew her quite well. She was a work colleague. Worked in the pharmacy for a bit. Lovely girl. Everyone liked her. Andrew?' She shrugged. 'I'm not sure. She worked quite often behind the bar at the pub – had done ever since the Billingtons moved in, except when she was away at university. Andrew would have seen her there. He pops in for a pint every now and then, or he used to.'

'Not anymore?' Jack asked.

'Er ... no. At least, I don't think so.'

'He stopped going in there after Freya Billington's death?'

Silence met Jack's question. Julie sat motionless, a rabbit in the headlights.

Beth cleared her throat. 'Mrs Green, to the best of your knowledge, was your husband having an affair with Freya Billington?'

'No!' The exclamation was vehement but Julie flushed crimson. 'I'd have known,' she added with less conviction.

The two detectives looked at each other. 'Is it a possibility?' Beth asked gently.

'No ... I don't think so. He wouldn't. Not after the last time.'

'The *last* time?'

She had said too much; she knew it as soon as the words slipped from her lips. Andrew would be furious! She tried to backtrack. 'It was a long time ago – shortly after we were married. He promised it wouldn't happen again.'

Beth nodded. 'I see. Would you agree it's possible your husband could have been lying regarding his whereabouts that weekend?'

'No ... at least, I don't know.' Julie was almost in tears. 'Why are you asking me these questions? Why don't you ask Mick and Steve ... and Andrew, for that matter?'

Beth stood. 'We intend to. That will be all for now, Mrs Green. We apologise for upsetting you. Thank you for your time.'

As she and Jack headed out, Julie scrambled to her feet to follow. 'Do you think Andrew was involved in ... what happened to Freya?'

Beth gave her a non-committal look. 'Thank you, Mrs Green. Have a good day.'

'What do you reckon, Beth?' Jack asked as they drove through the village. 'Could it have been Andrew Green?'

Beth shrugged. 'His wife obviously thinks it's a possibility, and Honoraria named him first, so we have to consider it. We know from the DNA test he wasn't the father of Freya's child, but perhaps she had more than one lover. And we'll need to take a good look at that DNA test ... perhaps ask him to provide another, just to be sure. But no, to answer your question, I don't think it was him. You know what I think, and Honoraria thought so too. But, before we confront Dr Holley, we'll see what Mr and Mrs Billington have to say.' They pulled up outside the pub. 'Hopefully, with this new information, they may remember something.'

***

Rick was slumped in the small, private snug of *The Lamb Inn* opposite his mum, a mug of tea in front of him. 'How's things?' he asked.

Sally Billington gave him a look. 'I could ask you the same question. What's up, Rick? Why are you moping around here on your day off?'

'Nothing's up. I'm fine. Just thought I'd come and check on you, see how you were.'

She shrugged. 'We're coping, I suppose. Taking each day as it comes. It doesn't get any easier.'

'No.' Rick tapped his fingers gloomily against his mug. 'It would help if the police came up with something new. I thought, when they re-opened the investigation, they would be able to give us some answers.'

'So did we. I can't bear to think someone who hurt our Freya could be walking around out there.'

'It wouldn't surprise me if they gave up on it again – the investigation, I mean. It's been a few weeks since Mrs Holley was found. Similar circumstances but they seem to have drawn a blank, yet again. I think we ought to consider making an official complaint,' Rick grumbled.

Sally sighed. 'I *do* believe the police are doing all they can. DI Honeysuckle has been very good about keeping us informed.'

'Hmph, informed about *nothing*. No progress. Hopeless!'

'Rick, what's up? You're usually the one buoying me up. It's not like you to be so negative.'

'Sorry.' He pulled a face. 'I don't want to bore you with my troubles.'

'Troubles?' Her face creased in concern.

'Not really troubles ... at least ... well, it's Emma.'

'Oh no. Have you had a falling out?'

'No, nothing like that. It's just this guy she's seeing.' Rick had hoped things had petered out between Emma and Max but the two of them had gone out together the previous evening.

'Max? The young chap who has just joined the practice? I thought you liked him.'

'I do.' He heaved a sigh. 'It's complicated.'

'Mm.' His mum nodded. 'I get it.'

'You do?'

'You're jealous. It's understandable. Emma is your friend and now she's spending time with Max, rather than you.' Sally smiled. 'You have lots of friends though, Rick. Get out there and enjoy yourself, rather than moping about here with me. Not that I'm not pleased to see you ...'

He scowled. 'It's more than that.'

'Oh.' She tried to hide a smile and failed.

'I don't see what's so amusing,' he huffed.

'Sorry.' She was instantly contrite. 'It's just you and Emma. You're perfect for each other. I've always known it and now you've realised it too. I couldn't be more thrilled. Now you just need to make sure Emma knows it.'

He was about to deny it, but then shrugged. 'Easier said than done. Max is on the scene now. It wouldn't be fair to come between them. First and foremost, Emma is my best friend. I need to put her happiness before my own.'

His mum snorted with laughter. 'Very noble! You sound like an old Mills and Boon novel! You're both adults, Rick. Tell her how you feel. I'm sure when she knows ...' The loud ring of the rear doorbell interrupted her flow. 'I wonder who that is. We're not expecting any deliveries today. Oh, it's the police. Perhaps they have news.'

She scurried to unlock the door. 'Please come in,' she said to the detectives. 'I'll fetch Gerald. Rick, can you make some more tea?'

'Nothing for us, thanks,' Beth Honeysuckle smiled as she walked through.

Rick sat down again and indicated for the officers to join him. 'Any news?' he asked.

'We'll wait for your parents to join us, if you don't mind,' Beth said.

An awkward silence ensued. At last, a flustered Sally appeared, husband Gerald in her wake, dishevelled in grease-stained overalls.

'Sorry to keep you,' Gerald said. 'I was just out in the workshop.'

'He likes to do up old cars. It's his hobby,' Sally explained. She frowned at her son. 'Didn't Rick get you some tea?'

'We're fine, thanks.' Beth sat straighter and gave them a warm smile. 'I'll get straight to the point. We have made a small amount of progress in our search of Freya's unknown boyfriend, and are once again considering the possibility it may have been a local man.'

'I thought you'd ruled that out?' Sally interjected.

'We interviewed those we considered to be possible candidates at the time,' Beth replied carefully, 'and took DNA tests, none of which were a match for Freya's child. However, we have reason to believe the DNA evidence may have been compromised, so we looked again at alibis. We now have cause to question the validity of at least two of those alibis.'

'Who?' Gerald's fists were clenched as he tensed for the response.

Beth shot him a look of apology. 'If you wouldn't mind, we'd prefer to ask you a few questions first. Freya had been working in the pharmacy at Wickthorpe Health Centre for seven months. Is that correct?' They all nodded. 'How was she getting on there?'

It was Sally who answered. 'Fine. It was just intended to be a temporary thing – a stop gap between university and a better job, to get some work experience. Freya was ambitious and wanted to wait until the right opportunity came along. Her degree was in microbiology and her long-term career plan was that field.'

'And had nothing suitable come along in those seven months?'

Sally frowned. 'To begin with, I think she just wanted a bit of a break from work. Her degree had been quite intense. When she finished uni, she spent three months travelling around Europe with her best friend, Cara.' Her face relaxed, remembering. 'They had a wonderful time. When they came back, Freya started applying for jobs. She had a couple of interviews and then an offer but she turned it down. It wasn't exactly what she wanted. Then, I noticed the pharmacy were advertising for an assistant so I mentioned it to Freya. It was just something to keep her occupied until the right job came along. Anyway, she started in November; said it was OK – a bit boring but at least she was earning and it wasn't going to be for long.'

'Seven months is quite a long time,' Beth commented.

'Yes.' Another frown. 'Gerald and I were a bit worried about that too. Somewhere along the line, she seemed to lose her motivation. She had been so career-oriented, but she stopped talking about other jobs and got a bit cross with me asking. That was the time she started spending most weekends away. We thought she was with Cara and other friends. We now know that wasn't the case.'

'We understand she also worked part-time here in the pub?' Jack turned the observation into a question.

'That's correct. She helped whenever we were a bit short-handed, quite regularly in fact. Business at the pub had taken off and we were very busy.'

'What did she do, when she helped out?'

Sally shrugged. 'Whatever was needed. She was popular behind the bar – always had a smile for every customer – but she did some waitressing too.'

'Is it possible she could have developed a relationship with one of the customers?' Jack asked.

Sally shook her head. 'No. A few of the men liked to flirt with her but she always handled herself well. Polite and friendly, but never over-familiar, if you know what I mean. Gerald and I were always there, keeping an eye on things, and none of the customers ever overstepped the mark. It was just harmless banter.'

'Was Andrew Green one of the men who flirted with Freya?'

Sally's eyes widened. 'Sometimes, but that's Andrew. He even flirted with me! As I said, it was totally harmless. And Andrew Green is married. Freya would never get involved with a married man.'

'You don't believe she would have embarked on an affair with Andrew Green?' Beth persisted.

'Definitely not!' Sally was growing indignant. 'I'm sure Gerald and Rick agree with me.'

They both nodded. 'If anything, she was embarrassed by his compliments. She knew how insincere he was,' Gerald said.

'He wasn't her type.' Rick added.

'Oh? And who would you say *was* her type?' Beth Honeysuckle turned her penetrating gaze to Freya's brother.

Rick shrugged. 'Who knows? I just know it wouldn't have been Andrew Green. He always seems a bit of a lightweight.'

Beth waited for him to expand further. When he failed to do so, she changed tack. 'Let's return to Freya's other workplace. How did she find working with Jane Holley?'

Sally wrinkled her nose. 'Fine,' she said again. 'I don't think Mrs Holley was much fun to work with, but otherwise ...'

'Did she talk about others at the practice?'

'Not much. I know she liked some of the nurses, and the receptionists, Hannah Whittle and Julie Green. Julie is Andrew Green's wife. That's another reason I know Freya wouldn't have become involved with Andrew. I think she felt a bit sorry for Julie.'

'Oh, why was that?'

'I suppose it was because Andrew was often in the pub on his own and Julie was always left at home with the girls. I remember her saying one night that Andrew didn't deserve his wife.' Sally gave a firm nod. 'Freya definitely wouldn't have fallen for his line. Anyway, to answer your original question, she didn't really talk about anyone else from the Health Centre. She didn't have much to do with the doctors although, when she first started working there, she used to make us laugh with some of her observations.' Sally chuckled. 'Freya had a great sense of humour. Some of the things ...'

'Did she talk about Dr Holley?'

'Seb? Oh, she considered him a bit of a god, like most of the village. There was one time when she had made a mix-up with a patient's prescription and Mrs Holley gave her a bit of a dressing-down. Poor Freya was mortified and became upset. She was on her way to the loo, practically in tears, when Dr Holley spotted her ... called her into his consultation room. It was at the end of the day and most of the staff had gone home. He was so kind ...' Sally's face glowed as she recalled the incident. 'Such a lovely man.'

Beth glanced across at Jack who was watching on, impassive as ever. She took a breath before continuing. 'Did Freya tell you any more about the incident?'

'Only that Dr Holley had made her feel so much better. He told her how impressed he had been by her; he could see she was going to go far.'

Beth nodded. 'Did Freya mention Dr Holley much after that?'

Sally shook her head. 'I don't think so.'

'She used to go on about him quite a bit to me,' Rick said. 'She couldn't understand how someone like him could be married to someone who was such as "a witch" – her words. Dr Holley was the golden boy, as far as she was concerned.'

'Would you say she developed a bit of a crush on him?'

'No,' Sally spluttered.

'Yes,' Rick replied at the same time. 'She did, Mum. She was always harping on. "Dr Holley that, Dr Holley this." She even started calling him

Seb. But that was a while back, in the early days of her working there. She did stop, thankfully!'

'When would you say she stopped discussing him with you?'

Rick thought for a few seconds. 'I'm not sure exactly. It would have been some time before she died. February, possibly.' He hunched his shoulders.

'Was it about the same time those weekends away started?'

'Inspector Honeysuckle, what are you getting at? You *cannot* be suggesting that Seb Holley was the man Freya was secretly seeing!' Silence. 'Oh my goodness, you *do* think that!' Sally clasped her hands to her mouth. 'That is completely ridiculous! Just because, maybe, she had a bit of a crush! Freya would never ...'

'I know it might seem a bit of a stretch, Mrs Billington,' Beth soothed. 'But Seb Holley is a good-looking man and we know your daughter greatly admired him. She met him through work and obviously had the opportunity to develop a close relationship with him. It is a possibility, given that set of circumstances, that she and Dr Holley began an affair.'

'Never!' Sally was white with horror. 'He's so much older ... and married. And Freya was gorgeous. Absolutely stunning. She could have had anyone. I feel sick.'

Gerald glowered from his chair. 'I'll go round there. Ask him. We'll soon find out if he was messing around with my daughter.' He bunched his fists.

'Please don't, Mr Billington. Please stay away from Dr Holley and let us handle this,' Beth interrupted, alarmed by his reaction. 'As yet we have no proof. We are just trying to discover if he is a possible match for Freya's mystery man. Your interference could wreck the whole investigation. I'm sure you wouldn't want that?'

'I just want him to get what's coming to him,' Gerald muttered, anger still simmering.

'If he is responsible for anything at all with regard to Freya's death, rest assured, we will make sure he gets the justice he deserves, Mr Billington.' Beth stood. 'Thank you all for your time. We will keep you informed of developments. And please do not do anything you might regret. That goes for all of you. We certainly don't want to be in the position of having to arrest any of you.'

With that threat still ringing in their ears, the Billingtons were left alone once more.

'I don't believe it. Not Seb. It couldn't have been!' Sally was still shaking her head.

'I disagree. I've always thought he was smarmy.' Rick picked up his empty mug. 'Come on. I for one could use a stiff drink. Dad?'

Gerald regarded him with sad eyes, all previous anger gone, leaving him as shrivelled as a deflated balloon. 'It's not going to help, son,' he said. 'Nothing can ever make this better.'

***

Honeysuckle and Everard headed back to the station, more upbeat than they had felt for a while. 'What next, Beth, given the case has been officially closed? Not that you happened to mention that to Mrs Green and the Billingtons, by the way.'

She glanced across. 'We get the Super to give us a few more days and we come up with a strategy to nail the bastard. We still don't have enough to arrest him, or force him to take a DNA test, but he's the link between the two women. I'd stake my house on it.'

'You think Ally Pally will roll with it, given we still lack anything concrete to pin anything on him?' Jack was referring to Detective Superintendent Allison Pallister, their superior officer.

Beth pulled a face. 'It's up to us to convince her. I think we've got enough.' She rolled the day's discoveries through her mind. Jack was right. It wasn't much. She hoped it would be enough.

However, when they entered the station, they found Pallister wanted to see them. 'There you are,' the Superintendent said drily. She was a slim woman, slight in stature, considered a fair boss and respected by her team. 'I was about to send out a search party.'

'Sorry, Ma'am.' Beth shifted uncomfortably as she met piercing, gimlet-grey eyes.

'I won't ask where the two of you have been,' Pallister's lips formed a tight line of disapproval, 'but there's been new evidence in the Holley case.

We now have a source for the email address purporting to belong to Stuart Bickerstaff.'

Beth sucked in a breath. 'Who is it, Ma'am?' she asked.

'It was set up by Peter Banyan. We've already checked Banyan out and, no surprise, he doesn't exist. However, the trail led to a company called Spark Electrics.' Pallister paused, waiting for a response.

'Should that mean anything to us, Ma'am?' Beth said.

'It should. Spark Electrics is a subsidiary company of Ryecroft Industries. I think you ought to bring Deborah Ryecroft in for questioning, don't you?'

CHAPTER 35

Ava Green hummed to herself, a secret smile on her lips, as she re-organised the greetings card shelves of their retail section. It was time to stop procrastinating; time to stop denying herself what she desperately wanted. She had come to a decision. Tonight, she would give Patrick his answer. She was going to say yes.

What should she wear? It ought to be something special but she had already given each of the new outfits in her wardrobe an outing with Patrick. He particularly liked the violet dress, she recalled. Said something about it matching her eyes. At the time, she did not point out her own assessment – that her eyes were a boring grey colour rather than violet. He was obviously flattering her. But the violet dress was one of her favourites. It would have to do.

'You're looking very smug about something,' Enid snarled from her chair. 'Care to tell me what you're so happy about?'

Ava smiled across at her. For once, her mother could do nothing to spoil her mood. 'Just thinking,' she answered.

'About what?'

'Oh, this and that.' Deliberately, she moved around to the far end of the shop, out of her mother's line of sight.

'Hmph.' The snort of derision followed her anyway. 'I hope you're not mooning over that con-artist American.' Ava did not respond. It wasn't worth it. Whatever she said, her mother would find some spiteful rejoinder. 'I've discovered some rather unsavoury details about his life in America, when he was with that woman he so readily threw you over for.' Enid's voice continued to weave its web.

Walk away, Ava told herself. Instead, she called back, 'I'm not interested, Mother.'

'Oh, I think you might be, but there … it's up to you. If you're stupid enough to make the same mistake all over again … I just thought you would want to know *exactly* why his marriage ended, especially before you do anything rash.'

Ava sighed. Best to get it over with. She would laugh about it with Patrick later. Stepping out from behind the shelf, she asked, 'What is it you want to tell me, Mother?'

Enid uttered a martyred sigh. 'I don't *want* to tell you, Ava. No one enjoys giving bad news.'

A sense of dread clustered around Ava's heart. *Bad news?* 'I'm sure that's true, Mother,' she said. 'Just tell me.'

'Your American told you he's divorced?' Enid began, concealing her glee behind a sombre demeanour. Ava nodded. 'Did he tell you why?' Another nod. Enid gave her a piteous smile. 'Did he tell you the marriage broke up because he owed thousands and thousands of dollars?'

Ava's eyes widened. Patrick had *not* told her that. 'Th … that's not true,' she stammered.

'It *is* true,' Enid ploughed on, relentless in her determination to destroy Ava's dreams. 'And that's not the worst of it. The reason he was in such terrible debt was because he's a gambler. He had gambled away all their money and much more besides.'

'Oh.' Ava clutched her hand to her throat. *That couldn't be true.* She knew Patrick. Except the gleam in her mother's eyes shone with conviction. Enid believed it. 'Where did you … how did you come by this information?'

Enid pretended to look shame-faced. 'I only did it to protect you, because I didn't trust that man. I couldn't bear to see you hurt all over again. I hired an investigator to do a background check on him. And he came up with that. I'm sorry, Ava. I did try to warn you.'

Ava could listen no more. Turning away, she fled up the stairs to the sanctuary of her room. Once there, she flung herself on the bed and stared, dry-eyed, at the ceiling, at the cracks snaking like veins across the greying expanse. Taking a deep breath, she tried to set aside her dismay at this latest revelation and consider it logically. Everything in life was flawed, either in plain sight like the ceiling, or hidden ... but the imperfections were there nonetheless. It was the same with people. Everyone had faults, weaknesses, shortcomings. Patrick was no different, much as she liked to think of him as her 'verray parfit gentil knight.' Gambling was an addiction, she knew; an illness. If Patrick was a secret gambler, she should try to support him. For a start, she would ask him about it tonight. If he still had a problem, it was better to get it out in the open and look for ways to get him help. Dr Holley was a trained hypnotherapist and had done wonders assisting people with all kinds of fears, phobias and addictions. She had every confidence he would be able to help Patrick. It niggled that he had not told her himself but who was she to sit in judgement? He may have had his reasons. She loved him. She would give him the benefit of doubt.

Head held high, she rolled off the bed and descended the stairs, determined to deny Enid the pleasure of seeing her upset. She would go out with Patrick tonight, as planned, and she would wear the violet.

But her answer to his marriage proposal ... well, that might have to wait.

***

After Ava had gone out – hopefully, to finish things with the American – Enid sat in her usual spot in her sitting room, two handsome men in front of her. Now they were ranged, side by side, she could see the similarities clearly. Blond, blue-eyed, tall, muscular ... *powerful*. Their mouths were almost identical: wide and perfectly shaped with even, white teeth. A lover's mouth, but one which could twist with sadistic cruelty. She had seen it often enough in her son. Now, she saw the potential for it in Dr Holley. The revelation pleased her.

'Thank you so much for coming, Dr Holley, and my sincerest condolences for your loss,' she said.

'Thank you. Please, call me Seb. After all, from what Andy tells me, we may be related.' He gave her his most winning smile, guaranteed to please any female, no matter how old.

Andy? Enid hated the abbreviation of her son's name but decided to let it slide. She smiled in return. 'Yes, Seb. You've read the book?'

'Indeed. Andy impressed upon me its importance. Most enlightening. I feel honoured you trusted me with it but I'm not sure why.'

Enid nodded. She had planned her speech in advance. Only she knew the importance of it, how crucial it was to get Dr Holley on side. Lives depended upon it. It was going to be difficult but she had every faith in her powers of persuasion. And she had right on her side.

'Because of the curse,' she began, her voice solemn with conviction. 'Since the day Martha Lightbody spoke those fateful words, the Holley family has been blighted. You read what she did to Roger Holley by her sorcery. Oh, I know the book seeks to portray her as an innocent but that was because it was written by one of her ancestors. She survived the drowning because she was a witch, just as the Ryecroft woman survived her trial by drowning.'

Seb pretended to look surprised. 'Deborah Ryecroft? Are you saying she's involved?'

'Yes.' Enid shot him a look of triumph. 'She is a Littlebody, through and through. Only a few of us know that her father, Elijah, was Mabel Littlebody's cousin. You noticed, I'm sure, that Martha Lightbody changed her name to Ruth *Littlebody*. This means Deborah Ryecroft is a pure-blood descendant of the Wickthorpe Witch.' She paused to let the information sink in, smiling inwardly at Seb's fascinated expression. 'As such, she poses a terrible threat to anyone who bears the Holley name including, I'm sorry to say, yourself. Look at what happened to your poor wife!'

Seb raised his eyebrows, his expression shocked. 'You can't think Deborah Ryecroft was responsible for what happened to Jane?'

'I am convinced of it. I know this will be a shock to you, Seb, coming out of the blue like this, but I have lived with it all my life. I know what the Littlebodys have done to this family – murder, rape, staged suicides, assaults, theft, blackmail, cheating ... you name it, they've done it. This is a war which has waged between the two families for almost four hundred years. And innocents have been caught up in it too, like Freya Billington. While a Littlebody lives in Wickthorpe, no one is safe.'

'Steady, Mother. You don't want to give yourself a heart attack,' Andrew interjected as Enid became increasingly breathless during her passionate speech.

Enid cast him an irritated glance. 'I'm alright, as long as I'm getting the message across.' She looked pointedly across at Seb, who appeared deep in thought.'

At last, he said, 'What about Mabel Littlebody? She lived in the village for years with no trouble.'

Enid had regained her composure. 'Not all Littlebodys are tarred with the same brush. It's the same with the Holleys. Only a few carry the responsibility of the curse. Mabel clearly was not involved. I am, as was my father before me. I believe Andrew is.' She glanced fondly at her son. 'And now, with Jane's tragic death, I believe you are. You're involved in this whether you like it or not. I thought it best to warn you, at the very least, but I hope you will help us.'

Seb ignored that. 'You said many crimes had been committed by Littlebodys against Holleys. Do you have proof of this?'

'I'm sure proof exists, if you want to look. I'm going by what my father told me, and his father before that. And I know what has happened in my lifetime. Louisa Littlebody, Elijah Ryecroft's mother and Deborah's grandmother, was a witch who caused us great harm by devious means. I remember her as an evil woman. She moved into Wickthorpe when she married Frederick Ryecroft and, straight away, awful things started to happen. That very first year, a young boy who had been playing with others by Dark Water Lake, fell in and drowned. Everyone said it was a tragic accident and it was never investigated, yet the boy's great grandmother was born a Holley. That was no coincidence. After that, a few years later, the village had a drought throughout the spring and all the farmers' crops failed. My father tried to warn villagers that Louisa was behind it but they refused to listen. Fortunately, Louisa died quite young, in mysterious circumstances, and all was quiet once more in the village. Until the Ryecroft woman was born ... and look what has happened since!'

'You say Louisa died in "mysterious circumstances." Do you know what happened?' Seb asked.

Enid shot him a coy look. 'Some sort of poisoning, I believe, but never proved.'

'Were Holleys involved?'

'I couldn't possibly say.'

'I see.' Seb's voice held disapproval. 'Obviously, I cannot condone any form of violence, but what you say is both interesting and worrying. I thought my wife had taken her own life. Now, I'm not so sure. Have you told the police?'

Enid snorted in disgust. 'The police? Totally useless in matters like these. They don't understand and they're certainly not interested in anything beyond what is right in front of their noses.'

'I can understand that. They have even questioned *me* in relation to Jane's death. As the husband, apparently, I'm the obvious suspect.' His tone was bitter.

'You need to be careful,' Enid warned. 'I wouldn't put it past the witch to try to frame you for her crimes. Littlebodys have done it before. There was one time when ...'

'But what can I do?' Seb interrupted. 'How can I protect myself? What do you propose, Mrs Green?'

'Enid, please,' she gushed. 'I know you said you can't condone violence, Seb. I totally agree. But desperate times call for desperate measures. What I'm going to suggest is extreme, I'll grant you, but we have to stop the witch before there are more deaths, and more innocent people getting the blame. She will not stop, that's for sure. We have to stop her. I have a plan to do just that, to end the curse, once and for all.'

And, lowering her voice, she outlined her proposal.

***

'You look so beautiful in that dress.' Not far away, in *The Lamb Inn*, Patrick took Ava's hand in his. 'I swear it is the exact same colour of your lovely eyes and that's the truth.' He gave her his heart–breaking smile.

That was her opening. 'And have you told me the *whole* truth, Patrick?' she asked, tugging her hand away.

'What do you mean?' His face full of bemusement, he reached again for her hand but she hid it under the table.

'Your marriage. Why did it finish? Why did you break up with Candice?' She tried and failed to keep an undertone of accusation from her voice.

He frowned. 'I'm not sure I understand. I told you the marriage was over, long before it was officially over. Part of that was my fault. I was young, stupid and momentarily infatuated by Candice, but I never really loved her, not the way I loved you. We should never have married in the first place. Both of us were unhappy. But I could lose myself in my work, which I always enjoyed. Candice ... well, Candice lost herself in other ways.'

Ava shook her head. 'The *whole* truth, Patrick. What are you *not* telling me?'

He threw up his hands. 'Candice had problems. Is that what you want me to say?'

'What about *your* problems, Patrick? The debts. The gambling. When were you going to mention those?' Her voice was cold as she glared at him across the small table set for a romantic, intimate dinner for two. A young girl hovered nearby to take their order and, realising it was not a good moment, beat a hasty retreat.

'But that was ...' His eyes narrowed. 'Who told you this stuff? Was it your mother, by any chance?'

'It doesn't matter who it was. The questions I want to ask are: is it true and, if so, why did you fail to tell me?'

He gave a heavy sigh. 'It's true we got into terrible debt and gambling was the cause.'

'Oh.' His admission deflated her. Right up until this point, she had hoped he would deny it, prove it was false.

'But,' he continued, 'what your mother *didn't* tell you was that the debts were accumulated by Candice, not me. *She* was the one with the gambling problem. I tried to fix it but I couldn't. We broke up and, eventually, I paid off the debts. End of story. I didn't tell you because it wasn't my story to tell. It was Candice's and I'm sure she would prefer me to remain silent about it.'

'Oh,' Ava said again. Hope began to blossom in her chest. 'So you don't gamble at all?'

'Never have, never will. I've seen the destruction it can bring. Do you gamble, Ava?'

The turnabout made her smile. 'Well, I have been known to have a flutter on the Grand National ... but I don't have to,' she added, somewhat anxiously.

His smile was back. 'I'm glad you asked me about it,' he said. 'I'm glad you didn't just accept what your mother had told you.'

She nodded. No point denying it was Enid. Tentatively, she brought her hand up, fingers trembling as they stretched across the table. He met her halfway, staring deep into her eyes with a look of such longing she felt she could burst with happiness.

'The answer to your big question, then, is yes.'

'You mean ...?' At the shy incline of her head, he whooped with joy. Then, to her utter dismay and embarrassment, and the delight of all the nearby diners, he leapt across the table, knocking glasses aside, gathered her in his arms, and kissed her, long and hard, on the lips.

CHAPTER 36

At eight-thirty, Deborah Ryecroft received a phone call from Wickthorpe Health Centre.

'Dr Holley would urgently like you to make an appointment to see him today,' a woman informed her.

'Why? What for? Is it the biopsy? The consultant at the hospital gave me the all-clear.' Fear clasped icy fingers around her heart.

'I'm afraid I can't say,' the voice said briskly. 'Would 9:15 be convenient? Or 4:45 this afternoon?'

'9:15,' Deborah answered. Whatever it was, she did not want to wait until later in the day.

'9:15 with Dr Holley. That's all booked for you.'

'Thank you.' Deborah's reply was automatic. Her brain was processing the suddenness and the urgency of the call. Perhaps there had been a mix-up over her results? A summons like that rarely heralded good news. She took a deep breath, trying to dampen her concern.

Dr Holley. Panic escalated as his name registered, and she forced herself to sit, slowly exhaling as she harnessed her nervous energy. Naturally, it was Dr Holley. This was a medical issue and he had referred her to the hospital. If there was a problem with her biopsy results, he would be the one to tell her. She took another deep breath. The doctor she had seen at the hospital was confident the lump was a cyst. No need to think the worst. It was the suddenness of the call, the unexpectedness of it, which had set her worrying.

She glanced at her watch. Soon she would have to leave for the 9:15 appointment. Still clutching her phone, she headed upstairs. There was just time to prepare – do her face, comb her hair, grab her bag. She didn't have long. The distraction of normal, routine tasks would help keep her calm. A glance in the mirror showed a face with no pallor and eyes dark with dread. Despite the pep talk she had given herself, anxiety slithered through her veins. No amount of foundation, mascara and lip gloss could conceal it. Her eyes skittered across to her bedside table. Martha's book was no longer there – she had loaned it to Honoraria – but it remained rooted in her consciousness, and she felt Martha's presence as a premonition, warning her, calling out to her ...

Stop! It was a doctor's appointment. Nothing else. And it was time to leave. Without a backward glance, she descended the stairs, slipped on coat and boots, and left the house.

***

Dr Sebastian Holley sat alone in his consulting room. Waiting. Preparing. His mind hummed with clinical precision. Everything was falling into place. It would not be long until the Wickthorpe curse was silenced, especially now he had the perfect scapegoats. His exit strategy had been in place for a while. Eventually, he would leave Wickthorpe. He was destined for better things.

Covering his tracks was something at which he excelled. It was an art honed to perfection over the years. Pleasure at committing crimes was only exceeded by the satisfaction of seeing others take the fall. It had started at school, an all-boys boarding facility in Oxfordshire. He had always been popular, possessed with the ability to win over peers and masters alike. Such unquestioning admiration allowed him to perpetrate acts of malice against targeted boys whilst framing others. Not too often. Not enough to raise suspicion, but sufficient to keep his scheming brain amused.

As a teenager, girls had been his target. How easy it was to seduce the pick of a local comprehensive! After a while, he chose to ignore those who simpered and fawned. He despised the way they pressed their scantily-clad bodies furtively against his in a pathetic effort to gain his notice. Instead, he focused on the less available girls – the attractive, intellectual virgins who pretended to ignore him. He chuckled to himself, remembering. None were immune to his charm. He had his pick, leaving his friends in awe of his prowess. Aged seventeen, in the first year of sixth form, they set him a challenge. *Miss Powers.* Even now, his loins tightened at the thought of her. A thirty-four-year-old chemistry teacher with the promise of a divine body beneath that white lab coat. She had arrived at the school that year and immediately become the object of common room fantasies. With her cool, crisp demeanour and no-nonsense approach towards the pupils in her charge, she was considered an inaccessible goddess. Boys wove lewd, late-night tales about her. Seb remained detached from it all, until one of his peers wagered even Seb would stand no chance with this latest object of desire.

Seb accepted the bet, excited by the risk involved. The prospect of sampling the mature delights of the sexy chemistry teacher, combined with the challenge of getting away with it, was just too good to turn down. It was a mission worthy of his abilities, requiring extreme cunning and caution.

He started by hanging back after chemistry classes, pretending he needed further help. Miss Powers treated him with courteous care and a teacher's diligent desire to educate. She liked him, he could tell. The groundwork was laid. The next step: persuade his father to fork out for extra lessons to give him additional time in Miss Power's company, one on one. Once that was accomplished, Seb quickly took advantage of the situation. She laughed often in his company and he knew his charm was working. Gradually, he steered their relationship into more personal territory, and fabricated tales of problems growing up to gain her sympathy. When he feigned tears, she hesitantly put an arm around him to comfort him – a major step forward. He continued to sob; she hugged him tighter. Her proximity excited him and he deemed it time to cease his crocodile tears. Swivelling in his chair, he gathered her into his arms and kissed her.

She stiffened with shock but had not pulled away instantly, much to his satisfaction. He apologised and said it would never happen again. She was upset and wanted to terminate their private lessons but, eventually, he managed to persuade her otherwise. And, at last, she succumbed, gasping in delight as his hands roamed her body, even while she protested that he had to stop.

Afterwards, he described the deed to his peers, followed by much back-slapping and envious congratulations. However, the boy who had set the bet, a gangly, pock-faced youth named Toby Swift, refused to pay up. He accused

Seb of inventing the conquest, and wanted proof it had actually happened. Worse, he cast doubts in the other boys' minds. The admiration and jeering compliments ebbed away.

It meant Seb had to repeat the experience. Not a hardship, but acquiring proof was more problematic. No phone cameras in those days. He *did* have an ordinary camera. Not easy, though, to take a surreptitious photo ...

In the end, he risked a late-night visit to Miss Power's ground-floor flat, in a building where the female members of staff on site were housed, and tapped on the window. Horrified, she opened it to tell him to leave and was unable to stop him from clambering inside. From then on, she was compromised. He could have forced himself upon her, but that was not his style. Instead, he pretended emotional turmoil; he couldn't sleep ... could barely bring himself to eat, he was so sick with love for her. He could not go on like that, seeing her daily but unable to touch her or to be with her. He had come to say goodbye, he said, brandishing a rucksack in which he had supposedly packed essential belongings.

For over an hour, she counselled and consoled him until her comfort turned into something more, as he knew it would. Afterwards, he had carried his rucksack into her small bathroom, removed his camera and taken pictures of the used condom alongside personal items in the cabinet on the wall including, most helpfully, a bottle of tablets with her name on the prescription label. Job done. Afterwards, when she was full of regrets and told him there could be no repeats of that night, he reluctantly conceded she was right.

Neither of them was ever caught. Miss Powers took up employment elsewhere at the end of that term and Toby Swift paid the bet. An excellent result ... except Seb felt Toby should pay a greater penalty for his declaration of doubt. Shortly afterwards, a stash of cannabis was discovered in Toby's room and he was asked to leave the school, despite his protestations of innocence. Seb felt he was invincible.

The first time he killed someone was also well-planned. Edinburgh, 2000. Maxine Darkins. The slut deserved it, no question. She had tricked him, told him she was on the pill, that he didn't need to take precautions. Having got herself pregnant, she had attempted to blackmail him into marriage. It was relatively easy to lure her to his house when he knew it would be empty, out onto the roof and give her a sharp nudge to send her tumbling. The adrenalin rush was insane, like nothing he had ever experienced before.

Meanwhile, he had been sleeping with Jane Hodrick, a reasonably attractive post-grad. Her maturity and cool aloofness had been her initial attraction. Then, he discovered her family lived in Wickthorpe, the home of the curse of which his father had long spoken. It was fate, he decided, and he had to have her, even though he was still seeing Maxine at the time. When things started to get tricky with Maxine, he knew Jane would provide an alibi. After the deed was done, he hurried over to Jane's, took her out for pizza and spent the night at her place, thinking that would put him in the clear, especially as he had ended his relationship with Maxine weeks before.

However, he had reckoned without Maxine's best friend. She informed police that Seb had invited Maxine to his student house on that fateful evening. He became the chief suspect, especially when it was discovered that the time of death was earlier than his appearance at the pizza place. To cover his tracks, he had to ask Jane to lie for him about the time of his arrival at her flat. He combined his request with a marriage proposal and, as she was madly in love and believed he could do no wrong, she was happy to oblige.

The police remained unconvinced and Seb continued to find himself under pressure. To prove his innocence, he engineered a DNA sample from one of his housemates, Neil, a heavy sleeper with a reputation for snoring. After a carefully orchestrated booze up, it was easy work to creep into Neil's room at the dead of night and swab the inside of his mouth. The next step was to swap Neil's sample for his own. Seb knew Fate was smiling on him when he saw the young, female officer assigned to do his test. A little flirtation and the pretence of a phobia was all it took for her to agree to him taking his own swab, enabling him to make the switch.

The memory of the buzz of that whole experience – that incredible, God-like sense of power – remained an itch. He *had* to feel it again. To kill again. And he had. Not often but enough. Different women, well away from home. Sex followed by killing – you couldn't beat it for the ultimate thrill.

Except, after a while, even that excitement began to fade. He needed even more risk, more danger. An eighteen-year-old patient in Surrey provided both. It was fun seeing just how far he could corrupt her, how far she was prepared to go for him. A very long way, it transpired. Power of a different kind. Before he could orchestrate her death, however, she made serious allegations against him, threatening his whole career. She had been his only mistake. He had left it too long before getting rid of her and been forced to think fast to diffuse the situation. Once again, Jane had covered for him. He had confessed the affair to her and she could see the wisdom in protecting him. Their marriage may be a sham but Jane knew on which side her bread was buttered. Their whole lifestyle was at stake and she was as keen as he to deflect any possibility of a scandal.

Being close to the edge, that was what he enjoyed. The extraordinarily vibrant and beautiful Freya Billington was another opportunity he could not pass up, especially as, in the meantime, the Wickthorpe Witch had returned to the village. Fate was coming to fruition. He listened to the talk about Deborah Ryecroft and knew this was a chance not to be missed. On a personal level, the opportunity to seduce a young girl from the village, *and* dispose of her afterwards, was delicious. The icing on the cake would be her drowning in Dark Water Lake, re-igniting the curse and acting as a precursor to a long-awaited denouement between him and Deborah Ryecroft.

His chance came when Jane publicly reprimanded Freya in the pharmacy. He managed to corner her for a private chat and soon had her blushing at his compliments. The seeds were sown but he remained as cautious as a cat burglar, merely bestowing her with private smiles and, when the opportunity arose, further intimate chats. Slowly, he succeeded in snaring her completely, so much so that it was she who made the first move.

Their affair was short-lived. There was no denying she excited him and it was a disappointment it had to end so quickly. When she tried to trap him into divorcing his wife for her, it was over. The motel in Oxford where they stayed was carefully selected for its lack of CCTV cameras – just one in the reception area and one in the car park, which he disabled beforehand. He booked the room in advance under the name of Taylor using a burner phone. Plans finalised, he met Freya in a supermarket car park in Ipswich and they drove to Oxford in her car, on back roads to avoid camera detection. Upon arrival, he gave her cash to pay for the room in full, while he waited in the car. All went to plan. The day was uneventful and she fell quickly asleep, thanks to a sedative he had dissolved in her apple juice. Then the real work began.

He fetched his kit bag and personal protection overalls from a holdall left in the boot of Freya's car. The next bit was all about timing and his skills as a hypnotherapist. Once he was fully prepared, and the effects of the sedative had worn off sufficiently, he woke Freya. She was still drowsy and very suggestible. His voice low and soothing, he persuaded her to drink several more cupfuls of apple juice laced with vodka. Within an hour, she was blind drunk. He was able to dress her, get her into the car, and drive to Dark Water Lake.

The weather was shocking but he found it only a minor inconvenience. Freya slept during the journey and, as before, he helped her to more apple juice, washed down with sufficient Silenor, a tricyclic antidepressant, to make her pass out. He carried her into the water, deep enough, and gently lifted her legs. Pleasingly, there was no struggle. He had judged things perfectly.

Afterwards, he discarded the empty vodka bottle and Silenor packet on the bank, along with her phone and the message he typed (unsent so no one would raise the alarm too soon). From there, he walked home. It was just after 4 a.m. on Sunday morning and Jane was asleep. The protective clothing and his boots were bundled in a black bag, for their safe disposal later, and hidden in the holdall; his clothes went into the washing machine. Once Jane was up, he persuaded her to drive him to Ipswich to retrieve his car and later had it valeted at a drive-through. Even though Freya hadn't been in his car that weekend, she had before, and he felt it imperative to eliminate any remaining DNA traces.

What he had not anticipated was that someone would see him and Freya together in Oxford. And Honoraria Simpson-Fairchild, of all people, the biggest busybody in the village! Suspicion fell on any man of her acquaintance when the stupid woman claimed Freya's 'mystery man' reminded her of someone she knew. Thank goodness he had been wearing his disguise! It proved meticulous planning was always required for such operations.

Fortunately for him, his previous, false DNA test put him in the clear, along with the staunch alibi he demanded from Jane. He had expected her to comply without question but, for the first time, she demanded answers. Although she did as he asked, it seriously affected their marriage, such as it was, and latterly, her mental health. As time went by, he realised she had guessed the truth. Fragile as she was, blabbing to Deborah Ryecroft and the bloody rector, he could not let her live. And he did not want her death, or Freya's, to be dismissed as suicides, despite setting them up as such. Jane's demise provided the opportunity, via the fabricated emails, to give the police a fall guy, or girl ...

However, since laying those plans, things had moved on. His phone buzzed.

'Deborah Ryecroft is here to see you, Dr Holley.'

'Thank you, Hannah. Send her in, please.'

CHAPTER 37

Deborah knocked lightly on the door of Dr Holley's consulting room.

'Come in and sit down.' The shark's smile of even, white teeth.

'Dr Holley.' Deborah gave him a tense nod.

'Seb, please. No need to be formal, not with me.' He relaxed back in his chair, his face and manner reassuring. 'And don't look so worried. There's no need.'

'You mean ... the biopsy?' Hope flared as she gazed into those hypnotic blue eyes.

'Mostly good news.' His voice took on its professional tenor. 'No cancer. The lump is some kind of cyst, as we thought.'

'Oh, thank goodness.' Relief washed over her. 'But you said *mostly* good news?'

'Mm.' He frowned. 'The pathology is inconclusive. We would feel happier if we could pin down exactly what has caused the cyst. It is unusual.'

'How do you mean?'

'As I said, nothing to worry about.' Another reassuring smile as he rose and walked behind her. 'But we would like to do another blood test, if you have no objection. It's always best to make certain nothing else is going on. I can do that for you right now, if you would like?'

'Of course.'

He pulled a small trolley to her right side. 'Would you mind removing your coat and pulling up your sleeve?' Feeling slightly bemused, she followed his instructions. There were phials on the table, she noticed, and a syringe. In the meantime, Seb had pulled on surgical gloves. When she was ready, he took hold of her arm. She had to steel herself to resist the urge to shudder. 'You'll just feel a sharp prick.'

Instinctively, she began to look away. As she turned her head, she imagined she saw something in the syringe. *That couldn't be right. He was taking blood, not giving an injection.* She opened her mouth to protest as the needle jabbed into her arm. 'There, all done.'

'But ...' There was something wrong with her tongue, and her lips had become incapable of speech. The room swirled grey and black.

'Just a little something to make you sleep. Nothing to worry about.'

Seb's voice sounded distorted, as if from the end of a long tunnel, and she struggled in vain to understand what he was saying. He was still speaking and his hands were under her armpits when blackness claimed her.

***

After the morning briefing, DI Beth Honeysuckle and DS Jack Everard drove to Greenways Farm to take Deborah Ryecroft to the station for an interview under caution. The new evidence, of Ryecroft's possible involvement in the Bickerstaff emails, had changed everything. Beth's superiors were hoping for an arrest, a view shared by her sergeant.

'I'm starting to wonder if there's some truth behind this whole Wickthorpe Witch thing,' Jack observed from the passenger seat as they turned into Green Road. 'Ryecroft seems to be involved in all the goings-on, one way or another. There must be a reason.'

Beth nodded. 'But is she behind it all, or is she a victim? She nearly drowned last summer, remember? We were there.'

'Mm. Makes you wonder if those Hampton-Browns were as crazy as we thought, doesn't it? Perhaps they knew the truth about her after all.'

'Or maybe they were part of the whole conspiracy against her.' They turned left into the driveway and Beth stopped the engine. She swivelled to face her colleague. 'My money says she's being framed and Dr Holley is our man.'

Jack's round face creased into a frown. 'I know you've been convinced of his guilt for a while but, even though we've spent a lot of time and resources trying to pin something on him, we still have nothing concrete connecting him to either of the drownings.' He shrugged. 'And, with this new information ...'

Beth's lips tightened. 'I know. We need to check it out. Come on.' She opened her door. 'Let's see what Ms Ryecroft has to say.'

There was no reply when they rang the doorbell. 'Her car is still here. She can't have gone far,' Beth said as she headed around the back of the house. 'She could be outside.' When they found the garden empty, they paid a visit to Tom Oldridge next door.

He was in his yard beside a self-propelled sprayer, talking to a small, wiry man in overalls. 'Alright, Ted. See how this load goes on.' He walked to meet the two officers as Ted climbed into the cab. 'Morning, detectives.' His greeting was affable but wary. 'What brings you here?'

'We wanted a word with Ms Ryecroft,' Beth answered. 'Would you happen to know where she is?'

Tom frowned. 'Why do you want to speak to Debs?'

Jack Everard ignored the question. 'Do you know where she is?'

'If she's not at home, she'll be out for a walk ... or in the garden,' he suggested.

'Where does she usually walk?' Beth asked.

'She usually cuts around the north of this field.' Tom pointed in the direction. 'She does a loop around the wood and comes back along Scarff's – that field over there. She's avoiding village footpaths,' he added with a wry twist to his lips, 'for obvious reasons.'

'Very wise,' Beth nodded. 'Did you see her come past this morning? From what you've described, we should be able to see her from here.'

'Yes, I often see her out but not this morning. I've been in the office most of the time.' The noise of the sprayer starting up meant he had to raise his voice.

'How long would you say this walk would take?' Beth shouted as the sprayer lumbered past and down a farm track, its booms neatly folded by its sides.

Tom shrugged. 'Half an hour or so.'

'Do you have her mobile number?'

'Of course. I'll ring her ... tell her you're here.'

'Thank you.'

He fished his phone from a pocket in his coat and pressed some buttons. 'It's ringing,' he confirmed. After a few moments, he spoke again. 'Debs, Detectives Honeysuckle and Everard are here and would like a word. Could you come straight home?' He returned the phone to his pocket. 'It went to voicemail,' he said.

'Right.' Beth's lips tightened. 'Jack will take the number and we'll leave you in peace.' She gave him a nod. 'Thanks for your help. Have a good day, Mr Oldridge.'

While Jack followed her instruction, she walked to the edge of the nearest field, her eyes scanning its perimeter for a walker. There was no one in sight and, with a sigh, she returned to the car to wait, her fingers tapping the steering wheel impatiently. After fifteen minutes, there was still no sign of Deborah.

'Try her phone again,' Beth said. This time it was switched off. At that piece of information, she started the engine. 'Perhaps she's called round to see someone. We'll head back, and you can keep trying her phone. Ask her to come straight to the station.'

***

With Deborah unconscious, Seb locked the door of his consulting room and slipped into protective clothing. He opened the external door to his room and clicked open the boot of his car, handily parked immediately outside for today's task. No one around; no one likely to be. This was a private car park. Still, he was not taking any chances. Speed was of the essence. He picked up Deborah's inert body and, after a final check, slipped her onto the plastic lining already in place, closed the boot and locked the car. She would be out for several hours – plenty of time before the next phase began. The prospect of that was something to be savoured. No rush.

Back in the consulting room, he found Deborah's handbag on the floor where she had left it. Inside, he found her phone and turned it off. A quick run through his mental checklist. Everything taken care of. He checked his watch. Not bad. Not even late for his next appointment. He buzzed through to Reception.

'Hannah, would you send Mrs Dalloway in, please?'

***

Tom usually had lunch at his house with Emma, but today decided to go across to Greenways Farm to see Deborah. He wondered if she had seen DI Honeysuckle and company. Hopefully, they had good news to share, like a breakthrough in the case, rather than another barrage of questioning. She had been through enough.

Whistling softly to himself, he headed for the back door. It was locked, as he expected. Her experiences last summer had made Deborah much more security conscious. He used his key and, after taking off his boots, padded through to the utility room to wash his dirty hands. 'Only me, Debs,' he called. There was no reply, but it was a large house. If she was in her study, she wouldn't hear him. He dried his hands and strolled through to the empty kitchen. 'Debs,' he called again. Silence greeted him. He was alone in the house.

Having decided Deborah must still be with the police, he made himself a mug of tea and found tomatoes and cheese in the fridge. He retrieved a loaf of bread from the freezer and popped four slices in the microwave for his sandwiches. He was troubled by the fact the police had kept Deborah for so long, and hoped they weren't giving her a hard time. Poor Debs. It was bad enough with superstitious villagers making accusations against her.

Having eaten his sandwiches, he tried ringing her but her phone was switched off. He shook his head, annoyed at DI Honeysuckle. What did she think she was playing at? Surely the interview couldn't have lasted all morning?

The first seeds of unease stirred in his stomach. The last time Deborah had disappeared, her phone was off. There was no harm in checking she *was* at the station. He found the direct number for Beth Honeysuckle and pressed the keys on his phone. She answered swiftly, a note of impatience in her voice. No, he was told, Deborah had not called them. Her phone had been switched off all morning. Tom was asked again if he had seen her or knew where she was.

That was when fear set in …

CHAPTER 38

Honoraria and Marcus had visited the Suffolk archives office in Ipswich, by appointment, hoping to find a record for the deaths of Martha and John Lightbody. They had discovered John and Martha's marriage took place in Kings Lynn in 1643 but, beyond that date, documentation for the couple seemed to have ceased entirely. After hours of fruitless research, they admitted defeat. There was nothing in the archives concerning the Lightbodys or their Littlebody aliases. A visit to the corresponding Norfolk archives office was planned for later that week but optimism was dimming. The book's assertion that the couple lived in Tocklewood for the rest of their lives was looking unlikely; their deaths were not registered there. It was a mystery.

Other facts were simpler to verify and there were further exciting discoveries. Whilst Prudence Harkness sadly died young, Saul and Elizabeth Makepiece from Tocklewood both lived long lives, and died aged seventy-three and eighty respectively. Phineas Tench was twice recorded in the parish records of Little Horseshoes: firstly, in 1646, when he wed Juniper Knight; and secondly, his death in 1667.

Honoraria and Marcus had concluded between themselves that the book's rather sketchy epilogue contained fabrication. The couple must have moved away from Tocklewood and may have changed their names once more. It was starting to look like they would never find out.

Wondering if Martha's persecution continued in Tocklewood, Honoraria had checked all the records for witchcraft trials, but none had featured Martha or Ruth. She and Marcus had discussed Marcus' theory of a continuing feud between the Holleys and Littlebodys. It was possible Roger's relatives, and later his descendants, may have sought vengeance for his demise. In a further newspaper search, this time focusing on later centuries, they had discovered an exciting match for the feud theory. In 1816, a duel was fought between Harold Holley and Elias Littlebody, with fatal consequences for Elias. Two months later, victor Harold was found in a ditch with his throat cut. Bernard Littlebody, brother of Elias, was arrested for Harold's murder, convicted and hanged. Given what was written in the book, those names could not be coincidence!

Despite their failure, to learn more of Martha and John, Honoraria found it all fascinating. She awoke each morning with a real zest for the day ahead, and she and Marcus continued to grow closer. Marcus seemed happy to spend every minute with her, the days in a bubble of contented research and nights in the throes of passion. Honoraria could scarcely be happier. If only she could find evidence of Martha Lightbody, or Ruth Littlebody, recorded somewhere in the annals of the past ...

***

After a long but successful operation on a greyhound, which had slipped its collar to chase a hare and been involved in a collision with a car, Rick had called in at the pub for a drink to see his parents. It was only as he was leaving, he spotted a couple in the corner, looking more than cosy together. Max Benson and some redhead, but not Emma. *Bastard!*

Poor Em! Despite his jealousy, he had always thought Max was a good bloke. Not anymore. Anger burned a fierce flame. Rick could scarcely contain himself as he drove home. However, as he turned into the drive and stopped the engine, his rage turned to anxiety. What should he do? Should he tell Emma? A friend would do so, but she was going to be hurt. He heaved a sigh. Best to get it over with. As he slid from his car, a tiny bud of hope burgeoned inside him. With Max out of the picture, maybe, in time, there would be a chance for him? The echo of his mum's words, 'Tell her how you feel,' whispered in his ear. Not yet. That would be insensitive. But soon ...

The house was dark when he entered. Emma was out, but obviously not with Max. He hoped she would not bump into him while he was with another girl. As he switched the kitchen light on, he wondered where she was. It was her turn to cook that evening and she had promised a new recipe. Frowning, he headed for the fridge and there, on the door, held in place by two magnets, was an A4 sheet of paper with his name at the top:

Rick
Am next door. Debs is missing.

He turned on his heel and made for the exit. *Debs missing – again!* He could scarcely believe it. The last time had almost resulted in her death. As he strode around the back, through the yard, and used the shortcut between the two houses, he uttered a silent prayer that Deborah Ryecroft would not be the next victim found in Dark Water Lake.

Tom was distraught. When Rick slipped through the back door, he found Emma with her arms around her father.

'She'll be alright. The police are out in force, searching for her. They'll find her, you'll see,' she soothed.

Tom failed to respond. His face was ashen with dread. Rick took one look at the pair of them and said, somewhat croakily, 'I'll make some tea, and then you can fill me in on what's happened.'

'Thanks, Rick.' Emma gave him a grateful smile as he busied himself pulling mugs from the cupboard. Once tea was made, he asked again.

'No one knows.' Emma bit her lip. 'She left the house sometime this morning, with her coat and her bag, and no one has seen her since. The police arrived at around 9:30 to speak to her, but she wasn't here and her phone went straight to voicemail. Dad left a message, saying the police wanted her to contact them. When he came here for lunch, the house was empty. Naturally, he assumed Debs with the police, but, after a while, he began to get anxious and tried her phone. By now, it was switched off. Eventually, he phoned the police. They hadn't seen her and were annoyed by her failure to contact them. Dad was really worried by then, but the police seemed more concerned she had done a runner. For some reason, Debs is now suspected of causing Jane Holley's death. Dad told them that was ridiculous but they said they had to investigate every possibility.'

'Dark Water Lake?' Rick had no need to say more.

'Dad has spent most of the afternoon there, searching. No sign of her, though. The police turned up while he was looking, so perhaps they are taking her disappearance seriously. I persuaded him to come home.' She threw her hands in the air. 'That's about it. Dad wants to go back. He's convinced someone has her and will take her there,' she grimaced, 'especially after what happened before. The place is currently crawling with police, so it's not likely in those circumstances. I can't help wondering ...' She paused and took a deep breath. 'Debs hasn't been quite herself recently. Maybe, she just needed some time out.'

Tom shook his head vehemently. 'That was worry over a medical issue which turned out alright. She was fine. It's not that, Em. Someone has her, I know it.'

Rick said nothing. He concurred with Tom. There was someone evil out there, killing women. He did not for one second believe his sister had committed suicide, and Jane Holley's death was also suspicious. If that killer now had his sights fixed on Deborah ... He swallowed, feeling sick, and took a slurp from his mug. The scalding liquid scorched his throat but helped relieve the nausea. 'Tea's up, guys,' he said at last, trying to sound encouraging. 'I'm sure the police will find her.' His words were met by blank stares. No one in the room felt optimistic.

The silence was broken by Tom's ringtone. He snatched his phone to his ear. 'Yes?' he snapped. Emma and Rick stood by, fidgeting with anxiety, their eyes fixed on Tom's face. With growing horror, they watched his features collapse with grief. 'I see,' he said finally. 'Thank you.' He ended the call.

Emma gripped Rick's hand. He could feel her shaking. 'Dad ...?' The word wobbled in the room's deathly pall.

Tom closed his eyes. 'No sign of Debs, but they have found her phone. By the lake. I need to go. They're extending the search and have started door-to-door enquiries in case someone saw something. A team of specialist divers are being brought in. They think they may find her body ... in ... the water.' His voice broke and he covered his face with his hands.

***

Seb poured himself a large gin and tonic, reflecting with satisfaction upon his day. He was invincible. No one could stop him fulfilling his father's greatest wish, and that of his ancestors before him – to avenge themselves of the curse bestowed by Martha Lightbody, the Wickthorpe Witch. He took a long sip of his drink, savouring the cool liquid on his tongue and the burn as it warmed his throat. Well-deserved for an excellent day's work.

He wondered if Deborah's mobile phone had been discovered. A chuckle rumbled in his chest. That would set everyone panicking. They would expect to find a body in Dark Water Lake. All in good time.

Everything had gone to plan. She turned up at the surgery, as expected, obviously in a tizz about her biopsy results, focused on nothing else. It was so easy. The proposed blood test was a master stroke. *The way she dutifully rolled up her sleeve and held out her arm to receive the needle ...* He smiled to himself. Unfortunately for her, not quite what she was expecting. It had been exhilarating, in the ensuing hours, to know he held the present-day witch in his thrall. Yes, he was doing his familial duty, but he was going to enjoy every second of it.

The glass was already empty. With a contented sigh, he eased himself from the armchair in the lounge to pour himself another. Just one more. He needed to keep his wits about him. It was possible, tonight, he would receive a visit from the police, although most likely it would be tomorrow. He had faith in their ineptitude. It would probably take them that long to discover he was the last known person to see Deborah Ryecroft before she disappeared. Meanwhile, they would be busy searching the wood and dredging Dark Water Lake. Sooner or later though, they would want to speak to him. He was ready, having catered for all eventualities – a chess grandmaster, in full control of the pieces in play. They would not find a body, of course. Not yet. Only he knew her current location – a small fishing lodge by Pentney Lakes in Norfolk. He had purchased the lodge three years earlier, using forged ID, and it had proved useful for entertaining guests. There had been two precursors to his current victim. Neither were now alive to tell the tale.

A smile flirted around his lips as he sank back in his chair, glass in hand. First steps accomplished. After morning surgery, he had driven home and walked the back way to Hundred Acre Wood. Once there, he crept through the undergrowth until he reached the bank by the lake, where he had abandoned Deborah's phone. He heard voices in the distance but was confident no one had seen him. After that, he returned to work. At the end of the day, he had driven to Pentney (avoiding main roads and cameras) to deposit and secure the still unconscious Deborah Ryecroft. Having ensured she was thoroughly bound and gagged, he returned home. A round trip of approximately three hours. He had made good time. It was now half ten and his grumbling stomach reminded him he had not yet eaten. There were at least three meals in his freezer, gifts from neighbours after Jane's death, but he decided to make himself a sandwich. Then bed. Saturday tomorrow. No work, but a busy day nonetheless. How he was looking forward to it!

CHAPTER 39

Residents of Wickthorpe were reeling at the latest news. *Deborah Ryecroft was missing! Police divers were searching Dark Water Lake!* The village grapevine suspected the worst.

A zone in One Hundred Acre Wood had been cordoned off, and a forensics team were busy at work. Some local people had volunteered to help and had been deployed to explore the less well-used areas of the wood. Most were genuinely anxious for Deborah, although some were enjoying the drama of it all.

'That must be where her phone was found,' Honoraria whispered to Marcus. She was decked in sturdy boots, fuchsia pink corduroy trousers and a Barbour coat, as befitted the drizzly weather. 'Look, there's Tom. Do you think we should go over and speak to him?' Tom Oldridge was visible, by the police cordon, conversing with an officer. Felix and Jules Goode hovered anxiously nearby.

'I don't think so,' Marcus advised. 'We're here to help. That would be intrusive.'

Honoraria emitted a loud sigh. 'Oh, you're probably right, but the poor man could surely use our sympathies?' She glanced again in his direction.

'Not at the moment.' Marcus took hold of her elbow and steered her away. 'There will be time enough for that if ... well, if the worst happens. Come on. We've been told to check the north side of the wood.'

'Poor, poor Deborah,' she gasped as Marcus ushered her along. 'I can't believe this is happening – not again! Still, I'm an optimist. They found her last time; they *will* find her this time. I don't believe she's ... in there.' She stopped to point at the water. 'She can't be. I just refuse to ...'

'Honoraria, enough talking!' Marcus interrupted firmly. 'I love you dearly, but there's a time and a place to stand and chat, and this is *not* it.'

'Oh!' She flushed pink with delight. It was the first time he had said he loved her. *Loved* her! Hardly the time or the place for that either, she thought, but still ...

They walked slowly on. When they reached the point where the path narrowed, he stood aside to allow her to lead. *Such a gentleman!* She tried to concentrate on keeping her eyes and mind vigilant, alert to any signs of disturbance, scraps of clothing, anything which looked out of place, as they had been instructed, but it was impossible. Those four little words kept playing a thrilling melody, over and over in her head, on a loop. *I love you dearly.* Having fully explored the phrase in all its glorious deliciousness, her thoughts travelled a relentless track to the point where she began to question his motivation. Did he mean it, or was it just an expression he used? Worse, did he say it to take the edge off his exasperation with her? Tiny needles of doubt began to prick. When she heard the words now, in her head, there were undertones of frustration and irritation. Her delighted spirits deflated with an inward groan. She was a fool to take such an offhand remark seriously, even if it was for just a few moments ...

But it *was* possible his words were deliberate. Maybe, he was now on tenterhooks to hear her response, to see if his love was reciprocated. He might think she didn't care for him in that way, but she did! Oh, she *definitely* did! Her mind now in turmoil, she came to an abrupt halt and spun around to confront his startled expression.

'What's wrong? Have you spotted something?' he asked.

'Marcus Monk,' she began, her face earnest and determined, 'you said back there that you loved me dearly. What did you mean by it?'

'Did I?' His eyes widened in shock. 'It must have just slipped out. I hadn't realised.'

'Oh.' Her shoulders slumped. 'You didn't mean it. Fair enough. I just wondered, that's ...'

'Of course, I meant it,' he declared fervently, taking her in his arms. 'I do love you dearly. Truly, madly, deeply,' he smiled, 'and passionately. I just had no intention of saying it in such an inappropriate setting. I was going to buy you roses, take you out to dinner, go down on one knee and ... oh, what the hell!' He stepped back, took hold of her hands and sank to the muddy ground. 'Dearest Honoraria, dare I hope you feel the same? Will you do me the incredible honour of becoming my wife?'

Honoraria emitted a squeal. 'Yes!' she squawked. 'Yes, I'd like nothing better. I love you too. Dearly, truly, madly, deeply, passionately ... and, of *course*, I'll marry you. Now get up, you fool. We'll *never* get that moleskin clean!'

***

Seb Holley, dressed casually in pullover, jeans and slippers, watched out of his upstairs window as two detectives emerged from the car by his front door. He smiled to himself. *Right on cue.* The bell sounded and he descended the stairs. Feigning surprise, he opened the door.

'Is there news about Jane?' he asked, his blue eyes full of concern.

Beth Honeysuckle gave him a tight smile. 'May we come in?'

'Of course. Sorry, where are my manners?' He stood aside to allow them entry and followed them through to the lounge. 'Can I fetch you some tea? Coffee?'

'Nothing, thank you.' Beth's face was guarded. 'We need to ask you some questions about Deborah Ryecroft.'

'Deborah?' He sat up straighter, his expression confused and troubled as he looked from one detective to the other. 'Why? Has something happened?'

'She's missing,' Jack Everard responded. 'Did you see her at all yesterday?'

'Oh no!' Seb had practised his look of dismay in the mirror. 'That's awful! I *did* see her yesterday. She had an appointment sometime in the morning.' He creased his brow. 'It wasn't my first appointment, but I seem to remember it was quite early. After 9:15 and probably before ten o'clock, I would say, off the top of my head. Sorry I can't be more specific. The details will be on the computer at the surgery, but I'm afraid it's closed today. When did she go missing?'

'We'll ask the questions if you don't mind, Dr Holley. How long was Ms Ryecroft's appointment?' Beth's lips formed a tight line as she awaited his answer.

He frowned. 'Ten ... fifteen minutes, perhaps. Look, am I under suspicion here?'

'And what was the nature of that appointment?'

'A medical matter. That's why people usually go to see a doctor.' Seb allowed a note of exasperation to creep into his tone. 'I'm sure I don't need to remind you, Inspector, that patient details are confidential.'

'What happened at the end of the appointment?'

'She left.' Seb narrowed his eyes. 'I'm not sure I see the point of these questions.'

'And how would you describe her state of mind when she left? Had she received bad news, for example?'

Seb relaxed his features a fraction, demonstrating that this was more the type of question he would have expected. 'On the contrary. It was good news. She was smiling as she left and thanked me profusely, I recall.' A modest shrug. 'I told her there was no need for thanks. I was just doing my job.'

'Is there anyone who would be able to verify this?'

He shook his head. 'I'm sure there must be, but I have no idea. It was a busy surgery. You would have to ask the staff and patients in the waiting area.'

'We intend to. Can you start by giving me the names of the other staff working yesterday morning?'

'I'll try.' Jack pulled out a notebook as Seb recited the names of doctors, nurses, receptionists, the practice manager, and other office and pharmacy staff.

'Thank you, Dr Holley. That will be all for now.' Beth rose to leave.

Seb also got to his feet. 'I hope you find Deborah soon. It would be truly awful to think something has happened to her,' he said fervently. 'Please let me know if I can be of any further assistance.' He accompanied them to the door. 'As a matter of interest, how did you know she visited the Health Centre yesterday?'

'We found her phone, dropped by Dark Water Lake, yesterday evening,' Jack replied before Beth could stop him. 'We tracked its location data. That was the last place she went before she disappeared off the grid.'

***

Seb found it impossible to stop grinning as he drove to Pentney later that same morning. He half wondered if the police would have someone following him, and took a circuitous route, which included pulling offroad. *No tail.* He nodded with satisfaction, knowing the police would have their hands full. As well as divers searching the lake, officers would be making door-to-door enquiries, asking if anyone had seen Deborah Ryecroft, and investigating all the names he had given them. Then, they would need to interview all patients who had appointments at Wickthorpe Health Centre on Friday morning – a mammoth but, ultimately, pointless task.

Licking his lips, he restarted the engine. The prospect of confronting Deborah Ryecroft was mouthwatering. She would be conscious by now, and completely at his mercy. His loins tightened in anticipation.

The old fishing lodge was a gem, completely secluded and accessible via a private dirt track. It sat well away from the fishing lakes, hidden in amongst the trees. No one would know it was there. He owned both the access and the acre and a half of woodland surrounding the property, which he had fenced with posts and barbed wire. There was almost no chance of detection, but still he exercised caution as he approached. One had to expect the unexpected.

All was exactly as it should be. He retrieved his bag from the footwell beside him and hoisted it out of the car. The lodge was a wooden construction, dark and sturdy. He undid the padlock on the door and stepped inside. It was complete darkness within. The hut had no electricity and the two windows were shuttered. He switched on his torch and made his way over to the narrow bed in the far corner.

'Deborah, my dear! How delightful to see you again!' Muffled cries sounded from beneath the merciless gag. His light picked up her pale face and terrified eyes as she writhed beneath the blankets with which he had thoughtfully covered her. He sat by her on the bed and propped the torch on a nearby ledge. 'How are you feeling?' His hand covered her forehead. 'Warm. No fever.' Gentle fingers probed the side of her neck and he checked the watch on his wrist. 'Heart rate raised, but that is to be expected. This must all be very frightening for you, my dear, but try not to worry. It won't be for long.' She ceased her noise and the struggle with her bonds. Her eyes pleaded with him. How he loved it, seeing her reduced to this! He felt himself becoming aroused, but ruthlessly subdued those urges. Not part of the plan. A shame, but there must be nothing on or within her person which could point the finger at him when her body was discovered. His false DNA sample was now compromised and it would be too much of a risk. 'Now, I know you must be very thirsty. I have brought you water and food, but for that I am going to have to remove this binding from your lovely mouth.' As he spoke, he softly stroked her cheek, enjoying her distress at the intimate gesture. 'For that to happen, you need to know two things. The first is that we are a long way from anyone's hearing. Screams will be completely pointless. No one will come. Do you understand?' She nodded. 'The second is that, should you choose to ignore my advice and make any sound at all, the tape will go straight back on and there will be no water and no food, nothing until I'm able to pay another visit. Who knows when that may be. Perhaps tomorrow but ...' he shrugged, 'it might not be possible. Your choice.' His lips curved in an encouraging smile. 'Do you agree not to make a sound if I remove this?' She nodded. 'Don't let me down, Deborah. Now, this might hurt.' His fingers tugged at the corner of the tape before he ripped it off in one sharp yank. He expected a tiny squeal of pain but, although she winced, she made no noise. Good. She was taking him seriously. He tipped the water bottle to her lips.

'Why are you doing this?' she hissed with a splutter as he withdrew the bottle. 'Is it to do with the curse?'

His shark's smile glinted in the torchlight. 'It doesn't take a genius to work it out. I'm a Holley; you're a Lightbody. I'm Roger to your Martha, and this time, sadly for you, there will be a different ending.'

She eyed him with contempt. 'We are *not* those people. You're mad to suggest we are. There is no such thing as the curse.'

He raised his eyebrows. 'How can you suggest that when, the moment you arrive in the village, the deaths begin all over again? You and I both know this is our destiny. This moment has been years ... centuries in the making.' He held a chocolate bar up to her mouth and she took a savage bite.

'I had nothing to do with those deaths, as you well know. Did you? Did you kill your wife?'

He heaved a sigh. 'Sadly, I could no longer rely on Jane's loyalty. I had no choice.'

'You're a monster!'

'Tut, tut!' He waggled a finger in her face. 'That's not the way to speak to me if you want more water.'

She could not prevent a longing glance at the bottle. To distract herself, she asked, 'Did you kill Freya Billington too?'

He clapped his hands slowly together. 'The West Suffolk Constabulary could use you on their team. They haven't a clue.'

'But why? She was just a young girl, with her whole life ahead of her.'

'I'm afraid she outlived her purpose. Now,' he held the bottle for her to drink once more, 'much as I'd like to sit and chat, I need to get going. Finish this, and the chocolate, and then I must bid you a fond farewell.'

She began to panic. 'You're not going to leave me here?'

'Sadly, I have no choice. The time is not yet right for our denouement. I'll be back, I can promise you that.'

'But,' she swallowed, 'I need the toilet.'

He nodded. 'Of course. We don't want you making a mess of the bed, do we?' He patted her shoulder. 'Don't you worry. I've thought of that.' He picked up the torch and moved to an adjacent corner of the lodge. When he returned, she saw he was carrying a metal bucket. 'All mod cons provided, your ladyship.' He sketched a mock bow.

'How do you expect me to use it with my arms behind my back and my legs tied together?'

'All in good time.' He unshackled her hands, gripping her tightly by her right wrist, and attached the cuff to a long chain which was fastened to the wall. He smiled as she flexed the fingers of her left hand. Did she not know he had done this before and knew exactly what she was thinking? 'By the way,' he announced idly, as he undid the cuffs around her ankles, 'there is no point trying to slip your hand in my pocket to steal the key. You won't find it.' He saw the spark of hope in her eyes fade away. 'You'll find I'm one step ahead of you,' he gloated. 'You are *not* my first house guest. There.' He retaped her mouth before she could respond. 'All done. Have a good evening.'

For a moment, he watched her tug at the chain and then, with a small salute, exited the lodge and relocked the padlock. Phase two completed.

CHAPTER 40

Monday morning. Two days on. Two days of knocking on doors, speaking to Deborah Ryecroft's friends and work colleagues, interviewing patients and staff of Wickthorpe Health Centre. Two long days ... and only dead ends to show for them.

Beth Honeysuckle called her team together for a morning meeting to review what they had so far. On the plus side, they were as confident as they could be that there was no body in Dark Water Lake. They had eliminated several possible sightings, and collated hundreds of statements. A huge amount of work had been completed ... but they were no further forward in discovering what had happened to Deborah Ryecroft. Had she been abducted and, possibly, murdered, or was her disappearance deliberate? Had Ryecroft been responsible for the two recent drownings and absconded? The search continued, but had been widened. Ports and airports had been alerted in case she was trying to leave the country. Every possibility had to be investigated, especially as many villagers were claiming 'the witch' had 'done a runner.' Beth did not share that opinion, but it could not be ruled out. Privately, she remained convinced that Dr Holley was somehow responsible. There had been no eyewitness claim to have seen Ryecroft leave the Health Centre, which was strange. Many had seen her arrive, and she should have exited via the crowded waiting room. However, a visit to the building had revealed further exits, including an external door in Holley's consulting room. This led to a private staff car park. They had invited Holley to the station again, for questioning under caution, but had been forced to release him without charge. He was adamant Ryecroft had left the way she had come, and merely shrugged when asked to explain why no one had seen her after her appointment. There was no concrete evidence to suggest he was lying, and a further search of his home proved fruitless. Again, they asked him to take another DNA test; again, he refused. No need, he insisted. His DNA was already on file. There was no point to another test. Police persistence regarding the matter amounted to harassment.

Meanwhile, the whole affair had turned into a media circus. The local press had soon got hold of the story and, once the news was out, reporters from national newspapers descended. Dr Holley was an amenable interviewee and came across well. The cameras loved him. On the front pages, he was portrayed as a victim, a widower who had lost his wife of twenty-two years. With tears in his eyes, he expressed his opinion that his wife had tragically taken her own life, although he welcomed the police investigation into his wife's death, and assured journalists of his full co-operation. He was then asked his thoughts on Ms Ryecroft's suspicious disappearance.

'I have no idea what has happened to her,' he said solemnly. None could doubt his sincerity. 'I pray for her safe return. This village has seen enough sadness.'

When it was put to him that recent events might be linked to Wickthorpe's centuries-old curse, he had no comment to make.

Honoraria Simpson-Fairchild was also in demand, much to her secret delight. Her demeanour remained studiously serious as she gave journalists the benefit of her considered wisdom on Wickthorpe's legend. She also provided a side story to the drama when she introduced Marcus Monk as her fiancé to journalists, and described his proposal, whilst searching for clues to Deborah Ryecroft's whereabouts, in Hundred Acre Wood. She was becoming quite the celebrity!

The story of the Wickthorpe Witch was a hot topic once more and old stories were raked up. Reports from the previous summer were revisited and many questioned the harsh sentences recently imposed upon the Hampton-Browns, the couple who had used the ancient method of 'trial by drowning' upon Ms Ryecroft.

The parents of Ayesha Khan, the girl who had drowned in 1988, were discovered in Birmingham, and they appeared on television, surprisingly upset about the disappearance of the woman everyone now claimed was responsible for their daughter's death.

'Deborah was a kind girl and a good friend to my daughter. We did not believe the story that she was a witch then, and we certainly don't now. My wife and I pray she is found alive and well,' said a sombre-faced Hashim Khan.

'Hmph,' Enid Green snorted at the television screen.

The news of Deborah Ryecroft's disappearance had her rubbing her hands with glee. *The plan was working.* She and Andrew had heard nothing from Seb Holley, but this was as expected. When Enid had divulged her scheme, Seb had initially dismissed it as absurd, and refused to have any part of it. It had taken all of Enid's powers of persuasion for him to agree to the witch's abduction. However, once convinced of his duty, he had been pleasingly decisive.

'Once it's done, don't try to contact me. I'm under suspicion from the police as it is. They may be monitoring my calls. I will find some way to contact you, a visit to the Post Office perhaps.' Enid had nodded at the wisdom of his words, happy to let him take the lead now she had secured his co-operation. 'I don't want to know what you plan to do to the woman once I hand her over to you. The less I know the better, especially if …' He paused, grim-faced, and shook his head slightly at Enid's set expression.

'You can't be thinking …' Andrew shot a horrified look at his mother. 'Not murder! I won't be a part of that either!'

'Don't be so lily-livered,' Enid sneered. 'You'll do whatever it takes. Naturally, we will try to persuade her to leave the village of her own free will, but if she refuses …'

Andrew's face drained of colour. 'I'm not doing it, Mother. I couldn't.'

'No.' She eyed him with contempt. 'Luckily, I am made of sterner stuff.'

Seb looked concerned. 'Presumably, we are *all* hoping it won't come to that?'

'Of course.' Enid looked down and scratched at her sturdy, wool skirt.

'Good. As I said, no contact.' Seb sketched them both a small bow. 'I can't believe I've agreed to this but if you genuinely believe Jane died because of her, because of the curse …'

'She did.' Enid responded with certainty. 'Such a tragic waste of a life, and more deaths will follow if she isn't stopped. All three of us are in danger.'

'And your daughter?'

'Pah.' Enid screwed up her face in distaste. 'The witch has befriended Ava for her own devious means, but my daughter is a fool. She is not to be trusted under any circumstances.'

'Understood.'

Seb had left then, leaving his co-conspirators on tenterhooks as to when he would act. They had not had to wait long. The good doctor had not failed them. Enid had wondered if he would prove trustworthy. It had been a big risk to involve him in her scheme for Deborah Ryecroft, but she knew she could not rely upon Andrew, and having read *The Life and Times of Martha Lightbody*, it became obvious to her that Dr Holley was Roger to Ryecroft's Martha. It was fate. Hence, not a risk at all. It was meant to be.

***

Tom was beside himself with worry. He had tried to persuade DI Honeysuckle to keep Dark Water Lake under surveillance until Deborah was found, so certain was he that her abductor would take her there. A police presence had been maintained on Saturday night but, once the divers had completed their search of the water, Honeysuckle said she could not justify it further. Budgets, she explained. The previous night, Tom had mounted his own vigil, despite attempts to dissuade him by his friends and daughter. He had concealed himself near the small clearing where cars parked, and kept watch all night. No one had come. By morning, he was grey with exhaustion and snappy with Emma when she tried to convince him to catch up on some sleep. In the end, she had left him. There were things on the farm which needed doing. When she popped by to check on him, later in the day, she found him asleep against a tree.

***

After the morning briefing, also attended by Detective Chief Inspector Allison Pallister, Beth had been summoned to Pallister's office. Throughout the exchange, she felt like a recalcitrant schoolgirl. Ally Pally was not happy to hear her team had no real leads.

'Two women are dead, a third is missing, and we still have nothing to go on, other than some nonsense about a village curse. I would suggest it's a straightforward case of two unfortunate suicides, and a woman who has buggered off somewhere without telling anyone. What have you got on Ryecroft? Have you investigated her company's finances?'

'Yes, Ma'am. Her business appears to be prospering. We don't think Ms Ryecroft's disappearance is work-related.'

'You *think* ... you don't *know*. What about her personal life? And those emails you traced back to Spark Electrics, a subsidiary of Ryecroft Industries ... the ones sent to Jane Holley before her death ... what else have you uncovered about them?' Beth remained silent and Pallister snorted her exasperation. 'Nothing! Meanwhile, we have journalists proposing theories and painting a picture of a clueless, inept police force. Does that about sum things up?'

Beth squirmed. 'Yes, Ma'am, but ...'

Pallister held up her hand. 'I have a press conference scheduled for eleven o'clock this morning. It seems to me you have spent far too much time on the doctor, and have nothing to show for it. I suggest you focus on the missing woman. Tear her life apart. Find out what is going on.'

'We are doing our best, Ma'am,' Beth said, her voice tight.

'Do better, Beth. That will be all.'

'Sorry, Ma'am, I know you feel we're wasting our time on Dr Holley, but I would strongly urge you to allow us to place him under surveillance. I would stake my reputation on his involvement in all of this.'

Pallister gave her a hard stare. 'I do not think you have much of a reputation to stake, Beth,' she said, her voice cold.

Beth squared her shoulders and maintained eye contact. 'I realise that, Ma'am, but we are getting closer to pinning something on him. The DNA test we have on record for him was compromised, and ...'

'Enough!' Pallister sighed. 'You had better be right, Beth. Alright, I'll authorise low-key surveillance of Dr Holley ... but make sure you don't neglect other avenues in this investigation. We need results. Is that clear?'

'Yes, Ma'am. Thank you, Ma'am.'

Beth left Pallister's office chastened but invigorated. Persuading Pallister to permit surveillance was a big step forward. If Holley was involved in Ryecroft's disappearance, they might catch him trying to cover his tracks. They may even strike gold ... he might lead them to her!

As she returned to her own office, Beth churned the facts over in her head. Deborah Ryecroft had vanished; the last person known to have seen her was Dr Holley; Dr Holley's wife, his alibi on several occasions, was now conveniently dead and could not be questioned; Honoraria Simpson-Fairchild had named Holley as a possible match for Freya Billington's mystery man; the DNA he had provided, which had put him in the clear after two suspicious deaths, was questionable. The evidence, albeit circumstantial, against him was mounting up. Dr Holley was at the centre of this whole thing – she knew it. He must have overpowered Deborah Ryecroft somehow. Could he have killed her right there in his consulting room? It was worth checking.

With renewed determination, she picked up the phone.

CHAPTER 41

Late Tuesday afternoon. Thirty-two hours on. A forensics team had examined Seb's consulting room, hoping to discover evidence of violence or a struggle. They found nothing inside, and extended the search to the outside area Again, nothing. And still no sign of Deborah Ryecroft.

Seb had been at work Monday and returned home at 6:10 p.m. He stayed in all night and reappeared the following morning, looking rested and assured. The same could not be said of the two officers in the vehicle parked nearby, watching his house. There had been moans from Beth's team about the surveillance being a waste of time, and Beth was under increasing pressure from above to call it off.

Investigations into Ryecroft's affairs had reached their conclusion. The computers she used at home and at her office in London had been examined by tech experts and yielded nothing of interest. Her financial situation was enviable; her personal life, according to friends, was in a good place. Deborah was happy, healthy (according to her medical records) and successful. Apart from the Bickerstaff emails, they had found nothing concrete to link her to Jane's death, and Beth did not believe she had left of her own volition.

She felt drained, and unable to shake off the sense that Seb Holley was one step ahead of them. Her hopes of finding Deborah Ryecroft alive had faded. It could be some while before her body was discovered, if ever. Despite all the team's efforts, they had, most likely, failed her. Yet there was still a chance. She gritted her teeth and insisted on giving the surveillance another night.

Her phone rang: PC Josh Stevens. 'I'm now outside Holley's house, Ma'am,' he said. 'Just thought I'd keep you updated.'

'Did he go straight home?'

'No. In an exciting development, he drove into the village and went to the Post Office. He was there for about five minutes before he went home.'

The sarcastic tone was not lost upon her, but she ignored it. 'Thank you, Josh. Let me know if he goes out.'

The Post Office. Could there be something in that? The Post Office was the residence of Enid Green, the woman behind the anonymous notes and the vandalism to Deborah Ryecroft's garden the previous year. Mrs Green had made no secret of her belief that Deborah was the Wickthorpe Witch and a danger to the village's inhabitants. Her son, Andrew, and another man, Philip Holder, had also been involved. Those three persons had been questioned when Deborah vanished. The Greens had alibis for the approximate time she went missing. Philip Holder had no alibi. All remained under suspicion regarding Deborah's disappearance. If Seb Holley was involved somehow with Enid Green ...

Her first instinct was to speak to Mrs Green – bring her in for further questioning. But if she did know anything about Deborah, would she reveal it under interrogation when they had nothing to use as leverage? Highly unlikely. And Beth could end up looking a complete fool. There was a strong possibility Holley had only visited the Post Office to purchase something innocuous like stamps. She sighed and shook her head. This case was driving her crazy, but she could not ignore that inner voice whispering to her that contact between Holley and Green was no coincidence. There just *might* be something in it. She *had* to act.

Decision made, Beth picked up her phone, wondering how on earth she was going to convince DCI Allison Pallister that it was imperative to extend the surveillance to include Wickthorpe Post Office.

***

Seb slipped out of his back door. He was dressed all in black, carried a rucksack, and made no sound as he crept along the hedge and crawled through a small gap near the far corner of his garden.

It was 7 p.m. Heavy clouds obscured any stars and there was little natural light, but he waited until he was across a field and beyond a small copse before switching on his torch. Ahead lay a half-mile walk to an old barn, where he had parked Jane's Renault Clio a few days before. It had been a risk, leaving it there, but he knew the owner of the barn, a patient of his, was currently in hospital having had stomach surgery, so it was unlikely to be detected.

He smiled to himself. Everything was going to plan. He had clocked the surveillance car, of course, and stayed in all last night, establishing the pattern for a routine he planned to replicate tonight. *Lights on. TV on. Music – quite loud. Lights off.* So easy to activate via his phone. A facile way to convince the watching police that he was having an evening at home. He had thought of everything.

Excitement fizzed through him and the mounting sense of anticipation lent a spring to his step. It would be a shame when it was over; he could not deny it. His whole life had steered an inexorable course to this point, and tonight would mark his greatest achievement. Within the space of a few short hours, he would terminate the Wickthorpe Witch, and the Greens would get the blame.

Seb would have liked it to have been just the two of them, him and Deborah, but Enid and Andrew would also be present to witness her death. It was a price he was willing to pay. Despite his protestations to Enid, murder had always topped his agenda. The fishing lodge would be burned to ashes, and then he would deal with the Greens. Timing was everything. Their disappearance, alongside the discovery of Deborah's body, would assure the police of their guilt, especially if he left a few clues along the way. Nothing could go wrong.

He chuckled to himself. The Greens were in for quite a few surprises this evening. Enid's plan had them taking Deborah back to Dark Water Lake, to drown her in the water there. It would have been a fitting end, he had to admit, to bring the witch back to where it all began. The symmetry of the scheme appealed to him, but sadly it was unworkable. Far too risky. News of Tom Oldridge's nightly vigil had reached his ears, and the police would be alert to anything happening there. Far better to end the curse in a blaze of glory, well away from Wickthorpe, where no one would happen along at an inconvenient moment. Three deaths in one night were enough of a thrill, even for him.

The barn where Jane's car was parked lay ahead, a dark, solid mass at the top of a short slope. His heart beat a steady rhythm as he navigated the farm track leading up to it. Walking was easier and he lengthened his stride. He wanted to have plenty of time to enjoy a final, intimate conversation with Deborah before he went to meet the Greens.

***

Beth sat in her office, reviewing the case so far and planning a schedule for the next day. All alleged sightings of Deborah had been followed up, and the search locally had been scaled down. Beth knew they were nearing the point where the case would be put on hold and other priorities would take over. Most likely, she would be facing an inquiry of her own, regarding her handling of the investigation. She would be lucky to keep her job.

Before Jane Holley's death, Beth had been working with a team from Ipswich on a drugs operation. The recent death from an overdose of a teenage girl, after a night out clubbing, meant this was now the top priority, and she knew her hours left working the Ryecroft case were numbered. Deborah was destined to become the latest addition to a long list of missing persons.

Whilst most of the team had gone home for the night, Jack was still there. After hearing about Seb's visit to the Post Office, Beth had asked him to dig up what he could about Enid and Andrew Green. Her gut feeling remained. They could be involved in Deborah's disappearance and in cahoots with Seb Holley. However, she was also beginning to wonder if fatigue was affecting her judgement. Currently, the cars stationed outside both the Post Office and Dr Holley's home had nothing to report. Residents were all in situ.

Her phone rang and she snatched it up. It was PC Barrunda from outside the Post Office.

'A car has just pulled up outside, Ma'am. A Honda Civic Hybrid, registration GV22 SBD. A tall man has just got out of the driver's side. In his forties or early fifties, maybe. Hold on ... a woman has just come from the Post Office. Also in her forties, I would estimate. They're hugging. Now he's walking her round to the passenger side and opening the door for her. She's getting in, and he's returning to the driver's side. What do you want me to do, Ma'am?'

'Stay where you are, and keep in touch.' Beth ended the call and hoped she had made the right decision. From PC Barrunda's description, the woman sounded like Enid Green's daughter, Ava, who ran the Post Office. Enid and Andrew Green were the people of interest.

Yawning, she stood and stretched. She was so tired she could sleep for a week. *Coffee.* She would take one to Jack and see what he had managed to unearth. Then, she would send him home. He, like her, had been working flat out for the past four days. She could not fault her team for effort, but they seriously needed results right now.

Jack looked how she felt, she thought, as she plonked a steaming mug on his desk. 'How's it going?' she asked.

He looked up and pulled a face. 'As you know, Andrew Green has previous. Arrests as a teenager and a spell in prison when he was …' He got no further as Beth's phone rang and she held up a hand.

'Give me a minute. Yes, Umar?' It was PC Barrunda again.

'Another car has just pulled up, Ma'am, and a fair-haired man has just gone into the Post Office. The car is a black BMW. Registration CR21 VHX.'

Andrew Green? A surge of excitement. Beth wrote the number on a pad and signalled to Jack to check it out. 'Thanks Umar. Let me know if he comes out, and prepare to follow him when he leaves.' She ended the call and looked across at her Detective Sergeant.

'That number is registered to Andrew Rupert Green,' he informed her.

'Good. I'm going to check if Holley is similarly on the move.' She made a quick call, before shaking her head at Jack. 'No, he's still at home. I've told Seamus to be ready.' PC Seamus O'Leary had taken over surveillance from PC Stevens earlier that evening. 'You were about to tell me Andrew Green served eighteen months for aggravated assault when he was in his early twenties.'

Jack rolled his eyes. 'After that, his record is clean. Married in 2014. Daughter of …' He paused as Beth's phone rang again.

'Umar?'

'He's now leaving the Post Office, Ma'am, accompanied by an elderly woman. Quite infirm. Needed his assistance to get to the vehicle.'

'Excellent. Prepare to follow. We're on our way. Don't let him see you. Stay well back … but whatever you do, don't lose him.' Eyes alight with hope, she turned to Jack. 'The Greens are both on the move. Come on. Let's see where they're heading.'

CHAPTER 42

It had been a wonderful day, Honoraria thought, and immediately felt guilty. How could she enjoy herself when poor Deborah was still missing? But she had. It was impossible to resist yet another happy glance down at her outstretched left hand, where a large sapphire, enclosed in a circlet of tiny diamonds, sparkled on her finger. The jewel matched her eyes, Marcus told her, his eyes alight with pleasure, when she tried it on in a gorgeous, little jewellery shop in Cambridge that afternoon. A perfect fit. Despite the expensive price tag, he insisted upon buying it for her. She sighed again with pure pleasure. What an extraordinarily fortunate woman she was!

Even now, she was resting on the sofa after their busy shopping day while her fiancé cooked supper. Her stomach rumbled at the prospect of fish pie. They had eaten lunch out, but she had only ordered soup and was now ravenous. Today, she had no thoughts of distracting Marcus from the task in hand. She was too hungry. Perhaps after supper, they would watch a film, something light and romantic, and afterwards ... A smile crept to her lips. Tonight, in bed, she would wear nothing but her new engagement ring.

Her thoughts were still wandering in that delectable direction as she scrolled through her emails. When one caught her attention, she exclaimed aloud. 'Oh, my goodness! Marcus, come and listen to this.'

'I'll be right with you, my love,' he called back. 'Just give me a moment.'

She reread the email as she waited. A lead in the search for Martha Lightbody! Over the past week, she and Marcus had found further corroboration of people mentioned in *The Life and Times of Martha Lightbody*, but nothing of Martha herself. However, it appeared someone else had! A fellow History Society buff, Georgina Compton-Finch, had shared Martha's story with her group in East Suffolk, along with Honoraria's appeal for information about her. Another woman in the group, Nina Maddon, said the name rang a bell. When it was put to her that, in all likelihood, she had seen it on the news regarding the recent deaths in Wickthorpe, Nina was adamant that was not the case. She thought she remembered seeing it somewhere else, but could not recall where. Several weeks had elapsed when, out of the blue, Nina rang Georgina. She and her husband had narrowed the sighting to a time, years earlier, when they had stayed in the small town of Swaffham in West Norfolk. They were visiting churches in the area, and Nina had seen the name Lightbody in one of them. Her husband had commented on it at the time. She had been trying to lose weight and, having successfully shed eight pounds, he joked that perhaps she should be called Nina Lightbody. As they could not remember where they spotted the name, they decided to return to Swaffham and revisit each church until they found it.

Such dedication! Honoraria was impressed, and a tiny bit jealous. She would have quite liked to have made the discovery herself.

Eventually, the couple located the name in St Andrew's church in the village of Bathersford. It was engraved on a tiny brass plaque, tucked away on a recessed wall, almost hidden from view. A photograph of the plaque was attached to the email, and Honoraria showed it to Marcus when he appeared from the kitchen, looking wonderfully masculine, despite being bedecked in one of her frilled aprons.

'Well, I never,' he grinned. 'Looks like we've found her.' He handed the phone back for Honoraria to enjoy another look. The inscription read:

IN MEMORIAM

MARTHA LIGHTBODY

1622 – 1686

A Good Christian Woman.

'I can't believe it!' Honoraria whispered, her eyes bright with the joy of discovery, and then her face fell. 'But we can't tell Deborah!' She closed her eyes and clasped her hands together. 'Please let her be found alive!'

***

Tom Oldridge turned haunted eyes towards his daughter. 'She's still alive, I just know it,' he insisted. 'I've got to stay here. Whoever has got Debs will attempt to drown her, just like last year. I'm not leaving. But thank you for the soup. Now, get your car out of here before anyone spots it.' His face was taut with exhaustion and stress.

'Don't worry. If anyone comes along, Rick and I will pretend to be a couple having a snog!' Emma replied.

'You wish!' Rick joked, relieved that darkness concealed the sudden redness of his cheeks.

She chuckled and turned back to Tom, currently hidden behind bushes by the car park area near Dark Water Lake. 'Rick and I will both have our phones on. Make sure you call us should anything happen.'

'I will. Don't worry.'

As they drove away from the lake and back towards home, Emma emitted a loud sigh. 'I have a horrible feeling that Debs is not going to be found alive.'

'I don't know.' Rich reached across to squeeze her hand. 'It's true that the longer she stays missing, the more likely she's already dead, but we have to stay positive. Debs came through last time; she can come through again. Do you remember, shortly after the Hampton-Browns had tried to drown her, that Debs said something about a woman watching over her? It was like a miracle. She believed the woman helped her survive the water.'

Emma snorted. 'I don't believe that, do you?' When there was no reply, she continued, her tone gloomy. 'Well, let's pray she was right and she *does* have someone watching over her. She needs a miracle right now.'

***

Deborah drifted in and out of consciousness. She was chilled to her core, but could no longer summon the energy to rise from the narrow bed and move her deadened limbs. How long had it been? Hours? Days? She had no idea. All she knew was the agony of extreme thirst, the mind-numbing grip of the cold, and tiredness. It was an increasing struggle to remain awake.

At the beginning, when she first woke, she had hoped for rescue. Tom would find her, somehow, or Beth Honeysuckle. A passer-by might wonder at the closed shutters, and hear her muffled cries for help. But, as time passed, indeterminate and progressively hazy, it became harder to sustain those thoughts. Despair was an all-consuming predator and, when combined with thirst, cold and fear, it had swallowed her fight for life.

She was facing death. She knew it. This time there would be no reprieve. Roger Holley had left her in no doubt of his intentions when he spoke so callously of killing his wife and Freya Billington. She moaned into the darkness. *Not Roger*. It was *Seb* who held her captive. Her mind was losing all sense of reality. Instead, it was filled with images of Martha Lightbody and the man who had pursued her so relentlessly. She was *Deborah*, not Martha. Martha had survived, and so could she ... except the bleakness of her current situation held her in a thrall of hopelessness. Her brief sparks of determination were soon extinguished.

Within the hut, the sounds of scratching and rustling were the only interruptions to the monotony of silence. Outside, occasional animal cries provided the soundtrack: the call of an owl; the bark of a deer; the scream of a rabbit under attack. For a while, she had imagined rats scuttling across the wooden floor, crawling over her body, nibbling at her face. Now, even those terrors failed to move her. All she wanted was to drift off to sleep, to a place where she could feel comfort, safety, love ...

The hum of an engine. Her eyelids snapped open, lethargy gone. Growing louder, more of a rumble. *Him!* With death imminent, she felt the sudden, fierce desperation to live. She struggled off the bed, feeling her legs buckle beneath her. Her tether prevented her from taking more than three steps. Previously, she had tugged at her restraint until her wrists bled, to no avail. Now, she tried again. She had to get away.

The engine stopped. She tensed, waiting.

'Only me, dear Deborah,' Seb called as he unlocked the padlock on the door. She shrank back onto the bed, hearing the glee in his voice and the jauntiness of his approach. 'What, no welcome? Aren't you pleased to see me? Sorry I couldn't make our date yesterday. Come now, don't sulk! I've brought water.' She heard the slosh of liquid in a bottle and turned towards the torchlight. Her raging thirst could not be denied. 'Good girl. Now, this might sting a bit.' She winced as he pulled the tape from around her head to uncover her mouth. One-handed, she had tried in vain to remove it herself in those solitary hours, but it had been fixed too tightly, and the edges were beyond her reach. The pain, as he tore it away, was excruciating but she remained stoically silent, denying him the satisfaction of witnessing her agony. 'There you go,' he murmured. 'Just little sips.' She took the bottle in her left hand and gulped greedily at the water. It spilt as he tugged it away. 'Just small sips, I said. We don't want you vomiting all over me, do we?'

When she had finished drinking, she stared at the shadowy planes of his cheekbones, trying to see into his eyes, to detect what he was thinking. A sudden smile revealed even, white teeth. The visage of an angel and the heart of a devil. Her nemesis. It was as if she had known, from their first meeting.

'Nothing to say for yourself? No last words? No curse you want to utter?' he chuckled, his delight rumbling around the small hut.

This was it then! This was where the Holleys and the Lightbodys engaged for the final time. It seemed a bit one-sided. The thought gave her an idea.

'Not much of a challenge for you, is it?' Her voice was barely a croak. 'Me chained up like this and you ...' Her words jeered at him. 'You can hardly call that a worthy triumph, surely?'

His lips curved once more in amusement. 'Nice try. However, much as I would relish the prospect of some kind of duel with you, I have other plans. Would you like me to share them with you?'

She shuddered. *Dark Water Lake.* The thought of sinking beneath those terrifying waters once more ... She wanted to scream, beg, promise him anything, but she knew his taunts were designed to provoke her. He would love her to supplicate herself on the altar of his domination. Nothing would please him more. Yet, she knew, no entreaty would move him. Her fate was sealed. He had said it himself. Instead, she clamped her lips together in a final act of rebellion. To the last, she would maintain her dignity and composure. At least, she hoped she could summon the strength to do so. She could not let him win that battle too.

'No? Ah well, it will be a lovely surprise.' He grinned. 'Perhaps not quite so lovely for you as me but ...' She felt him shrug against her. 'That's how this last hand has been dealt. Now, I have to leave you but, don't worry, I'll be back soon ... with a few of your friends.' She turned her head sharply in surprise. 'Mm, I thought that might get your attention. I won't be long. Be good, won't you.' He stepped away, before turning back and leaning over to smooth her cheek. 'Oops,' he murmured softly. 'I almost forgot. You didn't remind me, you naughty girl.' She reared away from him as he grabbed her hair, and forced her to face him. 'Tut, tut. Now, hold still.' More tape was roughly wound around her head and over her mouth. 'There, that's better.'

She sank back on the bed and registered his footsteps clicking on the wooden floor, the slam of the door, the rattle of the lock. Outside, the engine kicked into life and the car pulled away, leaving her empty of hope and overcome with despair.

CHAPTER 43

'Mother, we are going to persuade Deborah Ryecroft to leave Wickthorpe, aren't we?' Andrew Green's voice resonated anxiety. 'You're not really planning on killing her?'

Enid turned her head away, staring out into the darkness. 'I said so, didn't I?' she snapped back. If only her golden son had her backbone! He resembled her in so many ways, but possessed a streak of weakness, no doubt the heritage of his paternal genes. Such a disappointment! 'Just concentrate on the driving!'

Andrew's stomach churned and he wished he had refused to get involved. Things were spinning beyond his control. His mother had always been the only person who truly scared him, but he would never have believed she was capable of this. He wished he had objected more forcibly when she first revealed her plan. He had tried, thinking the doctor would share his horror. But instead, Seb, after some token reluctance, had taken Enid's side. Andrew had been shocked into compliance. At least, that was what he told himself. In truth, it had been fear of the backlash he would have received from Enid. Cowardice, pure and simple. And look where it had got him! He was aware they were taking a terrible risk. Had his mother considered, for example, that Seb could be setting them up? Even now, the police could be following! A quick glance in his rear-view mirror showed lights from a car some way behind, and his gut lurched again. He wondered if they had been followed since they left Wickthorpe, and cursed his lack of vigilance. After collecting his mother from the Post Office, his mind had been focused upon the enormity of what they were doing, and he had forgotten to stay alert.

The miles rolled on and the car behind was still there. Andrew licked his dry lips and wondered if he should mention it to Enid. Not yet. Could be nothing, and there was still some way to go. Enid had given him a postcode and directions to an abandoned outbuilding outside the village of Pentney in Norfolk. The instructions, which Seb had slipped to Enid in the Post Office that afternoon, also specified a time. 10:30 p.m. The sat nav predicted an arrival time of 10.04 p.m. so there was leeway to make a detour if necessary. Not that he had any idea what to do in situations which required losing a tail. The very thought of a car chase had his insides in knots. He might look the part, but he was no action hero!

His hands gripped the wheel a fraction tighter. *The lights were still there.* Was it his imagination or were they a shade closer? He wasn't sure. *God, it was hot inside the car!* Enid had turned the heat to maximum not long into the journey, claiming she felt chilled. *Little wonder, the ice chips she had running through her veins!* His fingers itched towards the temperature button and he edged it down a few degrees, hoping his mother wouldn't notice. At that moment, the car following him took a right turn off the road. Relief flooded his body. They were OK; there was no tail. The car lights even further behind did not concern him. He was pretty sure they hadn't been there earlier.

Emboldened by renewed confidence, he asked, 'How are you going to ensure Deborah Ryecroft doesn't go to the police the minute we set her free?'

Enid slowly rotated her head to fix him with a disparaging stare. 'I thought I said you should focus on the driving and leave the rest to me.'

Andrew sighed inwardly. Clearly his mother was going to tell him nothing. He just hoped she knew what she was doing.

***

Behind Andrew Green's BMW, DI Beth Honeysuckle and DS Jack Everard grew increasingly optimistic. Once they had caught up with PC Barrunda, who had been tailing the couple since they left Wickthorpe, Beth had radioed him with the instruction to take the next available turn, conscious that Green may have become suspicious of his vehicle. The young officer was instructed to rejoin the route but to hang well back, in case he was needed again.

'I don't think he's clocked me, Ma'am,' Barrunda said. 'He's been travelling at a pretty constant speed. Nothing erratic.'

Beth kept her opinion to herself. Barrunda had been following far too closely for her liking. Green must have been very preoccupied if he had failed to notice the same car behind him all this way, even with the cover of darkness. She hoped Barrunda's misjudgment would not make the Greens change their plans.

'Where do you reckon they're heading?' she asked Jack as she shifted in the passenger seat.

'Beats me. I don't often cross the border into Norfolk unless I'm taking the family up to the coast, and then we don't come this way.'

'We must be getting close,' Beth predicted. 'I can't imagine Deborah was taken miles.'

'If she was taken at all,' her sergeant commented dourly. 'We could be on a wild goose chase.'

Beth was only too aware of that fact. It was the reason she had not alerted colleagues in Norfolk when they crossed into that county. 'I've got a strong feeling about this,' she said.

'Ah yes, you and your intuition,' Jack nodded. 'Rarely wrong.'

Beth's lips twitched. She was convinced the Greens were up to something. The further they travelled, the more suspicious the journey became, especially at this time of night, but she was also niggled by doubts. PC O'Leary had reported all remained quiet at the Holley residence. Seb was in the house, the curtains were drawn, the television was on. This was not what Beth was expecting. With a frown, she radioed O'Leary for the third time since setting off.

'All as before, Ma'am. Our man hasn't budged since he got home. Looks like he's set for the night, but I'll stay alert, just in case.'

The crevices in Beth's forehead deepened. 'Seamus, do me a favour, would you? Go and knock on the door. Make up an excuse or something. I just want to make absolutely certain he is in there.'

'Roger that, Ma'am.'

Jack chuckled into the ensuing silence. 'You have a lot of faith in Seamus' creative abilities. I'd love to know what he comes up with.'

Beth did not respond. The wait for PC O'Leary to report back had sharpened her tension. Suddenly, she was sure Seb Holley would *not* be in his house.

'Looks like they're slowing in front.' Jack's observation brought her attention back to the road ahead, just as the BMW's left indicator began to flash. 'They're turning off. What do you want me to do?'

'Slow right down.' Beth checked her wing mirror. The road behind was clear. 'We'll follow, but not straight away.' They watched the car turn left. 'Pentney,' Beth read the sign. 'This could be it.'

As they crawled into the narrow lane, the radio crackled into life. 'He's not here, Ma'am.' O'Leary's voice sounded breathless. 'At least, he's not answering the door. I've been all around the house and made enough noise to wake the dead. Even if he'd been in the shower, he'd have heard me. And there's something else ...'

'What?' Beth snapped.

'I found footprints in a patch of longer, muddier grass out back. They lead through a narrow gap in the hedge. I'm sorry, Ma'am, but I think we've lost him.'

***

Seb watched Andrew's BMW pull up at the designated rendezvous twenty minutes early. He waited in the shadows, watching, his breath forming puffs of cloud in the cold air. An unexpected prick of apprehension teased his consciousness and he shivered. There was nothing to fear; he had all angles covered. Yet the sense of unease remained with him, taunting, impossible to pinpoint ...

With irritation, he shook his shoulders and returned to the task at hand, scanning the dark expanse around him, ever-vigilant. No sign of any other vehicle. Still, he waited. He had to be sure.

The two people in the car shuffled restlessly in their seats – mother and son. His teeth flashed white from his place of concealment behind the tumbledown barn. They were in for a few surprises this evening! First though, there would be the final showdown with Deborah Ryecroft. He would take care of the fishing lodge at the same time – burn it, along with the woman. A fitting end for the Wickthorpe Witch! The anticipation of it thrilled him like nothing before.

Then, those final touches, planting a few clues of the Greens' presence, which even PC Plod and Co would be able to find, and he would slip away, in the clear, with proof of being at home all evening courtesy of his police alibi. Oh yes, and the Greens would receive their last surprise.

A rustle in the bushes behind the car made him crouch lower, eyes narrowed, squinting at the shadowy foliage. Was someone there? He held his breath. The bush shuddered violently and a small deer erupted, darting wild-eyed across the track and into some trees beyond. He exhaled slowly. It would pay to continue his vigil a little longer. Experience had taught him extreme caution. And there was still that feeling something was amiss ...

For five further minutes, the bushes remained silent and Seb could wait no longer. He crept forward. Keeping low, he opened the BMW's rear, left-hand door and slid inside. 'Did anyone follow you?' he hissed.

'No.' Andrew swivelled to peer behind him. 'Where is she? Is she in the barn?'

'You'll see soon enough. Head on down the track. Keep your lights off.'

'But how will I see?'

'Drive slowly.' Seb's steely voice brooked no argument and Andrew meekly obeyed, his eyes straining to keep on the track. The earlier clouds had cleared and their path was lit by a silvery glow. As Andrew gained confidence, he pressed his foot a little harder on the accelerator.

'Not too fast,' Seb ordered. 'It gets narrower up ahead, and then we're going to take a left-hand turning.' They crawled forward. The route did indeed become less well defined and bumpier as it disappeared into dense woodland. 'Just past this bend, there's a narrow opening to the left. Take care or you'll miss it.' Andrew followed his instructions, wincing as branches scraped the sides of his BMW. 'Stop here!' At last, the cold voice from the back issued the order and the car pulled into a small clearing in amongst the trees.

Andrew and Enid peered out of the windows. Was that the outline of a building tucked away behind a row of pines? No, not a building, more of a hut.

'Is that where she is?' Enid asked, her voice eager with anticipation.

'Yes,' Seb drawled, 'and now we have a *burning* issue to address.'

***

Beth shivered as she picked her way through the trees, but she wasn't cold. It was excitement tinged with apprehension. She was pretty sure the Greens had come this way. The car had been easy to follow on foot as it lurched a drunken route along the rutted track, but then it had turned a corner and vanished from view. For a few seconds, her heart had plummeted as she stared in bewilderment at the empty track ahead. They must have turned off. Then, she spotted the gap in the trees. She was desperate to follow but, instead, stood waiting and listening. Jack should be along any minute in their car, but he seemed to be taking forever. She rubbed her hands together impatiently. If she didn't stay to show the way, Jack would be sure to miss the turning.

When they had driven along the lane towards the village of Pentney, they had been just in time to see taillights flicker up ahead to their left. The Greens had turned off somewhere. They had turned around and found the narrow farm lane the Greens must have taken. Beth had instructed Jack to switch off his lights and they had driven forward at a snail's pace. Pinpricks of light bounced up ahead, and were then extinguished. 'They've stopped. Pull over,' Beth had said. 'Just there.' She indicated a spot between trees to their right. 'A bit further. They may come back this way.'

From there, they had travelled on foot, keeping to the tree line, until they had reached a ramshackle farm barn. The BMW sat silently beside it.

'They're still inside,' Beth whispered as they crouched behind a broad trunk, a mere twenty metres from the target.

'Do you think she's in the barn?' Jack breathed.

There was no answer. The barn looked to be in an advanced state of disrepair – an unlikely place to imprison someone. At that moment, the bush nearest them had burst into life and a deer had leapt forward, heading first towards the car before veering off back towards the wood. Beth's heart had almost exploded in her chest and she had gripped Jack's arm. They had both held their breath, but there had been no movement from the car, and slowly, their tensed muscles relaxed.

'Looks like they're waiting for something,' Jack had murmured.

'Or someone.'

Suddenly, the car's interior light had flared and a shadowy outline appeared in the rear of the BMW. 'It's him!' Beth's voice quivered in the darkness. 'Holley! It must be!' The car engine had rumbled into life and she had scrambled to her feet, watching as it pulled slowly forward. 'They're on the move. Go back and fetch the car. Tell PC Barrunda where we are but with strict orders to stay put for the moment. We don't want him blundering on the scene! Hurry. I'll try to keep up with them on foot. No lights, remember.'

Now, she stood impatiently waiting for Jack to appear. They were going to lose them. Once more she debated following without her accomplice. 'Come on, Jack!' she fretted. At last, she detected the sound of an engine approaching. It was him. She stepped alongside the slow-moving vehicle and signalled to him to pull over. 'We'll go on foot. This way.' Cautiously, they followed the narrow track, tyre marks showing the way, until they reached the clearing. The BMW stood empty. 'Look, over there!' She pointed towards a small hut. 'They're inside. This must be it!'

Beth crept closer towards the wooden shack, tiptoeing away from the cover of the trees until she was pressed flat against the slatted side of the building. Crouching low, Jack stole in beside her. He pulled out his phone and pointed to it. She nodded a response. If Deborah was being held inside, they would need back-up. He moved away to make the call out of earshot and she skulked to one of the shuttered windows. If only she could see inside! Pressing still closer, she could hear the murmur of voices. A male laugh. No proof that Deborah Ryecroft was confined there, but such a stealthy meeting, late at night, miles from anywhere, *had* to mean the Greens and Holley were up to no good. She wondered how quickly help would arrive and hoped Jack told them to proceed with caution. With luck, they would be able to secure the building before its occupants were alerted.

Footsteps! Beth held her breath as an eerie creak signalled the door opening. She couldn't see who was there, and prayed Jack had moved far enough away to make his calls. Carefully, she edged back along the wall and peered around the corner. Whoever had exited the hut had disappeared. Fear tingled along her spine. She was exposed where she was. If he appeared from the other way, he would see her. *Dammit, where was he?* The crunch of a twig snapping on the other side of the shack sent her heart thudding. She risked another peek around the corner, just in time to see a tall figure step inside and close the door behind him. The man was carrying something in each hand. She swallowed. Back-up would be too late. Things were already happening. Unless she was mistaken, Seb Holley had just taken two fuel cans into the hut.

***

Oh God, not this. This was worse than drowning!

Deborah's eyes were wide with horror as she watched Seb Holley douse one side of her prison with petrol. Enid sat alongside her, toad-like. Andrew Green held a torch with shaking fingers.

'You're going to get her out first?' His voice quavered the question. 'You're not planning on burning her alive?'

'What better way for a witch to die?' Seb returned. 'She's already survived trial by drowning. Let's see how she escapes the flames.'

'But that's monstrous!' Andrew exclaimed. He tossed the torch aside. 'I won't be any part of this.'

Enid snatched it up. 'Man up, Andrew!' Her words spewed scorn. 'Seb is right. This is the way to end the curse. If we don't kill the witch and burn her in the hellfire of eternal damnation, our ancestors will be condemned forever. Your daughters. Have you thought of them?'

'I ...' Andrew tossed his hands in the air with a sigh of resignation. They were going to do it anyway, no matter what he said. He glanced across at the woman tethered on the narrow bed. Her face was deathly white, her eyes dark orbs of fear. For a moment, he felt pity for her, but hardened his heart and turned away. His mother was right. If she had to be sacrificed for the sake of his family, so be it. His mind was working overtime, considering his options, wondering if he dared to make a break for it and leave the deed to the other two. As far as he could see, it would be in his best interests to be well away from the hut when it burned.

***

Beth inched towards the BMW. It was unlocked, the keys tossed carelessly beside the gear lever. As carefully as she could, she pressed the button on the driver's door. It opened with a quiet thunk. The interior light flickered as she slid her arm in and grabbed the keys. She pushed the door to and scurried across the open space to the side of the hut. A dark figure awaited her and she froze, her breath caught in her throat.

It was Jack. 'On their way,' he hissed. 'What's happening?'

Grimly she told him of her suspicions. 'The Greens won't be driving anywhere in a hurry, unless he carries a spare ignition key with him, but I've no idea where Holley's vehicle is. Ssh!' They flattened their bodies hard against the hut as the door opened once more.

'I want to watch from here.' Enid Green's voice.

'Don't be silly, Mother. This place will go up like a tinderbox. It will be far too hot and dangerous to be anywhere near it.'

'Stand clear!' Holley commanded. The other two hustled towards the car, Andrew assisting his mother away amid her protests. 'This is one of the great historical moments,' Seb announced, his face alight with the knowledge of his power. 'The only tragedy is that just the three of us should bear witness to it. But, in years to come, people will remember the burning of the last Wickthorpe Witch. This is for Roger Holley and all her victims thereafter. The curse dies here.' He reached in his pocket and extracted a box of matches. With a flourish, he struck one against the side of the box, watching as the flame licked towards his hand, before throwing the match into the hut.

The effect was instant. The fire quickly took hold and roared a voracious path following the petrol trail. Beth glanced briefly at Jack and burst from her hiding place with a yell. Enid screamed. Andrew uttered a string of expletives before jumping into the driver's seat of the BMW.

'Get in the car, Mother,' he yelled.

Scrabbling for the keys, he realised they were missing. 'What the ...' He searched the footwell on both sides as Enid heaved her body into the seat.

'Drive!' she ordered. 'What are you playing at?'

'The keys ... they're gone!'

'Do something!' she shouted. In response, Andrew opened his door, jumped out and ran into the trees, leaving his mother cursing behind him, and struggling to lever herself from the car.

Upon realising what was happening, Seb crept into the shadows. The keystone cops had arrived, it would appear. But not in numbers. The game was not done.

Without hesitation, Beth rushed into the burning hut. She knew the culprits were getting away but her priority was the woman held captive within. With dismay, she took in the scene. Deborah was chained by handcuffs and attached to a ring bolted into the ground. Flames leapt all around, growing ever closer. Thick, choking smoke clouded the cabin. Beth took a deep breath of clean air and rushed to Deborah's side, her brain racing. What could she use to release Deborah? A panicked glance around yielded no inspiration. There was nothing. Desperately, she tugged alongside Deborah at the chain, hoping against hope she could pull her free. Jack emerged beside her and shook his head. Gripping her arm, he tugged her away. She resisted, unwilling to leave the stricken woman, until she realised Jack was trying to help. As he extracted something from his pocket and began picking at Deborah's handcuff, she barely registered the slam of the door and the click of the key locking them in.

'Get out, Beth! Now. While you can,' Jack spluttered.

She shook her head. *Not yet.* Seconds felt like hours as she watched him fumbling with the padlock. Her eyes streamed and she struggled to breathe. Then, suddenly, the handcuff fell open. The moment of elation was brief. Danger remained. They had to get out! Beth helped her colleague drag a barely conscious Deborah off the bed. Between them, they carried her to the door, dodging the wicked flames.

The door itself was also on fire and too hot to touch. 'It's locked,' she coughed. 'On three.' Jack nodded his understanding. 'One, two, *three*!' In unison, they raised their right legs and smashed into the door with all their might. It crashed open and they fell out into the night, gasping for air.

***

Seb Holley slid like a wraith into the murky depths of woodland he knew so well. The night had not gone to plan, but should end up to his advantage nonetheless. The witch and those meddlesome detectives would be incinerated, and the Greens would be detained by more police, doubtless already nearby. Meanwhile, despite whatever claims the Greens wanted to make, he would have his alibi, that he was at home all night, confirmed by the helpful police presence outside his house.

Still, he took every precaution, taking nothing for granted, weaving a stealthy route to the place he had hidden Jane's car. Despite being well-concealed, there was a small chance it might have been discovered.

He inched forwards, slow and steady, the ground soft beneath his boots. Danger lurked at every corner and his earlier unease remained, chafing his senses, seeking out his vulnerability. He gritted his teeth, annoyed with himself for his twitchiness. It was unlike him. He had no weaknesses, he reminded himself. He was invincible.

With a rush of renewed confidence, he stepped forward, tensing at the crack of a dry twig underfoot. *Idiot!* What was *wrong* with him? He was never this clumsy! He paused once more to listen.

'Andrew!' Enid was still shouting at the son who had so readily abandoned her.

Stupid woman! She would be the first target for the police. No doubt she would try to suggest she and her son had been kidnapped, or something like that. That might work for a while, but not for long. He had left his own piece of evidence in the wood. A smile curved his lips. No matter how loud they blustered, they would be well and truly stitched up when a forensics team found what he had left: namely, Enid's copy of Martha's book, her handwritten annotations included.

Jane's car was just around the next corner ... but a rush of premonition brought him to an abrupt halt. He was not alone; he sensed it with every fibre of his being. Statue still, muscles bunched, he peered into the darkness. Nothing; no sound; no movement. Slowly, he turned full circle. Still nothing. But someone was there. He could feel a deadly, skin-crawling presence nearby, wishing him harm. All senses on high alert, he stooped and removed the small knife he had strapped to the side of his left boot.

A laugh ... a woman's laugh. He felt it reverberate through him and swallowed, suddenly afraid. *What was happening?*

The moment passed and common sense reasserted itself. A flight of fancy, nothing more. He took a few cautious steps forward, and saw Jane's car, solitary, waiting for him. Relaxing his shoulders, he eased forward towards it.

He was a mere two steps away when it happened. *Did he stumble or was he pushed?* It was his last conscious thought. As he tumbled to the ground, his head crashed into something hard, and blackness descended.

There he lay, helpless and defeated, life ebbing away, a large, bloodied rock beside him ....

CHAPTER 44

Two weeks on, and the village of Wickthorpe was still trying to come to terms with the shock of Dr Holley's death, Deborah Ryecroft's dramatic rescue, and the arrest of both Andrew and Enid Green. Gossip abounded but, for once, not in the Post Office. Ava remained tight-lipped and held her head high, despite the mix of both condemnatory and pitying looks she encountered. She was helped through her ordeal by the constant presence of Patrick Velaman, supportive and loving. With him by her side, she felt she could face anything.

The people Ava felt sorriest for were her sister-in-law and beloved nieces. Poor Julie had been devastated at the news of Andrew's initial arrest, but worse was to come as further details emerged. Both Andrew and Enid were charged with the kidnapping and attempted murder of Deborah Ryecroft, but when detectives looked at Andrew's computer, they uncovered his dark, secret. Pornographic pictures of hundreds of young, teenage girls – some as young as thirteen – were discovered, some engaged in sexual acts with Andrew himself. This awful revelation had not yet reached the ears of the village gossip-mongers, but a distraught Julie had broken the news to Ava.

'It's so terrible! What am I going to do?' she sobbed.

'Tell your parents,' Ava advised.

'I can't! And what about the girls?'

Ava swallowed. The whole situation felt nightmarishly surreal. What could she say? 'Your mum and dad will help you to deal with it all, and protect the girls. Have you asked the police to try to keep it from the media?'

'They've assigned me a police liaison officer,' Julie mumbled through her tears. 'She said they'll do what they can.'

Ava tried to console her and pledged to do whatever she could, but harsh reality suggested it would take Andrew's family a long time to recover from the repercussions of his crimes.

If supporting Julie was difficult, seeing Deborah Ryecroft was going to be even worse. Ava felt quite overwhelmed by guilt when she heard what her mother and brother had done, and wondered how she could ever face Deborah again. But it had to be done. Deborah was now home from hospital, where she had been detained for treatment of the many injuries she had sustained, including severe smoke inhalation. Ava had waited a few days and then bitten the bullet. With trepidation, she knocked on the door.

Tom showed her in, his demeanour as affable as ever. 'She'll be pleased to see you,' he assured Ava. 'This way.'

Ava followed him through the house to a chair by a window, overlooking the garden, where Deborah was sitting.

'Ava,' Deborah smiled a welcome. 'How lovely to see you! Thank you for coming.'

Awkwardly, Ava handed over a bunch of yellow tulips. 'These are for you. I'm so sorry, Deborah.'

'They're beautiful! Thank you, and there's absolutely no need to apologise, Ava. You are not responsible for the actions of your family, and you *did* warn me, last year. No one could have predicted they would go that far and I don't think it would have happened at all if it hadn't been for Seb Holley. He was the mastermind behind it.'

'Really?' Ava was shocked. She had heard rumours that Dr Holley had been involved, but village opinion suggested he must somehow have been blackmailed into it. The people of Wickthorpe pronounced his death a terrible accident and a great sadness to them all. Enid Green and her son were the real villains, it was decided. Poor Dr Holley had been caught up in Enid's wicked web. Distraught following the terrible death of his wife, he would have been a vulnerable target. Another victim.

'Indeed.' Deborah succumbed to a coughing fit and it was a while before she could continue. 'Sorry. Can't talk too much as yet.'

Ava nodded and patted her hand. 'Please don't worry. I don't want to tire you out. I'll go now. I just wanted to stop by and ... you know. I'll let myself out. I hope you feel better soon.'

She walked over the road to Patrick's bungalow, soon to belong to her too. Patrick had insisted. They had set a date for the wedding but it would be a very quiet affair. After all that had happened, it could not be otherwise but she was more than happy. She loved Patrick; he loved her; and in the end, that was all that mattered.

***

'Sorry, I know I said I'd cook tonight but can I take a rain check?' Emma called to Rick as she removed her boots, her auburn hair dripping on the floor tiles.

'Rain check being the operative word,' Rick grinned at her, gesturing to the droplets of water streaming down the kitchen window. 'That's OK. Going anywhere nice?'

'Yes, Max has got tickets for ...'

'Max?' Rick exploded, his good humour instantly evaporating. 'I thought you weren't seeing him anymore.'

'Whatever gave you that idea?' Emma ceased towel-drying her hair and looked across at him, her face puzzled.

Rick flushed. 'Er, well ... you hadn't been out with him recently and ... oh, bloody hell, Em, you'd better sit down.'

'What's up?' Emma did as he asked. 'Rick, you're scaring me.'

Sorry.' He pulled a face. 'It's just there's no easy way to do this.' He swallowed and took hold of her hands. 'Em, I'm so sorry to have to be the one to tell you, but Max is seeing someone else.'

Her face broke into a relieved smile. 'You mean Sally? He's been seeing her for a while.'

Rick stared at her, open-mouthed. 'Why didn't you tell me?'

She shrugged. 'You didn't ask.'

'And ... how do you feel about that? Are you OK?'

'Of course. Max and I are just friends. We always have been.'

He frowned. 'But I'm sure you said ... you led me to believe you were dating! Why would you do something like that?'

'Perhaps I was trying to make you jealous,' she teased. 'Looks like it worked!'

'Don't be daft,' he scowled. 'Why would I be jealous?'

Emma raised her eyebrows. 'I don't know, Rick.' She sighed, instantly deflated. 'It was a stupid idea. We're just good friends. Why *would* you be jealous of someone I was dating? I just hoped ...' she broke off.

'What did you hope, Em?' he asked gently.

She shook her head. 'I can't tell you. It would ruin everything and I don't want that. Just leave it please, Rick.'

'I can't. You see ...' his blue eyes searched her face, 'I *was* jealous.'

'You were?'

'Yes.' He shrugged. 'I love you, Em. I guess I always have but I couldn't see it. That's me.' A wry grin. 'A bit slow on the uptake.'

'You *love* me?' He nodded. 'But I love you too. I have done *forever*! But you never seemed to notice me that way.' She stared at him in bemusement.

'As I said, a bit slow.' He hunched his shoulders. 'But I'm more than willing to make it up to you, if you'll let me. Come here, and I'll prove how much I love you.'

With a squeal of joy, she flung herself into his arms.

And he did.

CHAPTER 45

One month later

With its circular tower and thatched roof, St Andrew's church, in the small village of Bathersford in Norfolk, had a simple, rustic feel to it. It stood in splendid isolation, at the top of an incline, surrounded by large oaks. Built in Norman times, its flint walls were crumbling in places and it lacked the impressive majesty of St Mary's in Wickthorpe, but Deborah still felt a sense of awe as she gazed up at it from Tom's car.

'This is it,' she breathed. 'Martha's final resting place.'

She had a strong sense of Martha's presence as, arm in arm with Tom, she trod the gravel path towards the arched entrance. Doubtless, her imagination up to its usual tricks. If it wasn't for the small group of people, dressed in modern clothes, gathered by the doorway, it would have felt like stepping back in time.

'Good morning!' Honoraria called as they approached. She was resplendent in a three-quarter length emerald coat, black knee-high boots and an incongruous pink hat, set at a jaunty angle atop her curls. Marcus Monk stood stoutly beside her, and they were accompanied by another woman dressed all in grey. 'This is Georgina Compton-Finch. It's thanks to her and her friends we're all here today.'

'Georgie, please. You must be Deborah and Tom. I'm beyond excited to meet you.' She extended a plump hand. 'Honoraria has filled me in on the background of the infamous Martha Lightbody. Such an incredible story. It really does have everything. And to think that her history, the curse she uttered almost four hundred years ago, still has power today.' Her cherubic face became serious. 'I was terribly sorry to learn of your recent trials,' she said. 'Hopefully, the discovery of your ancestor's plaque will lead to some kind of closure.'

Deborah inclined her head in a gesture of acknowledgement. There was still no proof that Martha was her ancestor, but she was privately convinced of it. 'Are we any further forward in finding out if Martha was buried here, in this churchyard?'

'Well,' Honoraria chipped in, her tone brimming with excitement. 'Marcus and I have done some digging ...' She giggled at the unintended pun. 'Digging at the Norfolk Records Office, I mean, and we may have found some answers. We got nowhere looking for Martha Lightbody, so we changed tack. Instead, we trawled through the list of all the people buried in Bathersford from 1645 to the early seventeen hundreds. Whilst we found nobody by the name of Lightbody, we did discover a record of burial for a John Littlejoy in 1673, and another for an Elizabeth Littlejoy in 1686, which matches the date on the inscription inside for Martha. And Marcus spotted something else, didn't you, Marcus?'

'I did.' His deep voice rang out in the churchyard, as sonorous as a bass bell. 'I happened to notice, when Martha changed her name to Ruth Littlebody, she chose the Christian name of someone recently close to her, Ruth Fletcher, who had assisted her escape from Wickthorpe. From the surname Littlebody, it's not too much of a stretch to believe they settled upon Littlejoy, especially if the identity swap and the move to Bathersford were not things she would have chosen. Little *joy*.' He repeated, in case they had missed his allusion. 'And she selected the name Elizabeth. I had to go back to the book for that one – *The Life and Times of Martha Lightbody*, I mean – and there I was reminded of Elizabeth Makepeace, who had initially helped the couple settle in Tocklewood.'

Deborah nodded slowly, letting the information sink in. 'It sounds plausible. Elizabeth Littlejoy,' she murmured. 'I wonder why that information was left out of the book? I suppose we'll never know.' She smiled at the people around her. 'Shall we go inside?'

Honoraria bustled to the fore. 'Follow me,' she commanded. 'Mind the step.'

Inside, the church was plain and simply adorned. The pews were wooden benches and the whitewashed walls were dotted with arched windows containing clear glass. Honoraria led them to the south wall. 'It's over here,' she said, her voice hushed in deference to her surroundings. 'Quite hidden away. Very easy to miss it.'

When they reached their destination, they formed a semi-circle around the plaque, leaving space for Deborah in the middle, directly in front of the brass-plated inscription. She read the words silently, before repeating them aloud. 'In memoriam, Martha Lightbody. 1622 to 1686. A good Christian woman.' No one spoke, and Deborah reached up to trace the words with her fingers. After a few more moments, she repeated, 'A good Christian woman. Her faith was obviously important to her, perhaps even more so, considering the crimes of which she was accused. How could something like that happen to a good Christian woman?'

'Sadly, she was not alone in being accused of witchcraft. Many such as she, men as well as women, were unfairly tried and hung,' Marcus responded.

'Yes, and those who made their own medicines and cures were particularly vulnerable. In East Anglia, Mattthew Hopkins, a self-appointed Witchfinder General ...'

'Not now, dear,' Marcus interrupted.

'Oh, I suppose not, but, if you're interested Deborah, I have a wealth of information on the subject. I could ...' Another warning glance from Marcus halted her enthusiasm. 'Another time perhaps?' she finished tamely and was rewarded by a loving squeeze from her fiancé.

'I have a posy of flowers in the car. Tom, would you mind fetching them for me?' Deborah asked. 'There is no grave, so I think I'd like to leave them here.' As Tom strode from the church, Deborah murmured, 'She was sixty-four when she died. A good age, I suppose. I hope they were happy years, although perhaps not quite the "happy ever after" John Lightbody led us to believe in his book. I wonder why she and John changed their names and moved here?' she pondered. 'Something must have happened. It may well have had something to do with the feud with the Holley family. Perhaps someone came seeking revenge and they had to go into hiding.'

'We thought it might be something like that,' Honoraria remarked. 'As yet, we've found nothing in the newspapers of the time, but we'll keep looking. We did find a record for a Cecile Littlebody who married George Good in 1668 in the parish of Northrepps. That's not too far from here.'

'Cecile!' Deborah exclaimed. 'The same name as her friend ... in the book. Her daughter perhaps?'

'It's certainly possible,' Honoraria agreed. 'Martha and John must have moved away from their family. Something sent them into hiding, probably at a time in their lives when their children had grown and flown the nest. It could be that Martha's real identity was discovered and she was in danger once again of being hung as a witch. The law in England didn't change until the 1735 Witchcraft Act. Marcus and I have discussed it at length. We think that's the most likely explanation.'

'I suppose we'll never know for sure.' Deborah turned and smiled at Tom's approach. 'Thank you, darling.' She took the small bunch of colourful pansies, picked from her garden that morning. 'Do you think I could have a moment alone?'

While her companions moved away on a circumnavigation of the small church, Deborah tucked the flowers against the wall and closed her eyes, saying a silent prayer, secretly hoping for another sense of the long-dead woman. As she opened her eyes again, she chided herself for her foolishness. Ever since her experience in Dark Water Lake, when she believed Martha's ghost had helped her survive, she had felt inextricably connected to her story. Somehow, she had believed there would be a special moment of revelation, or some kind of commune across the centuries. It had not happened.

'Goodbye, Martha. Rest in peace,' she whispered.

Slowly, she followed the route the group had taken, pausing to read inscriptions on three other plaques on the walls, before rejoining them by the door. Collectively they left the building, Honoraria still chattering non-stop. 'I wondered, Deborah ... well, *we* wondered if you would be happy for *us* to write a book about Martha, using all the research we have compiled?' Before Deborah could answer, she continued, 'We've still got a lot more to discover, but it would make a fascinating book, with your permission, of course.'

Deborah smiled. 'I don't see why not. People should know the truth about her. That's what John Lightbody tried to do when he published his book – to clear Martha's name. Now we've found her, it would nice to think we could give her back her identity. She lost so much because of false superstition and ignorance.'

'And history has a habit of repeating itself, doesn't it? Especially in your case, Debs,' Tom added. 'Persecution, in any form, should be shown for the shameful thing it is. I think a book is a great idea, Honoraria.'

She flushed. 'Thank you, Tom. I can't wait to get started. Now, I'm feeling a little peckish, and I happen to know there's a nice little pub just down the road. I suggest we head there.'

'You go on ahead, Honoraria. We'll join you in a few moments,' Deborah smiled. 'I would just like to take a turn around the graveyard before we leave.'

'Oh, you won't find anything. Marcus and I have been all round it, and so has Georgie. It would be a waste ... oh, alright.' She pulled a face as her fiancé tugged her arm. 'We'll see you there. Carry on the way your car is facing and it's just round the corner on the left. You can't miss it.'

As the rest of the group made their noisy way back to the road, Tom and Deborah ambled through the graveyard in silence, arm in arm. Tom had mixed feelings about Martha Lightbody. In his mind, her story and her legacy were far too close to endangering the life of the woman he loved. He hugged Deborah a little closer against him as they strolled, picking their way through the older part of the graveyard, trying to make out inscriptions on the pitted stones, rubbed out through the ages. He had come so near to losing the woman he loved – not once but twice. Fervently, he prayed that Martha's history would not return to haunt them a third time.

Deborah's mind was on different things. Honoraria's talk of a book had tickled an idea she had been mulling over the past week. 'I'm thinking of taking up writing,' she announced as they stood by the grave of Agnes Newton, loving wife and mother, 1827 – 1865. 'Not a factual book, like Honoraria. I'll leave that to her. Fiction. Inspired by Martha's story but with different characters. Set in the past. What do you think?'

'Why not?' Tom smiled down at her. 'You excel at most things ... well, maybe not painting ... so why not give writing a try?'

She chuckled. Her attempts at art had failed to show much improvement. 'Yes, I think it's best to leave oils, acrylics and watercolours to those who have some talent using them, like Emma and Lewis. I love those three paintings Emma has done for me. They're so happy and vibrant with colour.'

'That's because she's happy. She has finally got her man, thank goodness.'

'A woman does not need a man to make her happy,' Deborah commented with a playful punch on the arm.

'True enough,' Tom agreed with a grin. 'Before you, I was perfectly happy.'

'Charming!'

'But now, I couldn't be happy without you.'

'Aw.' She smiled and squeezed his arm. 'Same here.'

They meandered for several more minutes before heading back to the church path. Deborah felt reluctant to leave. The place felt special to her because of its connection to Martha, but she could sense Tom was ready to go.

Shafts of sunlight cast splinters of brightness, dazzling and disorientating, between shadows cast by the trees. Deborah paused and blinked. The light was playing tricks on her eyes. She could have sworn she saw the shape of a woman. There it was again. She stopped and gasped. It *was* a woman, dressed in shawl and long skirt, dark hair tumbling over her shoulders. As she watched, the woman reached out to her. Was she smiling? Deborah wasn't sure. It was so hard to see in the shimmering light.

'Do you see her?' she murmured.

'Who?'

She blinked again. The woman had gone.

EPILOGUE

1686

Elizabeth Littlejoy shuffled across her small kitchen to set the clean plates upon the shelf. Every day, such tasks took a little longer and wearied her that bit more. It would not be long now until she was with her beloved John. The years since his death had been hard to bear but, looking back, her life had been filled with love. She had been blessed with the passion and companionship of a good man, the devotion of her children, and the joy of grandchildren including, recently, her first great grandchild. How fortunate had she been, also, to receive the selfless friendship of so many kind people! She could not have survived without it. Indeed, hers had been a life fraught with danger, necessitating both adventure and compromise, but she had no complaints. Overall, life had been good to her and she was more than ready to move to the next one.

Her failing eyesight and painful joints had taken away many simple pleasures in recent years: her morning walks, foraging for herbs, her needlework, her reading. Her ability to write was the first thing lost. When she, John and dear Josiah had settled in Tocklewood, she had started writing a diary. In it, she had recorded the episode in Wickthorpe, when she was so cruelly wrenched from her bed and forced to undergo trial by drowning. How long ago it was! She had continued, periodically, to write details of her life as they transpired – just those eventful or special moments, not every day occurrences. She found it relaxing and cathartic. Her children, and latterly her grandchildren, had liked to sit on her knee, or by the fire, listening as she relived those times, asking questions like children always did. She smiled as she thought of it now. Hopefully, Josiah, to whom she had given the diary, would pass it on to his eldest son, Robert. One day, it might even reach the hands of her great granddaughter, Elizabeth, named for her. *Elizabeth, not Martha.* Those days were long past.

She had given strict instructions to Josiah to allow her story to finish in Tocklewood where she had been happiest. Subsequent events were best left untold, she decided. Let it appear that her curse, and her troubles with Roger Holley, ceased once she and John settled once more in Norfolk.

Oh, she was tired! What a struggle it was to carry a mug of water to the chair beside the stove, to set it upon the table there, and to sink aching limbs into her armchair! Oft times she slept in that chair, the effort of getting to bed just too much by the end of the day. Now she sat, her drink untouched, remembering ...

She and John, as Ruth and John Littlebody, had been happy in Tocklewood for many years. It was only when the children had all married and left home that the past came back to haunt them.

It transpired that, after Roger had fallen from his horse and died, on that fateful day, his remaining accomplice had galloped back to Wickthorpe with a tale of how Martha had bewitched the horse, causing it to rear and unburden itself of its rider. Harold Holley, Roger's younger brother, had thereupon sworn vengeance and tried to find her. This quest had continued until the summer of 1670 when Harold had finally discovered where they were living and assembled a posse of men to arrest her. Luckily, her trusted, old friend, Ruth Fletcher, had dispatched a rider with a missive, warning her of Harold's intentions, and she and John had managed to escape. They had once again changed their name, this time to Littlejoy, and she had become Elizabeth.

This had been a sad time. Whilst she and John had each other, for years they dared have no contact with their family. Only Ruth was trusted with their new identities and place of abode. At last, in 1677, Ruth had written again, informing Martha that Harold had passed away, and Martha hoped that was the end of her troubles. Meetings with their children and grandchildren recommenced, initially infrequent and cautious, but eventually happening more regularly. Now she saw them often. Only yesterday, Robert and his wife, Mary, had brought dear, little Elizabeth to see her. Her wrinkled jaw slackened into a smile, remembering the child's sweet, chubby face, chuckling up at her. She had her eyes too, almond-shaped and hazel. Mary had remarked upon it. However, their visit also brought most unwelcome tidings. It appeared that the enmity between Martha and Roger Holley and, subsequently, his brother, Harold, had extended to other members of both families. Martha learnt that one of her grandsons had burnt down the house of Virgil Holley, revenge after his own home was set aflame. It was fortunate no one had been hurt in either incident but it appeared others were now threatening to get involved. How she wished she had never uttered that fateful curse upon Roger Holley all those years ago!

With unsteady hands, she took a small sip of water. Mary had been kind enough to bring her some cake yesterday and she had managed to swallow just a little, so as not to offend, but otherwise she rarely ate. Her appearance was gaunt and frail, she knew. She had seen the concern in their eyes and assured them she had eaten a hearty stew at lunchtime, brought to her by a kind neighbour, but she did not think they had been convinced. When they said goodbye, it was with sadness, as if they knew it was the last time they would see her alive. It probably was.

Was it *her* curse that the feud between the two families was to continue beyond her life? How she prayed it would not be so, and yet she feared it was what she deserved – so many lies had she told, to say nothing of the mortal sin she had committed.

Her eyes fluttered as she remembered that awful, final confrontation with Roger Holley. That too was in the diary – the tale of how they had fled from his pursuit and he had stopped them, on his horse, pointing a musket at John's head. Only she knew the whole truth of that day. Better her family believed the villain's death was entirely accidental, the hand of fate, the wish of the Lord. But it had not happened as she had written and told it.

Her eyelids closed. All these years later, guilt still burrowed in her heart. If she could relive that moment, would she have chosen a different course? Would she, given the same set of circumstances, repeat the lie she had told her husband? Once told, a spur-of-the moment decision, the deception was a weight she had carried for the rest of their lives together. Was it her own wickedness which now blighted the lives of her descendants? Was she the cause of the enduring feud with the Holley family?

Her head fell forward and her mind drifted, one last time ...

'Roger Holley!' I lift the blanket higher to conceal Josiah, mercifully still sleeping.

'The very same.' I hear smug satisfaction in his voice as he urges his horse closer and waves his musket at John. 'Release the reins, place your hands above your head where I can see them and step down from your perch. Packer!' he calls to one of his men. 'Take a hold of this horse. We don't want anyone getting ideas of escape.'

I tremble with fear. John holds Holley's arrogant stare and edges closer to him, ready to fling himself at the mounted man and disarm him. Unfortunately, Holley deciphers his intent and counters by aiming his musket at my head.

'Try anything and I shoot,' he snarls.

'Stop!' My voice rings out. 'Leave my husband be. This is nothing to do with him. I will come with you.'

'Don't move. Stay where you are. I give the orders,' Holley commands.

I refuse to obey. I know this man cannot be trusted. Instead, I take a step forward. 'This is between you and me. Or are you afraid I'll put a spell on you?' I taunt him.

'I said, stay still. Move again and I'll fire.' Holley urges his horse close enough to the cart to reach out a gloved hand, intending to push me to the floor.

At the same time, John launches himself from his seat. He hopes to grab Holley and wrangle him to the floor but misjudges the distance, cannoning instead into the horse's flanks and tumbling to the ground. I scream and Holley's horse rears up, hooves flailing. Desperately, Holley tries to control his mount and stay in the saddle but the horse rears a second time, even more violently. As Holley falls, he fires his musket, accidentally shooting Abel Packer, whose riderless mare gallops away into the night. Roger falls hard, hitting his head upon a rock, incapacitating him. I am forced to fling myself forward to catch the reins of our carthorse, Red, to prevent the frightened beast from trampling the prone figure of my husband. The remaining horseman casts a shocked look at the dead bodies of his master and accomplice, and flees in the opposite direction.

'John?' Having secured Red's reins, I leap from the cart to assist him and notice Roger has staggered to his feet. I see he is searching the ground for his weapon.

There is no time to hesitate. The bloodied rock is there, by my foot. I pick it up and rush at Roger, bringing the rock crashing down upon his head. It connects with a terrible crack and he falls once more.

Silence surrounds me and I realise the enormity of what has just happened. I have killed him, a terrible sin, and yet I feel only relief. He can no longer hurt me.

John's groans claim my attention and I help him to sit up.

'What happened?' he asks.

'Fortune smiled upon us,' I answer. 'By your brave leap, Holley was thrown from his horse, just as he was firing his musket. The wayward shot hit Packer and the other man fled. We are safe, my love. Holley is dead. He fell and hit his head on that rock, killing him instantly.'

John's eyes, previously fearful, shine with relief. 'Praise the Lord! He was indeed watching over us, my love.'

'Yes,' I say, my deception scoring grooves of guilt into my heart, as my murderous action had not ...

Consciousness flickered once more, hazy and difficult to grasp. One thing was certain. The deed was done and there was no going back. Roger Holley started the enmity between them, but her curse, and the murder she committed, began a war.

As she struggled to take her final breath, Martha Lightbody swore a silent promise to protect her family beyond her own death. And she uttered one last prayer:

'Blessed Lord, forgive me for I have sinned. Have mercy upon me,' she muttered, 'and let my curse die with me.'

ACKNOWLEDGEMENTS

Writing a novel, in my experience, is a journey beset with self-doubt. I am thankful for many people who have given me support and encouragement throughout the process. Special thanks must go to Sue, Sara, Mark, Jan, Lily and Alex who agreed to critique *The Lightbody Bequest*. I fully appreciate your insights, advice, comments and encouragement. My book would be a lesser novel without them. I am also grateful to my writer friends on social media for their selfless support and humour.

A special thank you to Camilla for the hours she spent researching tides and seventeenth century sailing boats in response to my question regarding how far they could travel around the north Norfolk coast in one day!

Thank you, Rob for designing the cover, and especially to Alex, my editor and proof reader. Any mistakes are entirely my own fault.

Most importantly, I would like to thank **you** for choosing to read *The Lightbody Bequest*. If you enjoyed it, please consider posting a review, however brief, on Amazon and/or Goodreads. Reviews are invaluable in helping other readers to find my books and I will be hugely grateful.

ABOUT THE AUTHOR

Carolyn Ruffles writes both contemporary and historical fiction, laced with mystery, romance and suspense. She loves reading and writing books which tell a compelling story: books with drama and emotional depth; books with characters who stay with her, long after their tale has ended; books about ordinary people embroiled in extraordinary situations and learning about themselves in the process.

Having retired from teaching, Carolyn wrote her first novel, *The Girl in the Scrapbook*, which was published in November, 2018. *Who To Trust*, followed in March 2020 and *The Vanishing Encore*, her third book, in 2021. The Lightbody Mystery series is her first duology.

If you wish to find out more about Carolyn, visit her website https://carolynrufflesauthor.com. By signing up to her readers' list, you will receive the link to a free short story, *Memories Forgotten*, about a subject close to her heart.

Carolyn lives in Norfolk with her husband Mark. When she is not reading or writing, she enjoys visiting interesting places, walking and gardening. She also loves spending time with family and friends, especially if there is a glass of wine involved!

OTHER BOOKS BY CAROLYN RUFFLES.

The Girl in the Scrapbook.

Who To Trust.

The Vanishing Encore.

The Lightbody Legacy.

https://carolynrufflesauthor.com

Printed in Great Britain
by Amazon

44330179R00185